D0464228

THE
CHILD
EATER

THE
CHILD
EATER

RACHEL
POLLACK

Jo Fletcher

New York • London

Jo Fletcher Books
An imprint of Quercus
New York • London

ISBN 978-1-62365-460-3

Library of Congress Control Number: 2015938653

Distributed in the United States and Canada by
Hachette Book Group
1290 Avenue of the Americas
New York, NY 10104

Manufactured in the United States

10 9 8 7 6 5 4 3 2 1

www.quercus.com

Dedicated to Martin, Jennifer, and especially Simon Greenman, who emerged into the world some years after the original story "Simon Wisdom."

And to Martha Millard, for her patience and encouragement.

Chapter One

MATYAS

Once, long, long ago, when there were still wise women and powerful men who knew things now forgotten, there lived, in a faraway land, a boy called Matyas. His mother must have chosen the name because his father appeared to dislike it. Sometimes, if Matyas' mind drifted from his chores, his father would slap him and call him "pious Matyas," and tell him, "You're not living in some church, boy. You work or you don't eat."

Matyas lived and worked in his parents' inn, the Hungry Squirrel, a small, dismal wood building on a dismal road that ran from the sea to the capital. Most of the inn's business came from travelers on their way from the port to the city, or the other way around. Sometimes, with the wealthier ones in their private carriages, Matyas saw the faces screw up in distaste, and then they would sigh, knowing they had no choice. Matyas always wanted to hit them, though if he was honest he wouldn't want to stay at the inn himself, but would have tried to travel nonstop to the sea.

Matyas had never seen the sea. He and his best friend, a girl named Royja, used to talk about it. They would sit on low stones in the dust behind the inn and imagine water. Vast stretches of water, so huge that great boats larger than the Hungry Squirrel would bounce and pitch across it for days, for weeks, and never see the dull dirt of land. They talked of women with fishtails and the heads of birds, who sang to sailors and drove them insane. And angels, or maybe demons, that rode on great fish that could swallow men whole, with room inside for the men to build homes, and fires to keep themselves warm.

When they tired of talking about the sea they imagined the cities they might visit if they could ever cross the water. Cities where the animals had taken over and now the people had to beg for bones at the feet of long tables where dogs lay on silk pillows. Cities where the buildings sang strange songs all night long and everyone had to go deep underground to be able to sleep. Cities where golden heads on silver poles lined the streets and would tell you anything you wanted to know. Cities where the children had killed all the adults and used the blood for magic spells that forced angels to give them whatever they wanted.

Royja was not just Matyas' best friend, she was his only friend. The daughter of the blacksmith who worked at the inn and lived in a one-room, dirt-walled building behind it, she and Matyas had known each other all their lives. Royja was skinny and wore clothes that were old and too big for her, and she was always dirty, her face, arms and legs streaked with mud and grease. Much like Matyas himself. Once, a rich family had stayed at the inn, and when Matyas and Royja saw their milk-skinned, plump little girl they had no idea what she was, possibly some animal fallen from Heaven that the lord and lady had dressed up as a miniature person.

Matyas cleaned the guests' rooms and carried firewood and swept the floors and brought the guests his father's watery beer and his mother's stringy food. He hated every moment. He was too good for this, too clever and talented. Sometimes he dreamed of himself as a great man, dressed in silk and gold and standing in a tower while, down below, the ordinary people would look up in fear and helplessness. Then morning would come and his father would kick him awake to begin his duties.

Matyas was gangly, with deep eyes and long lashes, and shiny black hair that always seemed to get in his face. He survived his work by mentally changing whatever he could. If he spilled food, he imagined the stain as a treasure map. If some monk or educated traveler left behind a scrap of paper, he pretended it contained the secrets of kings, or even better, a magic spell to carry him and Royja away from the inn to a place with gardens and fountains and high towers. Since he couldn't read, it was easy to pretend.

At night, after his chores had finally ended and he was so tired he knew he should just fall on his sleeping pallet by the stove, Matyas instead would wander the dusty hills and scrub flats and pretend he was on a sacred quest. Sometimes he took Royja with him; more often he went on his own. He knew he would never find anything, for who would bring a holy relic to such a place, let alone leave it there? Matyas simply could not stand the thought that he might live his entire life like his father, with no world beyond the streaked walls of the inn.

One night he and Royja stayed out late, sitting together against a dead tree that caught the moonlight in its spider-web branches. This time, instead of journeys on boats as big as palaces, Royja imagined they might find a cave in the earth, with tunnels that would open out to strange woods and palaces, and purple rivers, and trees like white ghosts, and a bright red rock as big as a village, and giant rabbits that carried human passengers in soft pouches in their bellies.

After a time Matyas fell silent and left Royja to do all the talking. She hardly noticed, waving her soot-stained arms as she described cities where every person had one leg and one arm and no face, or rivers where the dead swam back to the shores of the living. Matyas thought of that strange tower he saw in his dreams, how sometimes he was inside it but more often it stood so far away he could only see the shape and not any part of it. Now and then he would glimpse a small wrinkled face, high up in a window, see it for just a moment, the way a moth flits before your eyes so quickly you can hardly make it out.

When Royja paused, Matyas yawned and said how late it was—look, the Moon had set, and dawn was only a few hours away—and they'd better get some sleep before their chores began. At the smithy door they stood and faced each other with a few muttered phrases until at last Matyas took hold of her fingertips and kissed her, very slightly. She blushed and dashed inside.

Matyas yawned again and strolled to the kitchen door, only to slip around the side of the inn when he was sure Royja wasn't watching. It wasn't that he didn't want her to know, he just . . . he just wanted to see, and not talk. He had the strange sensation that there was something important he needed to discover, or do, and if he didn't find it now he would miss his chance, and all the rest of his life would be wrong in some deep way he would never understand.

He walked across scrubland, through mud hollows, over miserable parched hills. He didn't know how late it was—he thought the sky had begun to lighten, but dawn was still a good way off—but finally it seemed his journey came to an end before a tangled stand of blackened trees. He and Royja had seen this place before but never entered it. It wasn't that big, he could probably walk around it in less than an hour, but something about it kept people away, even repelled them. Matyas had once seen a woodcutter walk past it on his search for trees to chop and cure for the market. Rather than take his ax from his back and get to work, the man had made a fist, pointed his little finger at the dense trees, muttered something and hurried away. Matyas knew that gesture—he'd seen his mother do it after certain guests had left the inn. It was what you did to blunt a curse.

Matyas stood outside the woods and tried to stare within. A curse meant magic. If only he could see the center. For a moment he thought he saw light, or fire, flash inside, but it was so quick he wondered if he'd fallen asleep for an instant and dreamed it. It was very late, and he was very tired.

Tiny lights darted around him. This was certainly no dream but neither was it a torch. It was more like fireflies, except they didn't flicker. Matyas watched them, and as he watched they began to buzz, and in that buzz he thought he could hear a faint hum of voices, or maybe one voice formed from all of them together. "Matyas, Matyas," it said.

What? He swatted at them, angry that he'd let himself think a swarm of bugs could say his name. They moved around him easily. "Matyas, Matyas, Master Matyas!"

"Master?" he said out loud. "What do you mean? Master of what?" Nothing more came. The air went dark again, as if they'd never been there at all.

Stupid, Matyas scolded himself. Think some bugs could talk to him, say his name, call him *master*. He should have stayed home on his pallet, slept so he could do his chores and escape his father's stick across his back.

He didn't think he would make it back before the inn woke up and got to work but somehow he did. He even managed to lie down on his wooden pallet in the corner of the kitchen and pull his old torn sheet around him so he could pretend he was asleep when his father came to prod him awake.

To his great surprise he fell asleep—couldn't have stopped it if he'd wanted to—and soon a dream engulfed him. He faced the woods again, all the trees pressed tightly together like some sleeping beast with a thousand claws that might reach out and slash him. For a moment he was conscious that he was dreaming, and wondered if in fact he was awake and still at the woods, and the return home had been the dream. But then the woods parted, and a dark path opened before him, and he forgot anything else existed.

He never got to see what lay in the woods, for the dream shifted and he was standing in the snow, barefoot, his clothes torn, his hair long and filthy. All around him lay small pieces of paper, about the size of Royja's hands, with bright pictures on them, each one different. He found himself staring at one in particular, an image of what looked like a rich young man in green and gold clothes, dancing on a hilltop. Only there was something wrong with it. He bent down to look closer and discovered the face was missing—it looked like someone had slashed it out with a knife. Matyas gave a cry and jumped back.

He was walking down a magnificent hallway, the sort of room he and Royja had talked about so many times. The floor was a swirl of red and black stone, the walls a paler red lit by globes that gave off a cold, steady light. The walls rose so high, three times the height of Royja's father, that Matyas had trouble making out the ceiling, but it appeared to be a painting of some kind. There were angels, and bodies lying on the ground, and children with their arms crossed in front of their faces, as if to protect themselves. When he realized some of the angels were bent over to drink blood from the dead bodies, and the others were slashing at the children with sharp wings, he snapped his gaze away and focused on the room in front of him.

A stone door stood open at the end of the hall. Matyas hesitated, almost turned and ran away, but could not make himself leave. He heard a faint voice, a child, he thought, no words, just a cry or a moan. He stopped outside the door. There was someone inside, a tall man wearing a jacket and pants fashioned in a simple but elegant style that Matyas had never seen before. He stood next to a stone table and was doing something to a round object that lay on a silver tray.

A head. The round thing was a human head, a boy, his was the voice Matyas had heard. The man was cutting it, he had a stone knife, black and shiny stone, very, very old, and he was making tiny cuts all along the face. The boy's eyes flickered, saw Matyas. "Help me," he whispered. "Master, help me."

Matyas shook his head from side to side. *I can't, I can't*, he wanted to say but he was too frightened to speak. And then the man turned and saw him, and straightened up, and with the knife held loosely in his hand he smiled, his face gaunt, his teeth bright, and he said, as if to an old friend, "Ah. It's you."

Matyas screamed. He screamed so loud he woke himself up, and then a moment later his father's hand smashed into his face. "Stupid boy," his father whispered. "You wake up the guests, I'll make you sorry."

A few days after Matyas' dream, a strange man came to the Hungry Squirrel. Dinner had already been served when a soft knock sounded on the ash door that had been old—and dirty—when Matyas' grandfather was a child. Matyas looked at his father, who rolled his eyes and said, "Well, open it. And try not to scare them away." Matyas opened the door and there stood a short and stocky man, well fed, wearing a long brown robe like a hermit's, but softer, richer, with gold threads worked into the weave. His red-gray hair flowed out from under a white cap without a brim, while a red beard spread around his face and neck like an upside-down halo. He carried a staff that looked too thin for walking. Maybe it was meant to impress people, for he'd set a red stone into the top of it. The stone glowed with a faint light that dulled to darkness even as Matyas looked at it. On a strap across his chest the man carried a leather pouch with an eagle's head stitched into the flap. It must have contained all his travel needs for Matyas could see no luggage or bags in the dirt around the man's feet.

Nor did he see a wagon, or a horse. It was Tuesday, not one of the days when the coach came through, and if the man had not brought his own transport he must have walked. But from where? The nearest way-stop was a good three days on foot, and if he came from either the seaport or the capital, it would have taken even a young walker, with good supplies, over a week.

"I would like a room," the man said. "A private room, or as private as possible."

Matyas just stood there and stared for so long that his father shoved him aside. "Please, sir," his father said to the man. "Come in. Ignore the boy, he's ..." He wobbled his head side to side to indicate a simpleton. "We have a fine room for you. The best you'll find between the sea and the capital." He bowed his head a moment, then said, "Please, Master. Welcome."

Matyas stared. Maybe his father was right about him, for all he could do was stand there, with his mouth open like a fish. He did notice, however, that the few guests who sat in the tavern room did exactly the opposite, averting their eyes. And when the man passed Matyas' mother on his way to the stairs, she crossed her arms over her chest and held on to her shoulders, as if to protect herself.

As soon as Matyas' father had taken the man upstairs, Matyas rushed over to his mother. "Who is that?" he said. "Why did Father call him Master?"

His mother rolled her eyes. "What's the matter with you? Can't you see? The man's a wizard."

"A wizard," Matyas whispered. Then out loud, "Is that what Master means? A wizard?"

"Of course. Be careful, Matyas. If you make him angry, he'll turn all our food into stone and our wine into blood. And he'll turn *you* into a toad." Matyas shuddered, and yet he could not take his eyes off the staircase long after the wizard, the *Master*, had gone to his room. So softly no one would hear, he whispered to himself, "Matyas, Matyas, Master Matyas."

After he finished his chores, Matyas went behind the inn to meet Royja, as he did almost every night. She was there, of course, and as soon as he saw her he told her that a wizard had come to the inn.

"I know, I know," she said. "Jonana came to tell my father." Jonana worked in the kitchen with Matyas' mother, and liked to visit the blacksmith whenever she could get away.

"Did he ask you to stable his horse?"

"No." She shook her head, as if Matyas might not have heard her. They decided to look for any signs of how the wizard might have arrived. Near the inn, stopping some twenty yards away, they found the tracks of some large animal, a big dog, or maybe even a wolf. Royja said, "That's how he travels. He uses his wizard magic to summon some giant wolf to carry him. Oh, wouldn't that be wonderful?" Her face got that funny look that came over her sometimes, like she'd jumped into a dream with her eyes open.

"Or maybe he becomes a wolf himself," Matyas said. "He turns into a wolf so he can run very fast, and hunt if he gets hungry, and then when he gets close to where he wants to go he makes himself a Master—a *man*—again. So no one will notice."

Royja clapped her hands, softly to make sure no one heard and came out to yell at them. "Oh, I like that," she said. "That's even better."

Matyas thought suddenly, *She doesn't understand.* She'd never understand. It was all just stories to her. But if you could turn yourself into a wolf—or a boy into a toad—maybe you could become a bird. Then he could escape.

"Do you want to walk around?" Royja asked. That was what they called their explorations and their imagined adventures.

"I don't think so. My father might need some help. With the wizard."

Royja looked so disappointed he almost changed his mind. But all she said was, "All right," and then ran back to the smithy.

It was late in the evening before Matyas got a chance to go upstairs. His father poured a glass of thick blackberry wine—"Our own special drink," he would tell their guests, though Matyas noticed most took only a few sips—and ordered Matyas to, "Leave this outside the door. You can knock but very quietly. Never wake a sleeping wizard." His father laughed, as if he'd made some joke.

Matyas went up the stairs so fast his father yelled at him not to spill the wine, but as he approached the room he slowed down. What if the Master was sleeping, and Matyas couldn't see him? What if he was awake, and Matyas *could*? As he neared the door he saw it was slightly open, enough that a crack of light shone from inside. Had he made the jewel on his staff glow? But when Matyas pushed himself to open the door just a little bit further, he discovered that the great wizard had simply lit the oil lamp, like anyone else. Matyas peered inside.

The room was fancier than the others, or at least it tried to be. The bed, and the table, were larger, the table legs carved, the bed a four-poster with a drooping canopy. The single chair was also larger than usual, with a high back and arms that ended in lion heads. There was even an oval rug on the unpolished wood floor. But it was all rough, the weave in the rug too loose, the chisel strokes on the wood too obvious.

The wizard did not appear to care about these lacks any more than Matyas did. He had laid his staff on the bed, cast his cap on the table—he was mostly bald on top, with little tufts of white hair among the red—and now he sat in the chair, leafing through some loose sheets of paper, a whole stack of them. The pages, which contained pictures rather than words, reminded Matyas of something but he could not remember what. From a dream, he thought vaguely.

"It's no good," the Master said as he looked at one small sheet after another. "It doesn't fit, there's always something missing."

Suddenly he stopped. With both hands holding the papers as if they were birds that might fly away, he turned his head from side to side, even sniffed the air. Then, so fast there was no time for Matyas to set down the wine and run, the wizard jumped up, strode to the door and grabbed Matyas by the wrist, so painfully the boy had to bite his lip not to cry out. The wizard pulled Matyas into the room and slammed the door.

"Please," Matyas said, "don't turn me into a toad! I just wanted to look."

"Shut up," the Master told him. He had dropped Matyas' wrist and set the pictures down on the table, and now he appeared to be examining the air around the frightened boy. Despite his fear, Matyas also looked around. He saw that the lights had come back. Without thinking, he batted at them with his hands, to no effect.

"You won't catch them," the wizard said.

Matyas dropped his arms, shrugged. "They're just insects," he said.

The Master set his stack of pictures on the table and sat down heavily on the carved chair. "No," he said, "they are not insects. How long have they been coming around you?"

Matyas shrugged. "I don't know," he said. "A few days."

"Those lights are called the Splendor. Have you ever heard that term?" Matyas shook his head. "No," the Master said, "of course not. 'Splendor' is a collective title, like flock of sheep, or murder of crows." Matyas had no idea what the wizard was talking about. "The full expression is 'Splendor of Spirits.'"

"Spirits?" Matyas repeated, and looked again at the lights. "You mean like ghosts?"

"No, no. Ghosts are simply leftover images of confused people. They're not even actual remains, just . . . congealed imagoes that *think* they are trapped souls. The Splendor are third-order powers. They touch the world only at rare moments."

"And that's these little lights?"

"Oh no. The lights are simply markers. Tracks, really, the way prints in the dirt may show you a great lion has passed. If you could truly see them they would fill this room, this house. They would block out the night."

Matyas looked all around the room, up at the ceiling. He asked, "Can you see them? Truly, like you said?"

"No. No one I know has ever seen them in their true form. Well, perhaps one. But if so, she has never mentioned it, at least not to me."

She? Matyas thought. Were there girl wizards?

The Master went on, "The fact is, I have not seen even the tracks for some time. There are men who have studied, fasted, even cut themselves, for years just to invite the Splendor—those *insects* as you called them—to reveal themselves. I know of a man who drove himself over decades to amass a fortune only so he could give it away in one night, as a gesture to prove himself worthy. And you, an ignorant, filthy—"

"Did it work?"

Startled out of his speech, the Master said, "Did what work?"

"The fortune. Giving it away. Did the lights—the Splendor—show themselves to him?"

The Master laughed. "You know," he said, "I'm not sure. That is a very old story, and it only ever describes the effort, not the result. Perhaps the tellers thought the outcome, either way, would not be a benefit. Isn't that interesting?"

Matyas didn't think so. "Can you fly?" he asked.

"What? Of course not. No one can fly."

Matyas felt stupid and hoped his face didn't show it. Why did he ask that? He said, "There's wine. It's our best. My father sent me to give it to you."

The Master smiled. "Well, if it's your best, I can hardly refuse." Matyas stepped into the hall and brought in the glass. The wizard sighed and said, "So they're gone."

Matyas looked all around and saw that the lights had vanished. Anger flashed through him, as if they'd insulted him by leaving. Then he thought maybe he should run back into the hall, in case they'd followed him there and didn't return to the room when he brought in the wine. But he was afraid the wizard might slam the door. "I'm sorry," he said.

"No doubt. I am sorry, too."

Matyas set the wine down near the stack of pictures. "What are these?" he asked.

The wizard hesitated before he said, "They're called Tarot cards."

Matyas thought of the card games some of the travelers played in the inn, but these looked much fancier, more like paintings. He thought about the word. "Ta-row?"

A small smile, as if Matyas had performed some trick just by saying the word. "Their full name is the Tarot of Eternity. Supposedly, if you held the originals in your hands you could change the very structure of the world."

"What do you mean?"

The smile again. "Have you ever thought about the fact that the Sun comes up every morning, and that spring always follows winter?"

Matyas shrugged. "I guess."

"What if it didn't? What if the Sun, or the seasons, just did, oh, whatever they wanted?"

Matyas frowned. "I don't understand."

The wizard shrugged. "No, I suppose not. It doesn't matter."

Matyas reached out his hand. "Can I—?"

"No!" the Master said, then, "I'm sorry. What little power it holds works best when only one person touches it."

"But you said you could change the world."

"Yes, yes, the *original*. If I, if anyone, could ever hold that one—" He shook his head. "This—this is a copy of a copy of a copy. The true Tarot of Eternity has been lost for many hundreds of years. Maybe not lost so much as hidden. To protect us from seeing too much."

"Uh-huh." Matyas tried to see the top picture without being too obvious. It showed a rich young man in green and gold clothes, dancing on a mountaintop, or maybe it was the edge of a cliff. His head was tilted back and he looked up at the sky, as if he didn't realize he was about to fall off. His arms were out, so maybe he thought he could fly. As Matyas looked at the picture something twisted inside him, some fearful memory he could not quite bring to the surface. He asked, "What's wrong with him?"

"Wrong?"

"Doesn't he know he could hurt himself?"

"Maybe he doesn't care. Maybe he's running away and it doesn't matter what happens to him."

"Running away from what?" Matyas asked, but the wizard didn't answer.

Matyas wished he could toss the picture aside to see what lay beneath it, and the one beneath that. Instead, he said, "What good are they? If they're just copies of copies."

"They can reveal certain things. In a limited way. But mostly they represent hope."

"Hope of what?"

"Hope that the true Tarot will return to the world." The wizard closed his eyes for a moment, as if reciting a prayer. "It is said, 'Whosoever touches the Tarot of Eternity, he shall be healed of all his crimes.'"

"That's crazy," Matyas said. "How can you be healed of a crime?" The Master said nothing. "I'm going to be a wizard. A Master." The old man laughed. Angry, Matyas said, "The lights—that Splendor—they told me."

"Really?" Still smiling, the Master took out a rolled-up piece of parchment from his pouch, along with a small tube made of gold. There was a gold cap covering half the tube, and when the man removed it Matyas saw that the tube came to a sharp point, like a quill. Without dipping it into any ink, he inscribed some signs on the parchment, then held up the sheet in front of Matyas. "What does this say?" he asked.

Matyas wanted to hit him. "I don't know."

"It says, 'Those who seek wizardry might learn to read before they enter the Academy.'"

Matyas' hands clenched into fists, but before he could do or say anything the Master leaned back against the chair and closed his eyes. "I'm tired now," he said. "You should go. In the morning I will tell your father of the fine service you gave me."

Matyas was about to protest when the wizard waved a hand at him and he found himself heading for the door. At the threshold he turned and asked, "Can you really do that? Turn people into toads?"

The Master pointed a finger at him. No lightning or dark cloud emerged, but Matyas' body tightened, his throat became thick, his legs hard. He looked down at his arms. They were turning green. "Stop that," he managed to say. "Please." The wizard lowered his arm, and Matyas fell back against the door frame. A moment later he ran downstairs so fast he almost fell over his feet.

The next morning the Master left early, before anyone had woken. By the time Matyas came to the door with a plate of rolls and a pot of tea there was no sign of the man other than a small bag of silver coins. Matyas stared at the coins a long time, then finally grabbed three and hid them in his shoes. He brought the rest to his father.

Chapter Two

JACK

Once upon a time, in a town that came in fourteenth on a list of the "Fifteen Most Livable Cities," there lived a man named Jack Wisdom. The name was unfortunate, because neither he nor his family were especially wise. Some unknown ancestor, they joked, must have done something smart, and now all they could do was try to survive having such a difficult name. "We have to be more normal than normal," his father used to say, almost like a family slogan. Jack would roll his eyes when his father said that, annoyed for no reason he could understand.

Once, when he was a boy in English class, Jack doodled a family coat of arms, with lots of crossed swords and elegant swirls, and a flowering tree. He'd seen this sort of thing in a book once, and now as he looked at it he thought it was pretty good. But then, as if he couldn't help himself, he wrote across the top of the tree "More Normal Than Normal." Jack stared at it, then crumpled the paper and stuck it in his backpack.

Jack had not always lived in the fourteenth most livable city. He'd only moved there as a grown-up. Jack the boy lived in a housing development outside a town known only for a cough-drop factory and a halfway decent high school basketball team. Jack didn't play basketball. He didn't play any sport, really, though he liked to run and thought of trying out for track. But it was the running itself he liked, not having to make a competition out of it. Jack was never competitive, maybe because he had no brothers or sisters.

Young Jack was thin and tall, with dark brown hair that would have been curly if he let it grow. He had bony shoulders and long skinny arms and large hands and feet. It was hard to buy clothes for him, his mother complained: either they were too big or the sleeves were too short. Jack hoped he didn't look weird.

Young Jack liked to play in the woods at the edge of the development. He would wander around between the trees, pretending a broken-off branch was a sword, or a fallen tree a fort. Sometimes he would sit very still, pretend he was a small tree or a stone. If he did it right, the animals got over their fear and came out in the open. Woodchucks and raccoons would wobble past him, deer would crash through the branches (it amazed him how noisy deer were), and now and then he'd see a fox or a coyote. People thought coyotes only lived in the desert, but Jack knew this wasn't true.

The only problem was, when he spent time in the woods with the animals he sometimes had bad dreams. They started when he was around eight, right around the time when he began to go into the woods. At first they were just glimpses—a sudden burst of fire, distant screaming, a stone room with rough walls and floors and no door to escape. Over time they became longer, and more detailed. In one dream, wild animals, coyotes and wolves and foxes, hunted down all the humans and locked them in cages underneath the streets. In another, dead people were coming back. Not ghosts or zombies, just themselves, except they didn't know they were dead and wouldn't believe it when anyone told them.

Jack's mother tried all sorts of things—no television after eight o'clock, no comics at all, no scary books. She removed such things as pepper, oregano and bay leaves from all her dishes and made sure Jack drank a full glass of warm milk before he went to bed. The dreams just continued.

Jack's mom suggested that maybe they should see a doctor, but Jack's dad wouldn't hear of it. "We're Wisdoms, remember? Just imagine the jokes Jack would have to hear if people found out a Wisdom was getting his head shrunk."

"Maybe he just needs a pill or something," Mom said.

"No. No pills."

Jack's parents didn't think he could hear them but he could, even though they were in their bedroom with the door closed and he was downstairs with his homework. That night, when his mother brought him his milk he almost said, "Mommy, I don't want any pills," but instead he just drank silently. His mom looked about to cry and he didn't want to upset her.

That night Jack had one of his scariest dreams. It started out all right. He was walking in the woods, watching some birds fly in and out of the branches. Something large flew overhead, big enough to move a chill shadow across the path. Jack looked up to see if it was an eagle (he would have heard it if it was a plane) and for a moment he thought it was a man. Not hang-gliding or parachuting, but actually flying. But the sun made it hard to see, and then it was gone.

When he looked down again he was standing in front of a clump of gnarled, lifeless trees, their branches so entwined, like thick cables, it was impossible to see between them. When he looked at them a sick fear flooded his body, but he didn't know why. He wanted to run away, to wake up, but instead he kept looking. He could see something, a flash of light.

And then he saw a face, just that, skin all golden, surrounded by tight black curls, the eyes closed, the lashes so long they almost reached down to the tops of the cheekbones. Jack couldn't tell if it was a man or a woman and didn't care, he had never seen anything so perfect.

At first he thought a black tree trunk obscured the body, but then he realized it was a pole, polished ebony. The body wasn't hidden—it didn't exist. That wondrous head slept atop a black column hidden in the trees, had slept so long that dust, like flecks of gold, had gathered on the eyelids.

In his dream, Jack turned his head away for just a moment, but when he looked again the trees and the head had gone and he was standing in a high-ceilinged room, very cold, with a black and white marble floor and some kind of mural on the ceiling. Angels or something, like on the History Channel. He ignored them to look around for the perfect head on its ebony perch.

Now there was not one head but many, all on poles, all in shadows along the walls. Only, they were not beautiful. Their faces were twisted in pain. They were all children, Jack saw, the severed heads of boys and girls the same age as himself. Some were old and dried out—not just bloodless, but the skin shriveled and cracked. Others still had blood dripping from their necks, like fresh meat behind the butcher counter at the supermarket.

And now they all turned, and Jack realized they could *see* him. *Get out of here*, he told himself, but he couldn't move. "Jack, Jack," they chanted, "don't go back. Stay and heal the broken crack."

"I can't," he said. "I'm not the one."

"Jack!" they all shouted together. "Help us!"

"I'm sorry, I'm sorry," he said, "*I don't know how.*"

He woke up screaming, unable to move his body. He strained to free himself before he realized it was just his father's arms around him.

"It's all right," his dad said. "It's okay."

"No," Jack said. "I've got to go back."

"It was just a dream."

"But those kids. I've got to—"

"Shh," his father said, and held Jack so tightly the boy could hardly breathe. "It's just a dream, it doesn't mean anything."

"But I have to—"

"No. You don't have to do anything but forget it. Just leave it and it'll go away. I had scary dreams too when I was a boy. Everyone in this family has them. They don't mean anything."

It was Jack's father who first thought it might be the woods. He didn't know about the animals so he just wondered if maybe it was not good for a "normal boy like Jack" to spend so much time alone, in what Dad called "kind of a primitive state."

Jack didn't want to dream anymore, and he wanted to listen to his father, so he stopped going to the woods, stopped going out much at all after school, only watched TV or played on his hand-held Nintendo. Sometimes his mother would look at him with a pinched face and suggest he go outside, or call up a friend for a play date. Jack just shrugged and said, "I'm okay."

There was one game he played over and over, though every time he played it he thought how dumb it was, and, well, nerdy, and when he mentioned it to other kids at school they all claimed they'd never heard of it, which made him think no one wanted to admit playing it. The game involved a pair of squirrels, a gray and a red, trying to get out of a maze. You could move them together or separately, though Jack was pretty sure both had to escape in order to win. The fact is, he never actually did win, the squirrels never got out. Because there was a trick. Every now and then a door in the maze would open and a gray-faced man in a black suit would jump out and bite off the head of one of the squirrels. Dead. Game over. Try again.

Sometimes when Jack lost he would panic, and he would start the game again right away, desperate, for no reason he could understand, to try once more to save the squirrels.

Jack made sure not to tell his parents about the squirrel game, and how much he played it, for fear they might take away his Nintendo. But his parents seemed hardly even to notice how much time he spent playing his games.

One night his mother surprised him with a chocolate layer cake after dinner. A single candle burned in the middle. "Congratulations," Mom said, while Dad grinned at Jack's confusion. Mom said, "Last night was a whole month without any nightmares."

"Now that's something to celebrate," Mr. Wisdom said. He held up his glass of Diet Coke and waited for his wife and son to do the same. "To Jack!" he said as they clinked glasses. "More normal than normal." Jack wanted to run away, but he didn't want to let down his folks, so he made sure to smile and thank them and say something nice about the cake.

After dinner he was looking out of the window while he dried the dishes, and he noticed a pair of squirrels in the backyard. There was nothing strange about them. The place was full of squirrels, and chipmunks, and occasional deer, but these were a gray and a red, like in the game, and they didn't dart back and forth, they just stood on their hind legs, facing each other, as if they were having a conversation. "I'll be right back," Jack said, and put down the towel.

Outside he didn't know what to do, so he just stood there and watched them. It startled him when they appeared to watch him back. They turned to stand side by side, and then they looked up at him. Though he knew it was crazy to think these actual squirrels could have anything to do with the game, and almost as crazy to talk to them, he said, "I'm sorry I can't seem to win. To get you out of the maze." The squirrels looked at him. "I'll keep trying." Then, feeling really dumb, and ashamed, as if he'd let down his dad in some way, he went back inside and finished drying the dishes.

A few days later, a girl in Jack's class, Tori Atkinson, disappeared. The police came and talked to all the kids, and all the other parents held a meeting to demand that something be done and complain that their kids weren't protected. After the meeting, Jack's mom and dad told him he couldn't go out alone "for a while." Jack didn't mind. Now that he'd stopped visiting the woods there really wasn't any place he wanted to go. For a couple of weeks a policeman stood guard outside the school all day, but when nothing more happened, they sent him somewhere else.

Jack didn't know Tori very well. The fact is, Jack didn't really know anyone well, but Tori was the kind of kid who stuck to herself, didn't join any groups or say much in class. She was never found, and after six months her parents sold the house and moved away.

One day in gym class, when Jack was ten, he hit a home run. Jack wasn't a disaster as a baseball player—he was never one of the last kids to be picked by the team captains—but nor was he a home-run hitter. It felt so good to hear the cheers, even if they sounded a little shocked. As he rounded second base he heard the pitcher say, "Fuck!" as he hit his fist into his glove. Jack grinned at him and kept going.

That night Jack went back to the schoolyard after dinner. He just wanted to remember what it felt like as he walked around the bases and pretended he could hear the cheers. He was coming around third when he saw a man standing at home plate. The man stood very tall and stiff in a black suit. He was skinny, with bony hands that stuck out from his jacket cuffs, and a pale, drawn face, and gray hair combed straight back from his forehead. He didn't move, simply watched as Jack came to a stop.

For a moment both of them just stood there, facing each other, but then the man began to walk slowly toward third base. *Run*, Jack thought. *Go home.*

The man smiled, his teeth bright against his thin lips. He said, in a slow drawl, "Jack, Jack, don't go back. Let's just try to keep on track."

Jack couldn't move. It was exactly like that dream, the one with the black woods and all the children's heads, when he couldn't even try to move. He just stood there as this strange man came up to him and slowly walked all around him. Jack tried to speak but the gasping sounds that came from his throat weren't even words. Now the bony hands were touching him, only his head, his face, covering his mouth, pressing into his closed eyes. The hands smelled like something very old and hidden away for years. The skin was so rough it scratched Jack's cheeks, and Jack felt his tears roll over the gray fingers.

And then the man dropped his hands, and smiled, and said, "No, no, you're not the one. You're not ready. You're not ripe enough." He slapped Jack's face so hard, Jack's head snapped to the side.

Suddenly Jack was able to move. He ran as fast as he could and didn't stop until he got inside the house and slammed the door.

"Jack!" his mother said. "What is it? What's wrong?"

As soon as Jack had told his parents, his father called the police. They spent two hours searching the area, going up and down streets, knocking on doors all around the school. Nothing. Finally they came back and asked Jack if he was sure the "gray man" had really been there, if maybe, just maybe, he'd imagined it. Jack stared at the floor and shook his head.

The policeman looked at Jack's father and shrugged. "I'm sorry," he said. "I don't know what else we can do. If your son remembers something else—or of course if he sees the man again—make sure you call us." He sounded annoyed and trying not to show it. Suddenly he smiled slightly, just the side of his mouth. "You know," he said, "with all that family wisdom, maybe you guys could help *us* solve a crime or two." Before Jack's dad could say anything, he gestured to his partner. "Let's go, Becky," he said. "We'll let the Wisdom family sort things out."

"Dad," Jack said, "it's true. The guy was there. He held my head."

His father looked about to yell something. Instead, he turned around and walked to his and Jack's mom's bedroom and shut the door.

"Mom?" Jack said. "You believe me, don't you? He was *there*."

"Of course, honey," said his mother. "Of course I believe you." She pressed Jack's head against her shoulder, and Jack had the awful thought it was so she wouldn't have to look at him.

Later, in his bed, Jack wondered if maybe he *had* made it up. Maybe he'd dreamed it or something. "More normal than normal," he whispered. He would make his father proud of him.

Chapter Three

MATYAS

Matyas returned to the dark grove whenever he could. It was not easy, as his father seemed to find more and more chores for him, as if he feared Matyas was cheating him any time the boy did something for himself. And when Matyas could get away, Royja was often there, wanting him to tell stories with her about all the wonders they would see. But he did go sometimes, not sure what he expected to find. He looked for the lights—the *Splendor*, the wizard had called them—but except for one or two brief flashes there was nothing.

One night he was sitting on a bare hillock a little way from the grove, putting off the moment he had to return, when he saw a large object move against the moonlit sky. At first he assumed it was a bird, but as he stared at it a shock jolted him, for he realized it was a man. He was right! "No one can fly," that pompous old wizard had said, but look, there was someone flying!

As fast as he could follow on the lumpy earth, Matyas took off after the man. Several times he stumbled over rocks and bushes, only to get up and run faster. He could see the man clearly now, tall and thin with no shirt or shoes but only a rough brown jacket and torn and filthy pants. His hair was thick and dark and matted with dirt.

He descended to earth at the edge of the tangled and blackened trees. The wizard—a *real* Master, Matyas thought to himself, not like that red-haired fake—squared his thin shoulders and tilted back his head. "Come around me," he said. Matyas wondered if the wizard was talking to him. Did he know Matyas was spying on him? What terrible punishment would he enact? He remembered that moment when the old man—*this* wizard was much younger, only a few years older than Matyas himself—had begun to turn him into a toad. He was trying to decide if he should run away when the lights, the Splendor, appeared all around the man's body.

"Open the way," the wizard said. The lights moved toward the trees. Where they touched them, the black branches parted so that the wizard could enter. Matyas bent low and tiptoed forward, until he could see through the tunnel opened by the light.

After the sight of a flying man, he might have thought nothing could amaze him, but now he had to stuff his fist in his mouth not to cry out. In the center of the trees there was a circular clearing, the ground shiny and smooth like glass, and in the center of that circle there stood a black pole as smooth as ivory and inlaid with spirals of gold, and on *top* of that pole, perched like a bird, was a human head!

The face was strong, Matyas' idea of a warrior, with a sharp nose and high cheekbones, and yet it also appeared soft and gentle, almost like a girl's. The eyes were closed, with long lashes. Thick black curls set off delicate golden skin.

The man said something in a language Matyas had never heard from any of the inn's guests. The words all flowed together like white water over sharp rocks. *Wizard talk*, Matyas thought, but when the head answered, everything that had sounded hard or sharp vanished, and Matyas knew it was in fact the language of the head itself. A language of angels. He could have listened to it forever, until he died of hunger without even noticing.

The head and the wizard spoke together for just a few minutes and then the wizard turned to leave. Matyas barely had time to scurry around the curve of the trees and crouch down behind a rock. He looked up just in time to see the wizard rise back into the sky. Matyas stared and stared and thought how he wanted nothing else in the world but *that*.

The trees had closed up again, dark and vicious. It made Matyas want to cry to think of that beautiful head trapped in those hateful trees. He

stood at the edge of the wood for a long time, mouth opening and closing, until finally he called out, as firmly as he could, "Come around me!"
To his great surprise the Splendor appeared, stronger than ever, their
flash so sharp they sent bursts of light up and down his skin. Before they
could vanish he ordered, "Open the way."

The trees parted like high grass blown in the wind, and there, at the
end of the narrow tunnel, stood the head on its black and gold pole.
The eyes were shut again. They looked forever closed, as if the wizard had never been there. Matyas moved forward with tiny steps. He
longed to say, "I want to fly," but he didn't know the words. Even if he
knew how, he wouldn't have wanted to hurt that gentle language with
his clumsy teeth.

Then suddenly he heard that voice again, the lights speaking to him.
In a soft chant the voice said:

Matyas, Matyas,
Master Matyas,
Will you fly as
Straight and high as
A dark and lonely hawk?

"Yes!" Matyas cried, thrilled beyond his fear. He could see himself soar
through the sky, just like that wizard (except he imagined himself dressed
better, more magnificent). He would circle the inn, laughing as everyone
pointed up at him in wonder. And then he would take off, escape this
wretched world of the Hungry Squirrel and never return.

He waited for the head to say something but nothing happened. It
looked asleep. It looked like it would sleep forever. Matyas said, "Please.
Will you help me? Help me fly?"

Nothing in the perfect face moved, but it spoke, wondrous rolling
sounds, like liquid silver. "I'm sorry," Matyas said. "I don't understand.
Please."

Now the mouth curved in the thinnest smile, though the eyes stayed
closed and not another muscle twitched. It spoke again, but this time
the words were chopped, harsh. Matyas concentrated a moment, then
said, "That's the same thing. Isn't it? A different way of saying it, but the
same idea?" He had no idea how he knew that, nor what the two ver-
sions, either one of them, might have meant.

It didn't matter, for the effect was dramatic. The eyes opened wide—little puffs of dust came off them—and the voice, that glorious sound, cried out, in Matyas' own tongue, "How did you know that?"

With a great effort Matyas stood his ground. "I'm Master Matyas," he said.

The eyes looked him up and down. "Hardly," the voice said. "But the Splendor have come around you, no doubt for reasons only they would understand."

Matyas said, "Are you an angel?"

"*Angel?*" the head answered. "Do I *look* like a wing-slashing beast? *I* am a High Prince of the Kallistochoi!"

Matyas waited for more, then finally said, "I'm sorry. I don't know what that is."

The head—the Prince—made a sound of disgust. "How wonderful," he said. "Something new has come into the world. An ignorant Master."

"Can't you just tell me?"

The face looked startled a moment, then the Prince laughed. "Well. Ignorant perhaps, but impervious to insult. A valuable quality. Very well, then. The Kallistochoi are the original rulers of this world. Indeed, some have claimed that we created the Earth as a haven, but I cannot speak to that. Origins were never my concern."

"Haven from what?"

"The Great Above." When Matyas looked confused, the Prince rolled his eyes. "Heaven." He went on, "We were the First, the original beings to emerge from the Greater Light, behind the Curtain of the Creator. We descended only when the Creator brought forth the Lesser Lights, the Angels of Purity and the Demons of Desire. We wanted no part of their wretched war, and so we came *here*. We fashioned bodies for ourselves, taller than the giant pines, our eyes like oceans, our voices like hurricanes of wonder.

"Oh, how we delighted in this world. It was ours, and we poured all our beauty into it." He stopped for a moment, as if waiting for Matyas to say something. But the boy could not think of anything, and so the head continued, "For many turns of the Great Year, as the stars moved slowly around the Earth, we sailed the oceans and roamed the forests. We walked in the Garden of Origins and danced with the Guardians of the Seven Trees. And then the great disaster happened."

Again he paused, and now Matyas said, "What was that?"

"The war ended. The Host Triumphant cast the Rebels down into the Great Below. And then they came looking for us."

"Why?"

"To punish us, of course. For our refusal to take sides. They descended to this world in a thousand chariots, each one brighter than the Sun. Their vicious wings slashed open the sky itself, so that the jewels of Heaven rained down like hail. At long last, the Kallistochoi had no choice but to fight."

"Did you win?"

The Prince looked startled, then secretly pleased. The voice was scornful, however, as it said, "Obviously not. Would I be here, would I talk to *you*, if we had won?"

"I'm sorry," Matyas said, and was instantly angry at himself. Should a Master apologize?

The Prince said, "We fought with courage and ingenuity, but at last we fell. The Host did not cast us Below, however. Instead, they shredded our glorious bodies and left our heads on poles, immobile, forced to watch as our lovely world passed to the brutish hands of, well, creatures like you."

Matyas asked, "How many of you are there?"

There was a pause as the Prince closed his eyes again and appeared to listen attentively for some sound that wasn't there. When he spoke it was with such sadness that Matyas yearned to comfort him, though he had no idea how. He just listened. "I do not know," the Prince said. "I have been asleep for a very long time, hidden by the trees. As I listen now, I hear no songs, no whispers, no cries or laments. It is possible I am the last of the Kallistochoi."

"Will you teach me to fly?"

Once again there was that startled look. But the Prince said only, "Do I look as if I am seeking students?"

"Please. I need this."

"Well, if you *need* it, why don't you go and join the Academy?"

"Academy?"

"My, you really are ignorant, aren't you? The Grand College of Prophets, Sorcerers, Mountebanks and Fools." When Matyas said nothing, he sighed. "The school for wizards, in the collection of shacks and hovels you people call your capital."

"Why do I have to go to school? Can't you teach me right now? You're a High Prince!" Matyas was shouting, but it was no use, for the Kallistocha had closed those magnificent eyes and would speak no more.

He thought of knocking it off its perch, forcing it to answer him, but a sudden wind pushed him back, and the branches began to scratch at him, and he realized the trees were closing in, and if he didn't leave he might be trapped inside forever. As he was running along the narrow corridor, he heard the Prince call to him. "Matyas! We will meet three times, and the last shall also be the first." Matyas almost went back to ask what that meant but he had no choice except to keep going. He emerged onto the dull ground just as the trees locked back into place.

"Come around me!" he yelled, but the lights were gone and there was nothing but dark evening and the darker trees. "Open!" he commanded. "I'm Master Matyas." Nothing. Finally, crying, and angry he couldn't stop crying, he turned to go.

He was a good hundred yards from the trees when he heard the voice again. He didn't think it was the Prince—the sound was too harsh and thin. And he didn't see the lights, the Splendor, anywhere around him. It didn't matter, for only the words counted.

> *Matyas, Matyas,*
> *Master Matyas,*
> *Will you fly as*
> *Straight and high as*
> *A dark and lonely hawk?*
> *Or will you try as*
> *Ancients cry, as*
> *Children die, as*
> *No one dares to talk?*

"I don't care about any of that," Matyas said to the air. "All that crying and talking. And I won't just try. I'm going to do it."

Chapter Four

JACK

Jack Wisdom did his best to live up to his father's hopes for him. No more crazy stuff, he told himself. Normal. He stopped playing the squirrel game, stopped even thinking about the woods and the animals, and as much as he could, he stopped dreaming. If he did dream, whether it was children in pain, or rough hands moving over his head, he told himself it was only that, a dream, meaningless. Normal people just forgot it had ever happened. So that's what he did. It was, he thought, like casting a spell on yourself. A spell of forgetting. Forgetting the dreams and everything else.

He never hit another home run.

In high school, and then later in college, Jack dated girls now and then but not too often. Once, a girl named Rennie said to him, "What's it like under the mask, Jack? Where's the real Jack Wisdom?"

Jack shrugged. They were sitting in a coffee shop, and Jack took a swallow of his mochaccino before he said, "There is no mask. This is just who I am."

Rennie smiled and shook her head. "We've been going out for two months now, and I don't believe anyone could be so damned normal." She said it as a joke but Jack knew what was coming. A week later she broke up with him.

Jack studied software and for a while he thought of becoming a game designer. But it felt a little dangerous, or at least unwise, and so he took a job as a tech specialist for a small automotive accessory design company headquartered in the fourteenth most livable city. There he bought a white house with a porch, on a quiet dead-end street (a "cul-de-sac" the realtor called it) in the better part of town.

The spell stayed strong. He forgot all about the strange things that happened to him as a child, forgot the dreams, though at times it felt to him as if everything that had happened since he was a boy was really just a dream, as if any moment he would wake up. Screaming. But then the spell would come back, and he would banish such thoughts as, well, not normal enough for someone in the Wisdom family.

One winter day, he found himself driving in a part of town he'd never seen, with old houses of wood and even stone, most of them badly in need of paint and a new roof. Jack had no idea, really, how he got there, he was just on his way home from the store after work. Must have been daydreaming and took a wrong turn. He was about to swing the car around when he saw what looked like flames between two dilapidated brick apartment buildings. He pulled over and got out to investigate.

Then stopped when he saw it was just a group of homeless kids huddled around a small fire they'd made from bits of wood and other garbage. They all sat hunched over, hugging themselves in their dirty thin jackets and jeans. There was something wrong with their faces, Jack saw, marks of some kind.

Cuts, he realized. They all had a series of small cuts all over their faces. Some had red lines around their necks, as if someone had cut their heads off and placed them back on the shoulders for safe keeping.

Jack moved slowly away, his heart thumping with terror that they would see him. And in fact, before he could get to his car, all the children turned, or just swiveled their heads, and together they said, "*Jack, Jack, don't go back—*"

"No!" he shouted. "Leave me alone!" He ran to his car as fast as he could, locked all the doors and raced home. That night he dug out his old game player from a box of childhood things his mother had given him. Handling it with a paper towel, as if it might be infected, he took it out into the backyard and buried it. Only when he was inside again, with the door locked, did he feel his breathing begin to slow down. It was all right, he told himself. They were just some runaway kids. Probably they didn't even say that . . . that *thing*. Probably they were only begging and the wind distorted their voices. He poured himself some whiskey. Jack almost never drank, he kept the bottle around because he knew his boss liked it, and Jack thought he should be ready in case his boss came for dinner or a meeting. Now he drank it down, slowly, and on the last swallow he said, "More normal than normal."

That night he slept without dreams, and the next morning he felt as if nothing had happened. He drove a little more carefully on his way to work, but soon the whole thing was forgotten. His life was back the way it should be.

Only, he was lonely. Jack tried going out with women at work, or sisters of the guys at work, even once or twice the daughters of his mother's friends. Nothing ever happened. He'd considered dating services a couple of times. The people in the TV ads always looked so happy. Yet somehow the idea of it always felt unsafe, if not downright unwise. Who ran these things anyway? What did they really want? And so he'd never submitted his name.

Then, when Jack Wisdom was twenty-four years old, he met a woman who talked to squirrels in the park.

Jack had gone to a city halfway across the country on assignment from his company. He was there for weeks, and because his clients often needed time to try out his suggestions, sometimes he found himself free for an afternoon or even a day. At first he tried going to movies, or a sports bar to watch games on television, but both made him feel even more lonely. He didn't want to think what people might think of him, so he stayed away from such places. He tried watching television by himself in his hotel room but became too restless. So he began to take walks in a large park a few blocks from his hotel.

One afternoon he saw, some distance away, a woman on a park bench leaning forward with her hands on her knees as she apparently talked to a pair of squirrels, one gray, one red, who stood upright on their hind legs to twitch their noses at her. Occasionally she would laugh, as if the squirrels had made a joke, while at other times she nodded solemnly.

Sudden rage flashed through his body—how could someone act that way, didn't she care what people would think of her? And then the thought, *Get out of here. You don't need this.* But those very messages in his head, and that anger behind them, felt unnormal somehow—wasn't it normal to see someone else act weird? Why get so angry? So he stood and watched. Sparkling lights like fireflies darted all around her, illuminating her face in momentary flickers. After a few minutes, the woman gave each squirrel a small piece of bread, and then with a wave of her hand sent them away. As the squirrels dashed off to eat their prize, the lights also left, spiraling above the woman to disappear into the sunlight.

The woman was tall, with long red hair, curly and well cut but in no special style. She wore what looked like a heavy silk dress, deep purple streaked with yellow, and a blue shawl loosely draped over her shoulders. Around her neck a gold chain held a pendant that reminded Jack of the medical symbol of two snakes wound around a stick, except these snakes looked more real, and the stick had a kind of flaming crown on top.

Once the squirrels had left, Jack wanted to go and speak to her but he was afraid she would notice him staring, so he turned around and pretended to examine some flowers. When he finally looked again she was gone. That evening, Jack lay on his bed with the TV on, gazing at the ceiling, and he thought about the woman. *You've got to be pretty squirrelly to talk to squirrels*, he thought. It was one thing to play a game—and what would it have made him if he'd talked to her? Really, it was all for the best that he hadn't tried to talk to her.

The next day he went back to the park and she was there, dressed in blue this time, with a light gray jacket over her long dress. She was talking to the squirrels like the day before, and nodded, or gestured with her hand as if it was a real conversation. And once again, Jack turned and pretended not to see her as she got up and walked away. On the third day she wasn't there, and as Jack left the park he kicked a garbage can in his anger at himself for not speaking to her. That night he dreamed of her, his first dream in months, strange scenes that lasted only seconds. She was fighting with him, or she was standing in a cold room, surrounded by people so pale and miserable they might have been dead. Or she was holding something over a fire, and he was screaming at her. He woke up angry, and then sad. For a moment he thought he saw those odd fireflies in the room with him, but it must have been an after-effect of the dream.

Over the next two days, Jack's clients insisted on showing him the sights. *Just as well*, he thought. If seeing Squirrel Lady was going to make him dream again, better to keep busy. But when he finally got a free afternoon, he nearly ran to the park. At first he didn't recognize her, for instead of a long dress she wore jeans and a light ruby-red sweater, with her hair pulled back. In fact, it was only the squirrels that made him realize it was her. She leaned closer, as if they whispered secrets, and at one point he thought she was crying. When the squirrels finally scampered off, he made himself walk toward her with what he hoped was a casual stroll. "Hi," he said. "Those have got to be the friendliest squirrels in the park."

She smiled up at him. "All squirrels are friendly," she said. "But they're still wild. It's not good to think of them as actual friends."

He smiled back, hoping he would not appear either scary or pathetic. "You certainly seem to get along with them pretty well. It looked like you were having a great conversation." He laughed a little, to show he was joking, though not too much.

"Oh, they're good for news and gossip, but you know, they have their own point of view. They *are* squirrels after all, so you really have to sift through what they say for something useful."

She sounded so serious, despite a smile at the corners of her mouth, that he didn't know how to answer. He was never very good at small talk, anyway. So instead he just said, "Hey, look, do you think maybe you'd like to have a cup of coffee? I don't actually live around here, but I noticed a nice place a couple of blocks over."

The strangest look passed over her face, a sadness mixed with some kind of struggle. Jack was wishing he could just run away, maybe go and bang his head against the wall for pushing too soon, when she sighed, then smiled sweetly at him and said, "That would be nice. Thank you."

"I'm Jack Wisdom," he said as she stood up.

"What a wonderful name. Mr. Wisdom. Is there a Mrs. Wisdom?"

"No, no, not at all. I mean, my mother, but . . ." He let his voice trail off before he sounded even dumber.

She laughed. "That's all right. I knew you weren't married."

"You knew?"

"The squirrels told me, of course. They're really very observant."

"What?" He looked around, as if he'd catch them spying on him.

She laughed again. "I'm sorry, I really shouldn't tease you. My name is Rebecca. Rebecca Vale."

"There's no Mr. Vale, is there?"

"Only my father."

"Good," he said, then quickly added, "I mean, because I don't have any squirrels to give me that information."

As they walked out of the park, Jack said, "So you're a nurse?"

"No, I'm afraid that's a job that has never appealed to me very much."

"I'm sorry. A doctor, then?" *Sexist jerk*, he scolded himself.

She looked at him with a smile that might have made him feel foolish but instead lifted his body as he walked. She said, "Not a healer of any kind. Not even a pharmacist."

"Oh, sorry. It's just that necklace. Isn't it a symbol of the medical profession?"

"Yes, though in fact that's actually a mistake." She touched the pendant. "This is called a caduceus. In ancient times it was a symbol of prophecy. Of seers."

"Seers? You mean, like fortune tellers?"

"Afraid so."

He laughed, thinking she was teasing him again. "Great profession."

"Not really," she said.

From then on Jack spent every free moment with Rebecca. They went to movies, they walked around town, they even went to a museum where she surprised Jack with how much she knew about Renaissance painting. Sometimes that sadness would come over Rebecca, but then she would smile at him, or kiss him, and it would all be okay.

One evening they walked from Jack's hotel to a small park alongside the river, and as they sat on a bench watching a sailing boat, Rebecca said, "Jack, suppose you could do something really wonderful, something that would make you very happy. But suppose you also knew that it wouldn't last, that it would end horribly, that it would even destroy you. Would you do it?"

Jack said, "I don't know. I guess it would depend on how good it would be."

"The best," she said. "The absolute best."

"If it was as good as you, I'd do it in a second."

She began to cry and laugh at the same time. "Oh, Jack," she said, "I love you."

"I love you too, Rebecca. I never thought I'd love anyone the way I love you." He kissed her, and hugged her, and kissed her again. Because he felt so good, and because he wanted to dispel any sadness in her, he said, "And I don't even care what the squirrels say."

She laughed and clapped her hands. "Right. What do a couple of squirrels know anyway?"

The first time he went to her apartment he didn't know what to expect. He'd never been to a fortune teller's house before. To his relief there was no crystal ball, no weird symbols painted on the walls, no magic wands or lurid idols. There was, however, a small, round table, oak, with two polished candlesticks, one gold, one silver, and in between them a deck of Tarot cards on a blue silk scarf painted with images of stars. Jack had seen Tarot cards before. Back home, at the annual Christmas party, one of the company's patent lawyers liked to bring a deck and tell fortunes for whoever wanted it. Jack could never decide what surprised him more, that a lawyer would do that, or how many people, sensible people, his boss included, lined up for readings.

"Wow," he said to Rebecca, "you really are a fortune teller."

"Please," she said, "we prefer the term prophetic-Americans."

"So you really believe in all this stuff?"

She laughed. "I do it, of course I believe in it."

"So will you tell my fortune?"

"No." She took his hands. "Sweet Jack," she said, "you are a man who found love when he didn't expect it. Isn't that enough to know?"

"I guess," he said.

"Good. Then kiss the fortune teller."

Chapter Five

MATYAS

Over the next days, Matyas thought of nothing but the flying man, and the Prince, and above all, the prophetic voices. He had no idea how a swarm of lights could speak but he didn't care. Master Matyas, they'd called him, and promised he would fly, as straight and high as a hawk. Over and over he would stop in the middle of sweeping, or piling up wood, or emptying a guest's chamber pot, and look up, as if he could see the sky through the stained timbers of the inn, and he would close his eyes, and smile.

If his parents caught him they yelled, or hit him, called him a useless, lazy fool. In such moments, his body shook with anger, and his fingers twitched with the desire to cast some spell on them, burn them into lumps of ash and bone, turn them into miserable scurrying rats. How dare they hit him? He was a Master.

He wasn't sure what to tell Royja. If he told her about the Prince, or the flying man, or the voices and their prophecy, she might just laugh at him. Or worse, think he was making it up and respond with some story. Finally, he simply said he was going to leave, run away to the capital as soon as he possibly could.

Luckily, Royja didn't ask him why now, why such urgency. At first she said, "Take me with you!" and, "Don't leave me here alone. Please. If you went away I don't think I could live." She said this almost every time they went for a walk together.

"Of course," Matyas would say. "We'll go together." And later, "I could go ahead, get everything arranged. And then I'll come back for you. In a great carriage drawn by black horses. What do you think your father would say to that?"

After a time, what Royja said shifted. She asked him how he was going to do it, reminded him how far away the city was, and even if he stole food to take with him, it wouldn't last long enough to get him all the way there. And even if it did, what would he eat once he arrived? Where would he sleep? The city was hard and dangerous, everyone said so, didn't he remember those travelers at the inn who told of runaway children thrown into cages, or eaten by wolves who lived in the dark alleys between the buildings?

Matyas knew he had nothing to fear, for he would join the Wizards' Academy as soon as he arrived. Several times he almost blurted this out but he always stopped himself. What if she told his parents? She wouldn't mean to, but she might get angry and yell at them, "How could you hit him like that? Don't you know he's going to run away and become a wizard, and then he'll send a tribe of demons to devour you?" Then they would watch him all day, and chain him up at night, and he'd never escape.

To stop all her questions, Matyas showed her the coins he'd taken from the bag the wizard had left. They were standing on a flat patch of dirt and scrub brush about half a mile from the inn, under a hook Moon, when Matyas reached into his tunic and took out the coins in the pouch he'd made for them from a piece of paper left by a guest. "You see?" he said. "This is enough to pay for whatever I need."

Royja stared at them open-mouthed, as if she wanted to swallow them but didn't dare. "You *stole* them?" she said. "From a *wizard*?"

Matyas smirked. "Well, really," he said, "I stole them from my father."

"It doesn't matter. It's still wizard money. You could burn up the moment you try to spend it."

"No I won't! My magic will protect me."

"Your magic? What are you talking about?"

"Nothing," he said. He put the coins back. "It doesn't matter."

"I'm sorry," Royja said, and tried to take his hand, but he pulled it away and crossed his arms. "Please don't be angry," she said.

"Come around me," Matyas whispered, but there were no flickering lights, or any other sign of the Splendor.

Royja leaned closer, almost pressed her still-flat body against his hard chest. "I'm here," she said.

When she kissed him, a quick dart against his lips, he wanted to push her away but he only kept his eyes on the caked dirt and the low plants with their sharp leaves. When she did it again, his lips answered her, and a little later he was holding her shoulders as if she'd been the one who wanted to run off.

Later, they lay on a bare patch where they'd hurriedly swept away any pebbles or twigs. Royja's head rested on Matyas' shoulder, while he himself stared up at the sky, as if at any moment a wizard would fly overhead and Matyas would simply rise up to meet him. He wondered vaguely if the things he and Royja had done were what the guests at the inn (and sometimes his parents) joked about.

Royja said, "You won't leave me, will you?"

"Of course not," Matyas told her. To himself he said, *I'll come back for you. I promise.* It wasn't really leaving if you planned to come back.

Matyas' chance came on a cold afternoon in early spring. An elderly lady arrived at the Hungry Squirrel in a black and red coach. She was thin and stooped, and dressed all in black except for a white shawl that she draped over her thin hair. Frown lines were so deeply etched in the sides of her mouth that if she ever smiled it probably would break her face. As she stood in the doorway and looked around with disgust, she remarked how barren the road to the capital was, and how grateful she would be to return there the following night. When Matyas' father (in between bows to the old creature) sent Matyas out to bring down her boxes of luggage from the top of the carriage, the Master-in-training (as he already thought of himself) saw an unused iron grate on the back of the carriage.

That night he went for a walk with Royja. He hadn't talked for a while about leaving, and as a result Royja was more relaxed, waving her arms and giggling, and making up stories about the "fat sour-faced cow," as she called the old lady.

Matyas said very little, only guided her far from the inn, all the way to the grove of dead trees. "Oh," Royja said, "why did you want to come here? I hate this place." Matyas began to touch her, first her face, then her shoulders, then her breasts under her blouse. "Not here," she said, and twisted away. "I want to go somewhere else." But Matyas continued, held her and kissed her, and soon she sighed and dropped her resistance.

He didn't make a sound through all their thrashing and rolling, and stayed silent all the way back to the inn. At the door to the smithy he suddenly said, "I love you."

Royja stared at him, gaped really, her mouth open, as tears sprang from her eyes. "No," she finally said. "*No*. You can't just—*Please*. Don't leave me here all alone!" She looked like she would hit him, half raised her fists. But when Matyas didn't move, only stood and watched, Royja turned suddenly and ran into the smithy.

The next morning, after Matyas and the woman's driver had restored her boxes to their riding place, Matyas found his own place, squeezed into the narrow gap between the grate and the wooden back of the carriage.

For several minutes he held his breath and made himself as small as possible and wished he knew a spell to make himself invisible. Perhaps he did so without knowing it, for his father, after bowing, and cupping his hands for the coins the woman dropped at him, called out, "Boy. Where are you? Matyas! There's work to be done," and even though Matyas could hear him searching around the woodpile and around the building, it never appeared to occur to the man to look behind the old woman's carriage.

The ride was miserable. Metal wheels jolted on the rutted road, while dust, mud and horse excrement flew up into Matyas' face. He was terrified the whole time that some rider, or a carriage with swifter horses, would pass them, and someone yell up to their driver, "Do you know you have a boy stuck in your back grate?" Every two or three hours, they stopped and the driver helped the old woman step out to the side of the road where she relieved herself with loud grunts and sighs. Matyas shook with fear that the bored driver might wander to the back and spot him. He was sure what would happen then. The driver would yank him out, beat him and kick him, and leave him battered on the side of the road. Luckily, the old woman appeared to demand that the driver stay in constant readiness to help her back to her seat, for he never discovered their secret passenger.

They rode until late into the evening, pushing the poor horses so they would make it there in one day. There was a way station, a cabin with beds and a latrine outside, but as Matyas had guessed, the old woman clearly refused to stay in such a wretched place. The Hungry Squirrel was as low as she could bear.

When darkness finally came, Matyas felt a little safer, though he was hungry and all his muscles ached. Finally, late in the evening, they arrived at the outskirts of the city, and the biggest house Matyas had ever seen, had ever imagined. Years later, he would walk by this place in his wanderings around the city and laugh at how meager it was, but then he thought it a palace, with its white walls and gray shutters, its gables and turrets, its stone posts upholding a yellow balcony over the front door.

The driver jumped down and held open the carriage door. Matyas could hear the old woman complaining as she stepped out and took the driver's arm. He could hear her muttering and cursing the entire way up her mosaic-tiled path until they slammed the door behind them. Quickly, Matyas tried to uncurl himself. Only . . . only, he was stuck. He couldn't seem to move any part of his body after being jammed in so tightly for so long.

He heard the door again, heard the driver's heavy steps. In his mind, Matyas could see the man's thick shoulders, his large hands. He was whistling now, coming closer—

And then he was there, grinning down at Matyas, whose frozen body shook with fear. What would they do? He didn't mind a beating (as long as he survived), but what if they sent him back to his parents? The driver put his finger on his lips. Still smiling, he helped Matyas rise out of his iron tomb and step onto the cobblestones. "Better go quickly," he said, "before the witch sticks her head out of the window and sees you." Like a duckling in its first steps, Matyas wobbled down the street. He didn't even stop and relieve himself until he was sure he was out of sight of the old woman's house.

He got over his stiffness soon enough, but not his amazement. The city was so huge! He had thought it would be very easy to find the wizards' school, it would be the biggest and grandest of all the buildings. Instead, there were so many mansions and palaces and churches he had no idea where to look. Maybe the school would shine with magical power. Maybe they kept whole cages full of those colored lights he'd seen in the woods. When he spotted a building with a silver stairway that spiraled up the back wall to a roof garden, he slipped over the fence and scrambled to the top for a better view.

The city went on forever! How could there be so many buildings, so many people, all in one place? Sadly, nothing gave off so much as a shimmer. If he could fly, he would soar over the rooftops until he spotted the school. But of course—

"You!" someone shouted. "What are you doing there?" Matyas hurtled down the stairs as fast as he could.

Hours passed. As night faded to dawn, more people appeared on the streets, workers, messengers, merchants, but no one appeared to want to stop and talk with him, or if they did, they had no idea where the college of wizards might be. That had never occurred to Matyas, that the city might be so big people simply would not know where something was.

Or maybe they just didn't want to tell him. As he walked past people both grand and simple, he became aware of how much filthier he was than everyone in the city. His tunic and pants and sandals were not just rough-sewn and dirty, they were splashed with mud from the road and grease from the iron grate. A couple of times he passed beggars crouched against walls with their hands out. They glared at him, as if afraid he would try to take away their patrons. He thought of the three coins hidden in their paper pouch in his waistband and smiled. He wasn't sure how much money he had but he guessed it was more than any of these professional blind and lame people saw in a week.

And then he came across an old woman, bony, with matted gray hair and a face pitted from some long-ago disease. She slumped against the stone wall of a small building with cast-iron bolts on its doors, wearing a torn dress that was so faded Matyas could not tell its original color. Something about her made Matyas stop and look at her, the way her hands shook, the way she hunched a shoulder up, as if in pain. Her eyes half closed, she didn't see Matyas for a long time, but when she did she scowled and said, "What are you doing there? Brat. Get away from me."

To his own amazement, Matyas said, "Can I help you?"

The woman made a yelping sound that Matyas guessed was a laugh. "Help me? What can a stench-filled, starved rat do to help me?"

"I'm not a rat!" Matyas shouted. "I'm a Master!"

The yelps turned into a wheezing cackle. "Master of what? Rolling around in your own shit?"

Matyas grabbed at the coins in his waistband, held them in his open palm. "You think I'm just a beggar like you? Look."

The woman's mouth gaped open so wide it looked like a bottomless cauldron. "Oh please, Master," she said. "Forgive a helpless, miserable woman. Forgive me and help me. I'm starving and in so much pain I can hardly move."

A mix of pity and rage swept through Matyas, and before he knew what he was doing, he threw the coins at her as hard as he could.

In one swift gesture the old beggar snatched the coins from the air before they could strike anything, and almost in the same movement, she leaped to her feet and hobbled down the street. Despite her limp, she moved so fast she was gone around a corner before Matyas could even think to go after her.

Now he slumped down against the cold stone wall. *What did I do?* he thought. *Oh God, now I have nothing.* He put his hands over his face and cried.

He stayed that way for a few minutes until he suddenly sat up straight. "No," he said out loud. "I'm Master Matyas and I'm going to fly."

The first thing he needed to do was change the way he looked. On a small street of single-story houses, he saw a clothes line with freshly washed clothes. He grabbed a shirt and pants that looked the right size, then ran off to another street where he found a building with a cistern of rainwater behind it. Quickly he stripped naked, splashed water on himself and tried to rub the dirt away, then put on his fresh clothes.

He was still hungry and tired (and feeling like a fool for having listened to a head on a stick), but at least he had clean clothes if—when—he found the wizards. And then it struck him, didn't wizards study the stars? And if so, wouldn't they be on the highest hill? He found another house with outside steps to the roof. Instead of searching for a magical glow, he looked for hills and buildings that rose above the rest. There! He saw a stone wall on top of a hill, and behind the wall copper rooftops that looked like moss-covered stones on a riverbank. In the middle of them, a single tower rose into the sky. He recognized it immediately. He had seen it in his dreams.

Matyas walked most of the night. He might have tried to sleep except that he had moved into such rich neighborhoods, with buildings that looked more carved than built, and streets that looked polished by hand, that he feared they would set dogs on him just for daring to walk there, let alone trying to rest. *So wizards like money*, he thought and was not surprised.

At least he didn't have to go hungry. Smells of roast meat led him to porcelain urns behind the houses. Trash, he realized. The rich apparently threw away as much food as they ate.

At last he reached the wall. Could he be wrong? The buildings were made of ordinary stone and mortar, with iron gates, not gold, and no mysterious words or symbols, no explosions of multicolored fire, no talking heads stuck on poles. No wizards soared overhead. And yet there was that tower. He sat down by what he hoped was the main gate.

Chapter Six

JACK

They got married the night before Jack was due to go home again. Jack could never remember if he'd asked her, or if it was the other way around. It didn't matter. Nor did it matter that she didn't want a fancy wedding, didn't want any family present. She was the only one left, she told him (Mr. Vale had died, it turned out, and Mrs. Vale as well), and there'd be plenty of time for her to meet *his* relatives later, when she'd come home with him.

When they were filling out the papers, Jack suddenly thought about names. "Do you want to, you know, keep your own? It's okay. I know lots of girls, women, are doing that these days."

"Darling Jack," she said, "do you really think I would pass up the chance to be named Mrs. Wisdom?"

When they arrived at Jack's house the first time, Rebecca told him how sweet it looked, "full of Jackness." Inside, she moved from room to room like a child in a playhouse. Except—in the living room, she stopped and stared for several seconds at the fireplace.

"Honey," Jack said, "is something wrong?" For a moment he thought he saw those sparkling lights again, inside the fireplace, but if so they quickly vanished up the chimney.

"It's nothing," Rebecca said and began to talk about possible colors to paint the beige walls.

For two years they lived happily ever after. Jack's parents liked Rebecca immediately, and Rebecca was thrilled with her new family. Jack worried what people might think of his wife's profession or if odd people would be showing up at all hours. To his relief, Rebecca said she was happy to take a break from her work and just enjoy life. Every now and then she would see someone, mostly long-time clients who depended on her and didn't mind traveling for a consultation, but she promised to see them when Jack was at work and not to advertise. Jack never asked her about these people and she never spoke of them.

Once someone flew in from Japan, though he left before Jack could meet him. And once Mrs. Simmons, who lived across the street, told Jack how a pair of black cars drove up to his house and men in dark suits, some with old-fashioned walkie-talkies held up to their ears, went into the house and didn't come out for over an hour. Jack decided not to ask Rebecca about it. It was their agreement; he had said he didn't want to know, and he thought he should stick to it.

Sometimes Jack would come home to find Rebecca crying or tight-lipped and he wouldn't know what to do, how to help her. After a while she would sigh or rub her eyes, and then look at him with a soft smile, and everything would be fine again.

One night in early September, Jack woke at three a.m. to discover his wife gasping for breath, shaking. "Bec?" he said. "What is it? Do you need an ambulance?" He grabbed for the phone.

"It's okay," she said. "It was just a dream. Go back to sleep."

He thought how he hated dreams, but he wrapped his arms tightly around her, held on until she stopped shuddering. "It's okay," he echoed her. "It was just a dream." After a minute, she calmed down enough that he could let her go. She turned on her side, and Jack wondered, as he slid back into sleep, if she was still awake.

Five days later, terrorists attacked. Everyone Jack knew was weeping with frightened eyes, except Rebecca, who immediately began to organize local relief contributions. Jack never asked her about her dream.

He also never asked for any predictions about his work. Occasionally he would joke about "getting a reading" but never actually did it. However, sometimes at dinner he might tell her about a problem, or a pending decision, and the next morning she might casually make a suggestion. He never told her how these suggestions worked out, and she never asked, but once at a company picnic, when she met Charlie Perkins, Jack's boss, Charlie told her, "Your husband's really something, you know? Any time we can't figure out what to do, we just tell Jack and he comes back the next day with the right answer. I guess they don't call him Mr. Wisdom for nothing." Jack stared at the grass.

They were married for two years and seven days when Rebecca told Jack she was pregnant. He yelled and danced around and offered to go and get a case of nonalcoholic champagne. Rebecca said very little, only asked Jack to hold her. Jack hugged her for a long time, then said, "Sweetheart? Is this okay? I mean, the baby. I'm being a real jerk here, but I guess that's nothing new."

She shook her head. "You're never a jerk. You're sweet and lovable."

"I mean about the baby. I'm so excited I didn't even check how you're feeling about it. You okay? Because if not, and you want to, you know, do something, it's okay. Really."

"No, no," she said, then sighed. "Did you ever do something you knew would turn out, well, bad, just because you knew absolutely it was the right thing to do?"

He took her shoulders. "Sweetheart, nothing's going to turn out bad. I'll take care of you, and if there's any problems, we'll get the best doctors in the world."

"I'm not worried about that," she said.

"Then why are you so upset? You think I'll stop loving you 'cause there's a baby? I'll never stop loving you. Nothing can change that. I loved you the moment I saw you. I'll love you forever."

She stared at him. "You promise, Jack? Do you promise you'll love me no matter what?"

"Absolutely."

She closed her eyes. "Oh God," she whispered.

He held her again. "It's okay," he said. "You'll have a fine pregnancy and we'll have a wonderful boy or girl."

"Boy," she said, her voice muffled by his shoulder.

He let go slightly so he could look at her. "Are you sure?"

"Uh-huh."

"Did you get an ultrasound? I mean, it's okay, but I would have liked to have been there."

She gave him that sweet smile of hers. "No medical tests," she said.

"Then how can you—? Oh. Right."

She said, "Can we go and get that champagne now?"

The pregnancy went easily. Rebecca insisted on a midwife, though she agreed to see a doctor as well. The midwife, Jennie, said she'd never seen a baby so eager to be born. They named him Simon, for Rebecca's grandfather, though she'd never mentioned him before. "Simon, Simon," Rebecca half chanted, and held him so close Jack worried she might cut off his breath.

From his first moments, Simon looked at the world, and especially his mother, with curiosity and delight. Jack's cousin said, "He has your eyes."

"Come on," Jack said, "he looks like his mother. Lucky kid."

"Oh, the shape of his eyes, yes. But that slightly bewildered look? Jack, that's you."

It wasn't until a few days after the birth that Jack admitted to himself how scared he'd been that Rebecca would reject the baby. He didn't know why he'd thought that, but he was glad he was wrong. If anything, she went the other way, almost obsessed with spending every moment with her son. And yet, at the same time, Rebecca grew sadder and sadder. When she wasn't feeding or rocking Simon, she would stare out of the window, silently crying. Jack did everything he could to cheer her up. He brought her presents, he took her and the baby on weekend trips, he played with Simon with her, but none of it seemed to work. After four months he took her hands, and suggested, as gently as possible, that she see a psychiatrist. Postpartum depression, he said, was perfectly normal, it came from hormonal changes, and best of all, it was treatable.

Her smile was far sadder than tears. "Sweet Jack," she said, and touched her fingertips to his cheek. "This has nothing to do with my hormones. I wish it did."

It was late on a cold October night when the disaster happened. Curiously, Jack had been thinking of disaster when he went to sleep, for he'd been watching the late news, with reports of floods in Florida, earthquakes in California and Peru, and arsonists bringing down a library in Prague. When he woke up and smelled burning wood, he thought he was dreaming and was angry at himself for letting his control slip. But no, it was part of the "awake-world," as Rebecca some-times called reality. "Honey?" he said sleepily, and turned over to dis-cover she was gone.

From downstairs he could hear her voice. She was singing, or chant-ing or something.

Simon, Simon,
Rhymin' Simon,
Take the time an'
Stop the crime an'
Set the children free.

Jack said, "What the hell?" and got out of bed. The first thing he saw when he came into the living room was the Tarot cards. They lay on the floor, fanned out in concentric half-circles of color and action. And then he saw his wife in the epicenter, crouched down in front of the fireplace, her back to him as she leaned toward the high flames. "Bec?" he said. "What are you doing?"

She turned, her face a mix of rage and despair. "Get away!" she yelled, then, "Please, Jack. Trust me."

Only then did he see that she'd immersed her arms up to the elbow in the flames, and in her hands she held Simon, bathed in fire.

Jack screamed, leaped at her. With one hand she tried to push him away while the other held on to Simon. She was no match for him. He beat back her flailing hand and shook her away, then grabbed the baby from her. Clutching Simon against his chest he screamed, "You fucking lunatic!"

He thought she might try to fight him, or maybe run. Instead, she just stared at him. "Jack, Jack," she said, "I wasn't hurting him."

"Not hurting him? You were holding him in a goddamn *fire*."

"Feel him. Feel his skin, his clothes. Is he even hot?"

Jack started to shout again, but stopped. It was true, he realized. Simon slept peacefully against him, his beautiful soft skin pleasantly cool. Stubbornly he said, "You were trying to kill him. I got to him in time."

She shook her head. "I was trying to save him. But you're right. You got to him in time, and now it's too late." She jumped up and ran from the room. Jack didn't try to stop her.

He heard her weeping as he went first to their bedroom and then the baby's room to pack a suitcase, the whole time holding on tight to Simon, as if Rebecca might swoop in and snatch their baby the moment Jack set him down. But Rebecca never appeared, and when he'd taken what he thought were the essentials, he grabbed his keys and the suitcase with his free hand, then ran from the house.

That was the last time Jack ever saw Rebecca alive.

Chapter Seven

MATYAS

Matyas sat by the iron gates half the morning before the big doors swung open and four men stepped into the sun. They were young—younger than Matyas' father, at least. They all wore striped robes over white pants and plain sandals. One of them carried a staff with a jewel on top, like the one the Master had at the Hungry Squirrel. This staff was fancier, carved into a spiral, the yellow stone on top as big as a fist.

Matyas couldn't hear what they were saying and didn't much care. It angered him that they didn't appear to notice him standing just a few feet away. "Please, sirs," he said.

They all turned toward him. The tallest, a man with a high forehead and sandy hair and thin lips, said, "Who are you?"

"My name is Matyas. Sir."

"What do you want, Matyas-sir?"

To knock you down and walk on you. He said, "I want to go to your school."

A couple of them laughed but the tallest one said, "Go inside our school? For what? Whatever you are selling we don't need."

"I want to become a wizard."

The man's mouth gaped, then he and his friends burst out laughing. One of the others said, "Go home, boy. We have enough wizards, I'm afraid." Another said, "Did Johannan send you? Fat man with a skinny beard? Told you to come here and say that to us?" The tall one added, "We do not appreciate beggars making fun of us."

"I'm not making fun," Matyas said.

"Then leave."

"I want to learn how to fly." They burst out laughing once again. Matyas wanted to tear off their elegant robes and knock them down in the dirt. Instead he called out, "Come around me! Right now."

Lights appeared in the air, a scattering of fireflies that hovered around Matyas then vanished within seconds. The man with the spiral staff first looked startled when the lights appeared, but then he rested his stick in the crook of his elbow and clapped his hands in a large sweeping gesture. "Bravo. A true display of power." And then, "I have no idea who sent you with whatever glamour to summon a flicker of the Splendor, but I suggest you run back and tell him his joke was not very funny."

Matyas didn't know what to do. Beg? See if he could get inside the gate and hide? Tell them about the Kallistocha, the prophecy that he would fly? They probably would just laugh again. He was pretty sure he could get at least one of the men on the ground and kick him senseless before the others figured out how to pull him off. But suppose they conjured up a demon to eat him?

They had lost interest in him and were about to walk past—and Matyas was about to get down on his knees—when a dry, precise voice called down from above, "I will take him."

In one motion, the four all turned and stared up at the top of the tower. Matyas could make out a small figure in the single window. The man with the staff said, "Veil?"

"Yes, Lukhanan. You have identified me correctly. Your studies are progressing. Now, if you can keep the boy entertained long enough for me to come and get him, he can begin to work for me."

"But Mistress," Lukhanan said, and he appeared genuinely confused, "he's filthy. He'll steal everything the moment you go to sleep."

"Then I will have to stay awake. I will think of you, Lukhanan, and laughter will drive away drowsiness. Now hold him for me."

Matyas' mind jammed with thoughts. *A woman. What could a woman teach him? He called her "Mistress." That's like a Master. But maybe she's a demon.* When the gate swung open again, there was neither demon nor powerful sorceress, only a woman a little taller than Matyas himself. Her face was sharp and finely lined, with a wide mouth and narrow nose, eyes that looked very alert inside wrinkles, and gray hair pulled tightly back and held with a silver clasp. She wore a long, straight dress, as severe as a shroud, brown with gold and silver threads.

She looked at Matyas for what felt like a very long time, while he squirmed but managed not to look away. Finally, she turned to Lukhanan and said, "There. You see?" as if she'd won some contest.

Lukhanan rolled his eyes. "Look at him. He can't even read."

Veil turned back to Matyas. "What is your name?"

"Matyas." He almost said "Master" but stopped himself.

"Can you read, Matyas?"

"No, ma'am. Mistress."

"Wonderful. Then you will not need to unlearn anything. Or at least not as much." She turned and walked back through the gate, with Matyas running after her.

When they started up the narrow stone steps, Matyas said, "I dreamed of this tower."

"Did you? And does it look the same?"

"Well, I only saw it from the outside."

"Oh, from outside all towers look the same."

Matyas soon found it hard to keep up with her. After only one flight, he began to breathe heavily; after a second, his shoulders sagged and he had to pull himself up by the plain wooden banister; after a third, his legs wobbled and he didn't know if he could continue. Veil turned and looked at him as if to say, "Tired already? What use are you if you cannot even climb a few steps?" On the fourth flight, he thought for sure he would faint, and almost begged her to stop so he could catch his breath. No. He would not give her any excuse to send him away. Or laugh at him. With all his might, he managed to keep going. Finally they came to a low wooden door, unadorned, with a simple brass handle. Matyas almost wept when Veil opened it herself, for he had no strength left even to release a latch.

The moment they stepped inside, all Matyas' energy returned. He could stand again, and breathe easily. Curious now, he looked around. If he'd expected to see demons in cages, or angels trapped in circles of candles, or maybe eagle feathers as souvenirs from flights above mountains, he had to settle for a simple room with wood walls, two plain, unpainted chairs and a small white rocker, a rough wood table, a small fireplace and books, books, books, some on shelves, some piled on the floor.

Wedged in among the books were various objects, like small bells and thin gold sticks, along with various boxes and pouches, small statues of people and animals, and for some reason a lumpy black stone in a corner. A little, red wooden box, plain and faded, looking as old as Veil herself, sat all alone on a low wooden table. And that was all there was. No other furniture, and certainly no wondrous creatures. Two alcoves extended from the main room, one with a plain iron stove and rough pots, the other with a narrow bed and a lidded white porcelain chamber pot, with a blue curtain for privacy. Without thinking, Matyas blurted, "It's so ordinary."

Veil smiled. "Is it now? Then tell me, young Matyas, why you found it so difficult to climb the stairs."

Matyas stood up straight. "I didn't have any trouble."

"Oh? You looked in pain."

"I just told you, I was fine."

She laughed now. "Matyas, there was no shame in your weakness. I needed to test your talent and you have shown it. Remarkably so. Few practiced magicians could have made it even halfway up those stairs, let alone to the top."

Matyas squinted at her. Was she making fun of him? "It was just some stairs," he said.

"Look out of the window."

He peered out. "It's just the courtyard."

"Look again."

Shaking his head as if at a madwoman, Matyas took a step closer to the window. He saw blackness, deep night, though a moment earlier it had been sunny. As if from a vast distance swirls of gray emerged, shot through with sharp jewels of color. It all turned, arms spilled out, grew then dissipated like puffs of smoke, replaced immediately by fresh spirals. Matyas stared and stared. He could dive into it, swim in it—

Veil yanked on his arm. He growled at her, tried to fight her off, but she only held on tighter. He turned to tell her to leave him alone when suddenly he realized how off balance he was, that if she had let him go he would have plummeted right out through the window, down into—

Now, when he looked again, there was only the courtyard below.

Veil said, "Stairs can be many things, sometimes even a genuine ladder, which is to say a passage to the higher realms. The first flight took you beyond the Moon, the second beyond Venus, the third past

Mercury, the fourth the Sun, and the fifth, well, the fifth flight, young Matyas, carried you past the birthplace of stars. Only the very wise or the very foolish can survive such a journey."

"Don't call me a fool," Matyas said.

Veil nodded. "I would not do that. But let me tell you a saying from an old friend of mine. It goes like this: The scholar hears of the Gate and tries to undo the lock. The student hears of the Gate and tries to squeeze between the bars. The fool hears of the Gate and laughs. Without laughter, the Gate would never open."

"I'm not a fool," Matyas said. He glanced nervously at the window.

"Oh, no need to worry," Veil said. "While you stay here it will remain a dull tower leading to an old woman's crowded retreat. As I said, I wanted to test your talent. I am satisfied."

"Then teach me to fly."

"Fly? Who told you a wizard can fly?"

Matyas was about to tell her of the voice, the prophecy and the man he'd seen move across the sky, but something stopped him. So he only said, "It's why I came here."

"Patience," Veil said. "We will begin your lessons soon. Now I am tired and I would like my hair brushed." She sat down facing away from him and held out a small brush of pig bristles set into polished horn. With her free hand, she removed the clasp and her hair tumbled down her back.

"I'm not . . ." he started to say, then watched his hand take the brush. It felt warm and almost weightless. He ran it through her hair in long strokes, first jerkily, with anger, but soon smooth and rhythmically. He had no idea how long he'd been doing it when Veil murmured, "Thank you, Matyas. You may rest now."

He looked around, seeing hard floor everywhere, covered in books, statues and other odd objects. Where was he supposed to sleep? He'd have to twist himself like uncooked dough to find a spot. At least at the inn, his mother had given him a thin pallet and some torn sheets to set down in front of the stove.

He must have made some kind of noise, for Veil's head lifted and she turned to look at him. Matyas said, "I don't . . . I don't know . . ."

"Ah," Veil said. A finger pointed to the alcove with its small wooden bed, white pillows and a quilt of alternating squares of roses and squiggly signs.

Matyas stared, mouth open but unable to make a noise. He had never slept in a bed. Once, when a guest had left early, he'd sneaked into the room and lain down on top of the scratchy blanket. He couldn't remember now what it felt like. All that stayed in his mind was what happened when his father walked in and caught him. For days he could hardly move to do his chores, and when he did, he had to check constantly for any drops of blood that might leave a stain on a sheet, the floor, a dish.

Now he walked over to stand just outside the alcove where he could stare at the bed. It looked so soft! But suppose it was a trick! Maybe if he dared to lie down he would burst into flames, or snakes would rear up to tie him so he couldn't get away, and fire demons would roast him. He said, "Mistress—"

"Veil," she said, and when he looked confused she added, "There is no reason to call me Mistress. I prefer my name." When he did not continue, Veil added, "I apologize for interrupting you. What were you going to say?"

"I can't lie there! That's your bed."

"Ah," she said. "I see the problem. Matyas, I am very old, and old women often prefer to sleep sitting up. This rocker suits me quite well. And since I am not using the bed, it's for you."

Carefully, just in case it was indeed a trick, he lowered himself onto the bed where he lay on top of the quilt. A small sigh escaped him as he closed his eyes. He had never felt anything like it. For a moment he wanted to cry, something he had not done since before he could walk. But then that passed, and a moment later he was asleep.

Chapter Eight

JACK

It was barely six in the morning when Jack arrived at his parents' house. He didn't tell them what had happened—he couldn't bring himself to reveal how crazy she was, as if they might say I told you so, even though he knew they'd always liked her. So he just said that she'd fallen into depression and had refused help and had tried to harm Simon.

Mr. and Mrs. Wisdom loved Rebecca, but they loved their son more, and baby Simon most of all. Over the next days, Grandma took care of the baby while Jack's dad did his best to cheer him up, and every now and then suggest that maybe Jack should talk to her, maybe now she'd accept psychiatric help.

Jack didn't answer. He remembered when he'd had all those terrible dreams, and his mother wanted him to see a doctor but his father refused. *How would it look if someone from the Wisdom family got his head shrunk?* More normal than normal, that was what they were supposed to be. Well, Rebecca was as far from normal as it was possible to get. At times Jack wondered if he was back in his dreams, if he was still nine years old and trapped in an endless nightmare. But then he'd look at Simon, asleep in his crib or laughing at some silly face from Grandma, and he'd think how he could never have dreamed something so wondrous and pure.

And he thought of Rebecca, how much he ached for her. *You can't dream love*, he thought. *You can't command it, or control it. Even anger can't shut it off.*

Rebecca called every day. The first time, Mrs. Wisdom picked up the phone and when she heard Rebecca's voice asking for Jack, she got all confused and said she would check if Jack was there. "It's Rebecca," she whispered to her son, who stared blankly at the television as if it was a wall. Jack shook his head. The older Mrs. Wisdom told the younger that Jack wasn't there, she had no idea when he was coming back, and in fact had no idea where he was.

"And Simon?" Rebecca asked.

"He's fine," Grandma said, and wondered if she'd revealed too much. Or not enough. Could she have encouraged Rebecca to get help?

"Please tell Jack to call me," Rebecca said, and Mom promised and hung up. After that, they screened all the calls and followed Jack's insistence that no one talk to Rebecca, though her messages begged Jack to call her.

"Shouldn't you talk to her?" his father said. "She really sounds sorry." Jack shook his head. What if she said she was all better, and he believed her? And took Simon home, and then when Jack was at work—

One evening, Jack's father took him to a basketball game, leaving his mother alone with the baby. When the phone rang and Rebecca came on the machine, Mrs. Wisdom was tempted to pick it up, to see if she could get through to her daughter-in-law that she had to take the first step of seeing a psychiatrist. Like her son, she remembered, she couldn't help but remember, when she wanted to take him to a doctor, and she let her husband stop her. But this was different—Rebecca so clearly needed help. She was obviously heartbroken, and Jack was definitely in pain. Just as Jack's mother reached for the phone she realized Rebecca was saying something different this time, something crazy.

"Jack," Rebecca said, "please listen to me. Please. You have to remember. Nine years from now, a man will offer to take Simon on a special trip. To help him. *Don't let him do it*. He'll seem so kind and smart, and promise you every safeguard. Don't listen to him. Don't let Simon go with him. Please, Jack, you have to remember. I don't care what you think about me, what you tell Simon about me. Just don't let him do it. *Remember*." She was crying when she hung up the phone.

Mrs. Wisdom replayed the message three times. Rebecca sounded so desperate. But that very desperation, about something so obviously insane, was clearly a sign of her madness. Jack had a right to hear the message. Of course. But what would it do for him, except entrench him even deeper in anger? After the third time, she sighed deeply and erased the message.

Two days later, on a Sunday morning, Jack was sitting at the kitchen table, feeding Simon puréed carrots and occasionally snatching bites of a bagel and cream cheese. His mother had offered to feed the baby so Jack could relax—working long distance from his parents' home appeared to tire him even more than going to the office—but Jack wanted to do it himself. It was late autumn, and leaves swirled around the back porch. Jack's father stood at the window with his mug of coffee. He laughed and took a sip. "There's something you don't see every day," he said.

"What's that?" his wife asked.

"There's a pair of squirrels scratching at the back door like they want to come in." Louder, he said, "Sorry, boys. No nuts or berries available today."

Jack jumped up so quickly he dropped the spoon and Simon began to cry. Jack handed the baby to his mother then rushed to the window. "Jack?" his mother said. "What's wrong?" and his father said, "Son? What is it?"

Jack stood at the window, his mouth open as if he couldn't breathe. The squirrels turned toward the window, stood on their hind legs and tilted their heads up to stare directly at him. One was gray, the other red. "Oh my God," he said, hardly more than a whisper.

His father touched his shoulder. "Jack?"

The squirrels ran off now, along the path to the driveway and under Jack's car. Jack turned, stared at his father, and then his mother, as if they, not the squirrels, were strange and alien. Finally he said, "It's Rebecca. I have to go to her. She's dying."

His mother gasped, and his father said, "Dying? What are you talking about?"

Jack didn't answer, only ran for his keys. "Take care of Simon!" he yelled.

When he arrived home late that afternoon, Rebecca's car was in the driveway, and he didn't know if that was good or bad. At the back door, he dropped his keys twice before he discovered it was unlocked. "Bec?" he yelled as soon as he was inside the house. "Rebecca? Are you okay?"

The first thing he saw was the word *Remember!* written in red marker all across the blue living room wall. He stared at it a moment, shook his head and ran into the kitchen, the den—He found her on the floor of the bedroom, her red and black silk dress scrunched up around her knees, her face as empty as the rumpled bed, her hair bunched up under her neck. He wanted to rearrange her, lay her out properly, but he knew from television that that wasn't allowed.

He didn't even realize he'd squatted down until he saw his own hand touch her cheek, her neck, her forehead. Cold. She was cold and thick and empty. He lost his balance and fell back against the bed. *How long?* he wondered. *How many hours?* He tried to remember how long it took for a body to get cold but nothing came to him. Was she already dead when the squirrels showed up? Is that what they'd wanted to tell him? He'd thought they were summoning him, but maybe it was already too late. He couldn't decide if that made it worse or better.

He needed to call someone. 911? Was it an emergency if it was already too late? And he needed to call his parents, they would want to know. And Simon. He had to tell their perfect son that his beautiful, crazy mother would never see him again, never hold him—He shook the thought away. He didn't have to tell Simon. Not now, at least, not for many years. But he had to call the police, or the doctor, someone.

Abruptly he jumped up and rushed down to the basement, where a leftover half-gallon of paint stood on a wooden shelf with a couple of brushes. Upstairs he painted over the giant command to memory with great slashes of blue. No one would see her craziness, no one. Did she really think he would forget her? He wanted to shout, "How could you think that? You were everything to me." But his voice wouldn't work, only his arms and shoulders as they obliterated the insults of madness.

At last he called 911, and then his parents. They didn't ask how he'd known.

At the funeral, Jack's father and a cousin had to hold him up. At least it wasn't suicide. Brain aneurysm, the coroner said. Sudden, quick and unforeseen. "It just happens," he told Jack. "There's no way to predict something like that."

When they got back to the house, Jack let his parents take care of Simon and set up for visitors. "There's something I have to do," he said. He searched the bedroom and everywhere else he could think of for

Rebecca's Tarot cards. He wanted to tear them up, piece by piece. They were gone, or at least were nowhere he could find. Maybe, he thought, she'd come to her senses before the end.

Jack went home after that. His mother—once again the only Mrs. Wisdom—came for three months, not leaving until she was sure he was okay. Before she left, she helped Jack find a good day care for Simon, who was almost a year old. Jack resisted at first, said he was fine to work at home, but his mother told him he needed to get back with people. At the Happy Hands Center, Jack's mother did almost all the talking. Near the end, as they were filling out forms, Jack suddenly said, "You don't have anything to do with Tarot cards or anything like that, do you?"

Mrs. Beech, a large woman with muscular arms and tangled black hair, frowned at him. "Tarot cards? Now why would you think that?"

"Oh no, I didn't—" Jack stopped, not sure what to say.

"Maybe you'd be happier with a religion-based center," Mrs. Beech said.

"No, of course not. I just . . . I had a neighbor who was always throwing Tarot cards, and it just seemed . . . I don't know, a bad influence, I guess. I'm sorry, I shouldn't have said anything."

"Well, I can promise you we don't do anything like that here. We're pretty traditional."

"Good. Good. Thank you. Oh, one more thing. Simon has a kind of, I guess phobia, about squirrels."

"Squirrels?" Mrs. Beech said, and Jack's mother stared at him.

"When he was just a few months old, a squirrel scared him. He cried and cried. So if you see any squirrels around, could you chase them away?"

"Yes, of course," Mrs. Beech said.

Outside, Mrs. Wisdom looked about to say something, then changed her mind. In the car she said, "I'm so glad you're trying this. You know, Jack, Simon needs to be with other children as much as you need to be with grown-ups. I know it's hard, but really, it's for the best."

And maybe it was. Simon emerged into childhood sturdy and curious, with a wide smile that attracted other children as much as adults. He had his mother's curly hair and large eyes, his father's wide hands. He appeared to like puzzles, or at least objects you could put together into some kind of shape. He could play for hours, it seemed, with blocks, or the soft, colorful pieces of a baby jigsaw puzzle, arranging them into different forms, none of which made sense to anyone but himself. Though the other children liked him and often looked to him for directions, he was just as happy all by himself. He learned to read very early, and soon the house was filled with books aimed at much older children.

Jack had to be careful, though. He didn't want any fairy tales, especially stories about talking animals. It wasn't easy. From television to comics to toys, the child universe was filled with jabbering animals. But at least Jack controlled the books. And he always made sure Simon knew the difference between fantasy and reality.

One night Jack had a dream. He managed to keep them away most of the time—more than ever, he needed to stay normal, for Simon—but now and then one would sneak up on him. In this dream he went to check on Simon and lights were flickering all around his son's head. Simon laughed and grabbed at them, but they danced away from him. Jack ran at them, waving his hands as if they were flies or mosquitoes, and the lights streamed out through the window. When dream-Jack looked outside, he saw a whole line of squirrels staring at the house. He yelled and ran outside, only to discover more squirrels by the front door and all around the building. "Leave us alone!" he yelled, and woke in his bed.

Quickly he ran into Simon's room where the boy was sleeping peacefully, hugging a stuffed elephant his grandma had given him. Jack made sure the windows were shut, then glanced outside. The trees and the grass were clean and empty in the early dawn. Only, if he looked beyond the first line of growth it seemed to him that the trees became denser, dark and very old. He thought for a moment of when he was young, and "troubled," as his mother used to say, and his dad decided it was the woods. *Maybe Dad was right*, Jack thought. He glanced over at Simon asleep, then back at the twisted trees. Suddenly a light flashed within their dark heart, so bright Jack took a step backward. For some reason he thought suddenly of *Remember!* scrawled across the living room wall. He closed the curtains so he couldn't look at the trees anymore, and then he went to the kitchen to make a cup of coffee.

Chapter Nine

MATYAS

On that first day after his climb up the tower, Matyas awoke excited to begin his studies. Instead of instructions, however, Veil gave him a list of chores to do. All day he cleaned, or ran up and down the stairs, or just put books away. In the evening he cooked a carrot stew then once more brushed her hair until she fell asleep. This went on for weeks. Every time Matyas protested that he had not run away from home only to do the same work, Veil simply said, "When you are ready."

"I'm ready now," he would say—or shout—but Veil just ignored him or gave him another task.

Sometimes, when his chores took him downstairs and out into the courtyard, he looked around at the buildings and wondered what went on inside them. The Academy was not a large place, really, just a group of buildings set around an open square paved with stones worn smooth by generations of Masters and apprentices. Often there'd be no one around when Matyas made his way to the old stone well, or out through one of the gates on an errand, and he stared at the buildings, but at other times he saw apprentices studying, or practicing, or else the Masters them-selves, and he moved along, pretending to ignore them in the hope that they would ignore him.

Occasionally, if he thought the Masters weren't watching, he stared at their robes. The shape was usually the same, plain, made of heavy material that might be silk or wool, usually belted, sometimes with a rope, sometimes with leather shaped like a snake biting its own tail. What fascinated him were the colors, some just gray like the old wizard's that night at the Hungry Squirrel, but others bright red, or yellow, or blue, or mixed, maybe a red cloak over a white robe. What kind of robe would *he* wear when he became a Master? Something bright, and dazzling, so that people would have to shield their eyes when he passed them. He thought about Veil and that shapeless gray dress she wore. Anyone who didn't know her would think she was a beggar. Why did she do that?

If there was just one Master in the courtyard, he would always appear to be in a hurry, but if there were two or more they might walk together, their hands and heads in motion as they argued some doctrine or spell, or maybe just laughed at some joke only a magician would understand. Matyas watched them with a tightness in his throat, and an invisible hand pressed against his heart. *That should be me*, he thought. If Veil would just teach him—But then he would look at their boots or velvet slippers bound to the Earth, or the way the bottoms of the robes swept the stones, and he would think, *If they were real Masters, they would fly*.

Veil's tower was not only the tallest building in the square—by more than half, it appeared, though he was never quite sure, for some days it looked much higher than others—it was also the plainest. The tower was built, as far as Matyas could tell, of dull brick, the kind made with dirt and straw, while the other buildings were formed of some smooth stone that looked almost polished, as if someone had rubbed each one by hand. Matyas wondered if a tribe of demons had worked on them. The buildings had red metal roofs whose corners curled up into strange shapes, each one different, and marble steps, and large ornate doors.

Various stone or metal creatures stood guard, either in front of the doors or mounted right on the thick dark wood. There were lions, and what looked like dragons except they had women's heads, and sometimes just faces set into the door itself, faces all contorted like someone in pain, with gaping mouths and sharp teeth. Were they alive? If Matyas rushed up the stairs and tried to push open the doors, would the stone heads suddenly devour him? After a while, as he saw masters, and especially students, boys not much older than Matyas himself, go in and out without any obvious spells to protect themselves, he decided the statues and faces were just decoration. Later—months, years—he would come to understand that sometimes "decorations" contained a magic all their own, even if the people who passed by them every day, including those who should know better, had no idea. But in those first weeks, when he believed magic was all spells and miracles and changing people into toads, Matyas only cared if the statues *did* something.

And yet, even after Matyas realized no teeth would bite him in two, no lightning would strike him dead if he ran up the steps and kicked open the doors of what he learned was the library, or the great dining hall, or the Masters' Residency, he still stayed outside. For what if he marched inside to where the Masters sipped phoenix soup from crystal bowls and they all turned—and laughed at him? Better to wait and study and prepare himself. If only Veil would teach him.

Not all his chores were a burden. Or maybe it was better to say that some were burdens mixed with pleasure. Veil wanted everything kept clean of dirt, even dust, and that was a lot of work, but the *things* he cleaned, the statues, the jars, the endless books, these were a constant fascination. And a frustration, too, for he wanted to know everything, he wanted to read all the books, but every time he asked Veil to teach him she refused, or didn't even answer.

On Tuesdays and Fridays, Matyas went out through the Academy gates and walked down the hill to a street market a mile long, where vendors stood behind wooden tables piled high with cheeses and fish and cured meats, and green vegetables and berries in summer and root vegetables and apples in winter. There were bolts of cloth, including bright shimmering silks, and thick wools with strands of color woven in, and soft linens. There were spices and teas from across the waters and casks of wine and beer.

The first time Matyas came here, he stared and stared until he realized people were laughing at him and calling out things like, "Over here, country boy. I've got something really special for you." After that, he did his best to appear casual, but he still looked from side to side, not wanting to miss anything. He imagined how much Royja would have loved this, how if she was with him, he would blindfold her and lead her right into the center of the market, let her breathe the smells of the fish and spices, listen to the din of haggling. Then he would fling away the blindfold and watch her eyes blink in amazement. *Someday*, he promised himself. When he became a real Master and could send a coach drawn by horses made of moonlight.

At first the market people appeared to take him for a kitchen boy. They would say things like how much his "mistress" would love some special cheese or cake. Even worse, they looked at the simple things he bought, and his tattered clothes, and assumed the kitchen he worked in must be a very poor one. Sometimes they pretended to offer him exotic wines, or silver table ornaments, then laugh as he pretended not to hear them.

It didn't take long for Matyas' love of market days to turn to dread. He would try to look busy, cutting vegetables very small, or rearranging books so that she would not disturb him by sending him to the stalls. Finally she stared at him one Friday morning, her head tilted back slightly as if to see him from a different angle, while he pretended not to notice as he rubbed a soft cloth over a small stone statue of a woman holding a pair of snakes. "Matyas?" Veil said. "Is something wrong?"

Answers crowded his head. *I'm not your slave!* And *I didn't come here to buy cheese, I came to fly!* And *Everyone laughs at me. Teach me a spell to make them stop.* But all he said was, "I want different clothes." He felt himself turn red and couldn't look at her. Why did he say that? He didn't care about how he looked; he wanted magic and books. He wanted to learn to read all these great works he dusted every day. He wanted to study their secrets, not clean them.

To his surprise, Veil did not ridicule him, or threaten to turn him into a horned toad, but instead nodded, as if he'd said something very wise. "Forgive me," she told him. "Old women forget about such things. You are young, and need clothes that are fresh and clean, and proper to your station."

"Station?" he said. Did she mean servant? Slave?

"Yes, of course. You are, after all, an apprentice in the Academy of Wizards." His breath stopped for a moment, but Veil appeared not to notice. "Lukhanan would never forgive me if I allowed you to misrepresent our students to the world." She got up from her chair in that slightly stiff way she had, then walked over to a plain wooden box that stood on the floor with smaller, more ornate boxes piled on top of it. Carefully she removed everything, then lifted the dark brown lid to reveal what looked like blankets, and sheets painted with circles and diagrams of some kind. Matyas had not been in Veil's tower very long, but he had begun to suspect that nothing was ever quite what it seemed.

He wondered what she would produce for him. A great thick robe like the ones the Masters wore? A coat of many colors, maybe, and a hat with a red plume. In the end, it was simply a shirt of white linen with red ties across the front, undyed wool pants and a long sleeveless leather coat. "Here," Veil said as she held them out across her arms. "Your sandals should do for now. We'll see to proper boots when winter comes."

It took a moment for Matyas to reach out and take them, as if she might yank them away and tell him it was a joke. "Can I put them on?" he said once he had them safe in his hands.

Veil laughed. "Of course. I *was* saving them just for you, after all. I'm sorry I forgot. That seems to happen more and more, I'm afraid." Later, Matyas would think of the strangeness of what she'd said, for what did she mean by *saving* them? She'd only met him a few weeks before. But right then he just ran into his alcove, closed the curtain—he'd already grown used to the strange idea of privacy, something he'd never known sleeping alongside the stove in the Hungry Squirrel—and put on the new clothes. They fitted perfectly. After all, he thought later, hadn't she been saving them for him? The idea made him a little dizzy but he didn't care.

When he held up his old clothes he realized how filthy they were, how they stank, and the thought that he'd walked around in them for weeks filled him for a moment with shame, and then anger. And that too was odd, for during his whole life in his parents' inn he'd stunk of grease and soot and slop and never thought about it. But right then all he said was, "What should I do with these?"

"Do you want them?"

"No!"

Veil laughed, a sound so much fresher and younger than her old bent body. "Good. Then let the birds have them."

"Birds?"

She walked to the small window and beckoned him to follow. "Yes," she said. "What are rags to us are treasures to our friends." Slightly nervous at what he might see, Matyas bent forward to look out of the window. At first he noticed—relieved—the courtyard and the stone buildings of the Academy. Then he saw, high above them, birds floating on the warm air, outlined against light clouds. "Are you ready?" Veil said. Matyas nodded but held on tightly to his old clothes. Quietly Veil said, "Now, Matyas."

Matyas thrust the clothes out through the window with such force he nearly lost his balance and fell head first, but then he steadied himself on the window frame—or maybe Veil caught him, he was never sure—and he stood back to watch. For a moment the rags fluttered in place, held up by the same breezes that sustained the birds. And then it looked as if beams of light broke through the clouds and stabbed the fabric so that all of a sudden the clothes broke apart into tatters that blew away from each other. The birds swooped down, not one kind but many, hawks, an owl with a gray body and a white face, crows, herons, an eagle the biggest and a hummingbird the smallest. For a moment it looked as if they would fight each other but then each one appeared to get what it wanted, for they all spun away and took off into the sky, higher and further until at last the light and the clouds swallowed them.

Matyas watched them for a long time, watched the space where they'd been. His throat hurt in a way that made it impossible to think, and so he didn't try, he just watched. After a long time, he looked down at the courtyard, where the wizards and their students walked around, oblivious to the sky. He stepped back into the dimmer light of the room and looked at his arms in their clean white sleeves, as if he'd brought the clouds down to wrap them around his body.

Veil said quietly, "The market, Matyas. It's time for you to go and buy what we need."

At the foot of the stairs, Matyas stood a moment in the dark tower, one hand on the thick iron latch. What would he do if the apprentices, or the wizards themselves, gawked at his new clothes, made jokes, pointed and laughed? He wished he had the power to strike them all down, turn them into toads and rats. But then he remembered the owl, just the owl, as it took a shred of what had been his arm or his leg, he couldn't say which, and lifted up into the clouds. And he discovered he didn't care what anyone thought, or what jokes they might make.

Outside in the courtyard there were indeed some shouts and some laughter, though they died away quickly. Maybe it was because Matyas paid no attention, only looked up at the sky.

In the market, no one appeared to regard him differently at all. Oh, they joked, the usual offers to show him something special, and a couple indeed said how he must have got a promotion, or else done something truly special for his mistress—or master—but mostly it seemed they just didn't care who bought their cheese and fish and cabbage, so long as the coins were good.

No, it wasn't the clothes that changed the way the market people regarded him. It was something that happened a week later. Usually, Veil told him what she wanted and where to go for it and how much to pay, and gave him the correct amount of coins. The first couple of times she made him repeat it back, until he told her, "I'm not stupid," to which she apologized, and then only told him once. One day, however, she gave him a piece of paper with nine words written in a vertical column, the letters small and needle-sharp. Though he had no idea what the words said, Matyas had stared long enough at the books in the tower to observe that Veil formed her letters with a kind of flowing precision, free of the flourishes and ornamental style of most of the manuscripts. Matyas said, "If you'd teach me to write I could do this for you." He had no idea what *this* might be, and didn't care.

Veil ignored him. She said, "Take this to the very end of the market. You will see a table all by itself, and a man with a bald head and tattoos of birds on his arms. Give the paper to him, along with this." She passed Matyas a leather bag with what felt like twice the number of coins she usually gave him for everything they needed. "His name is Johannan," Veil said. "He will know what to do."

Matyas made his way through the usual jeers and fake offers and promises, but as he kept going, past the vegetables, the fish, the cloth, not stopping for the usual cheese or turnips, as it became clear he wasn't going to stop at all until he reached the end, a strange silence settled around him. He became aware suddenly that everyone was watching him and pretending not to.

It was easy to spot Johannan. His stall was indeed at the end, with an empty space between him and all the rest. The table appeared to be made from the same rough wood as the others, but was piled with boxes and jars of various sizes. On the ground beneath it stood three small chests of different metals, one iron, one bronze, the other silver. The day was cool, an early autumn chill, so that most of the vendors had jackets or shawls over their aprons, but Johannan wore only a thin yellow linen shirt with the sleeves rolled up, as if he could not bear to hide the bright plumage that adorned his thick arms. For he was tattooed, magnificently, an elaborate bird covering each arm. Years later, Matyas

would see such birds and realize they were called *parrots*, but now all
he could do was stare at the sharp detail of the multicolored feathers,
and think, just like those first couple of times at the market, how much
Royja would love to see this.

"Are you Johannan?" Matyas said.

"I believe so," the burly man said.

Matyas hesitated at the odd remark, then said, "I'm supposed to give
this to you," as he passed the paper to a thickly calloused hand.

Johannan studied the list, nodding once or twice. "And the money?"
he said.

Matyas showed him the bag but held tightly to it. "After you give me
what I came for."

Johannan nodded again. "A man of caution. Very wise. But tell me,
how would you know if I cheated you?" Matyas' face grew hot as he realized his ignorance was displayed all over him. Johannan laughed. "Don't
worry," he said. "I've never cheated Veil yet, and I'm certainly not about
to start now. If I ever visit other worlds, I would prefer the choice of
where and when to be left to me."

Matyas watched intently, as if his eyes alone could absorb the knowledge of all the powders and leaves and oils that Johannan assembled
so quickly it was hard to follow his hands. Smells swirled around him,
some sweet, some bitter, and one so sharp it seemed to cut Matyas in
half. That was when Johannan opened a jar containing a thick black
paste and spooned a tiny amount of it into a little silver vial. Matyas
gasped and sweat covered his face but he managed not to fall down or
even make any noise. At the nearby stalls, owners and customers alike
were coughing and retching, though no one yelled out for Johannan
to put it away, or to do his business somewhere else. Johannan himself
pretended not to notice.

When all the powders were in little envelopes and the oils and pastes
in vials, Johannan wrapped everything in paper covered with large letters and solemnly handed it to Matyas. Then he held his palm out. "The
money," he said. "Or do you want to check first that I did everything
correctly?"

"No," Matyas said, with as much dignity as he could manage. "If Veil
trusts you, then so do I."

Johannan smiled. "I'm honored."

Walking back through the market, Matyas pretended not to notice all the stares, the whispers of, "Veil! He works for Veil," and, "Not *works*, he's her *apprentice*. Veil must have disguised him to test us."

It was only when he had left the market noise and smells behind and was making his way up the hill to the Academy that it struck him. A test! Of course, but not the market people. *Him*. Veil was testing his loyalty, or his courage, or *something*, and now she was going to teach him to fly! That must be what all these disgusting powders and filthy oils were for. He tried to remember if the man he'd seen flying that night by the dark woods had any strong smells to him. He couldn't recall anything, but it didn't matter. Matyas was going to fly.

When he returned he ignored whoever might be in the courtyard and ran up the winding steps to the top of the tower. Veil was reading from a large black book with pages of stiff parchment and ornate over-sized letters that even Matyas could see belonged to some other alphabet than the usual. The letters looked somehow watery in the way they flowed in curlicues from one to the other. Usually Matyas would stare at any open page, as if, if he just looked at them long enough, with enough concentration, they would have to reveal their secrets. This time he only glanced at the book then excitedly held out the small leather sack containing all the powders, leaves and oils.

Veil nodded as she took the sack, then set it down on a wooden table next to her, alongside a glass bowl full of colored stones and what looked like an ancient dried lizard. "Thank you," she said.

"I got everything."

"I'm sure you did." He stood there until she looked up at him and said, "I believe you have work to do."

Matyas blurted out, "But what about my flying ointment?"

"Flying ointment?" She saw him look down at the sack, then back at her face. "Oh, I see. You thought all this was for you. I have other concerns than you, Matyas."

He felt his face turn red but refused to look away. "If you'd teach me, like you said you would, I wouldn't have to wait. I could do it myself."

"Do what yourself? Make a flying ointment?"

"Yes!"

"And then what? Leave me? Fly out through the window and not even say goodbye?"

"So you admit it!"

"Admit what?"

Veil was smiling, ever so slightly, but Matyas ignored it. "You want to keep me a slave. That's why you won't teach me. Or make me a flying ointment."

"Oh, Matyas, I have no need of a slave. Believe me, I've lived for a long time without you, and managed quite well."

"Then why won't you make me an ointment? So I can fly?"

"No such ointment exists. I've told you this. How can I teach you anything if you don't listen to what I say?"

Matyas' hands clenched and unclenched. The old woman was just playing with him, as if he was some small animal in a cage. He remembered how he'd gone to the courtyard one day and seen several apprentices practicing a spell on a frightened squirrel in a cramped wooden cage. Matyas couldn't tell what they were trying to do, but whatever it was, it must have been painful, for the poor animal would spasm, then shriek, while the boys all laughed.

Was that what Veil wanted him for, something to torture? If so, she was going to get a big surprise. When he learned to fly he would grab her—by the feet—and fly all around the courtyard, maybe over the whole city, until she screamed and begged him to set her down.

He must have been grinning at this idea, for Veil glanced at him and said, "I'm glad I can amuse you, Matyas. Now it's time for you to prepare our supper."

The whole time he was working, then eating, then cleaning, Matyas kept an eye on the sack. What would she do with it? If it wasn't for a flying ointment, what was it for? After he'd finished his chores and brushed Veil's hair—the usual signal for the end of the day—Matyas arranged himself in his narrow bed so that he could look out at the leather sack through a gap he'd left between the curtain and the wall. He'd have to pretend to be asleep, or Veil might not do anything. Luckily, he was good at that. Faking sleep was one way to avoid his father's drunken fists. It didn't always work, but at least he had a chance. So now he looked out through his own slitted eyelids, just as he used to do in the kitchen so he would know when to roll away from a sudden kick to the stomach.

Matyas had no idea when he fell asleep. He didn't even remember being drowsy. One moment he was watching the sack on the table, the next he had woken up to see Veil working a mortar and pestle made of green stone. He just stared, unable to move or even think clearly.

Whatever she was grinding in the bowl must have been very hard because she had to work the pestle so much her shoulders moved with the motion, and her long silver hair, still loose and flowing from the brush, swayed behind her like a thin curtain. Matyas tried to recall if any of the things he'd bought from Johannan had looked very hard. Weren't there a couple of brown nuts of some kind? Round, with a scratchy surface. He shook his head to try to remember. Why was it so hard to think?

If Veil's body strained at her task, her face showed nothing. There was only the light of a single stubby candle to reveal what she was doing, but he could see her expression clearly, as blank as the stone mask she kept on the wall next to the window.

After several minutes, Veil abruptly finished. One moment she was pressing the pestle down with all her might, the next she'd set the mortar on the table and straightened up to take a deep breath. Matyas shrank down under the blanket, but she took no notice of him. Twice more she sucked in air and let it out so slowly and completely Matyas unconsciously gasped for breath.

And then she was rubbing the paste she'd made all over her hands, and anger flooded Matyas. Flying ointment! She'd made it after all, just as he'd begged her to, but not for him! She'd stolen it from him. Lied, and taken it all for herself. He wanted to get up and knock her down, wipe it off her hands and onto his own. But he didn't move. He was suddenly so tired again that it took all his effort just to keep his eyes open. She was going to get away, jump out of the window and never return. Leave him with all her old books, piles and piles of them, and she'd never taught him to read.

Veil went nowhere near the window, only stepped over to a narrow wooden stand hardly noticeable among the stacks of books. At first Matyas thought the stand was empty, but then he saw it did contain one object, a red wooden box, unadorned but very smooth, about the length and width of Matyas' hand. Now he remembered he'd seen it before—that first day, actually. And he must have wiped the dust off it a dozen times since then, but it felt now like the first time he was looking at it. With all the statues, and elaborate books, and ornate bowls and sticks, the box was so easy to overlook.

Veil said something, and even though it was too low for Matyas to make it out, he could feel it, tiny sharp jabs all up and down his spine. Was it demon language? He was pretty sure it wasn't human talk. Something else she was hiding from him. He remembered how he'd thought the Masters had summoned demons to build their grand library and dining hall, but maybe it was Veil and the tower? Was he in a demon tower right that moment? Were the bricks made of dirt and demon spit—or worse?

He realized his mind was drifting away from the red box. It seemed to take a great effort to keep his mind on it. A spell. She must have cast a spell on the box. Or on Matyas himself. To make him forget. He forced himself to focus all his attention on the box and on Veil as she lifted the lid.

Voices. A murmur of voices, a whole crowd of them. Was this where she kept her demon slaves, imprisoned in the red box? Any moment now they would roar out, swarm all through the tower, screaming, biting. This was why Veil had taken him when Lukhanan and the others were about to throw him out—not as a student, not even a servant, just something to feed to her captive monsters. Maybe if he shrank down in his bed, closed his eyes tight, as he should have done all along, Veil would spare him. *Please, please*, he thought. She could send her demons out through the window to find some homeless beggar, maybe some old man too weak to stand up, who wasn't going to live long anyway.

No! he told himself. This was just Veil's spell, for hadn't the voices—the *real* voices, he decided—called him Master Matyas? Didn't they promise he would fly? Protection. He needed to protect himself. "Come around me," he whispered as softly as he could, and there they were, for the first time in weeks, tiny lights all around his face. The Splendor. "Stay close to me," he told them. "Don't let her see you." The lights moved almost against his skin.

If Matyas had been scared that even the Splendor would not be strong enough against Veil's demons, he was able to let go of his fear, just a little, when no monsters surged from the box. Instead, the voices died down, softer than a breeze, as Veil reached in and lifted out . . . not a hideous creature, not a dragon, not a jewel of captured starlight, but only a stack of thick papers.

At first Matyas nearly groaned out loud in disappointment. More paper! Something else he couldn't read. It always came back to reading.

But then he realized, he knew what these papers—these *cards* were. He'd seen the old wizard looking at them that night in the Hungry Squirrel. "Tarot cards" he'd called them. What was the name? Tarot of Eternity. If you had the original, he said, you could change the world. Or something like that. And that other thing, the one that made no sense— "Whosoever touches the Tarot of Eternity, he shall be healed of all his crimes." Only, the original was lost, hidden away by the great sorcerer who'd made them . . . Joachim, that was the name.

So had Veil found it? Maybe Joachim didn't *hide* the pictures, maybe Veil had *stolen* them. Was that it? Was she holding eternity in her paste-covered hands? What crimes would they heal her of? Refusing to teach Matyas to fly? If she could see all of time, she didn't show it, for she just held the whole stack between her hands, one below the pile, one above, as if to squeeze them together. She took three deep breaths, and each time the tower itself seemed to shudder, as if battered by wind. "Stay around me," Matyas whispered to the lights. "I need you."

Now Veil shifted her hands so that she could slide the pictures—the cards—in and out of each other. The effect of this simple action was dizzying, as if the room, maybe the world itself, was constantly forming and breaking, too fast to actually see anything change, only feel it. Finally she stopped, and Matyas had to hold in a sigh of relief. He wasn't sure that even the Splendor could protect him if he made a noise.

If Veil knew he was awake and watching, she certainly didn't show it. Instead, she held the stack in her left hand and lifted the top card with her right. A flash of light blinded Matyas for a moment, but still he didn't move or make a sound. When he could see again, Veil was holding the picture before her face, high enough for Matyas to see it over her shoulder.

The painting showed a naked boy and girl holding hands in an orchard where half the trees were bright with leaves and half looked dead and withered. The boy had golden hair in curls down to his neck, and his face and hands shone with light. The girl's pale skin glistened, and her long straight hair shone with silvery light. It gave Matyas a strange feeling to look at them, a kind of longing all mixed up with fear. He missed Royja all of a sudden, but forced himself to concentrate, to watch Veil. And as he watched, the old woman put all the cards but the one she held back in the box and closed the lid. A shock went through Matyas, and he thought of standing outside a beautiful palace and having someone suddenly slam the door. For a second he hated Veil and wanted to leap at her and knock her down for everything she was hiding from him, everything she denied him. So it was just as well that Veil, holding the picture of the boy and girl against her bony chest, simply walked to the door and left the tower.

Matyas could hardly believe it. She'd gone out and there was the box. He wanted to jump but it appeared he'd lain motionless for so long he couldn't move. "Give me strength," he said, and the Splendor moved all around him until his skin began to tingle, and then a moment later, he leaped up and dashed to the box.

No, first he needed the ointment. When he looked in the mortar there wasn't much left, but he managed to rub a thin residue on his palms and fingertips. He felt a slight tingling, pleasant when it started, exciting as proof that he was working magic. But then it became warmer and warmer, until suddenly it felt as if his hands were on fire. Frantically he shook them in the air, then rubbed and scraped them to try and get the poison off. It was all a trap. Veil had slipped some kind of fire poison into the residue. He ran and plunged his hands into the water bucket and felt a blessed coolness. But then they heated up again, even worse, and he realized she must have poisoned the water as well.

No, he thought. It wasn't poison, it was magic. Power, real wizard power, wasn't soft and gentle, it burned. He forced himself to stand there, with his hands in front of his face, the fingers spread wide, and steady his panicky breaths. The *trick*, he thought, was not to mind the burn. And as he did that, just breathed and watched his hands, the Splendor came around him, swirled all around his palms and in and out of his fingers, an ancient dance, until slowly the pain subsided and Matyas knew he was ready.

He turned to the box now, gently touched the fingertips of his right hand to the smooth wood.

He held his breath and opened the lid.

Chapter Ten

SIMON/JACK

Simon excelled in kindergarten, and then first grade, in all the ways a father wanted. His first-grade teacher, Mrs. Griswold, was amazed he could read whole chapter books. Hearing her praise, Jack nodded and smiled, proud of the hours he'd spent reading to Simon or tracing the letters with him, showing him how to sound out the words. He thought also of how carefully he'd chosen the stories, the ones he would read aloud to his son, and then the ones Simon would read for himself. Stories about boys—and sometimes girls, Jack wanted to make sure Simon didn't pick up the idea that girls were weak or frightened—who were brave and kind, and filled with wonder at the world. The real world, that is. Jack continued to screen out fairy tales, or stories of children with magical powers. He might choose a book about a child fascinated by the colors of butterflies, to help Simon develop a love of nature, or maybe a story of a girl who saves an injured horse from the vet's bullet, then nurses him back to health to win a race. That sort of book.

Just so long as the girl and the horse never talked to each other. Oh, the girl could talk. "Good horse, Shadow. You're going to get all better. I promise." Before he would buy such a book, however, Jack would read the whole thing, just to make sure Shadow never turned around and told Alice some secret about her cranky grandfather.

Over time, Jack's fears began to ease. Simon liked animals, same as most kids, but didn't try to strike up any conversations with them. He got along with the other kids, who seemed to like him, even follow him. It had been like that in day care, Jack remembered, and allowed himself a brief swell of pride, quickly followed by nervousness that he somehow might let his guard down, about what he wasn't sure. At home Simon did what any kid did. He played video games, screened by Jack for too much violence, and especially too much fantasy, and he watched a little more TV than Jack liked, but would turn it off to do his homework when Jack put on his Stern Daddy voice. He had friends in the neighborhood, and sometimes play dates with stable families, where Jack would occasionally go along and discuss business or lawns with the father. The mother might say how sad it was the first time she learned Simon's mom had died when he was just a baby, then usually let it go.

One Saturday, as he watched from the house while Simon and a boy named Marty laughed and threw snowballs at each other, Jack let out a long sigh. It was only then that he realized he'd been holding his breath for six years. *It's okay*, he told himself. Simon was okay. He was safe. Jack's beautiful child didn't even suffer from bad dreams. Well, no more than any normal kid. Suddenly, Jack laughed, loud enough that Simon must have heard it outside, for he turned around for just a moment, then went back to his game as a snowball hit him. "Not fair!" Jack heard him yell. "I wasn't looking."

Still grinning, Jack remembered how he'd made such a fool of himself with Mrs. Beech that first day in day care, how he'd told her Simon was afraid of squirrels, and then made sure the poor confused woman didn't keep any Tarot cards lying around. God, what must she have thought of him? It didn't matter, for hadn't Simon, beautiful strong Simon, achieved that elusive dream the Wisdom family had sought for generations? Simon Wisdom—more normal than normal.

For a moment Jack felt a strong stab of guilt, as if he'd betrayed his wife in some way. "No, Bec," he said out loud, softly. "This is good. It may not be what you wanted for him, but it's what he needs. Our little boy is normal."

But he was wrong.

One day Simon came home with a letter from the school. The second grade was about to go on the children's first ever field trip in a couple of weeks, and the school needed permission from one parent for each child. The destination was a place called "Animal World Petting Zoo." Jack wanted to tear the paper in pieces, but instead he kept reading as the letter gave the address and website, the bus arrangements (it was all during school hours), how many teachers and volunteer parents would be going along, money required for tickets and lunch—in short, everything a parent needed to know to feel safe and secure. Except, maybe, guarantees that the animals would not suddenly start talking to his son.

Simon must have seen his father's face, for he quickly said, "Please, Dad, can I go? It's gonna be so cool. Everyone's going."

Jack thought maybe he should sign on as a chaperone. But they didn't appear to need anyone else, and things had become busy at work, with a tight deadline approaching. And besides, he was being ridiculous, wasn't he? How normal would his son feel if he was the only kid not allowed to go on a field trip? Jack signed the paper, then took Simon out for ice cream.

On the day of the field trip, Jack was certain he'd made a terrible mistake. How could he ever have thought of letting his son—*Rebecca's* son—get close to a bunch of cuddly friendly animals? Should he just tell Simon he'd changed his mind and Simon couldn't go? He looked at him, and the poor little guy was so excited, talking nonstop even as he ate all his eggs and toast without any need for a prod. No, there was no way Jack could deny his son this, certainly not without some actual reason. Otherwise it would be as if . . . as if he was punishing Simon for his mother's craziness. And wasn't it just normal for a kid to want to go to a petting zoo?

Maybe he could cancel his meeting, Jack thought, to go along on the field trip. He was pretty sure they'd be happy to have another parent. But if he went, he would probably just drive everyone nuts by hovering around his son all the time, ready to grab him and run off with him at the first sign of any unauthorized animal conversations. He had to smile as he stood by the stove and sipped his coffee. He was being ridiculous, he knew. What would he tell his boss? "Sorry, Charlie, that presentation we've been working up to for six months? I've gotta blow it off. I have to protect my son from talkative sheep."

Jack walked Simon out to meet the bus. He gave his son a hug (not too long, he hoped), double-checked Simon had put his money for lunch and treats in a safe place, then watched as Simon ran up to where his friend Jason had saved him a seat. Jack gave Mrs. Coleman, Simon's teacher, his card with his cell phone number—just in case she'd lost the list with all the parents' numbers. He'd already checked that *her* number was safely programmed into his phone. The teacher smiled. "It's all right to be nervous, Mr. Wisdom. Every parent is the first time their child goes on a field trip. It's normal, really. I promise you, we'll take very good care of him."

Jack stood in the road and waved one last time at the bus as it turned the corner.

Somehow he got through the day. He even managed to do a decent enough presentation that his boss and the clients looked pretty happy as he turned off his PowerPoint and closed his laptop. Then he went home early to make sure he'd be there when Simon returned.

The bus was a few minutes late, a few maddening minutes with Jack at the edge of the picture window, where he could watch for it without being too obvious. Finally, he saw it, no black smoke bursting from the exhaust, no tires blown out. He forced himself not to run as he went outside to meet it. A moment later, Simon clambered down the steps. "Dad! It was so cool," he said. "All the animals, you could go right up and *touch* them. And they gave you these little bags of corn you could feed them. Did you know that baby goats are called kids? Isn't that cool? Oh, and they had these little pigs that were smaller than Mr. Harvin's yappy dog."

Jack listened happily as he took his son into the kitchen for a snack. "Oh, and some of the kids," Simon said, "I mean the real kids, not the goats, were kind of scared so they just kind of threw the corn at the animals and backed off, but I held it out and they came and ate it right out of my hand. It tickled and it was kind of slobbery, but it was really cool. Oh, and then Tommy Harmon slipped and fell into some poop!" He laughed happily as he ate his jam sandwich (he didn't like peanut butter).

Jack just smiled, and nodded, and contributed a few, "That's really great!" lines while he secretly waited for, "Oh, and Dad? This one little lamb came right up and *talked* to me." But nothing like that poured out of Simon's mouth, and after a few minutes, when Simon ran to the living room to watch TV, Jack leaned back against the sink, closed his eyes and whispered, "Thank you." He wasn't sure whom he was talking to.

The hammer fell on Jack Wisdom two weeks later. It was parent-teacher night at Mathers Elementary School, an event that Jack thought took place much more often than when he was a kid. The first couple of times, back when Simon was in kindergarten, he'd felt a little uncomfortable, the only single father among all the mothers and couples. By now, however, he'd grown used to it, even smiled at some of the admiring looks from the women whose husbands either had refused to come or fiddled with their phones when the teacher was talking.

Jack felt good on this spring night. Jessie, his favorite babysitter, was taking care of Simon, who actually listened to her, and Jack was pretty sure Mrs. Coleman would have some nice things to say about Jack's precious boy.

And so she did. She talked about Simon's reading skills, his curiosity, his politeness. And then she went on about what a natural leader he was. "It's amazing," she told Jack. "The kids all seem to look to him to tell them what to do." She laughed and added, "To be honest, I think I'm feeling that way a little myself." Jack felt his stomach clench, though he had no idea why. Mrs. Coleman went on, "Remember that field trip a couple of weeks ago? To the petting zoo? Well, we came to a certain corner, with the bus, you know, and Simon suddenly said, 'We have to turn here.' Well, of course I told him the driver knows where to go, and he was quite good about it, he just went back to playing some video game with Jason. But guess what? Two blocks later, we saw that a tree had fallen across the road. Can you believe it? We had to backtrack to the corner where Simon had said to turn! It was like he knew or something."

Jack didn't remember later what he'd answered, or how he'd survived the rest of the evening, only that he somehow got home, smiled as he paid Jessie and listened to her report and stood by the window to watch her drive off in her mother's Subaru.

Quietly he stepped into his son's room and watched Simon sleep. He stood there a long time, his mind jammed up, unable to think in any clear direction.

Should he take Simon out of school? He could home-school him, maybe hire a tutor. His parents would probably help with the cost. But Simon was happy in school. He was smart, well-adjusted, everyone liked him—a natural leader. Isn't that what everyone kept saying? Jack rubbed his forehead. He was being ridiculous, he knew. School wasn't the issue.

He went into his bedroom and picked up the framed photograph of Rebecca he still kept next to his bed. He'd taken it when they went back to the park where they'd first met. It was shortly after the wedding, when all the trees and sky looked filled with light.

"Oh, Bec," he said, "what have you done to our son? Is it true? Does he *really* have your eyes? That's what people said when he was a baby, that he had your eyes. Your red hair, too. He's turned out skinny like me, though. My nose, too, I'm afraid. Sorry." He felt tears begin and shook his head, as if to fling them away.

He said, "Is that what you did to him in that fire? Gave him your eyes? You said you weren't hurting him. Not physically. And you were right, of course, he wasn't even hot. But what about inside? What were you *really* burning into him? Jesus, Bec, if he's like you—I mean, what kind of life can he have—?" He stopped, took a breath. "I'm sorry. I just want him to be happy. I want him to be normal. Is that so terrible? No squirrels, no Tarot cards, just a happy, normal little boy."

It struck him that she might have answered, "But Jack, he *is* normal. Let him be who he is."

He closed his eyes and pressed the cool glass against his face. "God, Rebecca," he said. "I miss you so much."

Chapter Eleven

MATYAS

As he opened the red box, Matyas braced for a great rush of voices, maybe thunder and wind. But there was only silence. It was so quiet that Matyas felt a strangeness along his spine, and it took him a moment to realize that *everything* had gone silent, no wind outside the tower, no faint noises from the courtyard, no distant traces of the city. The world had lost its voice. Frightened he'd gone deaf, Matyas whispered, "Matyas, Matyas, Master Matyas," and was thrilled he could hear his own voice. Somehow, he decided, he had entered another world, where he was all alone with the pictures. *Alone with Eternity*, he thought. It should have scared him, but all he felt was excitement.

Reaching down to the stack of cards, he touched the top one with one fingertip, then immediately jerked it away. It was all right, the paper didn't burn, if anything it felt a little cold, actually, and slippery, like glass left out in winter. He picked it up and looked at the picture, a girl or woman in a white nightdress, like a burial shroud, sitting up in bed and covering her face with her hands, as if she was weeping.

He stared at it, aware that he didn't like it but not sure why. It was just a picture. It struck him then that the girl in the drawing looked like Royja, Royja grown up and unhappy, even though it was something drawn a long time ago, maybe hundreds of years. He didn't want to think about Royja, especially Royja weeping, so he set it face down on the table and looked at the next one, a man hanging upside down by one foot tied to a tree branch, with his hands apparently tied behind his back. A snake coiled around the branch, with its head descending toward the man's heart. Light filled the man's face, as if he could see some heavenly beauty at the foot of the tree.

Matyas looked at this one a long time, the snake at the heart, the serene face. Why wasn't he in pain? What was he seeing? Where did the light come from? Matyas remembered the Kallistocha from the grove of trees, and he wondered if this might be a picture of the High Prince. But this was a whole man, hanging upside down from a tree, and the Kallistocha Prince was just a head on a black stick. And as beautiful as the prince was, Matyas didn't think he was very serene, not peaceful and joyous, the way the man in this picture looked. Why was he hanging there? What did he know?

Finally, Matyas put it aside, for if he was going to discover the secret of flying, it certainly wouldn't be from someone tied to a tree. Holding his breath, he reached into the box with both hands and lifted out the whole set. They were much heavier than he expected, and he almost dropped them, but he managed to hold on, and with his feet, he moved aside books and jars and carved animals from the messy floor until he'd made a space big enough to spread them out.

He was about to put them down when he noticed there was one card left in the box, a picture of a woman sitting between two trees, a little like the two trees in the picture Veil had taken with her, except this one had jewels on the branches instead of leaves, white jewels on one, black on the other, but each one radiant. The woman sat on a stone bench mostly obscured by her long blue dress, which billowed out around her like clouds.

Her face at first looked empty, just darkness, until Matyas saw small lights and realized it must be the night sky with stars. Her face was the sky, and if you stared long enough, you could disappear into her dark and shiny skin. Matyas felt a longing that made him want to drop all the other pictures and only pick up this one, to look at it forever and never let it go. She was mystery, and beauty, the wonders of existence. Matyas thought how he could sit at her feet, as if she was really there, and stare at her, not eating, or moving, until he simply died and she would take him into the stars.

Suddenly angry, he slapped the picture face down on the floor. More tricks! Veil must have cast a spell on them. She knew if he learned to fly, he would escape her, he would be *better* than her, so she put spells all over the cards to distract him. Well, it wasn't going to work. Crouched down, he kept the night woman safely hidden but spread the rest of the cards on the floor.

So many! One on top of another, scene after scene—men, women, wolves, lions, lightning . . . He became light-headed, like the time he'd dropped a roast, right in front of the rich guests who'd ordered it so that his father had to throw it out, and then as punishment he wasn't allowed to eat for three days. But this wasn't a lack, it was too much. There—there was a picture of what it felt like, a man staring at seven gold beakers in the clouds, each one filled with something strange and wonderful, a dragon, a castle, a beautiful face that almost looked like the Kallistocha—

Matyas knew he had to concentrate. Somewhere in these pictures was hidden the great secret. It had to be there, otherwise why would Veil have put so many spells around it? With quick motions he moved them around, searching for what he needed. He realized he knew in fact what he was looking for, the picture, the card, he'd seen with the old wizard, the one that showed a young man in rich colorful clothes, dancing at the edge of a cliff. The Beautiful Boy about to Fly.

He found it finally, held it up with both hands before his face to scan it hungrily for secret messages. It was different somehow, or maybe he just hadn't got a really good look at the one the wizard had in the Hungry Squirrel. The Boy still held out his arms, with the fabric of his green and gold tunic billowing out like wings, and he still stood on one foot, the other raised behind him like a dancer. But now the sky was filled with faint spirals of different colors competing with the Sun, and the ground looked harder, and sharper, as if it might cut his feet through his thin boots if he couldn't learn to fly.

Matyas stared and stared at it, as if he could will himself to lift off into the spiral sky. If he couldn't do this, couldn't find out the secret, what would happen to him? Stay a slave to Veil, cooking, and cleaning, and brushing her ancient hair until one of them died? Or maybe she'd come back and see what he'd done and turn him into a toad. Maybe he already was a toad, maybe the wizard in the Hungry Squirrel hadn't really broken his spell, and everything that had happened since was some kind of dream, and he was just a toad, cold and sick in a swamp somewhere.

He focused his mind on the picture, the stiff paper, the bright, joy-ous colors. "Let me in," he said. "Please." Suddenly he remembered the strange words Veil had said, the spell in some harsh language that didn't even sound human. *That* was what he needed. He trembled just at the memory of hearing it—what would it be like to speak it? And how could he? He didn't even know what language it was, let alone the words.

He closed his eyes. Maybe he could remember the sounds. He con-centrated, made his mind like a room where he could close the door and window and keep everything out, everything but Veil's voice. He made himself think of nothing but Veil's sounds, the lips and tongue that would make those noises. It didn't matter what they said, it was just *sound*. Let *her* voice become his voice, his throat, his teeth, his tongue. Veil's lips were his lips . . .

He did it. He made the sounds, and for a moment exultation washed through him, because he knew, with certainty, that none of the appren-tices could do this, none of the *Masters* could do this. Just him and Veil. And Veil had studied it. So he was better—

Pain. It started as a slash on his tongue, then spread to his lips, his teeth, his cheeks, then his throat, his chest, wherever those sounds had touched he was cut open, as if someone had attacked him with a stone knife. *Help me!* he thought.

And then he was there. The pain was gone and he was there, right on the edge of that cliff, under a spiral sky. And because he was inside, he could see beyond the drawing, over the edge of the cliff to a deep valley hidden in clouds, and beyond that to icy mountains. He was alone, and he didn't know if he'd somehow replaced the Boy, or the Boy had already left, to soar beyond the spirals. It didn't matter. Matyas stretched out his arms, he opened them like great wings even though there were no folds of cloth to catch the wind. He was Master Matyas! Arms out as far as he could reach, he raised his foot and tilted back his head to the radiant sky.

And fell.

He fell through wind, his body tumbling in all directions as he gasped for air that went by too fast for him to grab it in his lungs. He fell through terror like a flood, through darkness and fire. He fell through shame, because if he could fly he wouldn't have fallen. The cards flashed around him, sometimes flat pictures but sometimes alive, as if he looked through a window. There was the Weeping Woman, and just as with the card, he turned his face from her, this time to see a man walking up a hill while a sad Moon covered the Sun. He saw a woman sitting against a tree and writing in a large book, and as she did so, flowers sprang up around her while impossible colors flooded the air. And he saw an old man, worn out and sick, slumped hopelessly against the wall of an inn as snow piled up around him.

He saw the Hanging Man, but now the light had gone from his face and he looked gray and cold. And he saw a wizard in a red robe, with a living snake around his waist for a belt, and a face that shone brighter and brighter. He saw this man several times, alone, or with demons chained to a block of stone, or with other people, whole crowds of people, beggars and wizards who walked alongside him, or sat around him, staring at the fire in his face that grew brighter and brighter until it dimmed the Sun. Even in his terror, Matyas understood that this man, this Master, had stolen the light from the Man Hanging on the Tree. He'd stolen the light but not the peace, for he was hungry, always hungry, and when he opened his mouth, and Matyas saw his stone teeth, he knew suddenly that this falling was only the smallest part of fear.

He searched and searched for the Beautiful Boy, for if Matyas couldn't fly free, maybe the Boy could save him. But all he ever saw was a wretched man in rags that looked as if they might once have been the Boy's bright clothes. It was just a glimpse, just a moment, as a pair of dogs bit the man and drove him away, but in that instant, sadness overwhelmed terror, and Matyas wondered if Veil was right after all, that "no man can fly." Then his fear swept back and banished everything else.

Just before he crashed, Matyas saw two things, almost lost in the wind and darkness. One was a card, the only one he'd set aside, the woman with the billowing robe whose face was the night sky. The other was in fact not a picture but a person. Or part of one, for it was the High Prince of the Kallistochoi. Both the card and the golden head were calling to him, singing, or shouting, but he couldn't make it out because—

He didn't even know he'd hit something until a different kind of pain roared through his side, and he cried out, and the sound of his voice made him realize the wind had stopped, he was no longer falling. Before he even looked around or tried to guess where he was, he felt himself for blood, for broken bones, the way he'd learned to do when his father had finished with him. Safe. He was unhurt.

Now he looked around him, felt the ground—no, the floor, for he was in some kind of building, which made no sense—had he fallen through a roof? When he looked up it was too dark at first to see anything. He felt the floor again. It was smooth, almost slippery, like the polished marble steps outside the wizards' library.

Slowly, carefully, he got to his feet, bruised but able to stand. The room had grown lighter, or his eyes had adjusted, because he could see around him now. The floor did indeed look like marble, a swirl of red and black, with the walls—quite far away on each side—a paler red. The room—or rather hallway, for it stretched out indefinitely—was lit, he saw now, by round lamps of some kind, about the size of half-melons, pressed high against the walls every ten feet or so. There were no candles inside, or any magical wizard torches; the lamps just gave off a cold, steady light.

Looking at all this, Matyas felt a sudden sickness that was stronger and harsher than the fear of falling through nothing, or the pain of hitting the floor. *I know this place*, Matyas thought, *I've been here before*. And, before he could even ask himself where those thoughts came from, *I don't want to be here*. He looked up at the ceiling, but turned away almost immediately. There was a painting that ran all the way down the long hallway, at least as far as he could make out. In the picture, angels with razor wings slashed at children who tried to cover their blood-soaked faces.

Matyas got on his knees and threw up, over and over, though nothing really came out, until finally his stomach stopped its convulsions and he could stand again. *Please*, he thought. *Let me out. I'm sorry*. There was no answer, no sound of any kind. When he began to walk, with no idea of where he was going, only the certainty he could not stay where he was, his sandals made a loud slapping sound against the floor.

He had gone a short distance when he saw papers, cards, scattered on the floor. For a moment he thought he was back in Veil's tower and relief almost brought him to his knees. But an instant later he saw he was still in the long hallway. He moved forward, though, because if the cards were the Tarot of Eternity, maybe he could use them to break whatever spell was holding him.

When he got closer he saw they were all the same picture, and it was the one he wanted, the Beautiful Boy about to Fly. Matyas rushed forward, excited that they might help him escape, and he'd already bent down to pick up the first one when he jerked back his hand. It was wrong. He knew it was wrong even before he saw what it was. They were all wrong. Someone had cut out all the faces, taken a dagger, or some other sharp blade, and hacked out the entire head, so that every card had a jagged hole above the shoulders.

"I have to get out of here," Matyas whispered out loud. "Please." But all he could think to do was keep walking.

At the end of the hall, a thin light came from a stone door that stood half open. It looked strange, this door, so crude compared to the marble floor, the smooth walls. The door was thick and rough, and stood only about a hand higher than Matyas. If he'd been as tall as Royja's father, or even Matyas' own, he would have to stoop low to walk through it. Matyas stood for a moment, looking at the door and the light. He didn't want to go to it, but when he turned around, he saw that the pale lamps had gone out behind him, so that only a few feet beyond where he now stood darkness swallowed the hallway. Almost against his will, or maybe with no will at all, like a marionette, he moved toward the door.

Now he could hear a voice, soft, a child, he thought, no words, just a sad cry or a moan. *I've been here before*, Matyas thought. But how could he . . . It was the dream, he realized, the one he'd had that night after the trees, and the Kallistocha, and the flying man. *Please*, he begged in his mind, *let me wake up*.

He didn't even realize he was standing just outside the door until it swung further open and Matyas saw *him*. Tall, in his elegant, close-fitting jacket and straight pants, with a gray shirt and some sort of red silk cloth tied under the collar. His face was softer than Matyas remembered from the dream, the bones less prominent, the skin pale but a little flushed, as if excited. His gray-black hair was cut short at the neck but thick on top, and brushed back to show his wide forehead. Incongruously, Matyas became aware of how skinny he himself was, how his bones stuck out, how rough his clothes looked.

The man appeared not to notice Matyas. He stood next to a stone table, doing something to a round object that lay on a silver tray. Suddenly Matyas remembered the dream, just an instant before he saw clearly what the object was. A human head. A boy, right around Matyas' age. That was the voice he'd heard, the wail, the head was *alive*, the man was cutting it, he had a stone knife, black and shiny and very, very old, and he was making tiny cuts along the cheeks, the forehead, all around the eyes and mouth.

Blood dripped into the boy's eyes but he managed to blink it away and stare at Matyas. "Help me," he whispered. "Please, Master, help me."

Matyas shook his head. He wanted to say, "I can't," but didn't dare, for what if the man heard him, what if he came next for Matyas? He needed to turn and run, back to the darkness if there was nowhere else.

Too late. The boy must have alerted the gray-haired man, for he turned now and smiled at Matyas, his teeth bright, the knife held loosely in his hand. "What do you think?" he said. "Is it ready?"

Sounds came from Matyas' throat, but he had no idea what they were. The man laughed and shook his head. "No, no," he said. "I would never eat *you*. We're too much alike."

"No!" Matyas managed to say. "I'm nothing like you." He looked around frantically, saw stone walls and a rough floor specked with ancient blood. And somewhere—far away, beyond the room, as if hidden deep in the wall—he saw the woman from the picture, the one he'd left face down on the floor. There she was, in her blue dress like clouds, her face the night sky filled with stars. But there was something different about her. Her hand! She was holding out her hand.

All he had to do was ask. Ask her to help.

The man appeared not to notice. He picked something up from the table, a piece of paper, Matyas saw, and then a second later realized what it was—the jagged head cut out of the Beautiful Boy. "There," he said. "Now we're ready."

No, Matyas told himself. *Ask her!* The woman was his one chance to escape, he knew this. But he knew something else as well. He would have to say what he'd done. There was no way around that. She couldn't help him if he didn't—*No*, he thought. Never admit anything. That was the one thing he'd learned, the single most important thing he knew. For just an instant, his father's massive fists rose up before him, scarred and greasy. And then they vanished to reveal, once again, the stone knife, the boy's cut and bleeding head. *Never admit—*

The Splendor came to him. The lights were faint now, half flickered out, but they were still there. Weeping, he nodded, and as if they'd been waiting for permission the lights entered his mouth and swarmed around his tongue.

The man placed the mutilated picture on the boy's forehead—

—and Matyas' voice cried out, *I'm sorry*. His voice, not the Splendor. They had come to help him but he was doing it himself—

—and the boy screamed as dark fire flashed from his forehead—

—*I stole them! Forgive me*—

—And Veil had hold of Matyas' shoulders and a moment later had thrown him across the room, away from the red box and the cards scattered all around the floor. He hit a wall and books fell down into his lap, but he just stared at her, his mouth open, his body flooded with gratitude that he was already trying to deny. *Never admit—*

"There," Veil said. "It's not wise to look too long into the Tarot of Eternity. An old saying but still a true one." Matyas could only watch as one by one she calmly picked up the cards and returned them to the box.

"It was you," Matyas said. "You were the picture!"

"The picture?" she repeated. "Matyas, I'm right here. You looked upset, and had your arm out, so I took hold of you."

"No," Matyas tried to say, "that's not . . ." Exhaustion overcame him. His eyes closed, his head drooped . . .

He woke up in his bed, hours later it felt like, to see everything back in place, and Veil in her rocker with yet another of her ancient books. Every object in its assigned place but one, it appeared. The red box, and most likely all its pictures, were gone.

Chapter Twelve

SIMON

Simon Wisdom was six years old before he realized he was different from other children. Before then it had not occurred to him that other kids didn't know their grandma was about to call before the phone rang, or when Daddy needed help with something, or when you shouldn't watch television because something bad was going to happen in the world. Once, in kindergarten, he came home bruised where a girl named Susan had hit him on the arm. "It's okay," he told his angry father, "she just needed to hit someone." When his daddy asked why, Simon said, "Because her mommy's hurting her." Simon knew his daddy was upset hearing this. He'd even known it would happen. He just didn't understand *why*. Didn't Daddy know what Simon was going to tell him? Didn't everyone know that Susan's mommy was hurting her? Daddy had said something about not knowing what to do, how he couldn't tell anyone because he couldn't explain how he knew. Simon couldn't understand that. Why couldn't Daddy just tell them?

It wasn't like Simon *always* knew what people were going to say. When Daddy asked him if he knew what people were thinking all the time, Simon rolled his eyes and said of course not, how could he know that? But when he did know he just assumed everyone else did.

Sometimes, like when he asked about Simon knowing what people were thinking, Daddy was angry at *him* for some reason, but again, Simon couldn't figure out why. Angry or maybe worried, because now and then Daddy paid extra attention to him, sitting and watching TV with Simon (even though Simon knew Daddy hated the show), going out for special weekend food on a Wednesday, giving him a toy for no reason. At those times, Simon could see his father was pretending he was happy when he really wanted to cry. Those were the moments when he really did know what his father was feeling, even sometimes what he thought, but even that seemed like a useless clue, like a piece of a jigsaw puzzle all by itself, without the cover to show where it went.

One of those times came after the field trip to the petting zoo. Daddy acted very strange after that, super-nice but angry—Simon didn't think his father's anger was about him, but he wasn't sure—and all worried, even scared about something. Simon knew it had to do with the tree that had fallen in the road on the way to the zoo, and—really weird—Simon's mom, who'd died when Simon was just a baby. But that was all he could get when he looked at his father's face. Was Simon's mommy hidden in the fallen tree? Could they go and look for her? She was dead, of course, Simon understood that, but still—

At one point, Daddy seemed to want to talk about it, but he didn't really say anything. It was a Tuesday night after the field trip and Daddy had made Special Pancakes, Simon's favorite (chocolate chips and bacon, yay). Simon knew that as soon as he had eaten his food, Daddy would come and sit next to him and talk. But what he said made no sense. "You know, Sweetie, everyone has special talents. Some kids can climb trees really well, and some are really good at Xbox, and some at math. And usually . . . usually it's good to show people when you're good at something."

"Uh-huh," Simon said between bites, so Daddy would know he was listening.

"But sometimes—some talents—it's best not to show them."

"Why not?" Simon poured himself some more orange juice. He liked it when Daddy made it fresh and let him have as much as he wanted.

"Because not everyone can do it."

"So what?"

"Well, people don't like it when you tell them things before they happen."

"But then they know." *And*, he thought, *didn't they know anyway?*

"It's just better if they don't, okay?"

"Okay," Simon said, and ate a piece of bacon that had fallen out of the pancake.

Simon was a practical person. Since he couldn't figure out what Daddy meant, he just didn't think about it, and sure enough, after a week or so everything went back to normal.

That was in first grade, when Simon was six. It was a year and a half later when he found out that his "talent," as Daddy called it, could get him in trouble. His teacher had sent him home with a perfect score on his subtraction test, with a note to his daddy saying how proud she was of Simon's progress.

Jack stared at the paper until Simon asked him, "Aren't you happy, Daddy? I got a hundred."

Daddy said, "Nineteen take away seven." When Simon didn't answer right away, his father sighed. "Simon," he said, "you don't really know this, do you?"

"I got a hundred."

"Yes, but you got it by reading the teacher's mind."

"Reading . . . ?"

"Knowing what was in her head. You don't really know subtraction, you just knew what the right answer was."

Simon moved back slightly. His father had spoken calmly but his body was vibrating with anger. Simon said, "But that's what you're supposed to do. Get the right answer."

"From the question, Simon. Not from the teacher's mind. It's . . . it's a kind of *cheating*." He said the word really hard, as if he wanted to slam his hand on the table.

"It is not!" Simon's own hands clenched into fists. "I'm not a cheater, I'm not."

"If you read the teacher's mind, that's cheating."

"No! I did what everybody does."

"That's not true. Most people don't get the answers that way. They have to study for them." He took a breath, controlling himself. "What you did, Simon—it's not fair."

"Yes it is!" Simon yelled, and ran to his room. Even as he said it, however, he knew his father was right. He thought about things kids said and the way they got scared of tests, and for the first time in his life he considered the terrible possibility that he might be very different from other kids. Maybe that was why his father was so angry.

His father left him alone in his room a long time, and when Simon came back downstairs his father was reading a book. It occurred to Simon that if he concentrated really hard he might know just what Daddy wanted him to say. But that too would be cheating, and suddenly it was really important to Simon that he not do that. So he just said, "I'm sorry, Daddy. I didn't know I was cheating. I won't do it again."

Daddy put down his book. "Come here, Sweetie," he said, and when Simon walked up, Daddy hugged him so hard Simon couldn't breathe.

When Daddy let go, Simon could see he was crying, and he said quickly, "I'm sorry."

"No, no," Daddy said. "I'm not angry at you. I was just . . . I was thinking about your mother. She would have been very proud of you."

Simon was surprised. He knew his father thought about his mother sometimes (Was it wrong to know that? Was it another kind of cheating?) but he almost never spoke about her. And there was a kind of anger in Daddy's voice, and Simon didn't understand that at all. Wasn't it good that his mother would be proud of him? But then he thought, why would she be proud of him for cheating? He waited, but his father said nothing more, so he said again, "I promise I won't cheat. Ever."

"I'm sure you won't," Daddy said. "You're a good boy."

Suddenly, Simon remembered the pancake talk last year. He said, "And I promise I won't say what's going to happen."

His father looked down at the floor. He said nothing for a moment, then, "You're a good boy. I love you."

Simon wondered if it was okay that he already knew that, but all he said was, "I love you too, Daddy."

Simon wondered that night if he missed his mother. Could you miss someone you'd never known? Sometimes he dreamed of her. At least he thought it was her. In the dream he would see a woman far away, like the other side of the school parking lot, but when he tried to run to her, so many buses or something would block the way she'd be gone by the time he got there. Once, when he was four, he dreamed he was walking with his grandma in the city, and he saw, across the street, a woman bent over a table, playing cards with somebody. Simon was sure it was his mother and wanted to go and see, but Grandma refused to listen, saying they'd be late for a party if they didn't hurry. In the dream he began to cry, and when he woke up he was gulping air and holding on tight to Mr. Axle, his favorite teddy bear, who was dressed in yellow overalls and carried a soft red wrench.

After Daddy explained about knowing the answers, Simon wondered if his mother didn't want to see him because he'd cheated. Or maybe because he wasn't like other kids. Could Daddy have told her? It was so unfair. He didn't know it was cheating. He'd thought everyone knew those things. But it was just him, his special talent, and nobody liked it. What good was a talent if everyone hated it? And what kind of world was it where you were the only one?

From then on, Simon did his best not to know things that other people didn't. Most of the time it was easy—you just didn't pay attention, or you thought about television or something. But other times, especially when his father, or someone Simon liked at school, was unhappy, Simon had to hold back from helping them by telling them what they needed to know. He reminded himself that it was cheating, and no one likes a cheater, but sometimes holding back made him feel kind of barfy, or feverish.

Early in third grade, a boy in Simon's class disappeared. His name was Eli, and he sat a couple of rows over from Simon but that day his seat was empty. Simon kept staring at it, even when the teacher told him twice to pay attention. As the day wore on, Simon started to squirm in his seat, for he felt like he could hear Eli's voice in his head, crying and crying. He tried to make it stop, for wasn't it a kind of cheating, even if it was just crying and not anything you could "read"? He tried, but he couldn't do it, it just got louder and louder. Now it felt like Eli was calling him, not with his name or any words at all, just with a great pain that begged and begged for help, for someone, anyone, for *Simon*, to find him and help him.

Simon could find him. All he had to do was follow the noise in his head. He could tell the teacher, and the teacher would call his daddy, and they would all go and get Eli so he could stop crying. Only, that was cheating, so Simon held his fists tight against his body and did whatever he could to ignore the sounds.

School let out early that day. Lots of parents came and picked their kids up instead of sending them on the school bus. Even Simon's daddy came, and said that they were going right home instead of to after-school care. Simon hardly paid attention, the noise in his head was so loud and he didn't want Daddy to know it was happening. He hated Eli, he wished he could grab him and yell at him to shut up, to leave him alone.

The crying stopped a few minutes after dinner. One moment it filled Simon's body, it filled the whole room, and the next it was just gone. Simon cried out. He couldn't help it—the silence *hurt*, it was like someone had hit him really hard in the belly, a pain so sharp he let out a scream before he knew he was doing it. His daddy jumped up from his chair, said something that Simon didn't hear, and a moment later was helping Simon stand. Simon hadn't even realized that he'd fallen, or that he was on all fours and trembling, like a sick dog. His father led him to a chair.

"What is it?" Daddy said. "What's wrong?" Simon didn't answer. When his father went to call the doctor, he said, "I'm okay, Daddy. I just felt sick suddenly. But I'm okay now." His father looked at him a moment, then put the phone down.

Two days later the police found Eli's body in a burned-out old house at the edge of town. Simon never really found out what happened, but everyone at school was talking about "scary things" that someone had done to Eli, and a couple of days later two state troopers, a man and woman in gray uniforms, came to assembly and warned all the kids against going away with anybody, even if he said their mothers or fathers had sent him. The grown-ups had their own assemblies as well. Twice that week his father went to a town meeting. He told the babysitter not to open the door for anyone, for any reason. Both times he came home upset.

A couple of weeks went by and everyone began to calm down. Kids went back on the school buses, the teachers didn't all hover in the playground at break, looking around nervously as if they were constantly counting to make sure no one was missing. Simon too began to feel better. For days all he'd been able to think of was Eli crying and crying and crying. He imagined his voice, very far away, saying, "Why didn't you help me? You were the only one who knew." Finally the voice was fading and Simon could hear the world again.

Jack Wisdom was having trouble of his own those two weeks. Like all the parents, he worried about his son's safety with a monster loose in their town, and like the others he tried very hard not to imagine *those things* being done to his own precious, beautiful child. Why would some-one—? The police said it wasn't even sexual; it was just . . . He'd taken the *head*—No, no, no, Jack would shake his own head very hard, trying not to let those thoughts, those images, take hold in him.

In those ways, Jack was pretty sure he was just like all the others. But a memory came to him, no matter how hard he tried to block it, and he was pretty sure it wasn't something that invaded any of the other parents' minds. He didn't tell anyone, not the committee demanding that the police catch the monster, and not the police themselves. For what could he tell them? He wasn't even sure it had really happened. For years he'd half-believed he made it all up—that's what his father had believed, and certainly the cops back in his home town—and then, as he got older, he did his best not to think about it at all.

It was that day on the baseball field, of course. The day he'd hit a home run and it had felt so good he'd gone back that evening, just so he could look, and remember the shocked cheers, and trot once more around the bases. And then *he* was there. Just standing there, at home plate, tall and stiff in his dark suit, his face all tight and pale. Jack hadn't thought about him for years, but now he could see him again, his gaunt face, his gray hair combed straight back. He could hear that taunting voice—*Jack, Jack, don't go back. Let's just try to keep on track*—but most of all, Jack Wisdom remembered the way the man's hands had touched him.

Just his head. They moved all over his face, the bony fingers covered his mouth, the rough skin scratched his cheek, pressed his closed eyes. Most of all, Jack remembered the way he couldn't move, couldn't stop the hands, until suddenly the man just slapped him and said, "You're not the one. You're not ripe enough." Somehow that had freed Jack and he ran home to his parents. *Not ripe.*

His dad had called the police, of course. That's what Jack would do if Simon ever . . . The police had looked, and found nothing, and somehow it had all become another joke on the family name.

Was Eli "ripe enough"? Was that what had happened? Had the gray-haired man come back and found what he wanted?

Ridiculous, Jack told himself. That was thirty years ago, and two hun-dred miles away. But what if it was true? *And what if Eli wasn't enough?*

As troubled as those thoughts were, they were not the only things that plagued Jack Wisdom during that awful two weeks after the police found Eli's headless body. Two, three times, Jack seemed to get lost driving home from work in this town where he'd lived for over ten years. He would find himself on streets with old wooden and even stone houses, most in bad condition, as if the banks had foreclosed on all the mortgages and then couldn't sell them at auction so just left them to rot. *The bad part of town*, Jack would think as he drove those streets he didn't know, and he would make a mental note to tell Simon not to come here, wherever here actually was.

It wasn't just the buildings that bothered him. He'd see kids, homeless and helpless by the look of them, slouched against boarded-up doorways, crouched together on corners, as if to share secrets, except they all just stared at the filthy sidewalk and didn't even look at each other. *Broken*, Jack thought. Broken children, thrown out like old household tools and gadgets that were once all shiny until they stopped working and it was easier to junk them than to try and get them fixed. Vaguely, Jack promised himself that this would never happen to Simon, his son would never end up like this. But then, unable to stop himself, he thought, *What about Eli?* Who'd been there to protect Eli?

Two weeks after Eli's disappearance, twelve days after the police found his body, Jack Wisdom drove down one of those broken streets and swore at himself for getting lost again and was about to turn around when he saw fire flash between two brick apartment buildings with broken windows. Something in Jack told him to run, told him, *You've been here before and you didn't like it, remember?* But Jack was a good citizen, he wanted Simon to become the kind of man who wouldn't ignore a civic duty, so he pulled over to look, cell phone ready even if he wasn't sure he could tell the police where actually he was.

He put the phone back in his pocket when he saw there was no out-of-control blaze, just a group of five or six homeless kids hunched over a weak fire made from bits of wood and trash. He should do something, Jack thought, get them some help, it wasn't right for kids to have to live like this. And all the while, some part of his mind screamed, *Run! You don't want to see this.*

He moved as close to the entrance of the lane between the two buildings as he dared and called out, "You kids need some help?" They couldn't have been older than twelve or thirteen, he thought.

They all turned their heads simultaneously, and it was then that Jack saw there was something wrong with their faces. Cuts. Every child had a series of small cuts all over their faces. Scars and dried blood covered them like chaotic maps. *Run*, his mind screamed, *you forgot this before, you can forget it again*. Some of the kids had thick red lines that ran all around their necks, as if someone had cut the entire head off—*Eli*—then finished with them, or maybe just decided they were useless and stuck them back again.

Unable to turn around somehow, Jack began to back away. Even as he hoped he might make it to his car and escape, he knew what came next, for he remembered now, remembered how they would put it all on him, as if somehow he could save them all, could have saved Eli. "Jack, Jack," they would tell him as he tried to leave, "don't go back. Stay and heal the broken crack."

And sure enough, they turned, and they looked at him, and he wanted to say they had the wrong man, he had no idea what to do. But instead of challenging him, they said something far worse. It was another chant that Jack Wisdom had heard before, seven years ago, by another fire, this one in his own living room as his wife held their baby boy in the open flames.

Simon, Simon,
Rhymin' Simon,
Take the time an'
Stop the crime an'
Set the children free.

"No!" Jack cried out. "You can't ask that of him. It's not fair, he's only a little boy. He's no good to you, okay? I . . . I stopped it. It's my fault. Whatever she was trying to do to him, I stopped it, so he can't help you. Leave us alone!" The children said nothing, only stared at him.

He ran for his car now, and thanked God he hadn't locked it, but he did lock the doors as soon as he was inside and started the engine, as if the kids would come and pound on the windows like zombies in some horror movie. None of them moved, however. As he drove away, he could see them around their makeshift fire, hunched over, helpless.

Jack drove the empty street until it ended at a T-junction, then turned right and kept going until he found himself in a part of town he recognized and could head home. "It's not fair," he said to the car. "He's only a kid, he can't do anything."

It took two weeks for Simon to stop hearing any traces at all of Eli, no more whispers, no more rustles of pain in the back of his mind. On that same day, Simon Wisdom's father looked strange when he picked Simon up from after-school care. Usually Daddy would ask him about school, or tell him what they were going to have for dinner (he wasn't really a very good cook, but Simon would do his best to sound excited), but now he just drove. He seemed to have trouble breathing. The fact is, Daddy had been acting kind of funny for a while, ever since the police found Eli. Simon didn't know what was bothering him, and didn't want to know, so he'd done his best not to notice.

And not to cheat. That was the most important thing, not to look inside Daddy and find out what was bothering him.

When they got home, Daddy pulled into the driveway too fast and had to hit the brakes to avoid crashing into the garage door. He said a bad word, then took a deep breath. "Simon," he said, then fell silent. Simon held himself really tight inside to stop from reaching out to touch what Daddy wanted to say. After a moment, his father said, "That little boy—Eli. Did you know . . . did you know anything about him? Where he was?" He stopped, then said, "Or what was happening to him?"

Simon shook his head. "No!" he said loudly. "I'm not a cheater."

"I didn't say that!" his father half yelled, as if they were in a noise contest. His face twitched. "I just meant . . . if you could have done something—"

"I'm not a cheater!"

"I didn't say you were."

"You said it was cheating to read people's minds."

"Well, yes. Yes, I said that. But—"

"I don't know anything. Okay? I don't know anything about Eli. He wasn't even my friend."

His father stared at him, then breathed deeply, as if he was trying to control himself. He said, "Sometimes in extreme circumstances, it's all right to do something that otherwise—"

"I told you, I don't know anything. Why can't you listen to me?" Simon began to cry, then rubbed the heels of his hands against his eyes, as if trying to push the tears back inside.

"Stop that," his father said, and grabbed his arms to pull his hands away from his face.

"I'm not a cheater, I'm not." He pushed hard against his father's grip.

Daddy wrapped Simon in a tight hug and held on until Simon stopped fighting him. "No, of course you're not," he said. "You're a good boy. I'm very, very proud of you."

Jack Wisdom held his son close, so Simon wouldn't see the tears flowing down his father's face.

Chapter Thirteen

MATYAS

"Where is it?" Matyas demanded. He felt cold and stiff, as if he'd been sleeping out in the scrub hills beyond the Hungry Squirrel, but he made himself jump up to stand over her. A glimpse out of the tower's small, square window showed the gray and pink of early dawn. All night! He'd been asleep all night; she could have hidden them anywhere. Something inside him felt a deep gratitude to her, and with it the absurd desire to kneel in front of her and put his head in her lap, but he pushed it aside. He could have saved himself, he was sure of it. It was just . . . just dreams. *Never admit anything.* To Veil's impassive face, he said, "What did you do with it?"

He half expected her to ask, "Do with what?" and make him say, "The red box," but instead she answered, "I've put that away. It was wrong of me to leave it out where you might get lost inside it."

"Inside it?" he said, trying to sound scornful. "What do you mean?" Veil said nothing, and Matyas felt his face heat up. He hated it that she always appeared to know so much about him and he knew nothing about her. He said, "Was that the original?"

"The original? No, of course not. That was only a copy of a copy." Matyas remembered the old wizard at his father's inn—*a copy of a copy of a copy*, he'd called his pictures. Veil went on, "The original has been hidden away for hundreds of years."

"Why?"

She looked at him standing over her before she answered. Matyas realized that he was leaning over her with his hands clenched, and he suddenly felt ashamed. She looked so small in her plain wooden rocker surrounded by piles of books. She wore a long, red-brown dress, as shapeless as all her clothes, the material old and worn. Matyas wondered suddenly if she was poor. Most of the Masters wore such glorious robes, and Matyas knew they had patrons for whom they cast spells or something. He'd seen the great carriages come up at night, their coats of arms glimpsed under the black bunting meant to hide them, and the elegantly masked men and women who hurried in and out of the wizards' private quarters. No grand visitors ever came to Veil. Was she as poor as she was old and frail?

She said, "Why hide anything?"

"Because it's precious and you don't want anyone else to have it."

Veil nodded. "Yes, that is certainly a reason to hide something. Sometimes, however, people conceal things because they are dangerous. Remember what I told you, Matyas. It is not wise to look too long in Eternity."

"Why not?"

She smiled, an action which hardened the network of trace-lines in her face. Matyas braced himself for something like, "Well, you should know *that*. I had to rescue you, didn't I?" But instead she just said, "You sound like a child."

"I am not a child!"

"Of course not." The smile vanished and she said gravely, "I apologize."

"Why isn't it wise?"

"Because you can get lost. And there are things hidden inside Eternity that are best not seen."

For a moment, Matyas saw again, as if he was back inside, the man with the stone knife and the boy's head covered in cuts. He had to force himself not to shake, so she wouldn't see his fear.

He said, "Who made them? The originals."

She smiled slightly, so quick he would have missed it if he hadn't been watching her so closely. "Would you mind sitting down, Matyas? It hurts my neck, I'm afraid, to tilt my head like this." Matyas didn't bother to get a chair, just toppled a pile of books and sat on the smooth wood floor. Veil sighed. "His name was Joachim. Joachim the Brilliant. Also called Joachim the Blessed, and occasionally Joachim the Beloved."

"What about Joachim the Baffled?"

Veil laughed, a surprisingly strong sound from someone so old. "No doubt," she said. "We all get confused at times."

"Did he make it so he could fly?"

"Matyas, haven't I told you—?"

"Yes, yes, no man can fly. Did Joachim make it so he could fly?"

"He made it so he could see Eternity."

"Then why are you hiding it, if it won't teach me to fly?"

She grasped the arms of the rocker and pushed herself to her feet. Matyas got up as well and stood in front of her, as if she might try to escape. But all she said was, "Enough. It is time for you to cook our breakfast. We can talk more about this later." She turned and bent down to choose a book from the stack Matyas had knocked over.

Matyas stomped to the small cooking area. Cooking! Chores! That's all she wanted him for. He was almost overcome by the desire to go back and knock the book from her hand, and see the shock on her face that he had refused her order. He might have done it, too, except he was never sure of what Veil could—or would—do if he really got her angry. At least, he saw, she'd made a small fire in the iron stove. He was about to pour water in the pot to make their porridge when he remembered that he'd soaked his hands in the water to cool the poison ointment she'd left in the mortar. Was the water safe? What would she do if he told her what had happened? He stared at the water, unable to see any oil or herb flakes. But that didn't mean—

"Matyas," Veil said, without looking up from her book, "the water is fresh. I brought it up from the well myself this morning, while you slept."

He didn't answer, only banged the ladle against the side of the pot as he spooned water into it. *Good for her*, he told himself. *Let her do some of the work for once.* The problem with her was that she was *lazy*. And then, against his will, he wondered, did she save him? Was it more than just a dream? He discovered he couldn't breathe, even had to hold on to the table to keep from falling. He stood up straight a moment later and took a deep breath. Did she notice? He glanced quickly behind him to find she had not looked up from her book.

Books. Something else she kept from him. If she'd just teach him to read, he wouldn't need her help for anything. She hid everything from him, reading, ointments, and now the pictures with all their precious secrets. As he returned to stirring the porridge, Matyas imagined finding the original Tarot of Eternity in some dark cave, or maybe a palace with slippery gold floors (he'd first have to kill some ancient dragon, or a horde of headless warriors), and when he had it, the palace/cave would dissolve and he would fly through the air, all around Veil's cold, dark tower.

He made a face at the gray, lumpy mush in the pot. Cooking! Carrying! When he found the original "cards," he would cast a spell on Veil and force *her* to do it all.

They were sitting at the rough oak table, where there was never anything but their bowls and spoons and a funny little stone figure of a pregnant woman holding her belly and sticking her tongue out, when Veil said, "Matyas, how did you know there was an original?"

His hand stopped with the spoon halfway to his mouth. A thick drop fell on the table before he could put the spoon back in his bowl. "I don't know," he said. "I just thought maybe . . . it seemed so powerful."

Veil sat back and clasped her hands in her lap, a quiet gesture, but somehow it made Matyas want to run. She said, "Don't worry, I won't change you into a dog or a monkey. Well, actually, a dog might be a pleasant addition." She saw him look at his hands, as if they might have thickened into paws. "Matyas," she said, "that was a joke."

"Oh."

"Tell me how you knew there was an original."

"I . . . I met a wizard once. He came to the Hungry Squirrel. That was—"

"Your parents' inn, yes."

"He was all by himself. He had one of those sticks."

"A staff, yes. Some find them useful to focus power. I believe Lukhanan has one he's quite fond of."

Matyas thought of the way Lukhanan marched around the courtyard, occasionally holding up his staff as if about to measure the sky. He said, "I wouldn't need one if you'd just teach me."

"The Tarot, Matyas. He had it with him?"

"Yes. He said they were a copy of a copy of a copy. Like yours." She didn't correct him and he went on, "And he said if you had the original, you could see everything all at once." And, he remembered, *Whosoever touches the Tarot of Eternity, he shall be healed of all his crimes.*

"Yes, and perhaps that is why Master Joachim hid it from the world. Or perhaps he had other reasons. At least he was good enough to allow a few copies to survive. It was said that if you placed the original and one of the first copies side by side you would have to turn yourself into an insect with a hundred eyes to see the differences."

When Matyas didn't respond, Veil sighed again and said, "This man you met, the wizard. I knew him, Matyas. His name was Medun. He was a great scholar, a true Master."

"Was he part of the Academy?"

"Yes. Until he was forced to leave."

"Why? What happened?"

"There was another Master, one who used his power in, well, an unfortunate way. He brought in poor young girls, beggars really, and told them he would transmit power and wisdom directly from his body into theirs. Do you understand what I am saying?"

"I think so."

"Yes, you are not as young as you look. Of course, there was no transfer, except from them to him, their youth and their innocence."

"And Medun did that?"

"No! Medun found out about it. He went to the Council of Governance, who run this Academy."

"Are you on it?"

"No, Matyas, I'm afraid I have different concerns. The other wizard, however, had friends on the council. They promised Medun they would investigate his charges."

"Was Lukhanan on the council?"

"Yes, I believe he was. Still is, in fact."

"And did they? Investigate?"

She smiled, for just a moment. "No."

"So what did Medun do?"

She was silent for a little while, then said, "He summoned something called a 'Singular Storm'—lightning and hail at a specific location."

"The other wizard's house."

"Yes. The man survived, but crippled, and with most of his power gone. He left the Academy."

Matyas asked, "What was his name?"

Veil shook her head. "No. There is a power in remembering names and there is a power in forgetting them. I prefer not to say his name in my home. Do you object?"

"I guess not." Matyas tried to remember if she'd ever asked his permission for anything. He felt somehow both proud and angry at the same time. He said, "What happened to your friend? Medun."

"Medun was called before the council. Some wanted to banish him from thought and memory, a truly terrible spell. The victim of it forgets everything, even his own name. If they had done that to Medun, his power would have remained but he would never have remembered it, and thus he would have stumbled through the world as helpless as an orphan."

Matyas stared at her. "That's horrible. It's all wrong. Medun was just trying to help those girls."

"Yes. Power and justice do not always march together. In the end, the council cast a spell that sent him into what is called a 'Wandering Exile.' He must travel from place to place, never able to remain in one location for more than a single night."

Matyas remembered when he came to the wizard's room in the morning and found only a bag of coins. He said, "That's still unfair. He was the one who was right."

"Yes, but poor Medun never understood the importance of having the right friends."

"Why didn't you stop them? Could you have stopped them?"

"Maybe. I didn't try, so I cannot say."

Matyas nearly upset the table as he jumped to his feet. "Why? Why didn't you try?"

Veil didn't move or unclasp her hands. She said, "Sometimes things must happen just as they happen. Even a terrible injustice may serve some unknown purpose. Perhaps Medun needed to go somewhere, *be* somewhere at a particular moment, and that could not have happened if he'd stayed in his study."

Matyas frowned, trying to follow flashes of thought that seemed to beckon him. He said finally, "I might not have come here if I hadn't met him." He remembered the Kallistocha telling him to go to the Academy, but it was Medun, an actual wizard, who made it feel possible. Suddenly he wanted to end this conversation, wanted not to think about it anymore. He almost knocked over the pot so he would have to clean it up, but he knew if he didn't ask he would still think it, over and over. He said finally, his voice tight, "Could I be the reason Medun had to leave? Did all those things happen to him—to those girls, and the wizard—so *I* would meet him?"

Veil looked at him for a long time and then smiled, so quickly Matyas was not sure he saw it. It was as if . . . as if she was *proud* of him. For what? Figuring it out? Matyas shook his head. He didn't feel proud at all. This was something terrible, something he didn't want to know. He thought of those girls, hurt by that wizard, and then of Medun, forced to wander the world for doing something right. Was it all so Matyas would come to the Academy? How could that be?

And what of the evil wizard? If the things he did were part of some great plan, did that mean he *had* to do them? Was he as innocent as the girls he hurt? If it was all about Matyas, was it all his fault? He whispered, as if afraid to speak too loudly, "Please tell me. Am I the reason?"

Slowly, as if she was picking her words with care, Veil said, "Everyone chooses their own actions. And yet, sometimes people's individual choices weave together, so that what each one does, whether for good or bad, allows others to be in a certain place at a certain time. This is how patterns form."

"Why am *I* so important?"

"Maybe you're not. Maybe you also have a purpose. A place in that larger plan."

"It would have to be a really large plan to pull in so many of us."

"That is not for us to judge."

"What is it?" Matyas demanded. "What's this great plan?"

"Matyas, do you think I am God that I can see how everything fits together?" Matyas started to answer before he realized he had no idea what to say. With a slight nod, Veil said, "If you have finished your porridge, perhaps you can clean up, then go and bring up some more wood for this evening's fire. And if you don't mind, I would like to return to my studies."

That night, as Matyas lay on his bed, he saw the Splendor, bright specks that darted all around his sleep alcove. Tracks, Medun had said. The lights were just their tracks, like wolf prints in the snow. If Matyas could see them in their full form they would crack open the tower, cover the sky. "What do you want?" he whispered. "Why do you come to me?" He had always thought it was because he was someone special, someone important. They came to honor him, and to help him fly. Now he wondered if it was because they wanted something from him. Would they force him to harm innocent girls? He thought of Royja and how horrible it would be if someone did to her what that wizard had done. Or would they end up banishing him, like Medun?

He remembered the voices, whispering at him, like insects in his ear, that great promise, that he would fly, that he would be better than everyone.

Matyas, Matyas,
Master Matyas,
Will you fly as
Straight and high as
A dark and lonely hawk?

But now, as he longed to hear that promise again, it was the second half that stuck in his mind, no matter how hard he tried not to remember.

Or will you try as
Ancients cry, as
Children die, as
No one dares to talk?

Chapter Fourteen

SIMON

Simon began to have bad dreams. There were people who changed into wild dogs when moonlight touched their skin. There were trees where men with burning faces hung upside down. Sometimes he dreamed of a stone tower in some old city. There were magnificent buildings all around it, with grand columns and statues of winged lions, but the tower looked lumpy and crude even as it stood over them. And yet, at the beginning of the dream at least, Simon liked to look at it, he felt both excited and peaceful at the same time. There was just something about it—it clearly was just dull stone, but somehow it seemed made out of stories, stories hidden all up and down the walls. In the dream, he would look at it for a long time, wishing he could go there and hide.

He'd be safe there. He couldn't cheat and read people's thoughts when he didn't want to if there was no one around but himself. Except— what about all those stories hidden in the stone? What if he started to read the building itself and couldn't stop? And then in the dream, the tower would explode, as if lightning had struck it, or just the pressure of all those stories was too much for it to contain. As it blew apart, Simon would discover it hadn't been empty after all, for a boy and an old woman fell screaming from the window.

As disturbing as the tower dream was, worst of all were the pieces of children. Sometimes Simon would dream that he was walking somewhere—in the schoolyard, in the town where his grandparents lived, in the street behind the old day-care house from when he was little—and at first everything would be fine, he'd be on his way to the drugstore to get candy, or on the baseball field at school. Then slowly he would discover he was lost, stuck in some place he'd never seen before. It would be late, with shadows that covered the bottom half of his body so he couldn't see his feet.

He would begin to get scared and look for markers of some kind, signs of safety or the way home. At first he would appear to get help: a branch would point along the trail; a candy wrapper would contain some message, even if he couldn't figure it out. Then the objects would change, become fragments of clothing covered in blood and grease, a basketball shoe that looked as if a dog had ripped it with its teeth. Soon he would begin to see actual pieces of children, a finger, bent as if to beckon to him, a leg with a scarred knee. Most terrifying of all were the tongues that twisted around like agitated snakes.

There were never any faces or mouths but the tongues still made a noise, a wailing sound, like children lost for a hundred years. Often Simon would wake up at this point, for he would imitate the sound while asleep, and then his daddy would rush in to save him.

"It's okay," Daddy would say each time, "it's all right," though it so obviously wasn't. "It's just a dream." Simon could still feel the cut-up pieces of children all around him, even if he could no longer see them. And he knew that Daddy was lying, that he didn't really believe what he said. Simon didn't have to cheat to know that—he could feel it in his father's stiff back, the way the muscles trembled even as Daddy tried to hold them steady. It wasn't okay. Nothing was okay.

Over the next year, Simon became more and more what his father and the doctor called "troubled." He began to fail tests and have problems at school, sometimes for not paying attention, sometimes for talking back or fighting. It seemed like he got in fights a lot. He lost most of his friends. Kids who used to run up to him in break now walked away when they saw him.

It was so unfair, he thought, *wasn't he trying so very hard not to cheat? They were just stupid*, he decided. *They couldn't read anybody even if they wanted to.*

Why would he want friends who never had to stop themselves from knowing what was going to happen, or what other people were thinking? Maybe Simon was a cheater but he wasn't dumb. He didn't need those dumb kids, he didn't need anybody.

His father took him to lots of doctors. There was Howard Porter, who'd been Simon's doctor his whole life. Dr. Howard, as Simon called him, was always kind, though sometimes he looked confused, or scared. Like Daddy. Then there were other doctors, ones Simon had never met before. Some talked to him, or asked him to draw things, or play games, or tell them about the dreams. Others attached funny wires to his head with gooey stuff, or made him lie very still inside a big noisy machine they said was like a spaceship, except that was really dumb because it didn't go anywhere. He called these "wire doctors," because of the things they stuck on him. He liked them better than the play doctors. The tests were weird, but he didn't have to do or say anything.

With the play doctors, Simon had to answer lots of questions, and that meant making sure he didn't cheat and know the right answer. One of them, Dr. Joan, asked him about his mother. Dr. Joan was pretty, with short blond hair and brightly colored dresses, but she never looked very happy. She would lean forward and smile a lot, but she also rubbed her hands as if trying to clean them or tangle and untangle her fingers. Simon knew it was not polite to stare, but he wished she would keep them still.

Most of all, he didn't know how to answer her questions. Was he angry at his mother? Did he hate his mother? Simon had never known his mother. She died such a long time ago, so how could he hate her? Did he hate his father? Why would he hate his father? Did he love his father? Did he know his father loved him?

When Dr. Joan asked things like that, Simon just shrugged. He could find out what she wanted him to say, of course. It would be so easy. And in fact, not doing it was hard, so that he usually left her office feeling tired and angry, and when his father offered to take him for pizza, Simon just wanted to go home. At least, he would think, he hadn't cheated.

Other doctors gave him medicines. They said the drugs would stop the dreams, make him less "angry," help him pay attention at school. The problem was, they also made him sick. It didn't matter which one it was, he would throw up and get a fever. They tried different colored pills (one of the doctors called them "magic beans," whatever that meant), they tried shots, but it was all the same, until finally his father cried and hugged him and promised not to give him any more.

His grandmother took him to churches where the priests sprinkled water on his head and said what sounded like magic words, but Grandma later said was just church talk. One priest held the sides of his head so tightly Simon worried the priest's fingers would leave marks, then flung his hands away and yelled, "Be gone!" None of it made any sense. None of it made any difference.

Throughout this time, the only kid who stayed his friend was "Popcorn Jimmy." His real name was Jimmy Aken, but everyone called him "Popcorn" because his mom always packed a bag of popcorn in his lunch. He and Simon had been friends since early in day care, and even though Simon was just as mean to Jimmy as to anyone else, Jimmy still hung around with him. "Weird and Weirder" was what some of the kids called them.

One day at break, Simon was off by himself, kicking pebbles, when he heard a whimper. Surprised, he looked around and saw that no one was there. He heard it again, and knew somehow it came from the other side of the school. At first he was horrified that he had left a crack in the wall he tried to keep up against cheating. He put his hands over his ears but that only made it louder, as if he was holding it inside his head. *Get out*, he silently ordered it, *get away from me.*

Then he realized the voice was Jimmy. For just a moment more he resisted, thinking, *Let him take care of himself,* thinking Jimmy would call him a cheater. And the crying, the fear, they were not that bad, really. Not like Eli . . . He thought of Jimmy screaming in his head, days long, the way Eli had done, and then just stopping . . .

Simon ran as fast as he could, nearly knocking over a girl playing kickball. When he got to the other side of the school, he saw Allen and Allen, two older kids who were gang types, shoving Jimmy between them and laughing. Jimmy's bag of popcorn lay scattered on the ground. *It's okay*, Simon thought, *it's just kids.*

"Leave him alone!" Simon yelled, and ran full force into the taller boy. Both he and Allen fell, but Simon got up first and threw a handful of dirt into the other Allen's face before he could take over the fight from his namesake on the ground.

Allen on the ground got up and stood beside his friend, fists clenched. Simon looked around, saw that Jimmy was hanging back and probably would run if the Allens attacked. Suddenly, Simon thought how unfair it all was. He tried so hard to be good, he tried and tried, all the time. And now—

Now he discovered, in one great sharp thrill, that he didn't care. With a huge rush, a cloud of sickness flew out of his body and Simon just stood there, grinning, his eyes electric as he stared at first one of the bullies, then the other. It was so easy!

Jesus, the bigger one was thinking, *what's he looking at?*

"Jesus," Simon said, "what's he looking at?"

Hey!

"Hey!"

How did you—? What the fuck—? What—?

"How did you—? What the fuck—? What—?"

Ah! My head. He's in my head. Get out!

"Ah! My head. He's in my head. Get out!"

Simon switched to the other Allen, who was looking from his friend to Simon. *What's going on?*

"What's going on?" Simon said.

Huh? Fuck!

"Huh? Fuck!"

Stop it, stop it.

"Stop it, stop it."

Oh, Jesus, don't think, hands, Mr. Blake, hands, no, stop, stop, stop!

"Oh, Jesus, don't think, hands, Mr. Blake, hands, no, stop, stop, stop!"

The two boys screamed together and scrambled backward, falling down and then jumping up as quickly as they could, afraid to take their eyes off Simon as if he might get inside them for good and never leave. Simon leaned forward, his body tight and at an impossible angle, as if a rod attached to the Allens held him upright. When they got to twenty feet, however, the rod snapped and Simon would have fallen face down if Jimmy hadn't grabbed him.

The Allens appeared to feel it too because they stopped their scramble to get away and looked around to see if anyone had been watching. When they saw no one was there, they stood up straight and hardened their faces. "Fucking weirdo!" one of them yelled, and the other repeated, "Weirdo!" Allen shook his fist and said, "Better watch out, weirdo," and Allen added, "Yeah! Watch your fuckin' back. Both of you, you sick little fucks." They tried to stroll off, hands in their pockets, but it was half a run.

Shaking, Simon stared at their backs, their heads, the angle of their shoulders and elbows, the jerkiness in their legs. Beside him, Jimmy said, "Wow, that was weird. I mean, it was *cool*. Just—you know."

Simon jerked around to stare at Jimmy, who looked suddenly like a drawing, a kind of cartoon version of something extremely complicated. Simon made a noise, then left his mouth open, and in that moment the sickness rushed back into him so hard he really did fall down now, seat first, onto a patch of dry grass. He wanted to get right back on his feet but knew if he did, he would just throw up, right on Jimmy, who nervously put out his hand to help, then pulled it back when Simon didn't take it.

"Hey," Jimmy said, "you okay?" Simon just stared at him, afraid to test himself at the same time that he knew he had to do it. He focused on the cartoon Jimmy, the outside, and discovered, as if he'd been given a great gift, that it held. "That was great," Jimmy said. "I mean—you know—cool. Thanks."

Simon nodded. It was okay to stand now. For a second he was scared that Jimmy would try to help him again, but when his friend held back, Simon realized, with both immense relief and a stab of sorrow, that he had no idea what Jimmy would do. Simon stood and felt the damp weight of the cloud inside his body.

Jimmy looked around. "Hey, you want to go and sit on the tree?" He nodded toward a tree that had fallen some weeks ago on the edge of the playground.

"Okay," Simon said. He didn't really want to sit. He wanted to run away. But he followed Jimmy and sat alongside him. They both stared at the ground.

"Hey," Jimmy said. "How did you know—you know, what those jerks were doing?"

"I didn't cheat!" Simon said. He remembered the thrill of tracking every flicker in the Allens' heads.

"Hey, man, I didn't say anything." Jimmy started to stare at Simon, then turned away. He laughed suddenly. "Look at that," he said, and pointed to where a pair of squirrels, one red, one gray, were eating the spilled popcorn. Jimmy laughed. "That's cool," he said, clearly relieved there was something else he could talk about.

Simon stared at the squirrels, his hands all sweaty. He knew his father hated squirrels or was scared of them or something because he shouted

and chased them away whenever they came anywhere close. Simon himself never thought much about them. Now he just stared at them as they
gnawed at the popcorn, almost the way he'd stared at the Allens. But
that was nuts, they were just squirrels. He kept on looking.

"Hey," Jimmy said, "you okay?"

But Simon paid no attention for the squirrels had lifted their
heads, together, and it looked just like they were staring back at him.
For a moment he became scared that he was dreaming again, and any
moment now the popcorn in the squirrels' mouths would change to
kid fingers, or tongues, and he would hear that terrible noise of all the
sad children.

But instead of the popcorn or squirrels changing into dead children,
Simon saw lights dart about the squirrels' heads. It was hard to see at
first in the sunshine, but they were all zipping in the air like fireflies,
only they weren't, they were just lights. Simon stared at them, for they
reminded him of something. Now he remembered—he used to see
them sometimes when he was little, before he found out he was bad and
had to control himself. What would Daddy do to him if he found out
what Simon had done? What if the Allens told on him?

Simon made himself focus on the lights. He hadn't seen them in so
long he'd forgotten about them. Not since Eli—He squeezed shut his
eyes and shook his head, forcing himself not to remember. It was so
unfair, every way he turned—

"Hey," Jimmy said, "you all right?"

The squirrels looked at him, and the lights jumped, and Simon knew
the squirrels wanted to tell him something, but that was so weird. And
wasn't that just what the Allens had said about him? *Fucking weirdo.*
He remembered once when he'd been at his grandparents' house and
Grandpa had put an arm around him and said, "Simon, buddy, when
your last name is Wisdom, you have to learn to be normal. More normal
than normal."

Simon was still staring at the squirrels and the lights when Jimmy
touched his arm. "Hey, you want to go back? The Allens are so stupid
they probably forgot about it."

Simon pushed him away. Immediately he turned to say he was sorry,
but something changed when he did that. He couldn't say what, it was
as if something broke, and when he looked back, the squirrels had run
off and taken the lights with them.

Jimmy stood up and raised his hands. "Hey, it's cool," he said. He started to walk away, then stopped, and a moment later turned around. "Hey, thanks," he said.

After lunch the next day, Simon grabbed Jimmy and said they should go around the side of the building. "Don't forget your popcorn" he said, sing-song, like a joke. The whole time they played, throwing pebbles at a tree, Simon looked around. No squirrels came. All that afternoon he wanted to hit Jimmy, or someone, but he kept himself still.

At night he dreamed of the woman again—his mother?—for the first time in months. He was on a field trip, to a museum or some other dumb place. The teacher (Mrs. Griswold, from back in first grade) took them to a giant dinosaur skeleton so big the bones looked like a city seen from far away. "In winter," Mrs. Griswold said, "the children let the dinosaur eat them so they can stay warm in its nice cozy belly. Then in spring, the dinosaur regurgitates them, like popcorn, so they can play in the sun."

From somewhere to his left, dream Simon glimpsed a flicker. When he turned he saw the dancing lights, just a few, and beyond them, under a doorway marked "Emergency Exit," stood a woman dressed in a guard's uniform. She was tall and pretty, with curly red hair, and she smiled so sweetly at him he wondered, once again, could she be his mother? He tried to run to her but there were so many kids in front of him, pushing, yelling.

The woman—Mom—was saying something, cupping her long, delicate hands around her mouth to call it out, but there was so much *noise*—the teacher, the kids, the dinosaur bones clacking together like those dumb wind chimes Grandma had outside the kitchen window. All he could hear was one word, "Remember!"

"Remember what?" Simon yelled. "What am I supposed to remember?"

For just a moment he could still hear her—"Remember!"—but then the woman, and everything else, the teacher, the kids, the dinosaur bones, they all got drowned out, for suddenly there was that sound Simon Wisdom hated more than anything in the world. The terrible crying and wailing. *No! Go away!* he thought. *Please.* For he knew what had to come next, of course. Pieces of children.

Yes, there they were, scattered all over the shiny museum floor. Fingers, toes, bloody strips of skin. And tongues. Tongues like snakes, tongues splashing blood like small hoses as they twisted around, trying to speak. "I'm sorry," Simon said in the dream. "I'm sorry, I'm sorry, I'm sorry."

He woke up to discover he was hitting his father, who was trying to pin down Simon's desperate arms. His father was crying himself now, and when Simon finally calmed down, his dad held on to him for a long time.

Shame filled Simon. Shame he made his father hurt like this, over and over. Shame he couldn't control his dreams. And somehow, shame he couldn't remember whatever it was the woman—*Mom*—was trying to tell him. He wished the lights were there but the air was flat and dull and wet with tears. Simon almost said, "Dad, I'm supposed to remember something but I don't know what it is." But that just sounded stupid, so he said nothing, and simply let his father hold him.

Chapter Fifteen

MATYAS

Matyas might have continued as Veil's kitchen boy for a good while longer if not for the taunts of the other students. At first they, and even most of the teachers, looked at him with respect, or maybe fear. It took a while for Matyas to understand this. Why would people turn away as he passed them, or even appear frightened? The only look he'd ever received from his father was disgust. As for his mother, she could go whole days without even glancing at him. So why did the apprentices, and even some of the masters, look so nervous when he passed them?

Slowly he understood. It wasn't him they were scared of, it was Veil. Veil, who didn't teach or attend councils, who was rumored to explore terrible secrets in her tower, who had not taken an apprentice in many years. And now she'd chosen Matyas. She'd even demanded that Lukhanan make sure the ragged boy stayed at the gate when he first arrived until she could come down from her tower to fetch him.

Knowing this, Matyas did his best to practice an aloof and superior air as he moved around doing his errands and chores. Over time, however, as those errands continued, and Matyas showed no sign of power or even knowledge, the students began to become more comfortable around him. At first they sniggered, then joked openly about such "magical" tasks as hauling wood.

One afternoon, Berias, one of Lukhanan's students, saw Matyas carrying two large water bags. "Aha," he said. "The sorceress' apprentice. Wouldn't it help to summon a demon to carry those for you?" His friends laughed.

Matyas wished he *could* call forth a demon, maybe something with a great bull's head, and lion's paws, and stone feet. Then he would order it to kick Berias from one end of the courtyard to the other. But since he had no idea how to do that, he pretended to ignore them and kept walking. Just a few steps. For all their brave talk, they wouldn't dare to follow him into Veil's tower.

Berias stepped in front of him to hold a sheet of parchment before his face. "Great wizard," Berias said, "would you read this for us, please? We find it too subtle for our simple skills." Matyas rushed inside, but not before laughter rolled over him. He was shaking as he closed the door and set down the water bags.

He left the bags and ran up the stairs. Veil sat in her plain chair, her hands folded in her lap, her eyes open, staring at nothing. Matyas slammed the door. It took a few seconds before Veil slowly turned her head. "Where is the water?"

"I don't care about that."

"You will when you get thirsty."

"Stop it. I want to know when you are going to teach me."

"When you are ready."

"You always say that! I'm ready right now."

"Indeed. And were you ready when you looked into Eternity?"

It took him a moment to realize she meant the red box. "That's different. You didn't warn me."

"Ah. So you are only *ready* when you have sufficient warning?"

"No! I mean, yes. No. You're just playing tricks. I have talent, you said so yourself. I want to start. Right now. At least teach me to read. How can I do anything with all your damn books if you won't even teach me to read?"

She looked at him for a long time, her face impassive. Finally, she said softly, "Matyas. Come brush my hair."

"No! I'm sick of taking care of you. Brush it yourself. Or let it fall out. I demand you teach me."

"My hair, Matyas. Now."

Should he leave? He could stamp out and show her he was not a slave. But then what? None of the other teachers would take him on, that was clear. If Veil turned him out for disobedience, he would end up a beggar. And he would never learn to fly. With a great sigh he picked up the brush and began to run it through Veil's hair.

At first he jerked it down as hard as he could, hoping the bristles would pull out tufts of hair, one for every time she'd refused him. Soon, however, the motion calmed him, and he moved the brush in long, smooth strokes.

Her hair became like water flowing all around him, first his hands, then his arms, then his whole body and all around him. He began to cry, he had no idea why, and his tears ran into the sea of the old woman's hair. The water sparkled, lifted, became weightless waves of liquid light. It poured over him, lifted him, until he dropped his arm and closed his eyes and let light fill him and carry him.

He was like the man in the picture, not the Beautiful Boy about to Fly but the Hanging Man. He might as well be upside down and tied to a tree with a snake for a rope, for just like that man on the tree, his face, his whole body, was all awash in waves of sparkling light. The light was fire but also water, and he opened his mouth, his whole body, to drink it in.

Within the light were shapes. No, not just shapes, letters. Letters all around, swirls and waves of them. They rolled over him, danced on his fingers, he tasted them, some sharp or salty, others voluptuous or sweet. And numbers, and formulas, and gestures and words.

He learned the language of demons and how to summon them (and why he shouldn't). He saw and heard the spirits of rocks and trees and places and objects he'd never known existed. He heard the cruel laughter of angels and understood the terrible pain of the Kallistochoi, the saddest tribe who had ever lived. He knew how to summon birds, and snakes, and lions. He could look behind the sky and under the night.

He saw Joachim the Blessed, and the creation of the Tarot of Eternity, and how Joachim used it to travel to the Creator Herself where he pleaded for helpless humanity. But when Matyas tried to see why Joachim hid the pictures, the waves of light grew dense and murky, and he had to look away. Then that too passed, and the wonders returned, and he found himself looking back through the ages, mystery upon mystery, all the way to the Creation of Names, beyond which no one, not even the Kallistochoi, were permitted to see.

Finally the waves ended and Matyas fell to his knees in a room full of books and relics, alongside an old woman sitting calmly in a narrow wooden chair. He opened his mouth to thank her but was shaking too hard to speak.

"There," Veil said, "didn't I tell you that you would be thirsty?"

Chapter Sixteen

SIMON

After school that day, Simon rode his bike to several stores until he found the right brand of popcorn. Then he headed for the schoolyard, where some kids were playing soccer. He sat down on the fallen tree. As soon as he opened the bag, they were there, the red and the gray, both on their hind legs with their front paws out. He tossed some popcorn on the ground and they grabbed it up a piece at a time. When he threw some more, however, they ran off a few feet, then stopped to look back at him.

He followed them into the small patch of woods that ran from the schoolyard to behind the drugstore. The trees were thick, with branches and thorns constantly in the way. The squirrels stopped next to an old oak hemmed in by upstart trees. Even though it was spring, a mass of rotting leaves lay at the base of the trunk. In his head, Simon heard, "Dig." He began to pull out clumps of leaves while the squirrels ate the popcorn that had spilled from the bag. Simon had no idea what he would find, but it gave him a kind of peace to stick his fingers in the dark dirt. A few minutes must have passed when he touched a flat, hard surface.

He moved the dirt away to find a blue cloth wrapped around a package about five inches long and a couple of inches thick. The cloth was stained but very soft. It looked like there were designs painted on it, but Simon couldn't tell with all the dirt. Excitedly, he unwrapped it.

Picture cards. They were just a bunch of people in dumb costumes doing dumb things. He realized what they were. Tarot cards. A couple of girls at school had brought some and were showing them off in the cafeteria, with lots of giggles and dumb faces. They went around to kids and waved the cards in their faces and said things like, "Let me tell your future," in a silly *woo-woo* voice. They even went up to Simon, who'd never needed a bunch of cards to know what was going to happen. He needed something to help him *not* know, and so he knocked the cards out of Ellen Lorenzi's hands. From the floor where she gathered up her cards, Ellen said, "I'll tell *your* future, Simon Wisdom. You're a stupid jerk and you'll always be a stupid jerk."

Now, as he held the old cards in his hand, Simon first thought he would throw them as far away as he could. Instead, something made him look at them more closely. They were worn, and a little ragged, yet still brightly colored, each one like a miniature story. Here was a picture of a man walking away from a row of brightly shining glasses that appeared to hold something rotten in them even though you couldn't really see it. And here was a man hanging upside down by one foot tied to a tree branch, with a snake for a rope. Light surrounded his face and he looked happier than anyone Simon had ever seen.

He sat down on the pile of leaves. The pictures made him a little dizzy, as if he was jumping from one place to another, like a character in a video game who can't stay on one level. When he closed his eyes, the pictures all spun around him and he had to lie down on the leaves. Even though they were dirty and wet, they felt like a soft bed where he could sleep and not be afraid of his dreams.

And in fact he must have fallen asleep, for he found himself in a dark grove of trees, tall and laced together like a fence. At first he felt trapped but then the squirrels appeared, and he followed them to an opening, a sort of gateway. It led to a dirt path, and at the end of the path was a garden, with red and white flowers and high plants that moved in the breeze. The air was fresh and sweet, a mix of flowers and fruit. Simon breathed deep and closed his eyes.

When he opened them he cried out, for in place of the squirrels, two children had appeared, a boy and a girl. They were younger than him, about eight years old. The girl wore a white dress, and her hair was so pale it might have been strands of silver. The boy wore a gold-colored, loose T-shirt over black pants. His short hair was thick and curly and blond.

Simon thought he should be amazed by their sudden appearance. Instead he just said, "Are you a prince and a princess?" and immediately thought how dumb that sounded.

They only smiled. "Something like that," the girl said.

"But you're also the squirrels?"

The boy nodded. "Yes. You get to see us as we really are."

"Cool."

They each took a hand, and the three of them walked along the path to the garden. There were roses and lilies and flowers of every color and season, and broom and heather, and green and brown and red herbs, and even patches of yellow grain. A waterfall fed it. The water came over a cliff far in the distance, gushed into a stream that vanished under the dirt to make the ground vibrate under Simon's feet. Though it all appeared to go on for miles, it also felt small and friendly. Simon didn't understand that, how something could be both big and little at the same time, but he didn't care. He didn't feel like a bad person here. He was happy.

He found a bench made of interlocking vines and lay down to casually shuffle the cards. The children stood on either side, swaying slightly. They made him think of two trees, silver and gold. He laughed. First they were squirrels, then children, then trees. What a funny dream.

He closed his eyes, and all at once he felt a warm and loving pressure, and he knew who it was, it was her, the woman, and he was sure now, she was his mother. She didn't hate him at all, she loved him. He wanted to open his eyes and jump up to hug her, but he was afraid she would go away again. So he just lay there and smiled until finally, even though he was already dreaming, he fell asleep.

He woke up in the woods a few feet from the pile of leaves and dirt, his back against a scrawny tree. He knew for sure he was really awake because he was filthy and there was a cut on his elbow. He didn't care. He looked down at the Tarot cards scattered in his lap. *So that's what they're for*, he thought. *Not to tell the future but to give you a safe place to get away.* He wrapped the cards in the blue cloth and stuck them in his backpack. Maybe he shouldn't tell his dad, he thought. Simon might forget and say something about the squirrels, and Dad had a real thing about them. Anyway, when he looked around, the squirrels were gone.

When Simon got home from his time in the park with the squirrels, the Tarot cards carefully wrapped and hidden in his pack, he found his dad at the kitchen table with some papers in front of him. Looking at the dirt and grass stains, Dad said, "Where have you been?" He had that tightness in his voice and Simon didn't have to cheat to know Dad was worried he had got into another fight.

"Out in the woods," Simon said.

"By yourself?"

"Yeah."

"You look like you've been digging for buried treasure."

Simon rolled his eyes. "Yeah, sure. Everyone knows there's no buried treasure around here. We're not exactly living on a desert island, you know."

Dad smiled. "Of course," he said. He looked at Simon a little funny. "Are you okay?"

"Yeah, Dad, I'm good."

Dad stared at him for a while, almost like the way Dr. Howard sometimes did, and this made Simon laugh. Now his father looked about to say something but stopped himself. Simon thought maybe *he* should speak, so he said, "I'm really good."

Dad glanced down, and when he lifted his head his eyes were wet. When he spoke his voice shook a little, but all he said was, "Well, why don't you go upstairs and take a shower?" He stopped, took a breath, then in that same funny voice said, "I'll start dinner. And make sure you put those clothes in the hamper."

Simon hid the cards, with the blue cloth still wrapped around them, in a box of old toys under the bed. In the shower, he found himself laughing as he remembered how the squirrels had changed into those weird kids. What a funny dream. And then he realized it was true. He *did* feel good. He felt better than at any time since his dad first told him he was cheating.

Jack Wisdom had no idea what had changed in his son. He didn't dare to ask. Maybe like people said, all the nightmares, the anger, were just a phase, because suddenly it was as if he'd got his son back. Simon smiled and laughed a lot, and over the next couple of months, his grades began to improve, and he even started making friends again. Jack told himself he didn't dare ask what had happened because he didn't want to make Simon self-conscious, or in some way jinx it. In fact, maybe he didn't really want to know. Whatever had changed, he was grateful.

A couple of times he thought of the strange kids he'd seen that day he got lost in that decrepit neighborhood on the other side of town. Had there ever been a danger Simon would end up like that? Jack didn't want to think it was possible, but he still thanked God it couldn't happen now. His beautiful boy was safe.

Simon never visited the dream garden again. He went back to the dead tree a couple of times, but didn't see the strange squirrels. It didn't matter. Every night, before he went to sleep, he took the cards from their hiding place and looked at them. Sometimes he quickly went through the whole deck, jumping from picture to picture like some superhero jumping between worlds. Other times he slid them in and out of each other, then selected one at random. He made up stories about them, or maybe the stories were already there, each picture a doorway into a tale. It almost felt as if *they* were telling *him* stories, like his dad used to do when he was little. It wasn't like there were voices or anything, but the stories just kind of appeared in his head. Sometimes they were simply of a place to go, like the garden with the squirrels who turned into children. Sometimes a group of them would lay out an actual tale, kind of like a comic where you didn't need any words to know what it was about. There was a boy who found a gold cup and a talking fish came out and told him to travel over the sea with a woman who covered her head so he never saw her face, until they came to an exploding tower . . . That one went on for a couple of days.

Other times the cards just made him feel a certain way. One day, when he'd been looking at them a little longer than usual, he stood up and suddenly the room, and the house, the whole world, it seemed, was filled with waves and waves of color. Except they were colors no one had ever seen before, colors that were somehow impossible, yet there they were. Simon wanted to run and tell his dad about them, but he was afraid that his dad couldn't see them, or worse, that he might suspect Simon was cheating in some way, seeing colors no one else knew about. So Simon just watched them all until slowly the world settled back to its usual dullness.

There were scary stories, too, or rather the beginnings of them. Sometimes a card, or more likely a combination of two or three, would open a door to a place Simon knew he did not want to go, like a reenactment of the terrible dreams of the children, or even a memory of Eli, as if the dead boy was still alive somewhere, hidden in the cards, and pleading with Simon to save him, forever and ever. But Simon discovered he could recognize when something like that was going to happen and then stop it by putting the bad cards back and smooshing them all around on the floor, face down, until nothing was left of the awful story. The sound of the cards moving in and out of each other was like a woman's voice telling him, "It's all right. You don't have to see that. You're safe."

None of the pictures had titles at the bottom or anything to say what they were called. Simon didn't really mind that, they seemed kind of cool just the way they were, but he remembered seeing titles on the ones Ellen had brought to school, and he wondered if maybe he should know what they were. He tried to make up his own titles, like "Upside-Down Tree Man," or "Talking Fish," but he was afraid he'd make a mistake and they wouldn't work right. So one morning, he asked his dad if he could have some money for a video game.

Dad looked at him a little nervously. "Which one?" he said.

Simon knew that grown-ups had some list of bad games, the ones with too much killing or bad words or sex. He said, "It's called *Knights*. You ride around on horses and kill dragons and stuff." That wasn't really a lie, because there were actual knights on horses in the cards (though no dragons).

Dad appeared to think a bit but Simon was sure he'd say yes. His dad was so happy that Simon had stopped getting into trouble that he probably would have given him anything. "How much is it?" Dad asked.

Simon had checked online for what Tarot cards cost, so he was ready. "Twenty dollars." Amazon actually said fifteen but sometimes things were more in stores.

"Well, that sounds fair," Dad said. He gave one of those half-laughs grown-ups sometimes did. "These days that's downright cheap. How about we go this weekend to pick it up?"

This was the tricky part. For just a moment Simon considered checking Dad's thoughts to know just what to say, but he quickly put the idea aside. He said, "Could I go myself? After school?"

Dad looked startled. Simon's school ran after-hours programs in the gym for kids without someone at home. You were supposed to use it for homework or clubs, but lots of kids just hung around, and none of the teachers seemed to mind. The school allowed kids to leave with a note from their parents, either to go with another grown-up, or even on their own if the parent said it was okay. The signature on the note would have to be checked against the signing cards the school kept for every parent.

Dad said, "Wow, you really want this game, don't you?"

"I don't need to do the after-school, it's not so much fun, really. And I promise to do all my homework as soon as I get home." He hoped his dad couldn't see him holding his breath.

"Well," Dad said, "you have been a really good boy lately. Maybe it's time to let you do something on your own."

Yes! Simon thought, but he kept his face and body still.

Dad said, "You'll come right home from the game store, right?"

"Sure, Dad."

"And you know where the extra key is, right?"

Simon nodded.

"But you can't bring anyone home with you. Is that understood?"

"I know."

Dad sighed. "If you have any problem, get Mrs. Volck from next door, okay?"

"I know, Dad."

Another deep breath, then, "Okay." Dad wrote a note on the memo pad, put it in an envelope, sealed it and gave it to Simon, who put it in his backpack's zipper pocket. "I guess you'll have to take your bike to school," Dad said.

"I'll be careful, Dad. I promise." Simon knew this whole idea was only possible because the store was not very far from both the school and the house, with only a couple of traffic lights in each part of the trip.

"And you'll come right home from the game store?" Dad said again.

"Sure."

"And you'll be super careful crossing intersections?"

Simon nodded.

"If anyone speaks to you, or asks you to go somewhere with him, even if he says I sent him, don't listen. Okay?"

Simon rolled his eyes. "Dad! I know that stuff."

His father hugged him. "Okay, then." He stood up.

"Dad? The money?"

His father laughed. "Right." Simon watched him take out his wallet and bring forth a bright twenty-dollar bill. "Here you go," he said. Simon put the money in his jeans pocket, not his backpack, and watched his father nod. Simon had lost a dollar when he was six, and Dad had told him then you never put money in your pack. Dad said, "Maybe if it's a cool game you can have Jerry over to play it with you."

Recently, Simon had begun hanging out with a boy named Jerry Lowe. He felt funny not playing with Popcorn Jimmy so much, but Jimmy looked just as happy to be by himself. And Jerry was cooler, and more popular. Simon liked the idea of inviting Jerry over, but not to look at his cards. He said, "Dad, for twenty dollars, it's just a one-person game."

"Oh," Dad said. "Sure. Well, maybe for something else sometime."

"Okay," Simon said. He shrugged on his backpack and headed for the door.

"I want to see that game when you bring it home," Dad said.

"Okay." This was tricky, but Simon thought there was a good chance Dad would forget about it. Lately, his father's work appeared to be taking up all his attention. If not, maybe he could show him some old game.

Simon got on his bike and headed toward school. When he'd turned a corner and was sure Dad couldn't see him, he stopped and pumped his fist in the air. "Yes!" he said out loud. He'd persuaded his dad to let him go to school alone, and without cheating. He almost wanted to tell his father what he'd done so Dad could be proud of him.

After school, Simon gave in his permission slip and pretended not to notice the kids watch him leave the gym and ride off on his bike. He rode straight to the game store, and was happy he hadn't needed to lie to his dad about where he was going. When he was there with his dad once, he'd seen a box of Tarot cards on the counter, mixed in with the RPG decks. He hoped they were still there.

Yes, there they were, and with tax they came to only $16.32. Simon bought gum and a Mars Bar with the rest of Dad's money and left the store. He wanted to rip off the shrink-wrap and look at them right away but decided it was more important to get home before his dad, so he put them in his pack and pedaled home as fast as he could.

The moment he opened the package he could see they were wrong. They were the same pictures—mostly—but they just looked, well, *wrong*: drawn too thick, the faces all funny, the colors too dull and too bright all at the same time. Simon wanted to tear them up and flush them down the toilet or something—but he reminded himself why he'd bought them, not for themselves but for the names.

Just as he'd remembered, the ones from the store all had titles at the bottom. Mostly they only said the suit and number, like "Four of Swords" or "Seven of Cups" (they were different from regular cards, no hearts and spades and things), and there were kings and queens, and—just as he'd guessed—knights, plus something called a "page," which appeared to be a person and nothing to do with books. The talking-fish card, in fact, was called the Page of Cups. Simon thought his name was better. And then there was a group with fancier titles: "The Tower" or "The Hanged Man" (the upside-down guy). These were the exciting ones, and when Simon looked at his own set—the "real" ones, as he thought of them—he realized he'd already known that group was special.

Some of the pictures showed naked women, and even though they didn't look much like the *Playboy* pictures some kid had brought to school in his backpack, Simon figured that was another reason not to tell Dad about them. At first Simon thought there were twenty-one of the special cards, since that was the highest number, but then he saw that one of them—his favorite, actually, which he'd called "the Beautiful Boy about to Fly" but now saw was called "the Fool"—was numbered zero, so that made twenty-two. He liked that, he didn't know why. Twenty-two just sounded like a cool number. And it was cool that something should be called *zero*.

Card zero, the Fool, was definitely his favorite. He'd liked the picture before, a young man walking or dancing on the edge of a cliff with his arms out like a bird, but this time he liked the real title better. Most of the others had fancy names, like "The Emperor," and they looked kind of serious, but here was a *fool*, and he looked so happy, even though he might fall off that cliff at any moment. Simon just knew nothing bad could happen to the Fool. And nothing bad could happen to himself either as long as he had the cards.

There were some scary pictures, or sad ones, such as a woman sitting up in bed, weeping in a dark room. This card had always made him sad, and now he saw it was called "Nine of Swords," and there were in fact nine silver swords mounted like a kind of ladder on the wall behind the woman. When Simon looked at the picture, he just wanted to put his arms around her and tell her it was okay.

There were angry cards, too, with people fighting, and there was even a card called "Death," which showed a skeleton dressed up in black armor like a knight and riding a white horse. Simon had never thought of it as scary, not even now that he saw its title.

Most of the cards from the game store were pretty close to the "real" ones, but two of them didn't match up at all. One of them was a card he liked a lot, though he wasn't sure why, and the other, well, the other disturbed him, though again, he couldn't really say why. The one he liked from the real deck was one of the strangest. It showed a beautiful head, with golden hair and a bright face, the eyes closed, the mouth open wide as if singing. There was no body—the head was mounted on a shiny black stick, with dark trees around it. There was nothing like it in the store deck, and Simon finally decided it had been replaced by something called "Judgment," a picture of an angel blowing a horn with people standing up in boxes and praying or something. So should he call the *real* picture Judgment, or just keep his own title—"Head On a Stick?"

The other replacement card was called "The Devil," and showed a scowling man with horns and goat feet holding a pair of chains like dog leashes that were connected to collars around the necks of a naked man and woman. The picture was just stupid, Simon thought, but he didn't feel that way about the card it replaced. That one—the "Devil," as he now thought of it—showed a handsome man standing in a stone room. He stood a little sideways but with his head turned to look directly out from the card, staring so intently Simon almost felt as if the man could see him. He wore a long robe of braided black and gold, which should have looked weird but didn't. A light shone around his face, which was set in a little smile.

Simon thought of him as beautiful somehow, which was a funny thing to think about a man, and yet . . . and yet he felt queasy when he looked at him and always put him back in the deck whenever he turned up. Sometimes he even forgot the man—the "Devil"—was there, and would be surprised if he suddenly came across it. All he knew was that he didn't want whatever stories the Devil wanted to show him.

There appeared to be a lot of forgetting going on those days. Just as Simon had hoped, his dad asked all about going out by himself, and cars, and not talking to strangers, and did he do his homework, but he never actually asked to see the game. He did say he'd look at it later, then he went into the kitchen to make dinner, which, since it was Tuesday, was cheeseburgers and potato salad. After dinner, he took out his laptop and his briefcase of papers and worked until it was time to put Simon to bed.

Two days later, Simon got rid of the Tarot cards from the store. He told himself he didn't need them anymore, he'd learned the names now, and it just meant two things to hide from his dad instead of one. But really, he simply didn't like them. He couldn't get over the feeling that they were wrong, like something that had forgotten what it was supposed to be. He took the game store cards to school with him in a brown bag, and when he passed the gray trash can by the door, he dropped them inside.

A week later, Jerry Lowe's mom and dad invited Simon for a sleepover. It wasn't the first time Simon had stayed at another kid's house, but it was the first in more than a year, since all his "troubles" began. Dad fussed around him, asked over and over if Simon was sure he felt okay about it, said there was nothing wrong with saying no, told him he could come home whenever he wanted, checked Simon had what he needed, until finally Simon rolled his eyes and said, "Dad, it's okay. It's cool."

And it *was* cool. Simon was all excited, Jerry had the best game station ever, and Mrs. Lowe had promised they could have pizza with whatever toppings they liked. Simon's only question was the cards. Should he take them? Sometimes he woke up in the middle of the night, all sweaty with his heart beating very fast, and looking at the pictures calmed him down. But suppose he did that and Jerry caught him? But if he left them home, his dad might decide to clean his room or something and discover them. Finally, Simon decided they were safe in their hiding place and he should just leave them there.

The funny thing was, it wasn't Simon who woke up all disturbed, but Jerry. And it was even weirder because when they were in their pajamas, and Jerry in his bed, and Simon on an air mattress on the floor, Simon asked what kind of dreams Jerry had, and Jerry said he didn't, he never dreamed at all. So it really surprised Simon when he woke up in the middle of the night to hear Jerry moaning and twitching his hands, just like someone in a nightmare. He wondered for a moment what to do, then finally touched Jerry's shoulder. His friend's eyes flew open and stared at Simon. "Hey," Simon said, "you okay?"

"There's a stone room," Jerry said. His face tightened, and he seemed to be trying to say the right thing. "No. Not a room. A long . . . long tunnel. Stone tunnel. There's things—things on the floor. Pieces of . . . things."

Simon jumped back. After a second, he said, "It's just a dream. It doesn't mean anything." Wasn't that what his dad always said? (*Remember*, the woman had told him.)

"Pieces of fingers," Jerry said, and snapped his head to the side, as if trying not to see. Simon knew that wouldn't help. Jerry went on, "And there's a man. Very tall. I can't see his face. He's got something on a table."

Simon grabbed Jerry's shoulder. The space-hero pajama top was sweaty, and he took his hand back. "Stop," he said. "It's just a dream." He wanted to feel inside Jerry, read his mind, Dad would say, find something to say to make him feel better, but really, just to make him stop. But that was cheating so he didn't do it, though maybe he was afraid if he went inside he'd never get out.

Jerry squeezed shut his eyes, but they opened right up again. His voice got very whispery as he said, "It's a head. It's a kid's head and he's—"

"Please stop," Simon said. "It's just a dream."

"Cutting it. Lots and lots of cuts, with . . . with a stone knife. Putting something on them—pieces of paper—pictures—" Suddenly, Jerry just closed his eyes, laid his head back on the pillow and a second later was asleep.

Simon went to his backpack and got out Dad's cell phone. *Call any time*, Dad had told him, but when Simon looked up at the Disney World clock over Jerry's bed and saw it was 4:20, he was afraid he'd scare his dad too much. And disappoint him.

Simon wished he had his cards. Why didn't he bring them? Stupid, stupid. He'd be good if he just had his cards in their comforting blue wrapper, with all their stories, their safe places. He lay back down on the air mattress and stared at the ceiling, trying to remember the pictures. *Remember.* He made himself think of his favorite cards, which was easier now that he knew their names. And it was easier somehow not to think of the one he didn't like, since the modern deck had replaced it with that silly picture of the angry "Devil." He made himself think of the Fool, his favorite, and doing so, fell asleep.

Jerry woke up first and knelt down by the air mattress to shake Simon's shoulder. "Come on," he said. "We've got some time to play before Mom makes breakfast."

Sleepily, Simon looked him over. "You okay?" he said.

"Huh? Course I'm okay. Come on, get up."

"You had that dream," Simon said.

Jerry laughed. "No, I didn't. I told you—I never dream." He went over and turned on his Xbox. "Let's go."

Simon stared at him a moment longer, then got up and grabbed the joystick his friend was holding out to him.

And that's where he was, hours later, after breakfast, after lunch and time outdoors shooting baskets, when his father showed up. Simon packed up his things, thanked Mr. and Mrs. Lowe, and he and Dad took off. In the car, Dad said, "So how did it go?"

"Cool," Simon said.

"You have fun?"

"Yeah. I beat Jerry two games in a row."

Dad laughed. "Good for you," he said, then, as if he liked the words, repeated, "Good for you."

Chapter Seventeen

MATYAS

From that day, when reading revealed itself to him like a flood of bright water, Matyas studied constantly. He still labored for Veil, but every other moment, he read and practiced, so much so that Veil took it on herself to reassure him that the knowledge, once given, could not be taken away. "You would have to forget yourself entirely," she said, "before you forgot how to read."

Matyas didn't slow down. He read Veil's books, some passages two or three times when he found he could understand the words but not what they meant. Slowly, over time, he began to read more quickly, suddenly remembering something he'd encountered a month before that had made no sense to him but now fitted perfectly with a new passage. As well as the books, he studied the strange objects that filled Veil's very plain tower home. He began to recognize such things as clocks that marked the slow movements of the stars rather than the Sun's swift dash, or a feather that was in fact attached to a bird who existed in some other world entirely but for that one feather poking into our world.

Sometimes he saw the lights, the Splendor as Medun had called them, but only for a few seconds. Medun had said they were not creatures themselves but the tracks of beings so great that if they entered our clumsy world of bodies and rocks, they would break open the sky.

Once, when he saw them while he was deep in a book half as big as himself, he wondered what it would be like to enter *their* world, and then he realized, it was the first time he'd seen the Splendor and did not immediately think of the promise that he would fly. He sat there for a moment, trying to decide what he should think about that—and then he returned to his book.

He read, he studied. And he began to practice. For there were spells in the books, and tricks, and ways to change things. He could make flowers grow out of rocks, or cause a page from a book to curl up and cry like a little child. He discovered that the spell Medun had begun against him, the toad spell, was not all that difficult to do, but once accomplished could not be undone. If Medun had not abandoned it, Matyas might still be hopping around behind the stove in the Hungry Squirrel. That is, unless his father had found him, for the master of the inn detested "vermin," as he called all small creatures, and crushed them or threw them in the flames whenever he could catch them.

Once, Matyas had made the mistake of not looking when his father had stamped his boot on a mouse. Matyas hadn't turned his head, he'd only squeezed shut his eyes, but his father must have been watching him, for he grabbed Matyas' face so hard the boy was scared his teeth would pop out to fall, all bloody, onto the dead mouse. "You don't want to look?" his father had said. "Maybe I should put my boot down on your coward face and throw you out with the rats and the garbage."

Matyas did his best not to remember such things, to stay safe inside Veil's books and his spells, but every now and then some moment would come back, maybe something his father had said to him, or his father's hand against his face when he was eating a piece of bread, or the terror he felt just before his father's foot reached his stomach. He scolded himself when he allowed such things to interfere with his studies. The point, he told himself, was simply not to think about his father, or the Hungry Squirrel. He thought of that life as little more than a bad dream.

Sometimes he thought of Royja and when they would sneak off to imagine another world. He remembered his promise to come back to her. When he was ready, and clearly that was not now, he was just beginning to learn. And yet, he had already found a better world, a real one. How could he return to Royja, who lived in dreams and fantasies? He became angry at her, imagined her grasping at his ankle, trying to pull him down with her.

Ultimately, all he could do was banish such thoughts. He was here to learn, and practice, and become a better wizard than anyone. Better than Lukhanan, better even than Veil (though as he thought about it, Veil never really *did* much of anything, did she?). He was Master Matyas, and he was going to fly, and leave his father, and even the wizards, even Veil herself, far behind in the lowly dirt. *Don't think about the past*, he ordered himself. Don't remember things that would only distract him. *Study. Learn what matters.*

He still labored for Veil. He owed it to her, he told himself, at the same time thinking how he really had more important things to do now than carry wood and buckets of water up four flights of stairs. And when Berias and the others taunted him, he imagined taking out some great scroll and reading it to them, just to see their faces. And then maybe he would open the earth beneath them, or cause their intestines to poke out from their bellies. Yet somehow he never did any of it, just ignored them and went about his business.

One day, as he was returning from the market with the moldy old cheese Veil liked, he saw a group of students arguing about a spell. It was a simple thing, a trick. You drew a picture of a bird on a flat stone, inscribed one of the Four Hundred Lesser Names, spoke the name in the right way and the bird would rise off the rock to flutter in front of you and sing exquisitely, at least for a minute or two. It was nothing, really, but the apprentices kept trying, and getting it wrong, and one of them, a skinny redhead named Caudfinn, looked ready to take his stone and smash it against the courtyard bricks when Matyas set down the cheese and walked up to them.

Berias rolled his eyes in that thick head of his that always reminded Matyas of a tree stump. Matyas ignored him and approached Caudfinn. "You do it like this," he said, then touched the other boy's drawing and spoke the name "sideways," as Veil put it, a kind of intonation that was neither the way the word looked, nor any of the obvious variations. Sideways. Instantly, all the pictures took flight and the air was filled with brightly colored see-through birds, their chirps so loud that even some of the Masters threw open the windows of their studies to listen, and wonder how so many clumsy students had accomplished something so tricky all at the same time. And Caudfinn and Berias and the others could only shift their stunned faces from Matyas to the birds and back, their jaws opened so wide that Matyas could not help but think of the abyss he'd once wanted to open beneath their feet.

He picked up the wheel of cheese and willed himself to walk at his ordinary pace, with his face blank, until he was inside the tower. Then he grinned and hopped up and down.

He calmed his face again when he reached the top of the stairs. What would Veil say, what would she do? Would she be proud of him, or angry for wasting time on a silly game? Or had she even noticed? It would be just like her to have been staring into some book the whole time and have no idea of the special thing that had happened out in the lowly world where she sent her apprentice out to run errands like a kitchen boy.

In fact, he found her, not with her eyes in a book but nowhere at all. That is, she was doing that strange thing where she sat in her small rocker, so still it might have been nailed to the floor, and looked straight ahead, at nothing. Matyas thought how lightning could strike the tower, throwing the two of them into the air amid a hailstorm of books, and Veil would not even know her body no longer sat in a motionless rocker.

He sighed and brought the cheese over to the white porcelain box that would keep it cool and fresh, then sat on the floor with a book, a small but difficult work bound in marbled red and blue and yellow leather. The work, by a Master named Florian, described the "color harmonics of the planets within the sky and the true body," and Matyas found it more confusing than anything he'd read in months. It wasn't just how difficult it was—it was certainly that—but something else. When he read Master Florian's words, he felt a strange energy that appeared to open up the very air in front of him and yet somehow threatened everything he was doing, like some strange trap.

At times he wanted to shove the book away, even run from it, and yet he kept studying, trying to understand it, for even without knowing exactly what it said it produced those strange sensations. Such sensations were new for Matyas. With all the previous books he'd studied, all that mattered was what he could do with them. Spells to cast, tricks, knowledge to raise him above everyone else. And ultimately to fly. What else was magic for? But this—this Master Florian—it opened layers and layers.

He was deep in the work when Veil stirred herself from her vacant stare. "Ah, Matyas," she said. "I trust that Esau gave you a good price on the cheese?"

Stupid woman, Matyas thought. Cheese! What color were the bird-songs on Jupiter? *That's* what mattered. He grunted an answer and stared at Florian's strange descriptions. Veil walked over to the small window where Matyas had originally seen her all those months before, when he was so desperate for someone, anyone, to take him as a student.

Might he have been better off with someone else (assuming anyone would have had him)? Of course, Veil knew more than anyone else, that was clear. And she had taught him to read—well, "taught" was hardly the right word—and now that he could read and had access to her books, he learned more every day. And true, sometimes she actually sat down and taught him something, such as how to speak sideways. But she still treated him like a kitchen boy. And she still insisted she knew nothing of how to fly.

And she never said anything about all his achievements. "Get the cheese, fill the bucket, build a fire," but never, "You did that very well, Matyas," or, "If anyone could understand Master Florian, it certainly would be you."

He felt color rise in his face at such thoughts and made sure he was turned away from Veil, lest the old woman catch him. Certainly he had never cared what anyone said about him at the Hungry Squirrel. If he could keep out of range of his father's fists, that was enough. But Veil was, well, different. And so was he. He knew things now, he had power, and he was sure it was only a matter of time before he learned how to fly.

Maybe Veil was jealous. Wasn't he the one who could summon the Splendor? He'd never seen them around Veil at all. He remembered Medun saying how no one had ever seen them in their true form, "Except maybe for one. And if so, she hasn't told me." Maybe he meant someone else, some other old lady. Someone who did more than just stare at nothing all day.

He was about to throw the book down—he hadn't understood a word—and stamp out of the room—maybe he ought to go and study with Lukhanan, what would she say to that?—when Veil half turned and said, "You should begin dinner. The Sun has returned, but only to say goodnight."

Now what was *that* supposed to mean?

"Oh, and Matyas, thank you for the bird concert. I suspect even Florian would have enjoyed it."

Matyas put his head down so she couldn't see his grin. "I'll go and cut the turnips," he said, and dashed into the tiny kitchen alcove so she couldn't see the pride swell his chest and color his face.

Months passed, then more months. Matyas' body grew and became strong, but his magic became stronger still. Though he still slept in the alcove in the tower, and did Veil's chores and carried her messages, he began, subtly, hardly knowing it himself, to teach. If in the middle of some errand he saw students—and even, once or twice, a teacher—struggling with something, he might stop and reveal what was missing. At first, even after he'd brought the birds to life, they would try to ignore him, or snigger to each other. For wasn't he little more than Veil's slave? Didn't he always appear with buckets of water or sacks of vegetables? He ignored these slights and helped them, and after a while, he noticed that their eyes would stray to him as he passed, hopeful, afraid or ashamed to ask outright. Sometimes he pretended not to notice, but more and more he went over to them, sat down and opened the way.

One day Veil filled an envelope with shiny green powder, sealed it and told Matyas to take it to a house on the far side of the city. As always with such errands, she said nothing about what the powder was, who would receive it or why. Nevertheless, Matyas enjoyed the walk through the capital's streets, some straight and wider than the wizards' whole courtyard, others bent and narrow, with walls that leaned over so far the two sides of the street nearly touched each other. He passed women wrapped in layers of yellow silk, and boys with hair so long that small sharp-toothed creatures lived in the coils. An aged fortune teller wearing several dresses at once promised to reveal Matyas' future. He walked over and whispered a formula in her ear that locked her mouth shut so tight she couldn't speak at all until he took mercy on her and withdrew his spell.

The address Veil had given him turned out to be a narrow, plain house set amid a row of wooden mansions with turrets and balconies in bright colors. His knock on the unpainted wooden door was answered immediately, as if the woman who opened it had been waiting on the other side. The tallest, and thinnest, woman Matyas had ever seen stood barefoot on an unpolished stone floor. She wore a black shawl that covered her head and shoulders to flow into the loose green dress that rustled against her body as if moved by wind. She said nothing, only stared at Matyas until he said, "Veil sent me." Still she remained silent. He took the envelope from his pocket and held it out. "She asked me to give this to you."

Long fingers with sharp nails plucked it from his hand. "Thank you," she said, then closed the door so swiftly Matyas had to jump back.

Furious, Matyas considered summoning a flame sprite to burn a hole in the door. Were all Veil's friends as crazy as she was? Why did he let her do this to him? Maybe he should just kick the door down, force Old Skinny to tell him what was in the envelope, why Veil wanted her to have it. He stood there a while then stamped up the stone street.

He stayed angry all the way back to the Wizards' Academy, determined to yell at Veil that she couldn't treat him this way. Usually, whenever he was in the courtyard and Veil had not demanded a quick return, he would look around to see if anyone was trying a spell or some other experiment. Today he wanted only to climb up the stairs and confront the old woman who treated him so badly. But then two Masters in their long heavy robes came up to him. "Good day, Matyas," one of them said. He was a stocky man with the shoulders of a wrestler, though in fact he was a scholar—the chief scholar in a way, for this was Horekh, head of the massive stone library that filled the entire north wall of the Academy. The other was a white-haired old man named Najarian, who had once been head of the council until he was pushed out by Lukhanan and his faction.

Not sure what they wanted, Matyas said, "Good day, Masters."

Najarian said, "Several of us have noticed the advances you've made, Matyas. Very impressive."

Before Matyas could think of an answer, Horekh said, "And while Veil, of course, can offer you her own great resources, we want you to know that the library is available to you if ever you might wish to use it. Would you like that?"

Matyas could only stare. So often he'd looked at the grand building with its black and white pillars, its green and red lions guarding the entrance, its slippery marble stairs leading to the dark wooden door that rose three times the height of a man yet appeared to swing open easily and silently at a touch, and he'd wondered what it would be like to run through it, grabbing books from the towering piles he imagined rising up in all directions. And now the Master himself was inviting him. "Yes," he said. "I mean, thank you. Yes, I would like that."

Horekh smiled. "Then perhaps you would like to come inside now and I will show it to you. That is, unless Veil expects your swift return."

"No," Matyas said, "Veil doesn't expect anything."

"Then come." Najarian stayed behind and watched as Horekh led Matyas up the slippery steps.

The inside was like nothing Matyas had ever seen. There was one huge room, with tables fashioned in the shapes of various beasts, and large wooden chairs whose high backs were carved with spells of knowledge. These were for the Masters, several of whom sat reading a book or a scroll. The apprentices, Matyas learned, studied in small cubicles along the sides, where they were expected not to make any noise, and to surrender any work a Master might have requested, even if the Master might not come to read it for a day or so. One apprentice, slim, with very short hair and dressed in a loose-fitting brown tunic and pants, sat on his bench in the middle of the floor at a bare table. Horekh introduced him as Alejandre, whose job it was to fetch the manuscripts when someone asked for them.

The cubicles held plain tables and benches, and simple oil lamps for which the apprentice was expected to supply his own oil. Above each of the Master tables hung a crystal globe suspended all the way from the ceiling by a silver chain. Each globe contained a bright silvery light. It took Matyas several stares to realize the lights came from creatures, captured sprites who glowed as they moved around in their cages. Some of the sprites took human form; others resembled hummingbirds, or beasts from some tiny zoo of light. One of the brightest lamps held two beings shaped like a man and a woman. Matyas thought they were fighting until he realized they were doing something else. He thought of Royja and immediately turned away.

The fact is, it wasn't the lamps, or the furniture carved with spells, or the tree-thick marble columns holding up the ceiling, or the elegant statues (great Masters of the past, he assumed, and imagined his own statue, taller than all the rest) that surprised Matyas the most. Rather it was the books and scrolls and papers themselves—that is, how they were stored. Matyas had expected something like Veil's unruly piles, only vastly higher. Instead all the works were stored neatly on endless shelves, tiers and tiers of shelves running along the walls and reaching up all the way to the ceiling. There must be thousands of works, Matyas thought joyously, and yet . . . it looked *wrong* somehow. Too neat, too ordered. And where were the carvings and powders and mysterious boxes, and stones and feathers and instruments that Matyas could never figure out how to play?

But still, so many books! So much to learn!

Matyas noticed that as Horekh showed him around, various people, both Masters and apprentices who otherwise looked lost in study, turned their backs as he passed them. Horekh appeared unaware of this until they came to a cubicle that was more elaborate than the others, with a cushioned chair rather than a bench, and a tapestry of the planetary spheres hung on the wall. The young man studying there wore the simple tunic and pants of an apprentice, but his were made of painted silk, with a gold buckle on a tooled leather belt. As Matyas walked by, he sniffed loudly, as if something had fouled the air, then he slammed his book shut and walked away. Matyas noticed that the book, a treatise on plants that bloom secretly at night under the new Moon, was one he'd read weeks ago. Still, he stared at the young apprentice, who made a show of leaving the building holding his nose.

Horekh sighed. "Please accept my apologies for Lord Olan's rudeness." *Lord?* Matyas thought. He knew that most of the students came from the nobility, but usually they surrendered their titles when they joined the Academy. "His family are our chief patrons," Horekh said, and now Matyas' eyes widened, for everyone knew that the king himself was the Academy's main supporter. Horekh saw his reaction and said, "Just so. But even if our illustrious patron supports our efforts—and appreciates the considerable advantage this gives him over his rivals—I'm afraid he does not consider the *work* we do suitable for one of his sons. Especially since we insist that Olan serve as apprentice, the same—" He smiled. "Or almost the same, as anyone else. Thus it becomes important for Olan himself to believe that magic somehow requires princely blood."

Matyas felt his face burn, especially as he noticed that all those who kept their backs turned appeared to be laughing into their books. He imagined transforming Olan into a moth then sending him into his father's palace where some servant would crush him. Or maybe he could cast a putrefaction spell that *Lord* Olan would find impossible to wash off.

Instead, he made himself focus on the library and all its wonderful possibilities. He asked Horekh, "Do you have the Tarot of Eternity here?" A few people sniggered or outright laughed but Matyas ignored them. He thought how wonderful it would be to learn all the secrets Veil had hidden from him.

"I am sorry," Horekh said. "Joachim's masterpiece has been lost for a very long time. Lost, or hidden away, for many believe that Joachim removed it from the world to prevent its terrible misuse."

Misuse? Matyas thought, but all he said was, "Do you have a copy?"

"No. There were only two copies ever made and both of them have vanished as well."

"Then what about a copy of a copy?"

Horekh shook his head and Matyas wondered if it was possible that the head of the Masters' library did not know that the old woman stuck in her tower owned such a copy.

Before he could decide whether or not to reveal his special knowledge—there might, after all, be a better time—Horekh said, "We did once have a copy of a copy of a copy. Sadly, someone took it away with him when he left our company. It was a true loss."

Medun. Matyas decided to conceal his knowledge of that story as well. Instead he only asked, "Do you have writings by Florian?"

The librarian smiled. "Yes, I have heard of your interest in those very difficult works. It's one of the reasons Najarian and I thought it worthwhile to invite you here to study. Veil, I am sure, owns a great number of Florian's works, perhaps especially the more difficult texts, but we may have something here that will help you."

Matyas said, with a certain pride, "I've been studying the Theory of Transcendent Colors." He noticed a few turn to look at him, for he knew this teaching was rarely attempted. Proudly he said, "Sometimes I'm sure I understand him, but then he escapes me."

Right away he knew he'd made some mistake, for there was a kind of collective intake of breath, then looks and smiles from one to the other.

In a gentle tone of voice that Matyas hated, Horekh said, "Has Veil never talked to you about Florian?"

"We've talked about the colors. And the songs of the planets."

"I see. Well, Florian was one of the original founders of this Academy. She was also a woman."

Matyas stared at him, somehow unable to move even as everyone around him, it seemed, burst out laughing. Then the spell that held him broke and he ran from the building.

He forced himself to walk normally across the courtyard, wondering if at any moment someone would come out of the library to announce to everyone how the ignorant kitchen boy was all puffed up that he was studying Florian yet didn't even know she was a woman. No such announcement came, but of course the story would spread through the Academy by nightfall.

He marched up the steps to find Veil in her rocker, staring at a long sheet of parchment that appeared to contain nothing at all, neither words nor diagrams. Normally he would have tried to grasp what she was seeing but now he wanted to yank it from her hands and throw it on the floor. He said, "Why didn't you tell me Florian was a woman?"

"Does it matter?" she said.

"Of course it matters."

"Are you suggesting that only a woman could have created the Theory of Transcendent Colors? And if so, can only a woman understand it? That would put you at a disadvantage. Luckily, there are spells that can remedy that." She was smiling, not a common sight.

"Stop it," Matyas said. "You know what I mean."

"Perhaps. There are two possible answers, Matyas. One is that in fact Florian's sex, and more broadly, her life history, have no bearing on her teachings. This is indeed true, but there is the other answer. It may be that there are, in fact, aspects of Florian's life that carry great meaning, though not for her doctrines and theories. And—"

"Aspects? What do you mean?"

That smile again. "I was going to say that it might be best if you uncovered those aspects for yourself."

"You're laughing at me." He should have known, it was just like her. She was no better than Lukhanan or any of the others.

The smile vanished, replaced by something even rarer—genuine concern. "Forgive an old woman," she said. "I confess that your enthusiasm sometimes amuses me. And there are times I treasure it."

Matyas had no idea what to say. Surprise, even gratitude, battled with anger in his mind. Finally he said again, "What are these aspects? The things about Florian. Besides that she's a woman." *Was*, he thought, but didn't correct himself.

Veil shook her head. "No. When you need to know them they will reveal themselves. And besides, it is not really so much about Florian herself as about *another* who was part of the story."

Matyas could hear the odd emphasis on that single word, a distaste, maybe even fear, though it felt odd to think of Veil as being scared of anything.

Veil went on, "Meanwhile, you have your studies. And I must return to mine. Who knows how much time I have left?" She cast her eyes on her empty parchment and all emotion vanished from her face, all movement from her body. If Matyas tried to talk to her, she probably wouldn't even hear him.

What should he do? He could walk out, but then he would have to return to the courtyard. Finally he just went over to his small bed where he'd left a long, thin volume of Florian that contained no text, only page after page of abstract drawings and diagrams. Briefly he wondered if he should go back to some of the other books, reread them not for their teachings, but to search out "aspects" that were so important Veil had to hide them from him. But then he would have to abandon the diagrams of the songs embedded in the fingers of the Outer Constellations. He forgot about the life and stared at the pictures.

For several weeks, Matyas did his best to forget about the library, though occasionally the image of the endless shelves of books would come into his mind, usually followed closely by the laughter that had chased him from the building. Then one night he found himself frustrated at reading the same passage over and over and he got up to look out of the small window. For the first time in weeks, he thought about flying, how wonderful it would be to step off the ledge and circle the courtyard, then take off and leave them all behind.

Ah, but then he would never solve the riddle of transcendent color. He remembered something he'd seen written on the edge of a page in one of Veil's books. "He who truly understands Florian understands the Mind of God." Had Veil written that? It didn't look like her writing—hers was usually fine and very precise, while this was large and a little rough. *Medun*, he thought now, and smiled.

Across the courtyard, lights flickered in a handful of the library's windows. Matyas glanced at Veil, who sat in her narrow rocking chair, eyes closed, her head dropped forward. Quietly he slipped out through the door and went down the stairs.

In the library's great hall, only a handful of Masters and apprentices sat in study. Most paid no attention to Matyas' entrance, but he braced himself as an apprentice got up from a small table and walked over to him. "May I help you with something?" he said, and Matyas remembered that Horekh had said someone would guide him to what he wanted to study. Alejandre was the one Horekh had introduced him to, but Matyas couldn't remember if this was him or someone else.

He said, "I'd like to see the works of Master Florian."

"Of course," said the young man who may or may not have been named Alejandre. He picked up a small oil lamp. "Follow me, please." Slightly dazed, Matyas walked with him to what he saw was a spiral ramp that wound around the hall to create the floors of shelves. They went to the very top, where there was a long row of dusty books. "Please forgive the untidiness," the apprentice said. "No one has come to test these books in some time." He smiled. "Too difficult."

Matyas stayed almost to dawn, leaving only so he could be back before Veil awakened. When he opened the door to leave, Najarian was walking up the steps. He looked startled but said nothing, only nodded to Matyas and went inside.

Matyas went to the library often over the next few weeks, though in fact Horekh was right—the vast collection did not appear to contain much he had not already found in Veil's unruly piles. It struck him one day that perhaps the books he saw in Veil's tower represented only a small part of her collection, with the rest hidden in some other layer of the world, like the man in the market who displayed a range of cheeses on his table but kept a great deal more in a large porcelain box. Veil's storage box would have to be in some different world, a "higher plane," as the books called it. Was that where she'd hidden the Tarot of Eternity? For a while he wondered if he might find the spell to unlock Veil's secret world, but his heart wasn't there. It was Florian that held him now.

And it was in Florian, on a chilly winter afternoon, with the red and green lions outside the library half covered in snow, that Matyas discovered the answer to a question he'd long ago forgotten. He was sitting at a small table Alejandre had arranged for him at the highest level, where the Masters kept the works of Florian, and on the table a book lay open. It was called *Origins of Origins* and it was, of course, by Florian. Matyas had read and in fact reread the three large volumes known simply as *Origins*, but this text was new to him. Judging by the dust on the marbled leather cover, no one had taken it down in a long time. He did not understand why, for compared to most of the Master's work, it was quite straightforward. It was written in poetry, and code, for it was Florian, after all, but still, much easier to penetrate than most. And it was short. It ran only a few pages, and would have been no more than one or two if the scribe who'd taken it down (Florian herself never wrote anything, but only dictated her teachings, so some argued that the notorious difficulties came partly from mistakes made in the writing) had not used such large and sweeping calligraphy.

From the moment he began, Matyas realized he was reading something special, the very beginnings of the world. And then he recalled, with a small shock, a strange thing Medun had asked him, all those months ago in the Hungry Squirrel. *What would the world be like*, the wizard had said, *if you could not know for sure if the Sun would come up in the morning, or that spring would follow winter?* Matyas had found the question so absurd he'd immediately forgotten it, especially after they went on to talk about flying, and changing people into toads. Now he saw that it was true.

In the beginning, Florian wrote, the Creator brought forth seven great Trees, each with its own quality, then gave them over to seven Guardians who would use the power of the Trees to create a perfect Garden for all the humans and animals who walked upon the new and shining Earth. Instead, the Guardians turned all of existence into a game, with no rules except their own will and amusement. The intended paradise became a place of desperation and fear.

This was the world that gave birth to Joachim the Brilliant. Others before him had stumbled upon aspects of magic and tried to gain enough power to battle the Guardians. Joachim understood that this was hopeless, and instead used all his skill to enter something called the Deep Woods, where he found a mysterious figure known as the Opener. Together with the Opener, Joachim created the Tarot of Eternity.

Using the images as "Gateways," Joachim—along with his disciple Florian—ascended to the Bright Palace of the Creator, where they begged Her to help them. And so the Creator changed the world. The Guardians retreated—"took refuge in the sky," the text said—and the world became a set of structures, knowable and predictable, ruled, Florian wrote, by "geometry and numbers."

Matyas read this and read it again and then got up to walk to the balcony and stare down at the various wizards and apprentices below. Najarian and some Master whom Matyas didn't know were walking silently past the statues of their predecessors. The glow of the sylph lamps lit up their robes as they moved. In the study alcoves, a new apprentice hunched over a book like a squirrel clutching a walnut. Matyas wondered suddenly if everyone knew these things, this Origin of Origins. Did all the apprentices learn it in their first year? Veil never told Matyas anything—he had to search and search, and hope he would stumble across basic knowledge before he made some foolish mistake and everyone laughed at him.

He wanted to run from the library straight to Veil's tower refuge and shout, "Why didn't you tell me this? You're my teacher—you're supposed to tell me what I need to know."

He didn't move. Instead, he held on to the edge of the table as if afraid to let go. He imagined Veil saying, "Why should I tell you things when you can discover them for yourself?" But it was not fear of what Veil might say that kept him there. No, there was something in the text itself, more a feeling than anything concrete. Was this what Veil had meant by *aspects*?

Because he had become a seeker, he tried to follow the feeling. The *Origin of Origins* stated that Joachim and Florian ascended in the "Chariot of Eternity." But as Matyas cast his mind back over the words—for he had learned the skill of remembering whole pages, word for word—he realized that here and there the text hinted that someone else had traveled with them. "We three" it said at one point, and, "Another"—the very word Veil had used, with distaste and even fear. When Matyas had first read these phrases he'd assumed they were scribal errors, but now, as he thought on them, he knew they were something else, a dark secret that disturbed him even to think about it.

Maybe he should ask Veil about *this*, he told himself. "Who was the Other?" he imagined himself shouting. "Who traveled with Joachim and Florian?" But he knew he wouldn't, for just the thought of it somehow made him so dizzy he might have fallen over the edge of the balcony if he had not been holding on to the table. When the weakness passed, he closed the book and returned it to its place on the shelves.

A few times during the next days, he thought briefly of the third traveler, someone who was not supposed to exist. Each time the idea seemed to stay less in his mind, until finally he simply forgot about it entirely.

Far from driving him away from Florian, however, the strange experience seemed to intensify his urge to understand her more elaborate teachings, as if to prove to himself that he had not abandoned her. He continued to read the same passages over and over, now in both the tower and the library, as if they might change by where he read them.

And then one afternoon, after all that study, he was standing in the courtyard, with his arms full of wood, when someone said something about the Moon caught on Veil's tower. He looked up, and yes, the crescent Moon appeared on its side right above the tower. He stared and stared at it, remembering a passage in Florian, one of those he'd never understood, describing how "the Moon sings its horns on the Gate of Stone."

Suddenly Veil's tower lit up with color, colors he had never seen before, all up and down the stones, every one a different color. Veil's tower wasn't made of stone at all, it rose on color after color, singing colors, harmonies never heard before because they were never possible until this moment, until Matyas could see them and hear them.

He stared at the sky and saw that it went on and on, layer upon layer of impossible colors that had never existed, and then he held up his hands and they were made of color and song. He looked down at the blazing sticks of color that lay at his feet where they'd fallen, and then the ground itself, and he realized that what had looked like solid dirt and stone now revealed itself as vast lattices and harmonies of color, reds beyond red and blues hidden inside blue, all of them singing to each other, singing to Matyas, singing *in* Matyas, singing in the world, in every face. This was the song the Kallistocha had sung, hidden in the dark colorless trees, trapped there by the warriors of Heaven, yet still able to sing.

Matyas held up his hands, fingers spread wide, and color and song flowed over the courtyard, and the statues, the stone lions, were revealed as glory upon glory. Color poured from his fingers and his eyes directly into the open mouths of all the wavy, shimmery forms that gathered around him. He was teaching now, giving truth, and didn't even know it at first, until he detected, beyond the figures sitting in the dirt, Lukhanan and Berias and Lord Olan, the only ones who had not surrendered their fixed forms to shifting harmonies of music and color. Only now Olan slid away from the other two and sat down, and instantly all his rigidity dissolved into brightness. Matyas laughed, and the sky rippled out through the spheres of the planets, and they were not shells surrounding the dead Earth but songs and shouts, calling to each other in layers and layers of harmonic color.

He saw lights amid the lights. Bright, sharp dots that hovered between the pillars, that *fitted* themselves among the listeners. The Splendor had come—not to help him, or protect him, but to listen. To learn.

Matyas had no idea how long it all lasted, for what he saw and heard changed time as well, so that instead of a steady flow it swirled and rose and fell and turned back on itself and flared up and died down.

Then suddenly, in the midst of everything, he saw a face: a fixed, hard form, bone-white, eyes like frozen fire. He could not look at it, he had never seen anything so terrifying, the end of all songs. *Another*. And so he closed his eyes, and turned his head, and when he dared to look again the world had returned.

Once more Matyas stood in the courtyard, ringed all around by layers of students, and yes, teachers. He tried to speak but found he was shaking too hard. What would they do to him? He realized, only now, that he had taken it on himself to lecture to the *wizards*—the Masters—as if they were just a group of stumbling apprentices. Maybe he should run for the tower, ask Veil to protect him. He didn't dare look at them and so he bent down to pick up a piece of wood.

Before he could touch it, however, one of the apprentices—Alejandre, he realized, the boy from the library—grabbed it and held it tight. "Please," he said, his voice hardly more than a whisper, "let me carry this for you." Matyas only stared at him. Then another picked up a stick, and another, until finally only one long rod of wood remained. Before one of the apprentices could grab it, Horekh himself stepped forward, the master of the library. He bent down and lifted the wood into his bony swollen arms. "Please," he said "we may not enter the tower, but let us walk with you to the door. Honor us that we may carry your burden."

Matyas found himself shaking so much he could hardly move, let alone speak, so he just nodded and walked the twenty or so paces to Veil's door, with the entire school flowing behind him. There he held out his arms for each one to place the wood like an offering to an oracle, or even a god. Matyas looked at them all, standing silent and still. When Horekh held the door for him he nodded once more and turned to go inside.

And that's when the shouting began. "Matyas!" they cried, "Matyas!" And then, "Master Matyas! Master Matyas!"

Somehow he made it up the stairs, even held on to the wood, though his whole body had dissolved, not into color and song, but only tears. Veil was waiting for him. Frightened she would scold him for his arrogance, or even worse, simply ignore him, he didn't speak or move. Without effort, it appeared, she lifted the wood from his arms and set it down before the small iron stove. Then she turned to him and smiled. "Florian is very pleased," she said. "She has waited a long time for this."

Neither of them mentioned the fact that Master Florian had died more than two thousand years before Matyas was even born.

Chapter Eighteen

JACK

Later in his life, Jack Wisdom would think of March 2 as the day he doomed his son. It was a Saturday, a month after Simon's birthday. Simon was on a play date at Jerry Lowe's house, and Jack was in a bad mood. The fact is, he'd been in a bad mood a lot lately, which made him feel even worse because Simon was doing so great, and shouldn't that be all that mattered? Sometimes Jack thought there was something wrong with him—worrying about work, because that's all it was, really, when he should be showing his son how proud he was, and happy. Work. Pressure and meaningless crises.

Except—there was an aspect about this crisis that disturbed Jack, and not least because it involved Simon.

Charlie, Jack's boss, had sent him home this weekend with a thick file that might as well have been marked "Danger! Massive Headache!" since that was what it had been for weeks, for anyone who had to deal with it. But the fact that Charlie had given it to Jack Wisdom to take home, well, that was more than just a headache. Now Jack just sat at the dining room table where Simon liked to do his homework and stared at the spread-out papers, occasionally writing some notes on a yellow legal pad, then angrily crossing them out. Charlie Perkins had asked Jack to work on the Kransky file for one reason only, and it wasn't Jack's ability to analyze. It wasn't even Jack he wanted at all, it was Simon, though Charlie had no way to know that.

Jack stared out of the window. A few trees were just starting to sprout new leaves, the fragile early signs of spring. Just one good ice storm and all that fresh life would come crashing down, probably taking out the power lines at the same time. Jack felt cold suddenly, dressed in what Simon liked to call his play clothes, old jeans and a blue hoodie with torn elbows. He should get rid of it, he knew, but he'd torn it when he was teaching Simon to ride a bike and inadvertently demonstrated how to fall off. Simon's laughter had been so infectious it hadn't even hurt.

Jack wished Simon was home, with him, right now. He was thrilled that his boy was doing normal things again, like play dates, but he missed him. And it would be a good excuse to do something fun, play catch, go to a movie, anything besides stare at that damn file.

It had started some two months earlier, ironically right around the time Simon began to emerge from his "slump," as Jack liked to think of that terrible period. Jack's company, Joyride Automotive Supplies, had taken a daring turn, moving from relatively simple devices like windshield wipers that contoured more closely to the glass to a whole new kind of seat belt. Using sensor chips located up and down the padded straps, the "intelligent" belts would adjust to a person's body, moving higher or lower, tightening or loosening as necessary. It was the first improvement in seat belts since the shoulder strap ("Bringing seat belts out of the Dark Ages," Charlie liked to say), and it would make or break the company. Everything was going well, no major glitches, good safety testing, and most important, some early interest from one of the smaller Japanese companies. And then one day, a letter arrived.

It came in one of those fancy envelopes that immediately said "lawyer" even before you looked at the return address. In this case, the counselor was a woman named Katherine Dunne, from a firm called Prescott and Bigelow, out of Boston. Prescott and Bigelow, it appeared, were patent specialists, and according to Ms. Dunne, Joyride's seatbelt design infringed on the patent of a certain Mark Kransky, an "independent inventor" who lived in Pittsfield, Massachusetts, and who, according to the letter, had spent fifteen years perfecting his "Comfort Strap" digital seatbelt system.

The letter had thrown things into an uproar. Joyride had always been a modest company, with a good history of using technical analysis to improve standard products—like the windshield wipers—but the seat-belt idea was on a whole other level. If it was blocked, or they somehow had to bring in this Kransky, well, no one knew what would happen.

Jack made himself a cup of coffee, then leaned against the kitchen counter, holding the mug in his hand without drinking from it. He didn't want to return to the table but he couldn't stop staring at the file. Originally Charlie had brought Jack in to lead the team working on the analysis of Kransky's patent. There were similarities, Jack reported, though not a complete match. And that was it, Jack had thought. His part was finished. Now it was up to the lawyers to determine the company's risk and liability. Jack expected to return to his regular work. Like everyone else in the company, he was worried about their future, but at least it was out of his hands.

Only, Charlie kept consulting him, talking about the case, complaining how it was driving him crazy, showing him the lawyer's letters and emails, asking him, over coffee and bagels in the morning, or Chinese food at lunch, "What do you think, Jack? What should we do?" At first, Jack was flattered, if a bit confused. He was an analyst. Business decisions, certainly legal matters, were not his area. He tried to tell himself it was because he'd been around so long, he and Charlie had seen the company grow together. But he knew that wasn't it. He knew exactly what Charlie wanted, even though Charlie himself didn't. Charlie hoped to call on a special talent his friend Jack Wisdom had. What he didn't know was that the talent was Jack's son.

The lawyers had thrown it right back on Charlie. They could resist Kransky's claim, let it go to court, and based on Jack's analysis of the design differences they stood a good chance of winning. But the costs would spiral up, and the case might delay production enough to scare off the market. Or they could try to buy out Kransky's patent and hope his fee wouldn't greatly lengthen the time it took to start making a profit.

On the Friday before Simon's play date at Jerry's house, Charlie called Jack into his office. As soon as Jack saw the file on his boss' desk, he knew what was about to happen. Ironic, he would later think, and imagined saying to someone, no one, "I must have been psychic."

Charlie, the kind of rounded, middle-aged man who talked constantly of how he needed to work out, gestured with a half-eaten chocolate doughnut at the file. "This thing is driving me nuts." And after a moment, "Maybe you can figure out what we should do."

Jack wanted to run from the office. Instead, he just said, "I'm not a lawyer, Charlie. I gave you my analysis, but I can't tell you what to do with it."

Charlie's head rocked up and down. "Yeah, yeah, sure. Of course. But you know how you used to come up with answers when it came down to a coin-toss? I got to tell you, Jack, this is one of those times."

So there it was. What they needed, what Charlie was talking about, was Rebecca. Jack remembered how he used to come home worried about something at work, some special problem that he might casually mention, maybe at dinner, or over a glass of wine. A coin-toss problem. And then the next day, maybe at breakfast, Bec would casually make a suggestion. They both knew what was happening, even if neither of them wanted to spell it out.

Until the crisis with the patent, Jack didn't even know that Charlie had remembered those "coin-toss" moments. The problem was, Jack had never told his boss it wasn't him, it was his wife. And now Rebecca was gone, so that was that.

Except, of course, there was Simon.

"Damn it!" Jack shouted out loud to his empty kitchen. "What the hell is wrong with me?" All those terrible months, all that suffering, and now Simon was finally coming out of it—all the *years*, really, of trying to protect his precious boy from his mother's sickness—how could he think, even for a second, of risking putting him back into it?

Only, did Simon have to know? Jack would never tell him to read anyone's mind, or to look into the future or anything so blatant, so *psychic*. But suppose it was a game? Jack could say he wanted to show Simon what Daddy did at work. Lay out the pages, describe the situation—he could make it like a fairy tale, with Kransky as the ogre. He smiled. Better make it an Xbox game, with Kransky an alien or something. He could say, "You're Charlie, facing the Kransky Monster. What do you do? How do you defeat him?" Maybe Jack could tell Simon he used to play this kind of game with Simon's mom.

Jack put down his coffee cup and began pacing the kitchen. It would be so easy. Simon wouldn't even realize he was "cheating," as he called it. But what would it do to him? What would it open up? He'd made so much progress, just the fact that he had friends again.

Could it help him in some way? *Bullshit*, Jack told himself. He was trying to help himself. Charlie would give him a bonus (*I could take*

Simon to Disney World), maybe even a share of the company (*Simon would be all set for college*).

He stared out of the window, only to see a pair of squirrels on their hind legs facing the house, as if they were staring back at him. Breathing hard, he opened the back door and yelled, "Get out of here!" as he made a shooing gesture with his left arm. Obediently, the squirrels dashed off and Jack was left feeling like an idiot. He hadn't reacted that way to squirrels in years.

Back in the kitchen, he opened the refrigerator to stare at some left-over spaghetti and meatballs, then slammed the door shut. Jack smiled, thinking of how Simon sometimes came home from school and looked into the fridge only to complain there was nothing "cool" to eat. He glanced back at the patent papers, shook his head. It would be so easy. He'd pick Simon up, take him home, or maybe out for pizza, and then show him the papers.

"Shit!" Jack said. He needed to distract himself.

A minute later, he found himself in his son's room. He smiled, took a deep breath and smelled the faint presence of his boy. There was the rumpled cowboy blanket (he could never get Simon to make his bed properly), Mr. Axle, the mechanic doll holding a felt wrench that Simon had had since he was three, and the elephant Jack's mom had given Simon. Schoolbooks and a few papers lay scattered over the small oak desk under a poster of a rock group in ridiculous outfits. A few comics were strewn across the floor, overshadowed by a stack of adventure books.

He bent down to pick up one of the books, a sea story called *The Tattooed Parrot*, and as he did so he spotted the cover of a wooden box under the bed. He pulled it out and saw to his surprise and delight that it contained a bunch of Simon's old toys. Jack had no idea he had kept them. He grinned as he picked up a couple of building blocks, then the green snap-on driver of a fire engine. He remembered playing with Simon in the living room when Simon was three, how Jack tried to make fire engine sounds, only to have his son roll his eyes and show him how it was done. Amazingly, Simon really did sound just like a fire siren. Jack smiled again. This was exactly what he needed.

Then he saw the blue cloth, and his stomach wrenched before he even realized what it was. By the time he'd begun to unwrap it he knew, but prayed he was wrong. There they were, worn and bent, even a little food-stained. Strawberry jam. Simon's favorite snack.

How the hell could they be there? Where had Simon found them? Jesus, Jack thought, when Simon was supposed to be doing his homework, or even playing his *Star Wars* game, or when Jack saw the flashlight and thought he was sneaking a few extra minutes with a book, Simon was looking at Tarot cards! After everything Jack had done to protect his child—just when he thought they were safe—this *infection*—

How was it possible? Jack remembered his frantic search through the house after the funeral. All he'd wanted was to find the cards and tear them up. She must have hidden them somewhere, like a goddamn time bomb. And now it had gone off. Suddenly he remembered that one word she'd painted all across the living room wall just before the aneurysm burst in her brain. "Remember!" Oh, he remembered all right. He remembered Rebecca holding their son in a goddamn fire. He remembered pulling Simon back before any harm was done. Now he had to do it again, save his boy from a sickness. His mother's sickness.

He wanted to run back downstairs, go and fetch Simon from whatever the hell he was doing with Jerry and wave the cards in his face. He wanted to scream at him, "Where did you get this . . . this *garbage*?"

Instead, he grabbed whole bunches of them and tore them in half. He took the cards and the cloth and stomped downstairs to throw them in the cold fireplace. It took him three tries to light a match and hold it steady enough to set them on fire. He sat on the floor and cried as he watched first Rebecca's cards and then her scarf disappear into fire and dust. Then for a long time he just stared at the ashes.

An odd memory came into his mind. He and Bec were at Lake Candlewick, sitting at a picnic table at sunset, drinking cheap red "vino" from paper cups and watching the light play on the water, when for no reason Jack had asked, "What would happen if you threw your Tarot cards into the water?"

He regretted it as soon as he'd said it, for he expected her to get angry. Or maybe she'd laugh and say she'd go and buy a new set. Instead, she stared at the water and said, "The Tarot of Eternity cannot be destroyed."

"What?"

Suddenly Rebecca had laughed, then covered her face in mock embarrassment. "Oh God," she said. "I just did that awful professional psychic thing, didn't I? Mystic pronouncements. Ponderous voice." She laughed again. "Sorry. I hereby promise not to do any more of that."

Now, years later, Jack stood up from the fireplace and said out loud, "Yeah, well, I think they're finally destroyed this time, Bec." He went into the kitchen to get a bottle of beer, shoved the damn Kransky file aside and sat down to drink, and stare at nothing.

He was still there, a second beer in his hand, when Carla Lowe called, her voice trembling with bad news. "It's Simon," she said. "I don't know what happened. Everything was fine. Really. The boys were playing that Conqueror game and suddenly Simon just yelled and fell over. I'm so sorry, Jack. They were only playing a game. Really."

"What do you mean, he just 'fell over'? Is he hurt? Is he in pain?"

"I'm not sure. I don't think so. He just shakes his head when I ask him. But he feels hot, Jack. You'd better come."

"I'm on the way."

Could it be the cards? Jack wondered as he drove through red lights to Carla's house. Did it happen when Jack burned them up? But that was crazy. How could—? It just didn't make any sense. Oh hell, what did he care if it made sense or not? If just destroying the cards could hurt Simon in some way ... *Damn it*, Jack thought, *why didn't I realize?*

He slammed the dashboard with the heel of his hand. No! If the cards could affect Simon that way, didn't that show what poison they were? Jack found himself furious at Rebecca all over again. He'd managed to save their son from the fire, but not from his wife's sickness.

Carla ushered Jack into the living room, where Simon sat curled up on the couch. He stared back at Jack with wild eyes. "Daddy?" Simon said. "What did you do?"

Jack bent down and pressed Simon against him. So hot—the cards flashed in his mind, burning and curling in the fire. He pushed the image away. "It's okay, baby," he said. "Daddy's here."

"I'm so sorry," Carla said again. "They were just playing, I swear."

"It's okay," Jack said. "You didn't do anything." He helped Simon get up. To Carla he said, "I'll come back and get Simon's stuff later, okay?"

"Yes, of course," Carla said. "Call me, please, when you get a chance, to tell me how he's doing." Jack nodded.

He called Simon's doctor, Howard Porter, from his cell, and by the time they got home there was a message about bringing the fever down. It took Jack half an hour to give Simon a cold bath and a pitcher of iced water. As soon as he could, he called Howard, but even as they talked, he heard his son moving around overhead. He knew what Simon was searching for. Should he run out and get a set of Tarot cards? No, he told himself, Simon had to get over this . . . this *thing*.

Oh hell, that wasn't it, and he knew it. If he really thought a set of cards would help his son, he'd track them down that moment, break into a store if he had to. Only they wouldn't be *hers*, would they?

Maybe he should get an exorcist, he thought. Can a dead woman possess her son?

The fever passed but not the agitation. Simon's nightmares came back, more frantic than ever. He cried out at night, flinging his arms around in his sleep. Jack never knew what Simon was dreaming, for now, when he woke Simon up, his son refused to tell him. Jack told himself it was early adolescence, but he didn't believe it. He had doomed his son and there was nothing he could do about it.

Jack took time off from work to be with Simon. When Charlie asked him, in between his sympathy and promises of any help he could give, if he'd looked at the files, Jack said he had no idea what they should do. "Listen to the lawyers," was all he could say. The lawyers apparently told Charlie to offer Kransky a settlement, which they did, and which he refused. The case dragged on for months. Jack Wisdom hardly noticed.

Chapter Nineteen

MATYAS

Matyas the Young, they called him. Matyas the Bright. Some, enthusiastic apprentices mostly, even compared him to Joachim the Blessed.

Horekh called him Matyas the Measureless, though not to his face. The first time Matyas heard the term, it wasn't from Horekh himself but someone quoting him, and even though he was in his study alcove, with his back to whoever it was, he imagined he could see the roll of the eyes, the twist of the mouth.

Matyas' old anger surged in him. Did Horekh mean he was incapable of even the simplest calculations? He nearly stood up from his desk to declare the exact *measurements* of the retrograde dance of Venus and Mars in the night sky, or how to calculate the precise moment of the year at which it was safe to perform the rite of Opening the Mouth of the Tiger. But then he stopped and went back to his studies, for it was a curious thing, this anger. Once so dependable, his only real friend, it now appeared to come and go, and he found himself helpless to hold on to it. It was probably for the best, he told himself. What good had it done for him? But without his anger, who was he? Matyas the Unknown.

A few days later, he heard Horekh himself use the title. Matyas was sitting at his table, but now with a Cloak of Concealment cast around him. Though he would not have admitted it—if there'd been anyone to ask—all the attention he was receiving made him uncomfortable in some odd way. So he used the "Cloak," which was not an actual cape, or any *thing* at all, but a spell that made it nearly impossible for anyone to see him, even when they were looking right at him. It was an ancient spell, and Matyas wasn't sure how many people knew it, even among the Masters. He'd only found it searching through some very old papers high up in the archives. So it was that he could see Horekh, but Horekh did not know Matyas was there when he brought a visitor into the library.

The visitor, a thick-accented envoy named Ulanov from some far-off Academy, first spoke vaguely about the wonderful collection of rare works and treasured secrets, a polite discourse that bored Matyas, so long as the man did not try to make off with anything. Then Ulanov said, "And what treasures your precious Veil must have, eh? Ah, but of course they are all locked away in her famous tower. Where none may go, yes?"

Horekh said, "Veil sees those whom Veil wishes to see." Matyas found himself smiling.

It was then that Master Ulanov said, "Then perhaps I could meet this wonder boy of yours. Matyas the Mighty, I believe you call him?"

Gravely, with no trace of scorn, Horekh said, "Matyas the Measureless."

"I see," Ulanov said, though clearly he didn't. Matyas, however, did. He realized now that Horekh meant to honor him, and the idea that this wise man, whom Matyas considered second only to Veil, should consider young, stumbling Matyas *beyond measure* both thrilled and scared him.

Horekh said, "If he chooses to meet you, no doubt he will present himself." He did not look in Matyas' direction and there was no reason to think the Cloak had failed, but Matyas still shrank down in his seat.

Puzzled, Ulanov said, "But he's only a boy. An apprentice."

Horekh laughed, as if Master Ulanov had said something foolish.

They moved on, both physically, as Horekh led his guest up to the higher levels, and in their conversation, now talking about the role of wizards in advising their respective monarchs, a subject that did not interest Matyas at all.

He tried to return to his manuscript but found himself unable to concentrate. Suddenly chilled despite that the day was actually quite warm, he pulled his jacket tightly around him. "Measureless," he whispered. Beyond measure. Something he himself might have said about Florian.

If the Master of the Archives spoke without sarcasm, that was not the case with Lukhanan and those loyal to him—a group that consisted primarily of his faction within the Council of Governance and anyone who aspired to it. They called him Matyas the Magnificent, with a knowing laugh or a twist of the lips. The expression didn't last long. Matyas first assumed that it was because no one paid them much attention, but then he walked past an apprentice who shrank back from him and muttered, "Magnificent," clearly with no idea the term was meant to carry scorn. Matyas did his best not to laugh. And then he just forgot, for as with anger, pride had become slippery. There was so much to think about, to read, to study, so many experiments to perform and spells to master.

He divided his time, without plan, between the tower and the library, sometimes staying in one or the other for days, only leaving the library to see if Veil needed him, leaving the tower only to bring her some firewood or a block of cheese from the market. For yes, he still did her chores, though often with helpers made of straw or mud and brought to temporary life, or by animating a few of the carved figurines—men, women, animals, angels—scattered among the books and scrolls. He roused them to action just long enough to tend a fire or cut radishes, then ordered them to return to their original place and position. The first time he tried it, he was terrified that Veil might catch him and accuse him of laziness, or cheating, or (worst of all, somehow) ingratitude. And yet he could not help but laugh and clap his hands as a naked man and woman, each about six inches high, labored to chop carrots, then hand them up to a golden-haired angel, all of eight inches tall, whose purple wings fluttered mightily to carry the pieces over to the stew pot, where he dumped them in boiling water and came back for more. As soon as they were done, Matyas hurriedly reversed the spell and returned them to immobility, still fearful Veil would burst in on him. As time went on, however, and Matyas used similar tricks more frequently, he began to relax, for somehow Veil never seemed to walk in at the wrong moment.

The old woman never asked him about his studies, at least not in the usual way of a teacher testing a student, or even, for that matter, a curious parent. At times Matyas thought she didn't care. *Now that I've gone past her—I'm not her performing monkey anymore—I know things—she's not interested.* But then, without warning, she would say something like, "Matyas, where do butterflies come from?" and Matyas, thinking of

Florian's teachings on the Lesser Origins, would say, "They arose when Mercury penetrated the second darkness of Venus."

"Ah," she would say. "Thank you."

He wondered, should he wear the robes of a Master? He remembered when Medun had appeared in the doorway of the Hungry Squirrel, how astonishing he looked in his long thick robe braided with gold, how Matyas' father had bowed to him, terrified as much as impressed.

Matyas had been so excited when Veil gave him his fine jacket and pants, almost embarrassed to wear them. Now he understood they were still the clothes of an apprentice—even if they never wore out, and somehow always fitted, despite that he'd grown a couple of inches since he started wearing them. Should he dress more properly? Some Masters wore heavy robes so thick the Master could fall asleep and his clothes would hold him up. Others wore fabrics that billowed behind them as they moved through the courtyard.

One evening he was walking through the city, far from the places Veil might send him, through narrow streets between houses held together with mud, streets full of loud children and angry mothers trying to control them. This was something new for Matyas—to leave the Academy, sometimes for hours, just to experience the city. Everything he saw fascinated him—the markets that ranged from stolen trinkets on filthy blankets all the way to carved and varnished stalls bearing the shields of the great guildhalls; the occasional platoons of soldiers in bright helmets and breastplates; the taverns, the churches, the shops of craftsmen and artisans.

On a street of narrow wooden houses with ornate carvings over the otherwise simple entrances, he noticed a simpler marking, of just a pair of scissors and a needle, above a polished door. He hesitated then walked up and knocked loudly. A young woman's voice called out, "Come in, please. It's always open for *you*."

Matyas frowned with his hand on the latch, then turned it and stepped inside. The room was not much wider than the entrance and long, running the length of the house. The only sunlight came from a window in the back wall. A young woman with long yellow hair sat at a table surrounded by fabric and oil lamps. Though most of the fabric was brightly dyed, much of it flowing silks or soft linens, she herself wore a plain white dress, long and unadorned and fitted to her body, which appeared graceful even as she simply sat with her work. She looked about fifteen, Matyas thought. His age. Royja's age.

"Just a moment," she said, with that slight lilt. With a flourish she finished a stitch then snipped the end of the thread with a pair of scissors shaped like a swan. "There," she said, and lifted her head, smiling. "Oh!" she said suddenly as she saw Matyas' curious stare. "Oh, I'm sorry! I thought you were—" She stopped herself, as if afraid to continue.

"Who?" Matyas asked. He found himself strangely annoyed at this unknown man who had inspired such anticipation.

She shook her head, then said tightly, "Please. I didn't mean any harm."

"How would you harm me?"

"Please, Master. Please don't hurt me." She shrank back on her stool, arms crossed over her chest.

Matyas said, "How do you know I'm a Master?"

Startled out of her fear, she said, "You're Master Matyas. Everyone knows you."

Matyas' mouth could not decide whether to grin or gape in astonishment. He thought about the way people stopped talking when he passed them, or moved away from him on the street. He'd never paid much attention, for why would he think anyone outside the Academy would recognize him?

He said, "Well, good," then stopped, waiting for a reply until he realized he needed to say why he was there. He pitched his voice a bit deeper than normal as he added, "I would like you to make me a robe."

Her eyes widened, whether from honor or fear he couldn't tell, but it seemed to take her a long time before she answered. "Yes. Yes, of course," she said. "Umm, what sort of fabric would you like? Of course, if you have your own, I mean, something special, something, you know, for a Master—"

"No," Matyas said. "No, I don't have anything."

"Of course. Of course. That's . . . that's good. I mean, fine." She swept her arm at the bolts of cloth. "I have . . . there are many—" Suddenly she began to cry. "Oh God," she whispered, and then, with her face turned away, "Please don't hurt me."

Matyas wondered if he should run from the place. Instead he just said, "Hurt you? What are you talking about?"

"Why me?" she burst out. "Why would you come *here*?" She fell to her knees. "There are . . . great artisans on Lokara Street. The king's own tailor would be honored to create a robe for you. I'm nobody. I'm nothing."

Matyas stared at her, wondering if he should cast a spell to dry up her damn tear ducts. For a moment he played with the thought of turning her into a cat. That's what she sounded like, a wailing cat. Finally, he said, "I don't know. It's just . . . I was walking . . . it felt right—your sign. Above your door."

It struck him suddenly that he needed to put her at ease, that she was somehow his responsibility. The thought excited him and made him very uncomfortable at the same time. "Will you please get up?" he said angrily. *Wrong*, he scolded himself. She stood—of course she did—but her whole body shook.

"Please," he said, in what he hoped was a soothing tone, "I don't mean you any harm. Really. I just want to hire your services." It struck him that he would have to pay her, and wondered exactly how he would do that. Veil never gave him any money, and while some of the Masters—the *other* Masters—took on paid tasks for the king or the army or rich merchants, Matyas had no idea how he would even set that up. Maybe he could do something for her.

His reassurance appeared to work, for she took a breath then said, "All right, then. Very good. We need . . . we need to start with the fabrics. And then the design. But first the fabric." She waved hesitantly at the only halfway decent chair in the house, made of some light-colored wood with the back cut crudely in the shape of a rose and lily. "Please, Master," she said. "It is all I can offer." Matyas thought of telling her about the rough benches in Veil's tower, or even the corner of the kitchen in the Hungry Squirrel where he used to sit sometimes when he'd finished his chores and his father hadn't spotted him doing nothing.

For the next hour or so, she laid out fabric after fabric on her work table, a process Matyas found surprisingly pleasant. At first she said nothing, only stammered that one was wool, another linen, but as Matyas became more interested she began to make cautious suggestions, saying for instance that blue might look better on him than green. Matyas thought of telling her how Florian wrote of blue beyond blue, of Blue Transcendent as the lover of red. Instead, he just let her show him the blue she thought would suit him.

They were a good half an hour into it when a knock came at the door. To Matyas' surprise, the seamstress put a finger over her lips, smiling as she did it. "Hello?" a man's voice called. Matyas couldn't tell how old it was. "Lahaylla? Are you there? It's me." Matyas could see *Lahaylla*—he realized he hadn't asked her name—suppress a laugh and found himself grinning. After a few moments, they heard someone walk away, and now both of them laughed, softly, and went back to studying fabrics.

They settled finally on a light shimmering blue in a pebbly fabric she called "raw silk." Next came what she called the "enhancements," trim to be used for patterns and designs. Here she brought out purple braiding and gold foil, and Matyas could only nod in appreciation.

"Very good, Master," she said. "Now—"

"Matyas," he interrupted.

"What?" The fear was back, and he realized how much he'd enjoyed having driven it away, at least for a while.

He said, "You don't need to call me Master. Just Matyas is good." It was what Veil called him, he thought, and Horekh, the only people who actually spoke to him on a regular basis.

She nodded. "Matyas," she said, her voice hardly above a whisper, as if she might be entering a trap.

"Good," he said, and added, "Lahaylla." She looked down but she was smiling. He thought of telling her that her name resembled words in several ancient languages, including a certain medicinal flower that bloomed only once a century in a land long since destroyed by a volcano, the volcano itself having been triggered by a war of wizards over that very same flower.

Picking up the purple and gold, she said, "I need to know your designs." When he just stared, she said, "The pictures. For the robe? I don't know . . . what a Master wants."

"Oh," he said, suddenly excited then. "Do you have any paper? And a quill? Or something to make marks?" He doubted she could write, but some of her clients might need to sketch an image. To his surprise she quickly produced several sheets of rough paper, a stone inkpot with gall ink already mixed and a nicely cut goose quill.

He closed his eyes a moment and breathed deeply, slowly allowing images to form on the "blank sky," as Florian called the canvas in our minds. Almost immediately he could see an entire composition, taken partly from his books, partly from things Veil had shown him, and even his own embellishments that he'd drawn in sudden moments of inspiration, late at night in the library or the tower.

He showed it all to her, a treasure such as no one had ever given her before. But all she said was, "Yes. I can do that. I think. Yes, I'm sure." He turned his face away a moment and was about to leave when she said, "Umm, Master? I mean, Matyas?" When he looked at her again she took a breath, then said, "I need—you know—to measure you."

He almost laughed, thinking of what Horekh might say to that suggestion, but then it struck him what she meant, and he felt his face grow warm. He said, "Oh. Yes. Do I need . . . do I have to take off my clothes?"

He saw a new flare of fear move across her face, and he thought suddenly of the wizard whom Medun had brought down through the Singular Storm, the one who'd told young women he would transmit magic to them. He wondered, *Does she think I—?* But apparently not, for a moment later her wariness changed to amusement as she said, "If you remove your jacket, that will be enough."

As he stood with his arms out for her to measure his shoulders, around his chest, the distance from wrist to wrist and the distance from his neck to the ground, he found himself deeply grateful he hadn't asked for pants to match the robe. He was glad too that she ran her tape across his back and not his front, but even so, when her fingertips happened to graze his palm he was fearful she must have seen his reaction.

If so, still all she did was step back from him and with her eyes cast down slightly said, "Thank you. It will be ready in seven days." He put on his jacket and was glad he could leave when she made a small sound and said, "Um—Master—sorry! Matyas—"

He stared at her, waiting, then finally said, "What is it?"

"I do not want to diminish the *honor*, but the fabric is, well, my most special. And the work, well, I will have to put everything else aside."

She looked so miserable. Was he supposed to soothe her in some way? Say something? What? No one had ever tried to comfort him in his life. Then he realized. It wasn't comfort she wanted, it was money. He was a Master, which meant he must be rich. He, who had never held any coins except to buy cheese and turnips for Veil. He'd thought of it before, but the excitement had driven it from his mind. Excitement that she'd appeared to share, but no, of course not. All she cared about was what she thought he could give her.

He stared at the arrogant little seamstress with her bolts of silk and gold. What had she done to get the money to buy all *that*? Who did she do it with? Why should *he* have to give her anything? Maybe it was payment enough that he didn't just turn her into some dreary brown moth. And anyway, why did she need money from him? Wouldn't she just run out into the street and tell everyone she could find about the "honor" of serving Matyas the Brilliant? Wasn't that enough?

All this ran like a river through him, but instead of letting it overflow into a flood of words or spells, he found himself saying, "How much do you . . . how much do you need?" He felt as ignorant and helpless as the first day Veil sent him to buy bread at the market.

Staring at the dirt floor, she whispered, "Twenty."

"Florins?" Veil had sent him once for a small bag of powder from Johannan's stall at the end of the market and given him two of the gold coins, the king's face engraved on one side, a crude image of a dove on the other. "Pigeons," the market people called them.

Lahaylla nodded without looking up.

Matyas said, "I'll bring them when I return. In seven days."

Chapter Twenty

JACK/SIMON

For three days after he brought his son back from Carla Lowe's house, Jack Wisdom hardly slept. Howard Porter came and examined Simon, an exercise as pointless as always. As always, Howard couldn't exactly find anything *wrong*, but he did give Jack some medicine to bring the fever down, and something to make sure Simon slept. Only, Simon didn't, not really. He was out for maybe half an hour, long enough for Howard to suggest "something for anxiety, or maybe ADHD" and for Jack to remind him they'd tried medicine and all it had done was make Simon violently ill, even have seizures. "You really want to go *there* again?" Jack asked, and Howard just looked down and shook his head.

A moment later, he said, "I don't get it, Jack. He was doing so well. I've got to tell you, it made me smile every time I thought of you guys. And now this. Do you know what set it off? Did something happen? At school maybe?"

I tore up his mother's Tarot cards. Jack shook his head. "No. Not that I know of. He wasn't in school, he was just at his friend's house."

Howard's eyes narrowed and he searched Jack's face, like someone trying to figure out a map in a foreign language. "Are you sure you can't think of anything?" When Jack didn't answer, he went on, "Sometimes in cases like this, when we can't find a . . . medical cause—" He stopped.

"Christ!" Jack said. "Do you think I'm *doing* something to my own son?"

"No, no," Howard said, actually taking a step back. "Of course not. But I've got to . . . Could something be happening at school? Is there any teacher that Simon seems scared of? Maybe in gym or something?"

For some reason, Jack thought of the man in the baseball field all those years ago, who'd held his head as if to measure it and then pronounced it "not ready." He remembered how the police had come, and they'd searched and searched, and when they couldn't find anything, they'd made the usual joke about the family name, and Jack's dad had become angry and accused Jack of making it up. He shook his head now and said, "No, there's nobody. At least, nobody he's told me about. You've examined him, right? You know, physically . . ."

Howard looked down as he nodded. "Yeah. No signs of . . . of anything."

Jack let out a breath he hadn't known he was holding. "Well, he's resting now. You can go, I guess."

Howard sighed. "Okay, Jack. Let me know if there's any change, okay?"

"Sure," Jack said. He didn't move as Howard walked toward the door. When he heard the door close, Jack thought of going to the fireplace and sifting through the ashes, as if he could somehow reconstitute the cards and bring them back to present to his son on a golden tray. He'd ask forgiveness and his beautiful boy would hug him and tell him everything was okay now. Somehow Rebecca got into the act, as Jack imagined her standing over them, her arms around their shoulders. Jack had no idea he was crying until a noise from Simon upstairs made him jump up and he felt the tears splash on his face.

Upstairs he found his son thrashing around, screaming something about fingers. Jack managed to grab Simon's arms and bring them against his body, which seemed to wake him up. The boy stared wildly at his father, and for a second Jack thought Howard Porter must be right to think such terrible things about him, for why else would Simon look at him that way, with such terror and hate? But Jack pushed the thought aside and chanted the world's most useless magic formula: "It's okay, it's only a dream."

It went on like that for weeks, as it had before, only this time Simon wouldn't talk to him. The fever broke after a couple of days, which allowed Jack to tell Carla Lowe it was some kind of forty-eight-hour bug, and thank her once again for her concern. He wondered what the other parents had told her about allowing her son to play with Simon. Did they warn her? And had she said, "Oh, he seems perfectly fine"? And was she kicking herself now for not listening? No more invitations came for play dates, and when Jack asked Simon, "How is Jerry?" (meaning, Are you and he still friends?) Simon just shrugged and said nothing. But then, that was Simon's response to everything Jack said. *Early adolescence*, Jack Wisdom told himself, again, and wished with all his torn heart that it was true.

Simon lost his appetite and sometimes refused to eat or threw the food on the floor. Jack yelled at him, ordered him to his room, then sat at the kitchen table and cried. Once, when they were eating pizza and Simon actually appeared to have an appetite, all of a sudden he threw up on the table. Jack ran over with a pot as Simon continued to vomit until all the food was gone and Jack feared blood would follow. Jack tried to steady his son but Simon pushed him away.

Simon gripped the sides of the table as if he'd fall over otherwise. "Daddy," he said, "what did you do to me?"

"It was only a pizza," Jack said.

"*What did you do to me?*" Simon shouted, then ran upstairs.

Jack slumped in his chair. He should clean up the mess. At least he was capable of wiping up vomit. Instead, he just sat there and whispered, "I don't know what I did. Really. It was only a deck of cards."

Every morning Simon lay in bed a long time, hoping something would have happened to the school, or Daddy would suddenly decide to stop forcing him to go. Finally, Daddy always came up and pulled the covers off him in that fake-fun way, as if this was just some dumb game, ha ha. It wasn't only that school was awful. The thing was, Simon never knew how it would go. Some days nothing happened; he sat there through Math and Geography and Social Studies, and with luck, the teacher didn't call on him and no one bothered him at lunch or during after-school activities. He could just sit by himself and pretend to read until finally Daddy picked him up and closed his eyes a moment when no bad reports came, and then took Simon for pizza or something, as if it was some big deal, like a birthday or something, when it was just dumb luck.

And other days . . . It wasn't his fault, that's all he kept thinking. He didn't want to cheat, he didn't want to know stuff. What did he care if Sally What's-her-name loved Arthur but was scared he'd laugh at her? What difference was it to Simon if Ms. Bowden's brother had a lump somewhere and was scared of doctors? At least Simon could understand that last part—he *hated* doctors, even Dr. Howard. Was it cheating if you didn't want to do it?

Even if it was just that, knowing things people didn't want him to know, cheating in spite of himself, he could get through it if he just had to stare at the floor, not look at anyone. It was like ignoring a gang of kids all shouting at you at once. As long as you didn't answer, they'd give up and go away. He knew about that because it happened sometimes. There were five of them, three girls and two boys (sometimes he got confused which was which, until he realized that they themselves couldn't decide and that scared them). When they started to grab at him and call him "Weirdo," or sometimes "Faggot," he just stood there and stared at the ground. Usually they gave up and walked away, fake-laughing as if they'd done something really cool. Once, one of the girls kicked him, and another punched his arm, and soon they were all hitting him, and Simon could see a teacher, Mr. Hunt, watch from the side until finally, when Simon's nose started to spurt blood, Mr. Hunt sighed and came over to chase the kids away. Even that wasn't so bad, it was just another day. The worst part was when his dad saw the plaster and wouldn't stop asking questions, until finally Simon told him—kind of—and Daddy went around making lots of noise, which Simon knew, without cheating, he only did because it was something he could *do*.

Days like that were just . . . days.

It was the other stuff that really made him want to stay home. Like when he looked at a kid and saw green rot all over him, or white things sticking out of his chest. Or that time in dodgeball, when Simon, who usually hid behind everyone else (he tried to pretend to himself that was why they chose him last, because he sucked, but of course he knew it wasn't), found the ball in his hands. He looked at it a moment then threw it as hard as he could at Caroline Hansen. When the ball hit her in the chest, he looked at it a moment then . . . fell apart. A hole opened in her chest and blood burst out everywhere, and in the middle of the torrent a small child, like some kind of antique doll, screamed and waved its arms for help. Simon didn't realize that he himself was screaming until he felt the gym teacher's arms around him. And then he just stopped, froze, became silent, because he knew how much Mr. Patton hated having to touch him, and Simon himself didn't want those angry arms touching him one second longer than necessary.

Everyone avoided him. In the hallways, everyone who was not actually yelling at him or hitting him moved closer to the walls when he walked past them. No one sat next to him in class, something his teacher, Ms. Bowden, pretended not to notice. She called on Simon as little as possible, only when she became scared his father would complain. As if Simon might tell on her.

The only person who seemed like he might be willing to be friends with Simon was Popcorn Jimmy. A couple of times, Simon could see Jimmy looking at him, in class, in the cafeteria. Simon pretended not to notice.

He did his best not to look at anyone, with one exception, and it wasn't Jimmy. It was Ellen, the girl who'd once brought Tarot cards to school to tell kids' fortunes. If she brought them again, would she let Simon look at them? Would they—he couldn't think of the right word—*work* for him? He wondered if he could somehow push her to think of bringing the cards. Would that be cheating? It wouldn't be the same as knowing what she was already thinking. *Probably*, he thought. He might have decided to try it anyway, except he was pretty sure it wouldn't help. They wouldn't be *his* Tarot cards.

Simon didn't look at people, and people didn't look at Simon. Even his teacher tried to look past him. He didn't mind. He understood. It wasn't safe to look at him.

But Jimmy looked, and then one day at lunch he came over to where Simon was sitting on the edge of a bleacher facing an empty baseball field. "Hey," Jimmy said. Simon didn't answer. "Can I sit down?"

"No," Simon said. Jimmy tried to say something but Simon told him, "Go away." He didn't have to look to know that Jimmy had slunk off, head down even more than usual.

He hated doing that. Simon didn't deserve Jimmy's friendship (even if it was because there was no one else). He hadn't even thought about Jimmy when there were other kids who wanted to hang out with him. No, it wasn't fair, but that wasn't the reason Simon had sent him away. He just didn't think it was safe for anyone to be friends with him. Jerry Lowe had started dreaming the terrible things, even if he didn't remember them when he woke up. Maybe Simon had stopped being friends with him just in time.

Simon told Jimmy to go away to save him, but he still hated it. A couple of times he glanced at Jimmy standing all alone, his hands in his pockets, and once he almost got up and walked over to him, but instead he made his whole body stiff, as if he'd turned to stone and couldn't move at all.

Back in class that day, Simon was not just scared, he was angry. It was so unfair! He didn't ask for any of this. He never cheated—well, almost never—and it wasn't like he wanted to dream, or any of it. He made a face at Ms. Bowden, who had asked some dumb question and now was looking around the room to pick on someone for the answer. Her eyes seemed to touch on Jimmy, then jump away, then come back. "Jimmy," she said, with a sigh, "how about you? Do you know how the War of 1812 started?" Jimmy slumped down further in his seat, as if he hoped he could disappear.

"Maybe it was popcorn!" Billy Ventner called out, and a bunch of kids laughed.

"That's enough!" Ms. Bowden said, but Simon could feel how much she wanted to laugh. And then suddenly, without wanting to, he could hear, or just know, everything she was thinking, and he found himself doing that thing again, like he'd done with the Allens, when he'd rescued Jimmy.

Christ, why do I have to get all the weirdos?

"Christ," Simon said, "why do I have to get all the weirdos?"

What?

"What?"

Oh my God, did I say that out loud?

"Oh my God, did I say that out loud?"

Stop it!

"Stop it!"

Jesus, fuck, get out of my head, you fucking creep!

"Jesus, fuck, get out of my head, you fucking creep!"

Then Ms. Bowden was actually speaking—shouting, in fact—with her left arm extended straight out to point at the door. "Simon! Principal's office! Right now!"

As he stood up, shaking from what he'd let himself do, Simon heard bits of laughter all around the room, and he was about to run out through the door when he realized, with a thrill, that it wasn't aimed at him—they were laughing at the teacher. Janie Higgins even whispered, "Cool," as Simon walked past her. At the door, he stopped and turned to stare one last time at Ms. Bowden. "Now!" she yelled, and Simon smiled as he left the room.

His excitement fell away almost the moment he stepped into the hallway. By the time he reached Mr. Chandruhar's office, he was shaking and finding it hard to breathe. He shouldn't have done that, it was the worst kind of cheating. Now his dad would hate him, everyone would hate him, and it hadn't changed anything, hadn't helped. Nothing could help.

He was wondering if he should just run away when Mr. Chandruhar called through the door, "Come inside, Simon." Simon jumped back—could teachers and principals *cheat*?—before he realized that Mr. Chandruhar must have spotted him through the frosted-glass window. Simon went into the office and stood just inside the door.

He wasn't there long, for the principal, it appeared, didn't really want to talk to him. He stared at Simon from behind his big metal desk. The wall behind him was crowded with pictures, some of his wife and kids but mostly photos of himself in a baseball uniform. Simon waited for the principal to say something until it struck him that Mr. Chandruhar was afraid of him. Ms. Bowden must have called him and told him what Simon had done, and he was scared Simon would do it to him, too. Simon cast his eyes down, as if looking up might tempt him. "I'm sorry," he said, and had to fight a grin.

"It's a little late for that, don't you think?" Mr. Chandruhar said. "I've called your father."

"What? No! *Please*."

"He's coming to pick you up."

"I'll be good. I promise. I swear. On . . . on my mother." Simon had heard kids say things like that, and even though he didn't know what it meant he knew it was supposed to be serious.

"You can wait in the detention room until he gets here."

"Please—"

"Go. Now."

Chapter Twenty-One

MATYAS

All the way back to the Academy, Matyas thought about money and his careless promise to pay Lahaylla twenty florins. The obvious wealth of so many of the Masters derived, no doubt, from selling their services to lords and bankers. And Veil—how she made him work and work, and paid him exactly nothing. Nothing! Kitchen slave. Whatever he learned, whatever spells he could do, that was all he was to her, all he'd ever be.

And what about Royja? She'd probably never even seen twenty florins at one time in her whole life. With her dirt-streaked face, her broken fingernails, her filthy shapeless dresses, she was worth ten of this—this *night flower*.

As he was walking up the long hill to the Academy, he suddenly felt dizzy, nauseous. He stopped and leaned against a building and could not help but notice how people moved away from him. Light-headed, wasn't that what people called this strange state? He wondered what Florian would make of the odd expression, and suddenly his anger dispersed, smoke in a gust of wind, as he imagined the great Master with her head transformed into radiant light, endless color streaming from her eyes and mouth, even her nose and ears.

He found Veil by the window, looking out at whatever Veil looked at. "I want some money," he said.

She turned to face him, something she did not always do. "Very well. How much?"

"It's not right. I've worked for you for years. Done everything. Even now. I'm a Master"—he felt foolish saying it, but it was too late, so he pushed on—"and all I get is scraps of food. It's not right."

"Matyas," she said, "I did not object to paying you. I would think that asking you how much you needed should have signaled my willingness."

"Then why have you never paid me?"

"Why have you never asked me?"

He was about to denounce her for answering a question with a question when he realized that the answer was the same to both. He'd never needed money before. But now he was a Master, and everything had changed. He said, "I want twen—thirty florins."

Veil nodded, and walked in that purposeful way of hers to a pile of books of such varied sizes they looked like they'd topple over at any moment. They'd been there, stacked on the floor, for as long as Matyas could remember. Reaching behind them, she lifted up a plain black wooden box about the size of a large roasted turkey, then set it down on the floor. Now she looked around and found a small bag made of chamois cloth and set that down near the box. When she opened the lid, Matyas stared in amazement. It was full of coins—pigeons, donkeys (half-florins, decorated with a bad engraving of a horse) and silver dukes (ducats), the coins Medun had left at the Hungry Squirrel.

As Veil counted out florins, Matyas could not contain himself. "Why do you have all that money?" he said.

Veil put the money in the bag and carefully tied the string. "How else could I give you thirty florins? Should I stand in the market and sell my books?"

"I don't know," Matyas said. "I thought—" He stopped.

"What? That I could turn cheese into gold? And not only gold, but actual coins stamped with the king's face?"

He didn't answer.

"I have lived a long time, Matyas. Once, like you, perhaps, I considered money beneath me, unworthy of a wizard. I saw others, those who courted patronage and cast spells for the rich, and I swore never to debase my calling. And then came a time when I needed money—it doesn't matter for what—and I had none. Since then I have occasionally done things, tasks worthy of your respect, I would hope, for those able to pay something. As you have done for me. Here." She held out the bag.

He took it, felt the weight in his hand, noticed a strange desire to open the bag, spread the coins on the floor and count them and recount them and inspect each one to make sure it was genuine. Suddenly, without plan, he said, "I want to fly. Teach me to fly."

"That again? I've told you, Matyas—"

"Yes, yes, no one can fly. But I saw it. I was there."

"And I was not. I confess, I do not understand what you saw, but I assure you, I hide no special knowledge, no secret text or spell. If you wish to duplicate this marvel you witnessed, you will have to seek it elsewhere." She sat down in her white rocker and clasped her hands in her lap. "Now I suggest you put your twenty, excuse me, your *thirty* florins somewhere safe so they do not fall from your jacket into the hands of some market pickpocket." A moment later, her eyes took on the blank look that signified he could say whatever he liked, she would not answer, perhaps not even hear him.

Matyas thought more and more about his appointment with Lahaylla. He tried to convince himself it was the robe that excited him, but it was her he saw whenever he thought of the approaching day. Several times he had to stop himself from rushing to her street, just in case she needed to ask him anything, maybe consult him on some detail of the design.

When the morning finally came, he woke early, made porridge for himself and Veil, then announced, "I have to go out." Veil nodded. "To the library," he added, instantly annoyed with himself for the lie. Veil said nothing. Matyas hoped she didn't notice him slip the pouch of coins into his jacket pocket. The night before, he'd laid them all out, then put them all back, then took out five, then finally another five. Lahaylla had asked for twenty—it might insult her to give more. He thought how his father would try to get "every last cent" from each guest, rich or poor, and told himself Lahaylla would never do that. He set them all out one more time, to choose the twenty whose gold shone the brightest, put these back, and hid the other ten under his thin mattress.

Lahaylla opened the door almost the instant he'd knocked, as if she'd been waiting with her hand on the latch. She wore a long, orange linen dress with wooden buttons all down the front of it. "Come in," she said, smiling brighter than the Sun. "It's finished." He reached out, as if to touch her arm, but she didn't notice as she rushed to her work bench to pick up the robe. "I hope you like it," she said. "I've never done anything like this before." She laughed lightly. "I wanted to run up and down the street and tell everyone."

"You told people?"

"No, no," she said. "Well, I had to tell my teacher. So she could help me with some of the stitches. For the pictures. But I made her swear secrecy, I promise."

Anger surged up in him—everyone on the street would be staring at him—only to subside as soon as she held up the robe. The blue silk fluttered slightly, the light breeze from the open window enough to bring it to life. Despite the dim room, it shone brightly, as if lit by an inner flame. He could hardly imagine what it would look like in the sunshine. Or under the grand array of magical globes that lit up the Masters' dining hall.

As perfect as the body of the robe was, the designs were the thing that froze Matyas with his mouth open. Precisely rendered (how many hours did she work on it?) in purple and gold along the chest and back and down the wide arms, there were geometric forms and planetary sigils mixed with flowing water and bursts of flame, and a tree whose trunk ran up the chest and opened into branches that flowed along the arms, only to change into shimmering snakes. All these were images any of the initiated might display, though Matyas could not imagine them rendered more gracefully in even the richest guildhalls on Lokara Street. Worked into them, however, concealed within the sigils and woven into the tree branches, were the secret marks of Florian, the signs that could open the trained mind to transcendent worlds of color and sound.

He stared at it, unable to speak, until Lahaylla nervously asked, "Is it good? Did I do what you wanted?"

"Oh yes," Matyas said. He tried to make his voice firm, and deep, as he added, "You did good work. Very well done."

"Thank you," she said. "Would you like to try it on? Is that allowed? I don't know much—well, anything, really—about . . . about Masters."

"It doesn't matter," he said, suddenly eager to reassure her. "This is very special." Then, "Do you mean I should put it on here?"

She nodded, and the slight movement caused the robe to shimmer. "If you would like."

He looked down at his tunic and pants. "I'd have to . . . we don't wear anything . . . I mean, we don't wear the robe over other clothes."

Her smile widened. "Oh, of course. I promise not to look. Really. I wouldn't want the sight of a Master to blind me. Or turn me into a pillar of salt."

"No, no," he said. "I didn't mean . . . nothing would happen, I just—" He stopped, seeing laughter build in her. Maybe he *should* turn her into a block of salt, he thought, but forgot about it when she moved the robe toward him.

"Put out your arms," she said, and when Matyas obeyed she laid the robe across them.

It was like holding sunshine and wind. Lahaylla watched him stare at it a moment, then said, "You can set it down—when you're ready, of course—and then change and let me know when it's safe to look."

He wondered if it would ever really be safe for someone untrained to look at him in this robe, but all he said was, "You're staying in the room?"

She smiled. "I'm afraid it's the only room I have. I could go up and down the street, but then you'd have to step outside to find me." When he still looked hesitant, she said, "I promise I won't peek."

Carefully Matyas set the robe on the bench. As he stripped down to his singlet and loincloth, he thought how no one, not Veil, not his parents, not even Royja, had seen him like this since he was a little child. Finally he took a deep breath, lifted the robe and put it on over his head to let it flow down his body.

For a moment it was like that day in the courtyard, when the true world opened before him, for he appeared to dissolve into light, color beyond color, music unheard since the Creation. He heard, became, the song, the voice of the High Prince of the Kallistochoi. Then the room returned, and he let out a long breath. "You can look now," he said. He added, "It's safe," and immediately wished he hadn't.

"I'm sure it must—" she started, turning, only to stop, her mouth open, frozen in midsentence. "Oh," she said finally. "Oh! You're so beautiful." Not *it*, not the robe. She reached out her hand, then pulled it back. "May I? Is it allowed?"

Matyas wanted to say no, wanted to run away. Instead, he just nodded. Her finger traced the pattern of the tree on his chest. "Oh," she said again, and Matyas shook like an actual sapling in the wind. Her hand hesitated, and then Matyas realized she was about to take it away, so he reached out to place his own hand over hers. They were touching just where the branches opened up, and Matyas knew that she could feel the beat of his heart shaking the tree. When she kissed him it was lightning.

He wrapped his arms around her, not so much an embrace as to anchor himself, as if they might lift right off the floor and crash through the ceiling. Was this it, then? The secret to flying? So obvious, and yet of course Veil couldn't give it to him! It had to be Lahaylla, soft, golden Lahaylla.

She stepped back from him and he worried that he'd hurt her in some way, misused her beauty. But all she did was look at him a moment, then down at her hand as it touched the top button of her dress. "Should I—?" she said. "I mean, if you want me to."

"Yes," he said, his voice nearly a whisper. Like a child, he added, "Please."

She smiled at this but he knew it was all right, she wasn't making fun of him. As she unbuttoned the polished bits of wood, Matyas began to lift up the robe. "No," she said, then, "I mean, please. Keep it on." She looked away. "Is that—?"

"Yes," Matyas said. "It's good."

Lahaylla let her dress fall to the floor. Underneath she wore only a white chemise, sleeveless, with tiny lace flowers worked into the top. She left it on and walked toward him.

Under the chemise her breasts rose and fell. Matyas wondered if they were large or small as breasts went. Sometimes he heard the other— the *apprentices*—talking about girls, about things they'd done to some servant, or some woman from the streets, and he knew that the size of the breasts was important, but he could never understand why. And he didn't know if Lahaylla's were the right size, though he thought they were perfect, like the proportions of the Sun and Moon that Florian discovered when she climbed into the sky. Then his mind had to add, *Larger than Royja's*, but the thought of Royja made him twitch so he banished the unwelcome memory.

Lahaylla arched her back slightly so that her breasts rose toward him underneath the thin cloth. He pressed his hands against them but she winced, and he realized it was too hard. He shifted the pressure, and yes, she smiled now, and sighed, and yes, he could feel their curve, and that was better, wonderful, he could feel her nipples in his palms. It was like . . . like holding the planetary spheres, the way the Creator must have held them.

They kissed again, longer, wilder. He stepped back to reach under his robe and untie his loincloth, letting it fall to the floor. Lahaylla appeared not to notice as she lifted off her chemise then brought Matyas' face down to her breasts, first the left, which was the Moon, and then the Sun on the right. For didn't Florian teach that every woman "recapitulated" the First Body, her breasts the Sun and Moon, her eyes the Fountains of Light, her cleft the gateway to the Ocean of Life? But it was one thing to know such truths and another to *know* them. Matyas had thought himself so wise, so learned. He'd never known anything.

Lahaylla shook and gasped as Matyas moved his hands down her body, along her belly and then between her legs. A wind pulled him to her—no, of course not, her hands had reached out, lifted his robe to reach behind him and pull him toward her.

He thought he would explode just from her touching him, but somehow he stayed hard, and strangely, when he was inside her, what he felt above all was *safe*. They were both crying now, and it was as though the robe surrounded both of them, the tree and the sky and all the secrets she had brought to life. Now he understood Florian's "Great Cry of Beginning." His eyes were closed but he could see Lahaylla with his hands, all the wonder of her. She was light, the light of origins, just as Royja was darkness, darkness and dirt. *No.*

In awe, Lahaylla whispered, "Oh, Matyas. Master. Master Matyas." Suddenly, against his will, Matyas thought of Medun. Medun, without whom Matyas might never have existed, Medun whose prison was the world, whose sentence was forever, all to protect women from a Master who had promised to give them . . . *this*.

He cried out as he pushed her away, and as he left her body—in the last second it was possible—it was like that moment when the Great Darkness came down over the Ancestors, so that they no longer beheld the planetary lights except through thick walls. Now he understood—and wished fervently that he didn't—why Florian "wept as if a thunderous river" the first time she beheld the truth.

"I'm sorry," he said, "I'm sorry, I'm sorry." He tried hard not to look at her, but her stunned face filled the room. As quickly as he could, he snatched up his clothes and was about to rush through the door when he felt the weight in the right pocket of his tunic. He managed to find the pouch of gold and would have tossed it behind him without looking, except he remembered the rainy day a duke had done that to his father, and then laughed as Matyas' father had run into the mud to pick up the coins. So he turned to her and she was sitting on the floor with her arms tightly around her knees to create a refuge for her face. She looked like a child, so small he could pick her up and carry her with him.

"I have the money," he said, and set the bag on the work table. "It's all here. You can count it."

"Get out!" she screamed. Matyas ran from the house.

He was two streets away when he became conscious of the Sun on the robe, light carried like wind through the branches and signs. He stopped in the middle of a hilly street paved with old gray stones. Thankfully everyone appeared to be off at whatever work they did, unless, of course, they were all inside, frightened to show themselves. He found a space between two wooden shacks where he could change his clothes. When he folded the robe, he found it was so thin he could hide it in the waistband of his pants.

When at last he passed through the Academy gates, he stared up at Veil's tower, for he wanted so much to run up and hide this thing that felt like ice against his flesh. But suppose *she* was there, and guessed what he was concealing? So he went to the library instead, where he could cast his spell, his Cloak of Concealment, and let himself breathe, for the first time, it felt like, since he'd left the seamstress' house.

He stayed there for hours, reading about sects known as Purificationists, those who sought to "give flower to the Tree of Purity" by "uprooting the Tree of Desire." The images were grand, but the actions were brutal: whippings, starvation, even self-emasculation. Matyas had always found such accounts not just unpleasant but incomprehensible. But now, as his body continued to react all on its own to any thoughts of Lahaylla, despite his shame at what he'd almost done to her, he wondered what it might be like to free oneself of such betrayal. Purification. The thought sickened him, but maybe that was all the more reason to contemplate it.

As so often, Florian saved him. It took some searching, but at last he came across a short passage about "Purity." She called it "a fool's literalism," a terrible misreading of ancient practices sometimes known as "the snake shedding its skin." The body is like a tree, the sage wrote, with a snake coiled at the base of the trunk. (Matyas thought of the design he'd given Lahaylla and shuddered.) The snake is said to drink the sap of the tree and spit it out like venom, so that some believe they must kill the snake to purify the sap. But the snake is life, and without it, the tree cannot flower. Train the snake, Florian wrote, so that it may give life to the sap and the leaves, and the flowers of the tree may open to the light of Heaven.

The passage comforted Matyas, told him he needn't be a slave to or a destroyer of his own body. And yet, he could sense some secret, something dark hidden under the reassuring words. When at last he left the library and made his way up the tower stairs to discover Veil mercifully asleep in her rocking chair, one sentence vibrated in his mind, like a low string tuned to the Earth itself so that it never comes to rest.

Beware the Tree that seeks to flower forever.

Chapter Twenty-Two

SIMON/JACK

The detention room was a classroom that wasn't used by any teacher. It had the usual rows of desks facing a whiteboard, but no posters or photos or maps, no models of poor-people villages, no gross pictures of the body, and no computer stations. The teacher's desk had no personal items and no clever displays that were supposed to spark pupils' "healthy curiosity" or "sense of wonder." The only thing on the desk was a plain wooden box with a lock on the front to hold the bad kids' cell phones so they couldn't spend their punishment time texting or playing games.

Mostly the room was used at the end of the school day, when kids who'd done something wrong had to endure an hour of silence while everyone else went home or to after-school activities. Simon had been ordered there before, but never during the school day. Mr. Chandruhar told his assistant, a pretty brunette named Miss Harrowey (the kids all knew how she'd refused to be called "Ms.") to take Simon to the room "and make sure he stays there."

"Hey, it's okay," the assistant whispered to Simon in the corridor. "I don't know what you did to Mzzzz Bowden, but I bet she deserved it." She blushed, as if she realized she wasn't supposed to say things like that, especially to a pupil being punished. Simon didn't care. His father was coming and he would find out what Simon had done, and hate him.

Miss Harrowey held open the door and told Simon, "Take a seat. Well, obviously." She didn't ask for Simon's cell phone. Maybe it didn't matter if you were just waiting for a parent to come. Simon stepped into the room.

And stopped. The room was full of kids! Every desk had someone sitting at it, all of them with downcast eyes, unmoving. And the room was much larger than Simon remembered—it appeared to go on and on, not very wide but longer than the gym. Simon turned around to look at the assistant. "Who are all these kids?" he said.

She rolled her eyes. "Very funny. Come on, get inside. I'm sure your dad will be here soon."

As soon as Simon had stepped into the room, Miss Harrowey closed the door behind him. He could hear her high heels receding on the hallway floor. All at once, as a group, the kids turned around and looked at him. There was something wrong with them. Something wrong with their heads. Cuts all over the skin. "Oh shit," Simon said out loud, "Oh fuck," and didn't even notice he was saying bad, big-kid words. *They're all dead.* Every single one of them, their heads cut in twenty places, with what looked like pieces of paper, or bits of cards, stuck in the cuts. "Help!" Simon yelled and tried to leave, but the door was stuck. "Please!" he called out to whoever might be listening. "I'll be good, I promise, I promise." But nobody came. If Mr. Chandruhar or Miss Harrowey could hear him they paid no attention.

The dead children began to speak, their voices empty and far away as they chanted:

Simon, Simon,
Rhymin' Simon,

"Stop it!" he yelled, and put his hands over his ears.

Take the time, an'
Stop the crime, an'

"I can't hear you," Simon called out. He tried saying, "La la la," the way kids did in the playground to drown someone out, but the voices cut through him.

Set the children free.
Simon, Simon,
Rhymin' Simon,

Simon knew he was about to scream. He didn't want to, somehow it seemed worse than any of the bad things he'd done, but he couldn't stop himself, he would start screaming and never ever stop.

And then he heard music. Singing. It rose above the chanting children—no, it flowed all around and through them, like water. Or light. Liquid light. Singing light. High and clear, a single voice filled with sadness and glory all mixed together. Simon couldn't tell if it was a man or a woman or maybe a child, but it didn't matter, nothing mattered except those perfect sounds. No, not just sounds, words. The voice was singing a song, and even though it wasn't English, or any language Simon could even imagine, he almost understood it. Not like you understand words, really, and not with his mind. Some other way.

The song ended—he had no idea how long it lasted—and when Simon opened his eyes he saw he was standing in a small empty classroom.

He must have sat down and time must have passed for there he was, in the back of the room, his mind somehow calm. He was vaguely aware of hills and trees, as if he'd been watching some nature documentary, when Miss Harrowey opened the door. "Your dad's here," she said. "Come on."

Instantly he was jolted back to all the awful things he'd done. Now they would tell Daddy and Daddy would . . . what? Ground him forever? Lock him in his room and never let him out? He didn't think his father would hit him or anything. Daddy had never hit him, not even when it looked like he really wanted to. But it didn't matter what Daddy *did*. All that mattered was that Simon had cheated, big time, and now his father would know. And hate him.

He stayed in his seat until the assistant rolled her eyes and said, "Let's go. It's not so bad. At least you get out of this place." She laughed in what Simon guessed was supposed to be a friendly way. "I wish someone would expel me for a few weeks."

Simon's dad was standing in the principal's office with his arms folded, his whole body like stone as he looked down at Mr. Chandruhar, who stared back at him, both of them silent. The assistant said,

"Here he is, sir," and gently urged Simon into the room, then quickly closed the door.

Simon flinched as his father spun around, but his face softened and he said, "Simon! Are you all right?" Simon couldn't speak until Daddy asked, "They didn't hurt you, did they?" And then Simon shook his head and whispered, "No, I'm fine. I just had to wait in the detention room."

"Mr. Wisdom," the principal said, "we do not 'hurt' children. Corporal punishment is not allowed in Chandler Elementary, and never has been."

Simon's dad glanced once more at Simon as if to double-check he was uninjured, then said to Mr. Chandruhar, "What the hell are you doing to my son? How dare you throw him out of school?"

Mr. Chandruhar stood up, his fists clenched, and for just a second Simon wondered if the no-hitting rule might not extend to parents. The thought of his dad and the principal in a fight suddenly made him happy, just for a moment, for the first time in weeks.

But no, the principal said only, "Your *son* is a disruptive influence. I can assure you—"

"Disruptive?" Dad said. "What the hell are you talking about? He's nine years old!"

"He causes trouble, he makes the other children uncomfortable—"

"What? *Uncomfortable?* You let my boy be insulted, set apart from other kids, you do nothing at all when older boys bully him—"

Mr. Chandruhar's voice rose. "We do not allow bullying. We maintain a zero-tolerance policy with regard to bullying."

"Like hell you do. And now it's not enough that you let the kids bully him, now you've got the goddamn teachers doing it."

"Mr. Wisdom, watch your language."

"And to cover it all up, you want to expel my little boy."

Reflexively, Simon thought how he wasn't little, but really, what did it matter? This was so cool.

"I assure you," Mr. Chandruhar said, "we are not 'covering' anything up, as you put it. We take expulsion very seriously here at Chandler Elementary."

"Oh yeah, I'm sure you do," Dad said. He held up a business card. "Here's something else you can take seriously. Jessica Green. Senior partner at Green and Blackmore. You heard of her? Her firm represents my company, and now she's really interested in what you're doing to my boy."

Simon had no idea who this was, but apparently the principal did, for he actually backed up a step and raised his hands. "Okay," he said, "let's calm down here. I'm sure we can work something out."

"You bet we can. Here's what the 'working out' is going to look like. I'm taking my boy home now so he can recover. Tomorrow he will return to class, where Ms. Bowden will treat him with respect and fairness. And if all goes well—if you actually enforce your zero-tolerance bullying policy—I will tell Jessica to put our lawsuit on hold."

"Mr. Wisdom, be reasonable. I can't just ignore . . . I have to be fair to Ms. Bowden."

"You know something?" Dad said. "That's just what Jessie said you would say. 'Reasonable.' That was the very word. She told me to tell you that she looks forward to *reasoning* with you."

Simon saw Mr. Chandruhar's hands clench and his jaw harden. But then a moment later he sighed and said, "No, no, I'm sure there's no need . . . I will tell Ms. Bowden to expect Simon to return tomorrow."

"And to treat him decently."

"Yes, of course. We treat all our students—"

"Come on, Simon," Dad said. "Let's get out of here." Simon grabbed his backpack and followed him out. In the hallway, Miss Harrowey was staring at her desk but couldn't keep a grin from filling her face.

Dad said nothing all the way to the car, and for a minute Simon expected he would punish him now they were away from the principal. But when they got to the car, Dad bent down and hugged him. "I'm so sorry," he said.

"Dad! That was awesome!"

Startled, Jack Wisdom separated and looked at his son. "Yeah, I guess it was." He held up his hand and Simon high-fived him. They laughed and got in the car.

"You want ice cream?" Dad said as they drove away.

"Sure. Dad, who's Jessie Green?"

"She's a lawyer who won a big bullying case over in Newtown."

"And she works for you?"

"Nope. Never met her in my life. I stopped by her office on my way here and picked up some business cards."

"Wow," Simon said. "That is so cool!"

Daddy laughed. "Yeah. Yeah, I guess it is, isn't it?"

Simon's good mood lasted all the way to the Sacred Cow Ice Cream Parlor, a hole-in-the-wall place in a small strip mall. Selling nothing but ice cream and frozen yogurt, "the Cow," as everyone called it, was a local institution in the fourteenth most livable city. In summer there'd often be a line all the way past the Subway sandwich shop, the pet store and the yoga center. Even today, in mid-April, Jack sighed as he saw a snake of kids stretching out from the door, some twenty or thirty of them, all around Simon's age. In June it might have been a Little League team come to celebrate a victory, but Jack was pretty sure Little League hadn't started yet, and besides, it was two thirty—shouldn't they all be in school? Giddy, Jack thought how none of *them* had an awesome dad to rescue them from the principal's office. He was about to ask Simon if he minded waiting when he saw his son staring at the line, all the old terror suddenly back in his eyes.

Jack said, in that forced manner he almost thought of as his normal speech, "Well, that's a shame. The line, I mean. Shall we try Dairy Queen?"

"I want to go home," Simon whispered.

"They're just kids" Jack said. "They only want ice cream. Like us."

Simon stared, his mouth open, until suddenly, all the children turned at the same time to stare at Jack's car.

"Take me home!" Simon yelled. "Now! Now! I want to go home."

Jack left the parking lot so quickly he nearly crashed into a truck. Neither of them said anything else all the way to their house.

Chapter Twenty-Three

MATYAS

She came in the old-fashioned Way of the Supplicant, on her hands and knees all the way from her narrow, fabric-laden home, through streets of stone or mud or brick, past hovels and mansions, oblivious to mud or offal, to guards and shopkeepers, as she made her way, inch by painful inch, to the Gate of Light at the top of the city. On her back, pinned to her white dress, she carried a simple drawing of the Lost Child, and even without words it was enough, people knew, they understood, for hadn't it happened before, time after time? As she moved through the streets, cutting her knees and hands, more and more joined her, rich as well as poor, for even the great might wake up one day and call helplessly for a child who would never return. They walked upright, but slowly, so as not to get in front of her, until finally, by the time she reached the Gate, where once a wretched kitchen boy had begged for entrance, they were two-hundred strong.

"Matyas!" she cried to the gatekeeper, a skinny apprentice who turned and looked behind him for help. "Matyas!" the crowd shouted, some with a raised fist, assuming the name was an accusation.

In the tower, Matyas could feel her coming long before there was any sight or sound of her. Keeping his breath even, he had pretended to study a text on the hidden names of the hours, but a kind of prickly sensation had washed over him, sharp heat that grew and grew until the moment his name rang out, and then the heat turned to ice, and it was all he could do not to gasp in pain. Even so, he might have ignored it and stayed in his book if Veil had not wandered to the window, where she said, "Matyas, a crowd of people appears to be calling for you."

"I'm studying," he said.

"They might not leave until you speak to them." Matyas sighed and stood up. When he was at the door, Veil said, in that same casual voice, "Perhaps you should descend in your office."

How did she know? Did she go through his things, look under his mattress when he was on some errand or at the library? No, of course not, he realized as he went to his bed and fetched the hidden robe. She was Veil, she just knew.

Though he'd taken it out a couple of times when Veil was away, he'd only held it up, somehow afraid to try it on again. Now as he took hold of it dizziness passed through him, and something beyond excitement. Behind him, Veil said softly, "Go ahead. It's time." Matyas nodded. He drew shut his meager privacy curtain and then removed his disguise to finally step forth as his true self.

"Good," was all she said, but he could see the rare joy in her eyes. Despite his fear of what was about to happen when he faced Lahaylla, Matyas could not help but notice the strange sensation of whole worlds moving with him as he descended the stairs, and when he emerged into the courtyard light, it was as if the tree on his body took root in the stones and opened its branches to the Sun.

Lukhanan and several other Masters were waiting for him. For just a moment, Matyas allowed himself a small smile of satisfaction as Lukhanan opened his mouth to begin some prepared speech then stopped to gape at Matyas' robe—his *office*, as Veil called it. Matyas realized that he'd never noticed how weighed-down Lukhanan's robe was, with all that brocade and actual gold.

Such thoughts vanished quickly as the Head of the Council recovered and launched his attack. "Matyas," Lukhanan said, "while we all respect how far you've come since we decided to give you a chance, the council has to protest this latest . . . this stunt. Maybe you believe you should bring the lower classes into this sacred precinct. Maybe you feel some misguided allegiance to your own, shall we say, *humble* origins." He spoke the word as if it was a euphemism for "filthy."

"I didn't summon them here. I don't know anything about this."
Liar, he accused himself.

"Matyas, they are chanting your name!"

Matyas could feel his face flush and realized Lukhanan could see it
as well. He said, "I don't know why they would do that." He tried not to
stare at Lahaylla. Soon everyone would know his crime.

Suddenly Lahaylla's voice rose above the crowd. "I come in supplication, as one who is desperate. I beg the aid of Great Master Matyas, for
he alone can help me."

It was the Ancient Formula of Supplication, carved, in fact, above
the very gate before her, though long since obscured by decorative flowers, dragons and planetary sigils. Some said it was the very origin of the
Academy, a place where the wizards might be gathered for those who
might need them. For a moment Matyas thought it a trick, a way to
dramatize how Matyas had misused her and the punishment she would
demand. But then he realized, belatedly, the desperation that had filled
her voice, and it struck him, for the first time, that she might not have
come to accuse him at all.

He strode to the gatekeeper. "Let her in," he said.

Lukhanan walked up close to him. "I'm warning you," he said.

Nervous, Matyas was about to try to explain when a breeze moved his
robe. He felt the tree pulse with his heart, felt the snakes slide along
his arms. The planets appeared to move in their orbits through his heart
and lungs. He looked at the girl who made this for him, who'd brought
the world out of his books and onto his body, and he knew that whatever
she wanted, even to accuse him, it was only what he owed her and would
always owe her. She'd given him his office. His skin.

"Open the gate," he ordered the keeper. Lukhanan looked around to
speak but glanced around, first at the Masters and apprentices gathered
behind him, then Matyas. Finally, he just stepped away.

Lahaylla entered as she'd traveled, on her hands and knees, then lay
face down on the stone mosaic of the planets in their true and secret order,
her arms out to the sides, her legs slightly apart, as if she was not on the
ground at all but flying, somewhere above all this human anger and sorrow.

"Arise and speak," Matyas said, grateful he remembered the old formula, even as he feared what she might say.

Lahaylla stood up stiffly and reached behind her to pull away the
drawing. "Great Master," she said, "my brother Rorin has vanished.

From his home, from everyone who knows him. Please, Master. Find him. Return him to his home. We beg you."

Matyas held the paper. Despite the simple drawing he could feel the boy, even see a glimpse of him as he closed his eyes. Around eleven years old, Rorin liked to run rather than walk, leap rather than step. He laughed often, especially when his sister or his parents tried to limit him in some way. At least, he used to. It took only a moment to realize that all these images were in the past. When he tried to see the boy now there was only a blankness.

Something was wrong. Even in the worst situation, even in death, something lingered, usually for weeks. He remembered how Medun had told him, all that time ago, that there were no such things as ghosts, only mindless spirits that attached themselves to a dead person's memories and emotions and believed they were that person. But there still should be traces of Lahaylla's brother, strong ones if it was only a short time since he'd passed. And that was assuming he'd died. Matyas simply had no idea what had happened to him.

He looked at Lahaylla. "When did you last see him?" he asked. "You or anyone."

Her eyes filled with tears but her voice held steady. "Three days ago. He went to watch the jugglers in the market and never came back."

"Did people see him in the market?"

"No," she whispered.

Matyas closed his eyes a moment. Yes, that was the last time he could feel the boy, almost exactly three days ago. He could feel Mercury's position in the sky, the wizard's way to give a time signature to an event. He looked again at Lahaylla, her face shadowed by fear, yet still with hope—and faith, he realized. Faith in Matyas, who suddenly wished he could hold her, protect her in the robe she'd made for him. Instead, he tried to make his voice both strong and optimistic as he said, "I will need to cast a spell. It may take some time, an hour or more." He looked at the crowd. "Can you stay with your friends?"

She looked back, hesitant, and Matyas realized she feared that if she returned outside the gate it would never open again. He said, "No one will bar the way, I promise you." He glanced at Lukhanan, who looked away, then at Horekh, who stood at the back of the crowd. Horekh nodded gravely. Matyas looked up at the tower, saw Veil in the window. To

Lahaylla he said, "I will be back soon." As he walked toward the tower door, the robe moved against his body.

Matyas was suddenly aware that he had no place of his own to cast a spell. He had performed many actions in the tower, some with Veil's instructions, more often on his own. But it was still her tower. The only place that in any way belonged to him was his small room in the library, and that only because he went there so often. The library was not a place for spells.

When he stepped into the room, Veil was standing facing the door, her hands clasped in front of her. It struck him that she looked exactly the same as when he'd first seen her, her body absolutely straight in a gray wool dress, ancient face of a thousand tiny lines, yet smooth and soft and somehow both blank and filled with expression. Her long silver hair moved in the air even without any discernible breeze. He thought of the times she'd made him brush her hair with that rough bristly brush, and of that one time that had changed his life, flooding him with letters and all they could give him. And then there were the eyes, small and sharp and vastly old.

He said, "I need to do something."

"I know. Do you have all you require?"

"Yes."

She closed her eyes a moment, and for some reason such a great sadness flowed from her that Matyas wanted to step up and hold her. But then she sharpened her eyes and nodded. "Very good," she said. At the door, she hesitated—Veil uncertain!—turned and said, "Be careful, Matyas. When we search for something, we do not always know what we will find."

A search spell is not a very complicated thing and it embarrassed Matyas a little that he had wanted Veil to leave. Somehow, around his teacher he always remained a student, despite all his knowledge and skill. Once she was actually gone, however, he shrugged off such thoughts and set out the powders, candles and stones that would mark the "true ground" of his work, a place that existed simultaneously in the world of light and the world of dirt. On this ground he placed stone markers for the four main gates of the city, the royal palace in the center and the Wizards' Academy in the northeast. Finally, he used a scrap of cloth to represent Lahaylla's home in the southern quarter, near the Summer

Gate, and some pebbles for the market with its jugglers, Rorin's destination when he'd left his sister.

Despite his ascendance to Mastery, Matyas kept his tools—his "attributes," as people called them—in a small oak chest fitted with a simple iron lock. As he lifted the box, he thought how embarrassing it would be if anyone saw him, the great wizard, hiding his magic under a servant's bed. He knew he should move into his own rooms in the Masters' Residency (would they take him? Yes, of course they would). And yet he found it hard to leave Veil. Who would buy her cheese from the market, cook her porridge, keep her hearth fire bright? Though he knew, of course, that she'd lived there many years before he'd stumbled his way to her, it was somehow hard to imagine.

From the bottom of his trunk, he took out a small knife in a black leather sheath. The black blade was double-edged, one too dull to cut bread, the other sharper than the glass scalpels the Academy supplied to the king's surgeons. The handle was made of some rough black stone veined with gold. Matyas had found it at the edge of the river, hidden among rushes in a place Veil had sent him to find five perfectly white stones. Of course she'd known the blade was there, maybe she'd even hidden it herself, but they never talked about it.

Matyas stood just outside the marker for the Winter Gate and "opened the way" by drawing the sharp edge through the air in front of him. He stepped into the circle, closed his eyes and felt the city all around him. The image came to him and he held it a moment with his fingers spread wide before his face. Energy rippled in them, tingling, eager to do their work. He said, "Unwind from me, my seeker threads, find me the boy, be he living or dead." Like young snakes the energy shot from his fingers and moved through the city.

Matyas knew that no one could see it, but anyone with training, even an outsider with talent or sensitivity, would feel them darting in and out of every street, every room, searching for the boy, for traces of him—fingers that might have touched him, ears that might have heard him, eyes that might have spotted him.

Nothing. The shadowsnakes returned to hover in the air, empty. He could feel their disappointment, even shame, like dogs that have let down their master. Matyas didn't understand it. Even if Rorin had left the city, the searchers would have found a trail. Even if he was dead . . . And then a thought came to him. He tried to banish it, it was impossible, but he remembered what Veil had said—*When we search for something, we do not always know what we will find.*

The command he had given was for a *creature*, something that lived or *had* lived. There was a much simpler version, one used just for *objects*. It made no sense, he told himself, and tried to abandon the idea, but he could not go back to Lahaylla and claim he had done his best if he hadn't tried everything. He thought suddenly of what he'd heard in the wood so long ago, the second half of the prophecy that had promised him he would fly.

Or will you try as
Ancients cry, as
Children die, as
No one dares to talk?

So now he held up his hands, as if to order the shadowsnakes not to leave, and did his best to reimagine Rorin, not as a boy but as some kind of lifeless puppet. No, not even that, just some mix of pebbles and dirt that purely by chance had come to resemble a child. Then, without even a chant, he sent the snakes on their way.

They came back almost immediately. There he was—there *it* was—a crumpled form against the back wall of some restaurant near the King's Officers' barracks. The vision lasted only a second, but it was long enough for Matyas to sense something missing. He concentrated, then gasped and opened wide his eyes. "Oh no," he said—and at the thought that he would have to show this to Lahaylla, "Oh God."

And then a voice floated up from his cellar of memory, icy, amused. "Ah. It's you." Matyas just had time to step out of the circle before he threw up on Veil's ancient wood floor.

The crowd was small. Only one Master walked with him, Horekh. The others either considered the troubles of common people not their concern or else they saw Matyas' face and wanted no part of whatever he was about to reveal. Horekh had looked at them all, then at Matyas, and said, "I will walk with you."

Matyas had sent away the crowd, told them to go home and not worry. It was the best he could do. He had tried, weakly, to send Lahaylla away as well, but she insisted, and so did a group of five or six, including an older man and woman who held Lahaylla's arms, either to comfort her or themselves. Parents, he guessed, and when they looked at him, he wondered what she had told them.

They found the boy—the *thing*—quickly enough, crumpled up right where the snakes had shown him. At first Lahaylla had thought Matyas was trying to trick her in some way. "What are you showing me?" she demanded. "Do you think this is funny?" The group around her looked angry, while Horekh just watched Matyas' face.

"I'm sorry," Matyas could only say. "I'm sorry."

She looked at him again, then back at the crumpled object against the wall. Matyas could see her take it in, maybe the clothing first, a tunic and pants of plain brown wool that she'd probably sewn herself, and then the shape, the thin arms, the narrow chest. "Rorin?" she whispered, for even though she could see, she could not feel. There was nothing left of him, it was as if he'd never existed. But still, she picked up the empty body, expecting to embrace it, hold it against her, and it was only then, when she unfolded the limbs, hoping to find some small remnant of her brother, that she saw, finally, what was not there.

"His head!" she screamed. "His head! What have you done with his head!"

"What happened to the head?" Matyas was speaking even before he came fully into the room. Sitting upright in her straight-backed chair, her back to him, Veil didn't answer. Matyas went on, "How could someone just . . . empty out like that? He wasn't just dead. He was gone. Completely. What happened to the head?" He'd been walking toward her, and now he spun the chair around, fearful she would just stare coldly at him.

Instead, her face showed a grief, a brokenness he never would have thought possible in her. He was silent, but only a moment, for then he said, "Why do I keep seeing this? Heads. Bodies. I don't know. I don't know what I mean. *Why don't I know what I mean?*" Images swirled around him, too fast for him to catch hold of them, Rorin, yes, but dreams, and visions—and someone else, a boy, back at . . . Halewin! Yes, that was his name, the cook's son, who'd vanished years ago.

And tunnels, and faces, and pieces of paper—and that voice, that terrible voice. "What's wrong with me?" Matyas cried.

She got up and walked to him, but he took a step backward, as if she might hurt him, punish him for something. But no, she only took his hands, her own so small and delicate. Lights appeared between them. The Splendor had come, the first time he'd seen them in months. For him or for her? "Oh, Matyas," she said, "I am so sorry. All this time I did not tell you—I told myself you needed to discover it for yourself. You needed to overcome the Forgetting. But really, I was hoping it would never happen. Please, come and sit with me. You've grown tall, knowledge nourishes you, and my ancient neck hurts from bending."

Matyas realized, with a slight shock, that he did indeed tower over her. When he'd first come, they were nearly eye to eye. He noticed, as he sat in the carved red chair opposite her plain white one, that the Splendor followed him. Despite everything, he had to make sure not to smile.

"Matyas," Veil said, "do you know the story of the Five Creations?"

"Yes, of course. The Creator tried four times to make the world and failed. She made a world of Fire and it burned itself up. Then She tried Water and all the creatures drowned. Next came Air, but everything fell apart and all the pieces drifted away from each other. So then it was Earth, but nothing moved. The Creator wept—frustration, the books say—and discovered She could use Her tears to bind everything together. That was the Fifth Creation, the world we live in."

Veil nodded. "Yes. That is what the books say. And no doubt there are many who believe it. Lukhanan, I suspect, has never questioned it. Nevertheless, the story is a lie."

Matyas stared at her. It had never occurred to him that the old books could lie. And yet, when he'd read that tale, hadn't he thought there was something wrong with it? How could the Creator stumble like that?

Veil went on, "When the Creator, blessed be Her face, began Her Great Work, it seemed a simple task. She created a world and beheld it, and it appeared good in all things. And then She discovered a flaw. There was something terrible in this bright world made from the Fire of Her passion. She could not simply erase it, for it appeared to be woven into the very fabric, and so She destroyed it, and started again. Now She acted with great care and compassion, and created a world of Water. And yet here, too, the flaw remained. So She destroyed this one as well. Now She planned and analyzed and measured before every step. Thus She created a world of Air, for Air is mind, as of course you know. And still there was the same terrible flaw. So She made an Earth world, heavy and dull, but it was still the same. Her tears, Matyas, were not of frustration, but a terrible grief."

For some reason, Matyas thought of Royja, but he pushed it away. He needed to concentrate.

"Finally," Veil said, "the Creator accepted what She could not change. She created a world of balance, and set within it two great trees. One was the Tree of Life, also known as Constancy, which grew into the light and brought forth all the creatures, animal as well as plant. The other, the Tree of Knowledge, known also as Variance, She made to grow down, taking the flaw into dark, hidden places where She hoped no one would ever discover it."

"What is it?" Matyas burst out. "This flaw—is it what happened to that boy?"

"Please," she said, and held up a hand. "Let me do this—" She took a breath. "The flaw is a spell. It's called the Spell of Extension, and with it a Master can live forever. This is what the Creator discovered—that it was not possible to create a living world that would not contain, deep within it, the Spell of Extension. She could not grow a Tree of Life without a Tree of Knowledge. The best She could do was hide the Knowledge in darkness."

Matyas thought of his dreams of tunnels. He remembered the dark places that time he'd stolen Veil's red box, thinking it held the secret of how to fly. For wasn't there a young man about to step off a cliff, without a care, as if the wind would carry him? Instead, he'd found himself in the dark tunnel. With bodies. With heads. With *him*. Now Matyas wanted to make Veil stop, before it was too late. Before he remembered. But it was already too late. He said, "The Tree of Knowledge. It's the Tarot of Eternity, isn't it?" The Splendor flared so brightly he had to squint, then it dwindled and went out.

"You must understand, Matyas. Joachim—"

"The Brilliant?" Bitterness sharpened his voice.

She nodded. "Joachim the Brilliant. Joachim the Blessed. He did not *know* of the flaw."

"Then what about the Kallistocha? The one who taught him? Did he know?"

For once, for just a moment, Veil was speechless. Despite everything, despite his desire to run, Matyas nearly smiled. Veil said, "Well, you *have* delved far. You are right, of course. Yes. Joachim did not just create the Tarot of Eternity. He was guided by a High Prince of the Kallistochoi."

If she knew—if she had any idea—that Matyas had met such a *person*, she didn't show it. When Matyas had first discovered this idea, that a High Prince had guided Joachim, he had wanted to run to Veil and find out if it could possibly be the same one. But he would have had to admit he'd hidden this experience for so long, and wouldn't he have appeared ungrateful after everything she'd taught him? And something else. He didn't want to share this knowledge, with Veil, with Horekh, with anyone. It was the only thing he had that was his alone. Now he said, "So the Kallistocha created it."

"No, no, you don't understand. No one *created* the Tarot of Eternity. The Tarot of Eternity has always existed."

Matyas sat back. "What? That's . . . that doesn't make any sense. You mean the Creator made it? Along with the world?"

She leaned forward to touch his hand. "Matyas, you know what I mean."

"No!"

"Yes. The Creator used the pictures to create the world. They were not a history but a blueprint. When the Creator brought Herself out of nothingness, the Tarot of Eternity was waiting for Her."

"But I saw it! It's just pictures!"

"What you saw was a copy of a copy. And even then . . ." She did not need to remind him how he'd become lost in them.

He said, "Did he know? The Kallistocha? About the spell?"

She frowned. "No one really knows. Joachim himself had no answer."

"Then did Joachim discover it?"

"No." She sighed. "Florian was not Joachim's only disciple. There was . . . another." There was something sharp in the air as she said that, like a shadow with knives.

Matyas said, "And this other disciple—he was the one who discovered the Spell of Extension?" What was it he'd read in Florian? *Beware the Tree that seeks to flower forever.*

"Yes."

"What was his name?"

"No one knows."

"What? Florian must have known."

"Matyas," she said carefully, "have you never wondered how Florian died?"

"Oh God," Matyas said. "He killed her. Because she knew his name!"

"It was more than that. He killed her, yes, but then he used her body to cast a Spell of Forgetting. He took his name out of memory, buried it under a great red rock where no one could ever discover it. It was the only way to ensure that neither Florian nor anyone else could ever block him from the Spell of Extension."

"Then what do we call him? Just 'the other'?"

She took a deep breath. "No. We call him the Child Eater."

Matyas jumped up and began to move about the room. He wanted to kick over her piles of books, smash her carvings, but he just couldn't make himself do it. "This is wrong," he said, not looking at her. "You're wrong. You shouldn't have kept this from me. It wasn't right."

"Matyas," she said, then stopped.

What? he thought. What lie or trick was she about to try now? But instead of some elaborate speech, or the opposite, a cryptic reference that she refused to explain, Veil did something astonishing. She began to cry. It wasn't loud, or gulping, the way Royja sometimes did, but there was no mistaking what filled her eyes. "You're right," she said softly. "Of course you're right. I knew it was impossible. And unfair. I couldn't help myself, I had to try."

"Try what? What was so important that you had to lie to me?"

Her voice came even softer now, almost a whisper. "I wanted to protect you."

Matyas opened his mouth for some sharp, furious answer but nothing came. All he could say was, "Protect me from what?"

"Oh, Matyas, watching you discover the wonders of Florian, even just your delight in simple spells, has brought back a joy I lost a very long time ago. I couldn't bear to corrupt that."

"So you were protecting yourself. Not me."

She looked startled for just a second, then said, "Yes, perhaps that's true." She shook her head slightly and the thin white hair came alive for an instant then settled back around her frail shoulders. She said, "I told you that the Child Eater seals himself off with a Spell of Forgetting, and this is true. But that spell works so very well because people *want* to forget. People like Lukhanan, those who think magic is all about power and prestige—"

"And money," Matyas said with a slight smile.

Veil nodded. "And money. They don't want to know about something dark and fearful in the heart of existence. If there were no barrier against memory, they would build one as soon as possible."

"You didn't forget."

"No."

"Are you saying I'm no better than Lukhanan?" He didn't wait for an answer. Instead, he turned his back on her and marched to the window. He knew what he'd said was unfair but he didn't care. Down below in the courtyard, the wizards and apprentices talked and argued and practiced as if nothing had happened that day.

He shook his head and raised his eyes beyond the Academy, beyond even the city walls, out past the Winter Gate to a flat, rocky area dotted with stunted trees and wooden platforms. The City of the Dead, they called this place. The platforms, about seven feet high with steps up one end, ran some ten feet long and three feet wide. Stained with age and blood, the Offering Tables, as people called them, had stood there for hundreds, if not thousands, of years. Overhead, vultures circled and glided, waiting for funeral processions to march from the city, wailing and ringing bells as they brought dead bodies to lay out on the platforms. The vultures took the meat, the Offering Table took the blood and the family carried home the bones.

At one time the whole area might have been busy, for people die all the time, but recently a young queen brought in from a land across the Southern Sea had introduced a new custom: burial. Now the nobility and the rich stored their dead underground, with stone monuments to impress future generations. It was only the poor and the old-fashioned who fed the vultures.

Matyas stared out, narrowing and focusing his eyes until he saw them: a small handful of downcast people, only three or four in the traditional white robes of a funeral, and at their head a young woman in a ragged dress. She held that thing in her arms, the empty puppet that had once been her brother. Matyas could not imagine how hard that was, but Lahaylla kept her body straight, her head high even as she marched up the steps of the Offering Table.

Matyas might have expected her to shroud the body in some beautiful fabric, if for no other reason than to conceal the missing head, but no, she laid him out exactly as he was when Matyas had showed him to her. She set him down without ceremony and immediately descended the steps to wait.

The vultures circled, arced, moved closer—and then climbed up again. Three times they moved down toward what looked like a body, and each time they soared up again, confused. Finally they simply gave up and went back to their patterns in the sky. Only then did Lahaylla begin to wail and sway and hold her head in agony. Thankfully, she was too far away for Matyas to hear her.

He turned around to stare at Veil. The old woman looked small and weak in her narrow chair. Matyas said, "I want to fly."

Veil shook her head. "I've told you—"

"No more lies!" He stepped toward her and she stood up to face him. "Why do you always think I'm lying?"

"Because you're so good at it."

"The world has limits," Veil said. "Structures. This is what Joachim and Florian created."

"And the *other*? He was there, too. Remember?"

"Yes."

"Break the rules. Tell me the secret."

She sighed. "Matyas, do you see that black stone in the corner, by the stove? Bring it to me."

"What?" He looked where she said, and yes, there was a black rock, about twice the size of his foot, just past the stove where he'd cooked their meals every day for years. He remembered now that he'd seen it when he first arrived, and probably hundreds of times since then, but he appeared to have forgotten it. He said, "If I bring it to you, will you teach me to fly?"

She shrugged. "We will see."

In two steps he was there. When he tried to scoop it up it wouldn't move and he nearly pitched head first into the wall. He squinted at it. It was a trick, of course, like that climb up the stairway. He summoned all the spirits that hovered at the ends of his fingers to bring energy into his arms. He bent down and pulled so hard the veins in his neck threatened to break through his skin and send his blood flying in all directions. When it still wouldn't move, he summoned the spirits who slept under the tower to wake up and push from below. Slowly he felt it stir, half an inch, an inch. Then he heard terrified shouts, from the courtyard, he thought, but when he listened, he realized they came from people all over the world. He dropped the stone and sent away his helpers. Exhausted, he had to lean against the wall to stand up.

Veil said, "You see? How can you expect to perform miracles when you cannot pick up a single stone?"

Matyas said, "*That was the night sky*. You crazy old woman, you wanted me to bring you the sky! What would have happened if I had done it?"

When she smiled, flickers of light came through her skin. "Then maybe you wouldn't need to fly."

Matyas launched himself toward the alcove where he'd slept for six years. He grabbed the box from under the bed, quickly checked to make sure everything was in it, then held it against his chest as he rushed past her toward the door. He left the suit of clothes she'd given him under the bed.

"Matyas—" Veil said, but he didn't stay to hear the rest. At the top of the stairs he hesitated, worried she might turn it back into celestial steps and he would never reach the ground. He didn't care, he realized. He raced downward and thankfully they remained ordinary wood.

Outside, in the bright courtyard, a few people looked curiously at him, and at the wooden box he clutched so tightly. Then they looked away again and returned to whatever important matters were moving them through the day.

Chapter Twenty-Four

JACK

With the fear of the mythical Jessica Green hanging over him, Mr. Chandruhar did not try again to expel Simon. He did, however, send him home twice more, both times for fighting. Both times the principal greeted Jack with a defiant stare, arms crossed, certain that if necessary, he could summon witnesses to testify that it was Simon who hit first, Simon who had attacked some helpless innocent, Simon who was in fact the bully.

Jack did not have the strength to argue. He knew, he *believed*, with all his heart that his son was not some kind of violent sociopath. Simon had never been one of those children who tortured the neighbor's cat, who set fire to things. It agonized Jack that he had to even think of such things. Simon was a good boy. Until . . . until the troubles started, Simon had been a happy child. He'd had friends. Got good grades. Natural leader, isn't that what the day-care woman had called him? *What the hell had happened?*

Jack couldn't believe that tearing up a stupid deck of cards could actually make his son sick. It made no sense. It had to be a symptom, not the cause. If Simon wasn't already sick, he wouldn't have reacted that way. Period. In fact—how could Simon have known? Jack kept going back to that moment when Carla called to say Simon had been taken ill. It was just after Jack destroyed the cards, certainly well before Simon came home and searched for them. So that proved it, right? Because if Simon didn't even know what his father had done, that couldn't have been what made him sick. So when Howard Porter asked Jack if he could think of anything, any incident, large or small, that might have thrown Simon into such a terrible decline, Jack could only shake his head, with a thoughtful expression molded on to his face, and say no, there was nothing.

Sometimes, when he thought Simon was safely asleep—as if, Jack reminded himself, sleep could ever be *safe* for Simon Wisdom— Jack would go to his own bedroom and pick up the picture of Rebecca he kept on his dresser. There she was, in the park where they'd first met. *Look at her*, he thought. Smiling, bright, no sense of . . . You could look at this picture and almost believe his dad's favorite slogan had finally come to life: *more normal than normal.* "Oh, Bec," he whispered. Was it his fault? Had he ignored all the warning signs? Indulged her too much? Laughed away all the psychic talk—or worse, pretended to believe it, in some misguided attempt to support the woman he loved?

If Jack had made Rebecca get some kind of treatment, maybe they could have . . . what? Stopped her trying to burn their infant son in the fireplace? When he thought of that night, he pressed Rebecca's picture against his chest, as if he could not bear to look at her, but even less to let her go. He thought of that awful, sick message splashed in paint all across the living room wall. "Remember!" Did she really believe he'd *forget*?

Howard Porter wanted to send Simon to specialists. More specialists. All they ever did was upset Simon even more. What was the point? he asked Howard. With a forced optimism, the good Dr. Porter explained that they would provide more information. Such as what? Jack asked, and Howard said the sudden onslaught of symptoms without any clear cause suggested the possibility of seizures.

Jack stared at him, as if to say, *That's what you call good news?* To which Howard said, all in a rush, yes, because if it was seizures, they might not be curable but there was treatment. Drugs. More drugs all the time. Better drugs. Hardly any side effects at all. *Better and better*, Jack thought bitterly, but agreed to let Simon undergo more tests.

Simon, however, did not care for the idea. Expecting this, Jack had suggested sedation, but Howard pointed out that they were scanning

Simon's brain patterns. So Jack tried the age-old parental three-pronged attack: assurances of no danger or discomfort, firm commands and, of course, bribes. Oblivious, Simon thrashed so much on the table that they had to strap him down, like . . . like a lunatic, Jack thought. A screaming lunatic in a straitjacket. At any moment he felt ready to demand they stop this torture and release his boy. But with Howard Porter at his side, occasionally gripping his arm, as if to reassure him—or restrain him— Jack let it carry through to the end. By then, Simon had in fact stopped resisting. When at last they unstrapped him and Jack rushed forward to help him off the table, Simon said nothing. And continued to say nothing for three days.

When the tests came back negative for epilepsy and any other signs of seizure, Howard insisted that this too was a positive step. "At least we've ruled something out," he tried to say. Too exhausted to speak, Jack just hung up the phone.

A month after the "MRI incident," as Howard called it, Jack received a letter from a Dr. Frederick Reina. The letterhead said "Reina Institute for Pediatric Neuro-Psychiatry," with an address in Wisconsin. "Dear Mr. Wisdom," it began, "I hope you will forgive this unsolicited letter. My colleague Dr. Howard Porter and I were discussing cases recently at a conference, and he mentioned your son's deeply troubling condition."

Anger surged in Jack that Howard would treat Simon as some kind of interesting study. Upstairs at that moment, Simon was sitting on his bed, just staring at a blank television, and *Dr. Porter* thinks it's okay to *chat* to some stranger . . .

He took a deep breath and allowed hope to push the anger aside. The letter went on to say that Dr. Reina had seen such cases before and had good results with an intensive treatment he had developed at his Institute. Then it listed Simon's symptoms—the nightmares, the outbursts, the behavioral changes, even what Dr. Reina called "a fixation or terror of the paranormal." *Who is this guy?* Jack wondered, for he was pretty sure he'd never discussed Simon's "fixation" with Howard—or anyone, for that matter.

The letter ended with the news that Reina was about to visit the area on personal business and might he come and examine Simon? No charge. If Dr. Reina, with Jack's agreement, of course, decided that treatment might prove beneficial, they could discuss a plan. He went on, "I do not know, of course, of your financial circumstances, but I have never turned away a child in pain for monetary reasons. Restoring your son to health is all that matters."

Jack didn't know what to do. Something in him wanted to tear the letter into small pieces and call Howard Porter to scream at him. But maybe Dr. Reina could really do something. He called Howard and asked him about Reina.

"I don't know that much about him," Howard confessed, "but he seems to know the field really well."

"You don't know him but you told him all about Simon?"

"Yes, it's a little strange, I know. He just seemed to understand, and I found myself telling him. Maybe he can help. I've got to be honest with you, Jack—I've run out of ideas."

"Why didn't you tell me about him?"

"I'm not sure. I guess I was embarrassed I told him so much. I know your concern for privacy."

Jack paused, then said, "Did you tell him anything . . . anything about the paranormal?"

"What? No. What are you—? Jack, please don't tell me you're going to some quack promising miracles."

"No, no," Jack said, then, "you think I should do it? Let him examine Simon?"

Jack could hear Howard take a breath before he said, "Yes. Yes, I do."

The letter listed a website, Reinainstitute.org. Jack called it up and saw photos of a large stone building in a woodland setting, more like an elegant estate than a hospital. It didn't say much about Dr. Reina's methods, but there were photos of smiling kids, and letters from grateful parents, and endorsements from prominent pediatricians, some of whom Jack had heard of from his own research. They mentioned the "slightly unorthodox" approach of what they called his "total immersion therapy," but added that the results were "nothing short of phenomenal."

There was a video as well, a couple around Jack's age sitting on a couch with a boy who looked a year or so younger than Simon. They talked with him a moment or two, just long enough to demonstrate how cheerful he was, how normal. When they asked him about Dr. Reina, the boy's face lit up and he said, "Doctor Reina's *cool.*" Then they sent him away and their whole manner changed. The woman began to cry and the man put his arm around her, then he started crying as well. They told how three years ago Eric had changed, apparently overnight. He pulled away from them and all his friends, he couldn't sleep without screaming nightmares, he even became violent with other kids. And he started obsessing about . . . "strange ideas" was all his mother would say.

They'd tried everything: therapy, drugs, prayer. (*Just like me*, Jack Wisdom thought.) And then they found Dr. Reina. For a moment neither of them could speak, and then it was all "miracle," and "astonishing turnaround," and "blessing." The video ended with the man nodding vigorously as his wife said, "Thank you, Doctor Reina. Thank you, *thank you*." Jack watched it three times, then clicked on "Contact us" and sent Frederick Reina an email.

Frederick Reina arrived just five days later. He was a tall man, handsome, with greying hair around a young face, so it was hard to tell his age. He wore a dark gray suit with a blue striped tie, "banker's clothes" they would have said at Jack's office. He had a large gold ring on his left hand, stamped with some kind of insignia. His fingers were very long, Jack noticed when they shook hands. For just a moment, Jack had the strangest reaction, a feeling that he knew this man from somewhere, knew him and wanted to slam the door on him. All that vanished when Dr. Reina smiled at him. The man was so confident yet caring. And he'd come specially just to help Simon. What kind of person would Jack be if he didn't trust him? What kind of father if he didn't take a chance? It wasn't like he had any other options.

Jack had hoped Howard Porter could sit in on the consultation, but that morning an emergency had summoned Howard to the hospital. Maybe it was for the best. Simon might have refused to cooperate if too many grown-ups, too many *doctors*, ganged up on him.

When Simon first came downstairs at his father's summons, he shrank away and Jack feared he would run back to his room. Instead, Simon only squinted, as if he had trouble seeing Dr. Reina clearly, but when the doctor smiled and held out his hand, Simon appeared to relax and walked right up to him.

Jack was about to sit down next to his son when Dr. Reina said it was best if he talked to Simon alone. "I'll be right upstairs," Jack said to Simon, who looked very young and frightened. The thought, *Something is wrong*, came into Jack's head, but then Dr. Reina nodded to him, and trust dissolved Jack's fears. "Just tell him whatever he needs to know," he said. Simon nodded. *Help him*, Jack thought as he left the room. *Please help him.*

Upstairs in his bedroom, Jack saw a pair of squirrels on a branch outside his window. Dots of light bounced around them as they stared at him. He opened the window and threw an old ballpoint pen at them, and they ran down the trunk.

The session lasted nearly two hours. Jack sat on his bed the whole time, hands together between his knees. He thought of phoning Howard, just for support, but he wanted to be ready for anything Dr. Reina—and Simon, of course—might need from him.

When Dr. Reina called him, it was all he could do not to leap downstairs three steps at a time. Simon was still sitting on the couch, his head bowed. Jack thought, *What have I done?* But when he looked at Dr. Reina, the man was smiling. Could it be? Could Jack finally have found someone who could help his son?

When he let the doctor wave him into the kitchen, the news sounded anything but good. "The situation is serious," Dr. Reina said. Simon, he claimed, was suffering from a deep inner conflict that was causing his psyche literally to attack itself in a kind of autoimmune response.

"What conflict?" Jack said.

"We will not know this until I begin treatment. Of course, with your permission."

Jack was having trouble breathing. "You think you can help him?"

"Oh yes. I can work with Simon to relieve his inner pain. I assure you, he will become once again the strong and healthy boy you have missed."

"Oh God," Jack said, "that's incredible. That would be so wonderful."

Dr. Reina held up a finger. "I must warn you, Simon is in a critical condition right now. He must come to my Institute immediately."

"Yes. Yes, of course."

"I return in three days. I will come for Simon then. You must have him ready."

Jack thought of people he'd have to call to get away at such short notice. "No problem," he said. "We'll be all set to go whenever you tell us."

"No, no," Dr. Reina said, "Simon must go with me alone."

Jack leaned back. "No. No, I can't. He's never been separated from me. Never."

"Exactly." Dr. Reina nodded, as if Jack had given a correct answer. "You are deeply entwined in his psychic world. He needs to break from that world so he can heal himself. Do not worry—he will not become distant or hateful. On the contrary, I assure you he will return with his love for his father liberated."

"Maybe I could get a hotel room somewhere near your Institute."

"No. Simon must make a full break from his current psychic universe, and at the same time know firmly that his home awaits his healthy return. You are the essence of that home."

"Wow," Jack said. He sat down on one of the oak table chairs. *Don't do it*, he thought, and, *I can't just send him away*. Suddenly he imagined he could hear Rebecca, very distant, very faint, as if on a bad cell connection. "Jack! Remember!" Remember *what*? he wanted to shout. Instead, he looked at Dr. Reina. The man appeared so calm, so confident. And what had Rebecca ever done but hurt Simon? What had *Jack* ever done but hurt him? This Reina was the first person to offer any hope. He said, "All right. I'll have him ready Monday morning."

Dr. Reina stayed a few minutes more to discuss payment. It was steep, of course. After all, this was residential treatment they were talking about. But it wasn't as bad as Jack might have feared, and Reina said there would be no charge until Jack agreed there had been clear improvement. And if Jack wished, he could pay in installments for as long as two years. Jack thought how he would pay his whole life if this man could help his son.

After Dr. Reina left, Jack called Howard Porter. "That's wonderful," Howard said. "I knew he could do something. I just knew it."

"But Howard, we don't really know anything about him."

There was a pause. Howard sounded confused when he said, "Yes, I guess that's true." Then he seemed to brighten as he said, "I just have a hunch. This could be a real breakthrough."

Jack promised to let him know as soon as there was news. He hung up and took a deep breath. Time to tell Simon.

Jack found his son in his room, sitting on the edge of the bed, bent over with a book about a lost land of pirates. Jack sat down next to him. "Simon," he said, "what did you think of Doctor Reina?" Simon shrugged. "He wants to help you." No answer. "He says he *can* help you."

Simon whispered, "No one can help me."

"That's not true. You're going to get better. I promise. And I think Doctor Reina's the one to do it." He paused. "Monday," he said finally. "He's going to pick you up and you're going to travel with him to his Institute."

At last, Simon looked up. "No, Daddy," he said, "please. *Please don't make me*." He sounded six years old.

Jack hugged him. "He's going to help you."

Simon struggled free. "No! You can't make me."

"I can and I will. This is ridiculous. He says he can help you."

"Please." Simon clasped his hands, as if in prayer.

Jack stood up. "I'm in charge. It's my responsibility to make sure you get better, and that's what I'm doing. After dinner, we'll start packing."

Chapter Twenty-Five

JOACHIM/FLORIAN/ANOTHER

In the Times Before Time, Heaven belonged to the Angels and the Deep Darkness to the Rebels, who had tried and failed to seize power. In between lay the Earth, the World of Living and Dying, ruled by the Seven Guardians, who treated all mortals, male and female alike, as amusements, to help or hurt whenever it suited them. Each of the Guardians possessed a great Tree—or perhaps the Trees themselves were the original beings, and the Guardians simply branches that had gained the power to separate and move around and instigate events. The Trees all grew together in the Garden of Origins, at the center of the world. They were:

The Tree of Constancy, known also as the Tree of Gold
The Tree of Variance, known also as the Tree of Silver
The Tree of Brilliance
The Tree of Desire
The Tree of Incitement
The Tree of Gifts
The Tree of Limits

Of all these, the most important were Constancy and Variance, for they ruled the Sun and Moon, yet even their Guardians did as they wished, and human beings could count on nothing.

Joachim the Brilliant, also known as Joachim the Blessed (though others say the Blind, for the great mistake he made at the height of his success), sought to change the world. He knew he could not battle the Guardians, so he took a different road. He entered the Secret Woods and allied himself with an Outcast, a High Prince of the Kallistochoi. This became known as the Union of Above and Below. There has only ever been one such union. To attempt to repeat it is strictly forbidden. Those who have tried became known as the Uabi Heresy, and if any Uabi has succeeded, he or she has never revealed it. As to why a Kallistocha Prince would join with a human, no one really knows. Some say he took pity on wretched humanity. Others claim he saw in Joachim something more than human, as if a free Kallistocha secretly walked the Earth disguised as a man. Still others suggest the Prince wished to spite the Heavenly Victors who had stolen his body and imprisoned his head on a black pole, for he knew the Victors had given the Earth to the Guardians.

Out of this joining came the Tarot of Eternity.

Joachim had two disciples, Florian the Wise, and . . . Another. This other became the Hidden One, who is said to have buried his name under a Red Rock at the furthest reach of the world. Joachim allowed each of his disciples to create a Copy of the Tarot of Eternity, and together the three made the Great Journey. They pierced the curtain that hid the Creator from Her Creation. Florian and even the Other stood with bowed heads, afraid to look, but Joachim saw and spoke with Her, face to face. The Angels opposed him and said the Creator should cast him down with the Rebels. But Joachim insisted that he did not seek power for himself or any other human. Instead, he asked the Creator to change the world, not for his sake, or any other human, but for Herself, for only a world of laws and cycles could truly praise its Creator.

The Creator granted Joachim's plea. The world shifted and the Guardians diminished. Where once they had stood as towering beings impossible to look at, they became almost like children. The five Lesser Guardians left the Earth to move among the distant stars. We can still see them, sometimes visible, sometimes obscured, as the planets— Mercury, Venus, Mars, Jupiter and Saturn. Some say that without their Guardians, the five Trees withered and died; others that the rulers uprooted the Trees and planted them in the sky. The only ones left were Constancy and Variance, grown small now along with the Guardians who belonged to them. Many believe that the Guardians of Gold and Silver had secretly supported the humans and even hidden themselves behind the seat of the Creator to plead for Joachim against the Angels. Certainly the Sun and Moon have remained strong, while the Five have become small and faint.

When the Three Masters returned, Joachim spent his time in contemplation, or perhaps in communion with the Splendor, the great beings known as the Hidden Mystery, for only their tracks show, like flashes of light. Joachim's withdrawal later became known as the Great Mistake, for had he stayed in the world, he might have stopped the Other before it was too late.

Florian used her Copy of the Tarot of Eternity to discover the Colors Beyond Light, the Music Beyond Sound. She found the Five Basic Spells and used them, in turn, to create the original Academy of Wizards. Before the Great Corruption, she allowed one of her disciples to create a Copy of a Copy. Many years later, this disciple, or a descendant, created a Copy of a Copy of a Copy. This was given away, or stolen, and it too vanished.

Florian found the Five, but the Other found the One: the Spell of Extension, buried deep in the world's soul. Some say the Guardian of Incitement revealed it to him during the Ascent, that the Guardian knew he could not stop them but came out to battle just so he could plant the discovery in the Other's mind. There is no way to know, for the Other became secretive, silent, almost as withdrawn as Joachim himself. Might Florian have stopped him if she'd realized what he was doing? Nobody knows. If she'd found out—and roused Joachim—maybe the two of them could have saved him.

The other made multiple copies of his Copy, for in fact it was the Tarot of Eternity itself that made the Spell of Extension possible. Not all of it, though possibly every piece plays a part, but one picture, one "card," in particular. This card was called the Dancer, or the Flying Boy. The spell corrupts this picture, and thus all the others.

Only when it was too late did Joachim realize what had happened. Because of the Spell of Extension, he removed the original Tarot of Eternity from the world, and even though Florian's Copy remained pure, she too took her Copy to the Place Beyond Place. The Copy of a Copy, however, remained, so that some record would survive beyond the distortions of the Spell, for those copies made to enact the Spell of Extension serve only one purpose—to drain the lives of children, destroy every part of them, so that the Corrupter might live forever. Because of this, and because his true name remains hidden, he became known as the Child Eater.

Some say the Child Eater will indeed live forever, unstoppable, devouring child after child, for after all, the Spell of Extension is a poison at the heart of the world. But some say that a single child will destroy him. The Child of Eternity.

Chapter Twenty-Six

MATYAS

For a long time, Matyas stood in the courtyard, holding his few pos-
sessions tightly in his arms. He realized he was breathing heavily but
couldn't seem to stop. People walked past him, apprentices mostly,
but also one or two Masters; some stared, but most hurried by. Finally,
Matyas went to the library where he found Horekh in the first-floor
arcade, a portfolio of ragged parchments spread out before him. He
looked up expectantly, but when Matyas just stood on the other side of
the table full of texts, he said, "Matyas? Do you need something?"

"I need a place," Matyas said, and then, as if he was not sure he'd said
it out loud, "I need a place. A room, rooms. Where I can sleep. And
study."

Horekh nodded. "Of course," he said. Carefully he gathered up
the parchment sheets and put them back inside their gray leather
case. Matyas recognized it as a collection of accounts of journeys "in
the body" supposedly made by Joachim to the realms of the planetary
spheres, but most likely forgeries written some five hundred years after
Joachim's death. "Come with me," Horekh said.

Halfway across the courtyard, Matyas stopped when he realized they
were headed toward the grand palace of the Masters' Residency. When
Horekh appeared not to notice and kept on going, Matyas moved to

keep up with him. An apprentice was washing the thirty-two marble steps leading up to the door. He shrank away as Horekh and Matyas passed him. At the top, Matyas looked back at the young man, who kept his eyes down.

Inside the grand hallway, they moved quickly over the black and white tiled floor, past the gold and silver statues of the Armies of the Sun and Moon that some said were older than the Earth, but which Matyas knew were cast at the founding of the Academy, though possibly by *rohati*, builder-spirits summoned by Florian that were indeed far older than the world. Finally, they came to a small room where all the furniture was made of stone—slate, onyx, granite. A small, heavyset man stood with his back to them at a wide basalt table where he stared at a group of jade figurines of different shapes set in a grid of interlocking hexagons.

"Malchior," Horekh said quietly, and the man turned around with a smile and then a slightly puzzled look when he saw Matyas. Malchior had thick black hair that made him look younger than his sixty-some years, while his low, thick body made him look like one of the wrestlers Matyas had seen compete at street markets. His robe was stiff and green and brown, so that it looked like it was formed of wood and dirt and vines. He'd come from overseas, Matyas knew, and still spoke with a thick accent, though Matyas suspected he did so deliberately, for the tones and sibilances only appeared to get harsher each time Matyas had overheard him in the library.

Malchior was the Steward, the Master who kept the Academy strong and rooted to the Earth. He rarely left the Residency except to go to the library. The first time Matyas saw him, Malchior had come to the library and ordered everyone to leave. To Matyas' surprise they obeyed, and it was only later that Matyas learned the Steward had come to perform the Spell of Anchoring in the tunnels underneath the deepest cellar. Done among the skulls and hands and preserved hearts of dead Masters, Anchoring was said to preserve the Academy's connection to the physical world. Without it, the library, the Residency, maybe even Veil's tower, might simply dissolve into light and then disappear, as if their very presence in the world was always an illusion. Matyas knew that some of the Masters considered this possibility a superstition, used to keep the apprentices in awe of their surroundings. And yet, when Malchior said, "Leave," everyone left.

Horekh said, "Matyas needs rooms, Steward. I suspect he will not care so much about elaborate furniture but he will require shelves for books." He smiled slightly. "Many books."

Malchior looked confused for a minute, then said, "Yes, of course." He walked to the door and said, "Please, Master. Follow me." It took Matyas a moment to realize Malchior was talking to him and not Horekh, then he hurried to catch up.

Despite Horekh's suggestion of simplicity, the room Malchior took him to contained a four-poster bed of carved walnut, tapestries and paintings, a polished chest of drawers with gold handles, a wide walnut table inlaid with marble, four brass chairs that looked as uncomfortable as they were elaborate, and a life-size jade statue of a tiger sitting back like a dog waiting for instructions. Yellow brocade curtains framed a large window overlooking the courtyard. There was a single bookcase, ceiling-high and as wide as Matyas' arms stretched in both directions. Malchior said, "I hope this will suit you."

Matyas nodded. "Yes, of course." Then, a moment later, "No. No, take everything out." He swept his arm around, as if Malchior might not have understood him. "Bring me a small bed. And a plain table. Wood but not carved. And more bookshelves." He looked directly at Malchior. "Will you do that?"

"Yes, of course."

Matyas had to struggle not to grin. *Of course.* As seriously as he could manage, he said, "Good. I will be in the library." On his way out, he suddenly saw lights flicker around the bed canopy. The Splendor had come to welcome him, and for once he saw Malchior's calm face open with amazement. Now Matyas did allow himself a smile, but when he returned, hours later, to his now cell-like room, the lights were gone.

Matyas studied. He began before dawn and continued so late it sometimes felt as if one day ran into the next, and soon they overlapped each other and whole weeks became lost. At first he thought he would continue with Florian, or even the Child Eater, but he decided all that was a trap, a trick to keep him from his true subject: flying. The Spell of Extension was terrible, of course. He could understand the Creator's tears, and if he could have saved Rorin or brought him back, he would have grabbed the chance. But it was too late for Lahaylla's brother, and if Joachim himself could not have stopped his own disciple, how

could Matyas even think to attempt it? And besides, what did it all
have to do with him?

> *Or will you try as*
> *Ancients cry, as*
> *Children die, as*
> *No one dares to talk?*

Try how? What was he supposed to do? No, Matyas knew very well
what he needed to study. Flying. Books, scrolls, letters, parchments soon
overflowed the shelves Matyas had asked Malchior to provide for him.
He found treatises on artificial wings, with details on what kind of feathers to use, and the best wax to avoid melting as one got closer to the Sun.
Matyas thought these latter comments showed a misunderstanding of
the Sun and its sphere so profound they revealed the authors' worthless
ignorance. Others suggested bat wings as a model, with the warning that
any wizard who used such wings must do so only at night, for the bright
day would cause the leather wings to dry up and crack.

Matyas was slightly more impressed with the idea of shifting aware-
ness directly into a bird, a hawk, for example, so that you felt the air as it
soared and dived, saw through its finely honed eyes. Matyas could lean
back and imagine himself as a hawk—*a dark and lonely hawk*—an idea
so bright it made him dizzy. He could do this, he was sure of it. Only . . .
the man he'd seen that night in the woods had flown and landed as himself. Not a hawk with a man's mind, not any kind of trick, but a true
flying man. Matyas went back to his studies.

He took his meals alone, in his room or at the library: simple meals on
plain dishes, brought by apprentices who were often older than he was,
and who either looked at him with awe or refused to meet his eyes. Malchior invited him to dine at the Masters' table, and he tried it—once. The
gold plates looked all wrong, there were too many utensils and it annoyed
him that he didn't know just *what* he was eating. He listened around the
room for something, any comment at all, that might interest him, but all
they talked about, apparently, was politics and money.

He began to think about Veil, more and more, it seemed, as the
weeks went by. At first it was with anger: anger at all the tricks she'd
played on him, all the humiliations. Anger at her using him like a slave.
Anger at her secrets. Most of all he just thought over and over how she

pretended to teach him but kept back the one thing, the only thing he really needed from her. Veil knew all the magic there was to know, whatever she pretended when he asked her. There was simply no question about that. She probably even knew the hidden name of the Child Eater (not that he cared about that). Flying existed, and so Veil had to know about it. When she said she didn't, she was lying.

Sometimes he stood in the courtyard and stared up at the tower, shaking with clenched fists as if he could will her to appear in the window so that he could bring down lightning on her. Or maybe he would turn her into a toad, the way Medun had almost changed him all that time ago. He didn't notice how everyone fled the courtyard at such moments. He saw only the tower, with its empty window.

And then, slowly, something terrible happened. He began to miss her. At first it was just twinges, a flash of a thought quickly drowned in a fresh wave of rage. After some weeks, however, he could no longer deny it. He tried to tell himself it was only her books, the shelves that opened into chambers that opened into tunnels and caves, all of them crammed with words. And along with the books there were all the wondrous objects, some of which he could bring to life to watch them work, or dance, or do strange things he could never quite understand. Finally, however, he simply had to admit it. It was not just her books he missed, but Veil herself.

He missed seeing her in her narrow rocker, her hands folded in her lap, her eyes far, far away. He missed the odd things she would say, or the way she stared at a single page for over an hour and then go through the next twenty in less than a minute. He even missed cooking for her, the simple vegetable stews he prepared in her iron pots. And he missed brushing her hair. In recent months she had not asked him very often, but he always remembered that moment when he'd run the plain brush down her hair and unleashed a flood of letters.

And yet these thoughts and memories also fueled his anger. After all her mistreatment of him, he still longed to see her? Had she cast a spell on him, did she control his thoughts, his feelings? Now when he stared at her tower, it was with a mix of longing, rage and fear.

As for Veil herself, the old woman became even more reclusive than before. Sometimes people would indeed see her standing in her window. It appeared to happen, or so people said, when Matyas was walking below, but if so he never noticed, and no one dared to tell him. At rare moments, she ventured out to dart across the courtyard on some unknown errand as quickly as possible, like some woods animal crossing a road. Once she even showed up at a council meeting and sat at the back, as small and quiet as a child. Matyas wasn't there, he never attended such things.

In his confusion of feelings around her, Matyas sometimes wondered how she lived without her slave to bring her water and food and lay a fire for the cold nights. There was no sign she'd found any new street boy. He pretended to himself that his concern was sarcastic, a derisory thought on how she'd treated him. And yet . . . One afternoon, drinking tea with Horekh, Matyas asked in as casual a manner as he could how Veil sustained herself. To his surprise, Horekh smiled and shook his head. "Ah, Matyas," he said, "don't you know the three forbidden questions? What is the name of the Creator's older sister? Where was your mother before the Creation of the world? And most difficult of all, what does Veil eat?"

"But I have seen her eat—ordinary food. I spent years cooking for her."

Horekh sipped his tea, brewed with the leaves of an ancient plant that "opened the warehouses of the mind," as an old saying had it. Horekh said, "As inspired and well taught as you are, there are times . . . Do you really think Veil needed your rice and cabbage?"

"Then why would she—?"

"Perhaps she wanted you to feel comfortable. After all, *you* needed to eat."

That night, Matyas spent a long time thinking about Veil, remembering the times he'd seen her eat and the times she'd simply nodded when he'd told her dinner was ready and continued her study.

One time he caught sight of her in her window. Maybe it was the influence of that disturbing conversation with Horekh, but it looked to him that she had grown thinner. So much for *that* idea, he thought. Of *course* she needed to eat, the same as anyone. The same as him. But as he continued to stare, he thought how it was not skinny so much as . . . He frowned. Her *substance* had grown thinner. Light shone through her, as through a translucent painting of an old woman. Was it the light of day or from some other world?

That was the next to last time he saw her. The final time came a few weeks later. He'd been thinking about her more and more, sometimes unable to sleep or even study. He tried to go without food or water, just to see if it was in fact possible, but could not last more than a week. It was all a trick, he decided, it had to be, though if someone had asked him just *what* was a trick, he might not have been able to answer.

He passed the winter like this, with a kind of pressure slowly building through the cold and snow. At times he found himself wondering if she was warm enough. The Residency and the library were both supplied via grates from large fires in the cellars, but Veil's tower had no such luxury. As far as Matyas knew, no one was bringing her wood from the pile just outside the Gate of Light. That had been one of his jobs, of course, and no one had replaced him. Then he would get angry all over again that he even cared. If she didn't need to eat, maybe she wouldn't freeze, either. Or maybe she knew some spell to warm the tower. But if that was so, why did she send him down into the courtyard to pile wood in his arms and stagger back up the stairs?

Finally, on a bright day in early spring, after weeks when he couldn't sleep, or read, or think, he left his room and strode into the courtyard to shout up at the tower, "Veil! Show yourself!" He did not notice the tremor in the buildings, or the way two apprentices carrying a pile of books dropped everything and ran into the stables.

And there she was, thin and straight in the window, impassive as always.

Neither of them spoke a word, or even moved. Matyas stared up at her for a long time, days it seemed, and maybe it was, or maybe it was hours, or just minutes. He did not see that the Sun had grown dark blotches, or that the ground trembled, or that people were yelling at him. Finally, when he thought she was about to turn away, he spun around so she would not be the first. Only then did he notice the fissures in the ground and the people throwing up or leaning against walls which themselves looked shaky. With a gesture Matyas steadied the buildings; with another he sealed the cracks in the earth. As for the people vomiting, they could clean themselves. He strode to his room and slammed the door, then went and sat heavily on the edge of his bed. He stayed there for what felt like a very long time.

Three days later, the council came to see him. He had not left his room in all that time and so they had to come and knock on his door. Despite everything, he smiled as he noticed that they had left Lukhanan behind and brought Malchior in his place. He thought Veil might enjoy that—if she ever enjoyed anything.

Their demands were simple. Either Matyas stop his "duel" with Veil or leave. When Matyas asked, "What duel?" Malchior rolled his eyes.

Matyas said, "Why don't you ask Veil to leave?"

Angrily, Malchior said, "This is a serious matter, Matyas. We have no time for verbal games."

Matyas considered. It struck him suddenly that he had in fact been thinking of leaving the Academy, thinking of it for a long time really, and only his obsession with Veil had kept that thought from becoming a plan. In truth, he was fairly certain he had exhausted all their resources. If he really wanted to fly, he would have to find some other kind of magic. Keeping him here was somehow just another of Veil's tricks.

He set out the next day, packing only a sleep roll, a few basic texts that he carried more for comfort than knowledge (he could recite any of them by heart), a knife, a sheaf of papers, a pair of quills and a block of ink. At the gate, he looked back at the tower one last time. She wasn't there. *Goodbye then*, he thought. *Goodbye.*

That night he made camp on a green and yellow hillside, by a soft stream. He found some sticks and set them on fire by writing a sacred name in dust on his finger and blowing it at the sticks. He closed his eyes and called a rabbit to come and give its life to aid his quest, but when he opened them a woman stood before him.

Tall and thin, she had white hair so long it graced her ankles as it moved back and forth like a gentle wave. Her black skin was smooth and bright, almost polished, and her eyes were blue flecked with gold. She wore a green dress covered in tiny mirrors that reflected the campfire light back and forth between them, as if it had caught the flames and would never let them go. Matyas knew stories about that dress, those mirrors, and he knew not to look too closely, for if any of the fragments caught your gaze it would bounce it back and forth, and even if you walked away and never saw the woman, the mirrors again, your image, your eyes, would remain trapped in that infinite maze.

Matyas knew the stories for he knew who this was, though he never expected to meet her. For wasn't she dead all these two thousand years? "Mistress," he whispered and bowed his head. "Great Florian. My heart thanks you for the blessing of your appearance." It was the Standard Formula of Acknowledgment should any seeker receive that greatest boon, a visit from the Lady of the Mirrors. It was also true.

Matyas knew that Florian the Wise had appeared this way when she returned from her visit to Forever, the Queen of the Dead. Florian had gone to the Land of Rock and Shadows to talk with Joachim, and although nobody knew what they'd said, Florian would sometimes ever after appear to seekers in need of help. She would not solve their problems, it was said, but give them just enough to send them further.

Should he ask or simply wait for her to offer assistance? After a few moments, when she said nothing, he spoke, hardly above a whisper. "Mistress," he said, "I have followed you, devotedly, all my life." And it was true, for his life had not begun until he discovered her. "Now I seek the great secret. How to fly. Please. I have seen this, I know it can be done. Teach me."

She didn't answer right away, and for a moment she grew faint. He thought he could see the evening through her body, the trees and hills behind her, until he realized the land here was flat, the bushes sparse and low, like the scrubland around his parents' inn, so that what he was seeing was *someplace else*. And then the green dress returned, and she spoke, in a voice surprisingly high and clear. "I shall speak and you will listen. You who are my truest disciple." His mouth opened, eager to answer, but he stopped himself. "You need to find a True Ladder. Only then can you climb to the place of beginning. And I will tell you something else. You are doing two things wrong. The first is that you are looking in the wrong place."

He wanted to ask where the *right* place was, but again knew to keep silent.

Florian said, "And the second thing—"

But right then a spark flew up from the fire toward his face, and without wanting to he cried out. Just a small noise, but it was enough, for if Florian indeed had finished relating the *second* thing, Matyas had not heard her. Once again she began to fade, her skin just as dark but translucent, like rice paper. He could see her veins and arteries like tubes carrying liquid light. Now instead of a hilly landscape, he saw a garden in her dress, with two bright trees, and a boy and girl holding hands.

"Mistress!" he cried. "What is the second thing? What am I doing wrong?"

Suddenly, inside Florian's garden world, Matyas saw a man, far away but coming closer. His left hand loosely held a stone knife. *No*, Matyas thought, *not him!* Then everything inside Florian turned to light, blinding Matyas and forcing him to cover his eyes. When he could see again she was gone.

The fire had burned out, not even a glow remained, as if hours had passed. Matyas paid no attention, only turned around and around. "Mistress!" he called out. "Come back. Please! What was the second thing? What am I doing wrong?"

No answer. He began to shake but forced himself to stop, to think. Even if he didn't know the second thing, he knew much more than when he sat down by the fire. He knew he needed to find something called a True Ladder. He could not remember seeing a mention of such a thing in any of his books, but now that he knew about it he could find it.

And he knew that he was looking in the wrong place. Well, that much he'd figured out on his own. Wasn't that why he'd left the Academy, left Veil? So now all he had to do was find the *right* place, where someone could lead him to the True Ladder. Suddenly he had a good idea of where that might be.

As he repacked his small belongings, it struck him that he could guess what the second mistake might be. The wrong place and the wrong person. Veil would never tell him, she'd never even hinted at a Ladder. But after all, despite all her great knowledge, she was just a wizard. What Matyas needed was a Prince. Smiling now, he set off, his back to the Academy, his face toward a dark grove of twisted trees.

Chapter Twenty-Seven

SIMON

On the first night before he was due to go with Dr. Reina, Simon met an old woman in the attic. He was lying in bed when he heard a sad voice call his name. For a while he tried to ignore it, even put his hands over his ears, but when that didn't help, he got up. "It's not fair," he said out loud, but it felt like he had no choice.

He walked up polished steps to a wide attic room lit by thick candles mounted on gold sticks shaped like trees. There were shining tables and carved chairs whose arms were shaped like animal heads, bears and wolves. In the corner, an old woman sat all by herself on a plain wooden chair. She wore a white dress so bright it reflected the candles like a soft mirror. Despite her elegant clothes, she wore no shoes, and her feet were worn and bent. Her hands, resting on her knees, were slim and graceful. Currents from the candlelight lifted her thin hair which looked like white gold, and yet her lined face looked impossibly soft, like a child who'd grown instantly old.

She said, "You have to go, you know. You have to break the chain."

"I don't know what you mean," Simon said.

"You do, you do," the woman told him. "There's so many. Thousands. Over and over."

Simon began to cry. "I don't want to go. Please. Please don't make me." He ran downstairs and threw himself in bed with the covers held high. He lay there a long time, then went to wake his father.

"What is it?" Jack said immediately.

Simon told his father what had happened, then said, "I don't want to go, Daddy. I don't like Doctor Reina. I'm scared."

His father sighed, said, "Simon, it was just a dream."

"No! It was real."

Daddy looked away, and Simon didn't have to cheat to know his father was trying not to cry. A moment later, his father got out of bed. "Come on," he said. "I want to show you something." They went to the end of the hall where a small door opened to the unfinished crawl space that was too low for an attic and only served to store old computers and other things Simon's dad intended to sell or recycle. "You see?" Daddy said. "No fancy attic, no old woman. It was just a dream, Simon. That's all it was." When Simon looked away, Daddy gently turned his face so Simon had to look at him. He said, "This is why you have to go to Doctor Reina's institute. So you can stop being scared of your dreams. Don't you see, Sweetie? You have to get better." Simon pulled away and ran back to his room where he slammed the door.

On the second night before he had to leave, Simon found a factory of dead children. He was lying in bed, tired, but scared to fall asleep, when he heard that awful cry of agonized children. It was the sound from his dreams but he knew he was awake. "Go away," he whispered. "Leave me alone." The sound grew louder until Simon knew it would not stop until he went to look for it. He put on his bathrobe and slippers and went out through the back door.

There were no pieces of bodies to leave a trail, like in his dreams, but somehow he knew where to go. He walked for a long time, shivering in a chilly wind, until finally he came to a large brick building, very old, with chipped paint and broken windows. The sound of weeping children filled the sky. *Run*, Simon thought, but instead he found a metal door that creaked open when he pulled with both hands.

Inside he saw a giant room, very long and wide with a high ceiling and steel-beamed walls. Dust and a smell of grease filled the air. It was hard to see in the dim light from the doorway, but after some time he could make out two long rows of metal tables, and on each one—each one—heads! They were filled with children's heads! Like products waiting to be picked up and delivered to customers!

Simon gagged. He thought he would throw up or faint. He had to feel his way back to the doorway, for the awful sight filled his mind as if the heads could float up in the air and blind him. Just as he found the way out, the heads all spoke, fifty or a hundred voices. "Go!" they cried. "Break the spell!"

Simon ran all the way home. This time he went straight to his father.

"Simon," Daddy said, "it was a dream."

"No!" Simon screamed. He showed his father the dirt on his slippers and bathrobe.

"Oh, Sweetie, you must have been sleepwalking." He shook his head. "That's . . . that's a new one."

"I wasn't sleepwalking. I *saw* it." He got down on his knees and clasped his hands together, as if in prayer. "Please, please, please," he said. "Don't make me go."

Daddy began to cry. He pulled Simon's hands apart, gently lifted him off his knees. "I'm sorry. We have to do this. You've got to get help. I don't want to send you away, please believe me. You're my boy, I love you. But I don't have any choice. I don't know what else to do."

"Then don't do anything!"

"I can't, I can't. I can't just watch you suffer so much and do nothing."

On his last night at home, Simon Wisdom met a woman made of light. He had fallen asleep after an hour reading a book while his father sat on a chair alongside the bed. When Simon woke up, his father had gone and there was a soft light in the chair, as if the full moon had taken his father's place. Simon smiled at this funny idea, and was about to go back asleep when he heard a soft voice from downstairs, reciting a poem:

Simon, Simon,
Rhymin' Simon,
Take the time an'
Stop the crime an'
Set the children free.

Simon tiptoed past his father's room and on downstairs to the living room. A woman sat in Grandma's angelback chair (it was really called a wingback but Simon used to think Grandma looked like a queen of angels and the sides of the chair were the tips of her wings). The chair was pink with blue threads, and the woman wore a blue dress, soft and long, like an angel's robe. Tiny lights sparkled all around her and for a moment Simon thought she actually was made of different colored lights, like on July Fourth, when they would make a flag or even some-one's face out of fireworks.

He felt calm as he sat down across from her. She was so pretty, and she looked at him so kindly. He wanted to go and hug her or even sit in her lap. But if she was really made of light, she might disappear if he tried to touch her. So he just sat politely and said, "Why did you call me that? Rhyming Simon."

"Oh," she said, "because you're such a perfect poem."

Simon didn't know what to reply to that, so he just said, "I'm Simon Wisdom."

The woman nodded. "I know. I'm Rebecca."

Simon's throat made a noise. He said, "That was my mother's name."

The woman nodded. "Yes."

Now Simon did jump up, but the woman—his mother—raised her hand. "I'm sorry," she whispered. "I wish, I wish I could hold you, but it's not allowed." Then Simon knew it was true, that she wasn't really there, and he began to cry. "It's all right," his mother said. "I'm so happy to see you."

"My dad wants to send me away. Can you tell him not to do it? Please. He won't listen to me."

"Oh, darling, I can't. I've tried, believe me, but your father doesn't know how to hear me. I tried to leave him a message a long time ago, but it got lost. Please don't be angry at him."

"I . . . I met some other people. They said I *had* to go. To break some-thing." His mother didn't answer. "But I'm scared," Simon said. "I don't like Doctor Reina."

The lights in her face dimmed a moment, then grew bright again, only it was the kind of cheerfulness that grown-ups put on when they want to pretend everything is fine. "I'm going to tell you something important," she said. "If you do what I say you'll be safe." Simon nodded. "When you go with Doctor Reina, you need to do two things. First, pay attention."

"Pay attention to what?"

"Everything. Things will not be as they appear. Look carefully, and listen, especially at night. Do you understand?"

"I think so."

"Good. I'm very proud of you. And now the second thing. Make sure you do not eat or drink anything. Anything at all, not even a drop of water."

"What if I get hungry?"

"Don't give in. It will go away. If he watches you, wait until he's distracted, then get rid of some of the food so he will think you ate it."

"What if he doesn't get distracted?"

She smiled, and it was such a happy sight. "The squirrels will take care of that."

"Oh wow," Simon said. "You know about the squirrels?"

"Oh yes. They're old friends of mine."

"I had a dream about them once."

She smiled again. "Did you?"

"Uh-huh. In my dream, they weren't really squirrels, they were really *kids*, a boy and a girl."

She nodded. "Yes, they changed a very long time ago."

He thought for a moment. "So it wasn't a dream?"

"No, Simon. It wasn't a dream."

"Can they change back?"

"Maybe they will, darling Simon. Maybe you can help them."

"Wow," Simon said again.

It would be dawn soon. The morning light began to dim his mother's face. She told Simon to close his eyes, and when he did, he felt warm arms hold him against a soft, full body that smelled of flowers, as if she lived in a garden. *I thought she wasn't allowed*, Simon said to himself. Maybe he just had to keep his eyes closed. He didn't open them until several seconds after the arms let go. When he finally looked around he discovered, just as he'd expected, that he was alone. He thought he should feel bad, but somehow it was okay. He went back to bed where he fell into a peaceful sleep until his father came to wake him.

To Jack Wisdom's surprise, Simon woke up in a good mood. And hungry. He asked for pancakes and eggs and then a grilled cheese sandwich, and he drank three glasses of milk. Jack thought maybe his boy was okay, maybe he could keep him at home. As if the very thought threw some kind of switch in him, he found himself furious and wondered if Simon was playing a trick on him. Was he forcing himself to eat and act cheerful so Jack wouldn't send him away? Was he reading his mind to know what to do? Maybe he was planting stuff in Jack's head, controlling his thoughts.

Jack made himself go into the living room and sit down. *Why am I feeling this way? What the fuck is wrong with me?* He felt completely out of control, as if someone had cast a spell on him or something.

With great effort he calmed himself. He didn't want the last time he saw his son to be filled with anger.

Dr. Reina arrived at 9:30, strong and positive in an off-white suit and a maroon tie. His greying hair was brushed back, his face shone with warmth, confidence, compassion. He smiled at Simon, who stared at the floor, and shook hands with Jack. "Everything packed?" he said. Jack nodded. To Simon, Dr. Reina said, "Well, young man, it looks like we are going on a trip. I hope you like sitting up high in a big car because that is what we are going to do." He sounded so cheerful and positive, Jack was sure he had made the right choice. And yet there was a panic in him that he had to fight to suppress.

He held Simon for a long time before he finally let Dr. Reina lead him out to the white Mercedes. He could still change his mind, he thought, as the door closed, as the engine started, as the thick wheels began to carry his son away from him. Instead, he just waved goodbye, even though Simon sat very still in the front seat and didn't look back. "I love you!" he yelled after the car. "I love you, Simon!"

Just as the car turned the corner, Jack saw a strange sight. Two squirrels ran down the road, side by side, for all the world like dogs chasing a car. Jack thought he should be angry, go and chase them or something. Wasn't that the very last thing he wanted to see? But the part of him that was in full panic somehow calmed, just a little. He walked back to the house and sat down and closed his eyes. He wasn't sure why, but for the first time in many weeks, Jack Wisdom felt a stir of hope.

Chapter Twenty-Eight

MATYAS

He could have gone by coach. They would have taken one of his ten florins and given him a few ducats back, but somehow he didn't want to arrive that way. So he used the Unwilled Stride, a way to let the Earth move your feet at great speed and with little effort. In the midst of his journey, with trees and stones a blur, he remembered how he and Royja had seen tracks outside the inn the night Medun had come, a dog or a wolf, and imagined he'd turned himself into a beast.

If he could fly, he thought, he wouldn't have to move across the Earth at all. But then, if he could fly, there would be no reason to go, not there, at least. Even without flying, he arrived in less time than it had taken him to make the journey out, when he'd hidden behind a grille in a rickety coach.

He stopped a good distance from the building, among a small stand of trees, where he could cast his Cloak of Concealment spell and just watch. It was evening, the sky a dull purple that looked just right for the dusty road, the sparse trees, the unpainted stables and the rickety inn itself. Was it always that small? That shabby? The foolish sign, a crudely painted squirrel holding a giant acorn, creaked slightly in the occasional breeze. He remembered hearing his mother tell a guest once that the previous owner had seen the name, or maybe just the picture, in a dream.

Candles flickered in the narrow windows. That had been one of his jobs, to keep the candles fresh in their filthy glass holders. He remembered how he'd let one burn out once so that someone's dinner went dark for a minute or so before Matyas could rush up with a new candle. That night his father kicked him so hard he coughed up blood and then had to scrub the floor so it wouldn't leave a stain. He was five at the time.

He stared at the door, its red paint now faded to a dull brown. If he concentrated just a little he could hear voices, a good crowd, it appeared. Then he remembered it was Thursday, coach day. There'd be people resting on their way to the city.

He could leave. He hadn't come for them, after all. He could go and see the person he needed to see and then take off again and no one would know. Instead, he went up to the door where he reached out twice for the handle, only to surprise himself by knocking.

His mother opened it. Matyas braced himself, thinking he could still run before she began to scream at him, or whatever she was going to do. Dressed as she always was, in a black dress and a plain white apron with her gray hair pulled back into a tight bun, she stared at him, her eyes running from his face to his robe and back again. And then—just as she'd done that other time—she crossed her arms over her chest and bowed and said, "Master. You honor us deeply. Please enter."

Matyas followed her, dazed. Did she really not know? Maybe if she actually looked at him, he thought, for in fact she kept her eyes down, and if she had to glance his way she didn't raise them higher than the tree of signs painted on his chest. But hadn't she seen his face in the doorway?

As they walked through the room, people hunched over their beer or looked away, some making signs of protection. "Wizards," one man said in disgust, only to have his friends frantically whisper him quiet.

His mother took him to *that* room, of course. Maybe from now on they would proudly name it "the room of the Masters."

"This is our best room," she said. "Reserved . . . reserved for our most important guests."

"Yes," he said, and wondered if his voice would give him away.

If so, he couldn't tell, for she just asked, "May I bring you anything?"

"No. Thank you."

She bowed her head and shuffled awkwardly from the room as if frightened to turn her back on him.

Alone, Matyas turned around and just looked at everything. There was the high-backed wooden chair with the badly carved lions' heads at the ends of the arms, the cheap oval rug with its off-center designs, the absurd bed with its droopy canopy. He thought of the room Malchior had given him in the Masters' Residency, the tapestries, the huge bed, the jade tiger, and how he'd told them to remove everything. He shook his head, his mouth open. When he looked at the chair again he could almost see Medun, the stocky body in his brown and gold robe, the white skullcap, the red beard like an unruly flower bed. And the hands, thin and strong as they slid the pictures in and out of each other, the copy of a copy of a copy, searching . . . for what? Something to break the spell? Wandering Exile, forced never to spend two nights in the same place. It had sounded so trivial when Veil described it to him, but now Matyas could hardly imagine it.

There was a knock at the door, quiet, hesitant. Matyas almost ignored it but then he stepped across the room, opened it—and there he was. Bent over slightly (unless he was just trying to bow and not very good at it), mostly bald, his face above the beard stubble (he never did have the patience to shave properly) all scratched for some reason, the thick shoulders in his ill-fitting shirt. And the hands—those hands!—callused, with enlarged knuckles, they held a small tray with a stemless wine glass and a small carafe of wine. Like his wife, he kept his eyes low, didn't look up as he said, "Master. We would like to offer you our best wine. Blackberry. We make it ourselves. If you want . . . if you wish something to eat, we will be happy to serve you. Anything you like. My wife is a very fine cook."

His voice hoarse, Matyas said, "The wine is enough. Just set it down on the table."

"Yes, Master, of course." He did as he was told and quickly left.

How could he not know? There was a mirror on the wall opposite the bed, chipped glass in a heavy wooden frame. Matyas stared at himself. He was taller, his shoulders straighter, his whole body more muscular. And he had the robe, of course, no torn shirt and pants but a cosmos of signs and wonders flowing across his body. And there was something else. He was clean. No grease, no mud, no ashes. No blood.

Oh God, he thought. He turned away from the mirror, thinking to sit down, but instead just stood there, unable to move. There was so much he could *do*. Tighten the throat so he couldn't breathe. No, let him breathe but make it too narrow to eat, so he would slowly starve to death over days, maybe weeks. Or heat the blood, slowly, hotter and hotter until he burned to death from the inside. Or set his feet and hands on fire. Or freeze them so they broke off and he couldn't walk or feed himself.

Or change him. Change him into a toad—no, a mouse, and let someone's boot crush him in the kitchen. Or some small, helpless creature that Matyas could set outside for an owl, or a hawk, to tear him to pieces. He heard the inn's sign creak in a gust of wind. A squirrel! He could change his father into a squirrel!

He sat down on the bed now, squeezed shut his eyes and tightened his fists against the laughter that would never stop. There was a spell that could do that. He could make his father laugh and laugh and laugh until he convulsed into death.

Get out of the room, Matyas told himself, *the room, the building, now*.

He opened the door just enough to see that neither of them was in the main room, then he cast his shielding spell around himself and hurried down the stairs and out through the door. A man sitting alone turned his head as if he felt Matyas go by, then shrugged and returned to his ale.

Once outside, Matyas realized he'd been holding his breath and made himself calm down. *Everything is good*, he told himself. All he had to do was go where he needed to go and then he could leave. ("Wizards," he imagined his father saying. "They show up all high and mighty and then they just sneak off when you're not looking. Good riddance to the bastards, if you ask me.")

And maybe he would have done just that and not thought any more about it if his path had not taken him alongside the stable and if he hadn't seen her there, feeding the coach horses. Still, she had her back to him and he could have just walked on. Instead, he stood and watched, not even using his shield, until she finished her task and turned around.

In that moment before she faced him, he discovered himself terrified that she too might not know him—terror and hope, for she was the last, and if she couldn't see it was him he was free. But she turned and stopped and dropped her wooden feed bucket, and he knew that he was caught. They stood there for a while, about twenty feet apart, and when he took a step toward her she moved back, so he stopped and waited.

And looked. Was she always that short? Was her hair always so greasy, and cut as if she'd just slashed at it? Were her clothes always so thin and worn and too small? She'd grown fat. Her belly pushed against her dull brown dress. No. Not fat.

She looked him up and down. "So," she said. "You got what you wanted."

"I . . . I came back. I told you I would."

She laughed, and he grimaced. *Stupid*, he scolded himself. When did she acquire the power to make him feel stupid?

"You look . . . dazzling. Can you . . . can you do things?"

He glanced around, saw a stray piece of wood that must have fallen from someone's arms on the way from the woodpile to the fireplace (one of his jobs). With a gesture he shot it up to eye-level, spun it around so fast it almost vanished, then let it fall back to the dirt.

"Ha!" she cried, and clapped her hands, and for just a moment it was her again, *them* again. And then she shook her head, and he could see her squeezing back tears.

"You could come with me," he said, and became terrified she'd rush to say yes.

She made a noise, looked away for a minute, then down at her swollen belly. "Even if you wanted me . . ." she said.

"Who is it?" he asked. "I mean . . ."

"I know what you mean. His name is Kark. Your parents hired him after . . . after you ran away."

Somewhere in the ancient archives there was a story, *The Man Who Was Replaced*. It told of a brutal king whose subjects begged a wizard for help. Rather than execute the king, or even imprison him, the Master simply created a benign substitute and caused everyone—the courtiers, the advisers, even the queen—to think this replacement was real. No one knew what happened to the original. Matyas said, "This Kark. Do my parents—?"

"Beat him?" She shrugged.

"Then why does he—?"

"Stay?" She looked around. "I suppose it's better than starving."

Matyas nodded toward her belly. "Is that your first?"

She laughed. "Third. A boy, a girl and now whatever this is." When she saw alarm flash in his face, she said, "Matyas, the oldest is four."

"Oh." He'd been gone nearly six years. "You could still come with me," he said.

"Stop it!"

He stepped back, and as if she couldn't help herself, she moved forward, keeping the same distance between them. "Matyas," she said, and had to stop, take a breath. "It's all right. You did what you had to do. To get out. My father never . . . It wasn't the same for me." When he didn't answer, she said, "Go. Do—Whatever it is you came for, do it, and then—just go."

He hesitated, then nodded and turned. He was only a few steps away when she called out, "Matyas!" He spun around. "Is it true?" she asked. When he didn't answer, she said, "Does the palace float in the air? Are the mansions made out of flowers? Are the royal family descended from swans? Are there streets that turn around and around and no one ever gets out?"

He smiled and said, "Yes. It's all true."

Royja laughed, and clapped her hands. "I knew it," she said. "Thank you, Matyas. *Thank you.*"

"Royja—" he said, but she held up a hand.

"No. You have to—" She ran into the stables. He heard a horse neigh, and beneath that the sound of weeping.

Like everything else, the dark grove looked smaller than Matyas remembered it: still dense, twisted, caught up in a kind of cloud of hate, just not very large. Matyas could walk around it in less time than it would take the Sun to pass over it from one end to the other. He wondered how it had looked to the Flying Man as he came down from the sky.

He stared at the trees, so tightly woven, impossible to enter without some kind of help. What had happened here? He did not doubt that the Heavenly Victors had placed the High Prince in as harsh a place as possible, part of his punishment for not taking sides in the Great War of Darkness and Light. But what made this place the worst they could find? What happened here? He tried to probe the trees with magic but it proved as useless as sight.

He shrugged. Not his concern. Was this the right place, the right person? That was all that mattered.

"Come around me," he said. When nothing happened he invoked the Voice of Command, an amplification spell that could cause rivers to run uphill. Still nothing. For the first time it struck him that he might not get inside. Without help . . . But wasn't he stronger than a knot of trees? His hands clenched and unclenched, his whole body tensed in preparation for an all-out attack.

And then the lights came. The Splendor. Stronger than any time since he'd first seen them, they swarmed all over his body. "Open the way," he said, and just as those other times, for the Flying Man and then for Matyas himself, the lights briefly blocked his view of the trees, and when the lights vanished there was a pathway. The black branches arched over it, straining to close the gap, but couldn't do it. Matyas took a breath and walked inside.

It didn't take very long to reach the center, to reach the prisoner. A golden head perched on an ebony stick of polished darkness. Beauty beyond male or female, beyond even the Sun and Moon, the High Prince of the Kallistochoi was a remnant of an age before the world hardened into the dullness of wood and metal, water and stone. Eyes closed. The skin smooth and motionless. Sleeping? *Dreaming?*

Matyas found himself overwhelmed by a desire that could blot out everything—to dream like a Kallistocha. Angrily, he pushed it aside. "Wake up!" he commanded. Matyas had learned the Kallistochoi Phases, the term used for the Seven Primary Tongues, and now he spoke in the tones sometimes called First Palace.

The eyes stayed closed but the lips widened ever so slightly, the suggestion of a smile. "You've been studying," the Voice said. "You honor me." Matyas was so caught up in the music it took him a moment to realize the Prince had used the Child Phase, as if Matyas was acting like his father.

Embarrassed, Matyas switched dialects to the Inner Chamber. "Wretched head of the once mighty and beautiful!" he sang out. A text in the library had given this as the Proper Formula of Recognition, but as soon as he'd said it, Matyas was uncertain.

The eyes opened like great swans lifting into a sunrise. "No, no," the Voice said. "You were doing so well as my mother. Or is that father? Those sorts of distinctions become lost after a time." He cast his eyes downward, where once there had been a body.

Feeling less and less in control, Matyas switched to the Flatlands Parade, the Phase the books called the simplest for humans to emulate. "Thank you for receiving me," he said.

The Prince smiled, and Matyas thought he might have seen the slightest grace of kindness. The Kallistocha murmured, "I could not exactly run away." His eyes scanned the wide path the lights had opened and the way the trees leaned in as if they yearned to snatch Matyas and tear him apart. The Voice said, "The Splendor appear to favor you. Have you ever wondered why?"

"No," Matyas said without thinking.

"Perhaps you are useful to them."

"Useful? What do you mean?" The eyes closed and the head tilted slightly, as if the Prince was drifting back into its vast sleep. "How about you?" Matyas asked. "Are you useful? Were you useful to Joachim? It was you, wasn't it? Who gave him the Tarot of Eternity?"

The eyes opened again, summer returning to a frozen world. "Ah, Joachim," the Kallistocha said. "Joachim the Brilliant. Joachim the Blessed. The Bountiful. The Bewildered." He had switched to Matyas' own language, a move that frightened Matyas, though he was not sure why.

As if to lure him back, Matyas stayed with the Flatlands. "You taught him?"

"Yes." The Prince had returned to Inner Chamber, and Matyas felt safe again.

"Why?"

"Perhaps, as you suggested, I was being useful."

"Useful how? For what?" No answer, and Matyas felt as if once again he'd taken a wrong turn. He should just ask what really mattered but he could not seem to help himself. He said, "Did you know about the Spell of Extension?"

Again the slightest smile, though Matyas had no idea why. "Yes."

"Then why did you give Joachim Eternity? The spell couldn't work without it—you need that one picture."

"Yes."

"Then why?"

"Would you banish magic, Matyas? Would you give up everything because of a single flaw? After all, the Creator persisted, so why not Her lesser beings?" His eyes moved across Matyas' robe in a way that made Matyas want to cover himself with something dull and ugly. "You wear the Tree of Ascendancy, the Tree of Signs and Snakes. Would you tear it from your body that you might burn it and scorch all the knowledge from your mind? I might offer to do it for you, as you appear to think I should have done for Joachim, but as you see . . ." The eyes drifted upward. "Perhaps the branches would help."

Matyas too looked up, and saw that the trees were leaning closer. Not much time left. He remembered when he'd come here before and had to run before the branches could get hold of him. *Now*, he told himself, *you have to ask now.*

"Tell me the secret!" he blurted out, not even sure what language he was speaking.

"Haven't we been doing that? What secrets do you wish now?"

"Flying! Tell me how to fly. Tell me how to find a True Ladder."

The High Prince laughed so loudly the trees shrank back before leaning in again. "Flying? You would ask a *Kallistocha* how to leave the Earth?"

Matyas stumbled back as if a hand had shoved him. *Are you an angel?* he'd asked that first time, and the head had answered, *Do I look like a wing-slashing beast?* "Oh God," Matyas whispered, "this is the wrong place!"

The Prince's laughter chased him from the woods. When he was safely outside, and the trees had closed again, he sat down on a wide rock, ignoring the rough surface. So sure. He'd been so convinced, and all he'd done was rush from one wrong place to another.

He stood up, took a breath. The night had grown chill, and he realized he was shaking. Beyond the hills he could see the glow of the inn. Should he go back? He could warm himself, sleep and leave before anyone saw him. Or he could say goodbye to Royja. It would be easy enough to cast sleep over her children, and this *Kark*, whoever he was.

No. There was no time. If Florian said he was looking in the wrong place, there had to be a right one. There were other Academies, after all, other scholars. Hermits, wise men, keepers of secrets. He knew of one such place, in fact, the College of Trees. With the Unwilled Stride, he could reach it in just three or four days.

He began to run.

Chapter Twenty-Nine

SIMON

Simon wasn't sure how long the journey lasted. His dad had told him they were going to Michigan—"the Great Lakes" Simon had said, and his father had nodded, proud and a little surprised that Simon remembered something from Social Studies—and it would take two or three days. And yes, he remembered big hotels with nothing much around them, and very clean rooms, with large beds, and Dr. Reina saying, "I'll be right next door, Simon. Please remember to knock on the connecting door if you need anything. And especially if you have a bad dream, yes?"

Simon hadn't answered, and after Dr. Reina had gone, Simon locked the connecting door, but when morning came he woke early and opened it, because after all, what could he do? He had no idea where he was and he didn't want to disappoint his dad, and besides, his mom had said it was going to be okay. He opened the door because he didn't think it was a good idea to make the doctor angry.

He remembered as if it was all one time (though he knew it had to be two or three), sitting on the too-large bed, with piles of too-soft pillows propped up behind him and watching cop shows. Somehow it was always cop shows—silent, unstoppable men and tough-talking women, and people chasing people, and children locked up in dirty warehouses, and bad people with scars and tattooed arms and very short hair being shot dead, and the tough woman cop holding the screaming child and saying, "It's okay. I've got you. You're safe now."

Simon remembered the trip but it was all detached, like something in a video game or another cop show. "Did you sleep well?" Dr. Reina asked him each morning and Simon said, "I guess," and Dr. Reina said, "No bad dreams?" and Simon said, "No," and Dr. Reina said, "You see? Already you are getting better." And then they would get back in the car and continue.

The only thing Simon could say for sure was that he didn't eat anything. No food, no water, that was what his mother had said. He tried to tell Dr. Reina he wasn't hungry and just wanted to stay in his room, but the doctor insisted Simon go with him to the hotel restaurants, which were always very clean and bright, with cloth napkins and large shiny silverware. "Have whatever you like," Dr. Reina said, "my treat. You can have steak, or hamburgers and French fries, if you like. Pizza, ice cream—you choose." But when Simon said he didn't want anything, Dr. Reina didn't appear to mind.

The second night (at least, Simon thought it was the second), Dr. Reina told Simon, "You need to eat to get well," and suggested Simon order something from room service. "Ah, you will like this," he said, as if Simon didn't know what room service was. "They come all the way from the kitchen to bring whatever you want on a covered tray. Just for you." With the doctor standing over him, Simon ordered a bacon cheeseburger, fries and a large Coke. "Very good," Dr. Reina said. "Now we are moving in the right direction."

Simon feared that Dr. Reina would wait for the food to come, but the good thing about room service, he knew, was that it took a really long time, so he just turned on the TV and waited, and sure enough, after a while Dr. Reina went to his own room. When the food came, Simon tried to remember if his mother had said he mustn't *touch* it, but he was pretty sure she'd only said not to eat or drink anything. He cut up about half the burger and about a third of the fries—too much might look suspicious—and flushed them down the toilet. *Let the alligators have them*, he thought, remembering some kid who'd claimed that hotels all had giant gators in their sewers from tourists who bought them as babies in theme parks and then flushed them down the toilet. Simon poured about half the Coke down the bathroom sink. In the morning, Dr. Reina checked the room service tray and smiled happily. "Very good," he said, just like the night before. "Now we are on the right track."

Everywhere they went, people appeared to like Dr. Reina. They smiled at him, and said nice things, like, "You folks have a wonderful trip, okay?" Sometimes they even gave Simon little presents, like a toy truck or a chocolate bar. Simon wondered if it was okay to eat something that someone other than Dr. Reina had given him, but he decided it was best to be safe, so he threw away the candy bar, and the truck, too, as soon as he could.

At a gas station somewhere off the interstate, Dr. Reina talked with a woman filling her SUV. When the doctor went inside for something, the woman walked over to where Simon sat slumped in his seat. Through the open window she said, "I just think it's great that you and your granddad are taking a trip together."

Simon slumped lower. "He's not my granddad," he muttered.

"Oh," the woman said, "I'm sorry. Your dad?" Simon shook his head, and wondered if she'd try "uncle" or "cousin." Instead, she looked over at the store, where Dr. Reina was talking to the Arabic man at the cash register. Simon sat up slightly as he saw alarm flicker in her face. When she said, "Do your parents know you're with him?" he wondered, if he said no, would she call the police? Would they send him home?

He was trying to think of what to say when Dr. Reina came walking back to the car, smiling. "Ah," he said, "I see Simon has made a new friend."

The woman looked confused, struggling as she tried to hold on to a worry that appeared to be melting away. "I hope you'll excuse me," she said, "and not think me horribly rude—you hear such stories, I'm sure you understand." Dr. Reina nodded as if to reward her concern. "If you don't mind my asking, how do you know this boy?"

"Of course, of course," Dr. Reina said, with another warm smile. "I am, in fact, his doctor." He took out a folded sheet of paper from his jacket pocket. "Here, I show you. A letter from Simon's dad, with a photo of the two of them, you see, and a photo of his dad's driver's license. Just for the proper identification."

The woman looked at it so quickly Simon couldn't imagine she had time to read anything. And—it was hard to see—but he wasn't sure there was actually anything *on* the paper. If so, the woman did not appear to notice. "Oh my God," she said, "you must think . . . I'm so sorry!"

"Not at all," Dr. Reina said. "We need more such concerned citizens like you, Margaret. I applaud you."

"Um, thank you," the woman said, and Simon didn't have to cheat to know what she was thinking, how she'd never said her name. Simon looked quickly at Dr. Reina, who apparently had realized his mistake for he moved quickly to get into the car and start the engine.

Simon wanted to stare at Dr. Reina, but he made himself look out the window. How did he know that woman's name? How did he . . . did Dr. Reina *cheat*? Was that how he knew what to say to Dad? Did he know what Simon was thinking? Right now? Simon's breathing began to speed up. *Stay calm*, he told himself. But what was the point, if the doctor knew what he was thinking? Suddenly he understood why his dad hated it when he cheated. It was so creepy! He wanted to run and say he was sorry. But he couldn't, he was stuck in this car, with this . . . this *doctor*.

But then he remembered his mother. *You'll be safe*, she told him, *as long as you don't eat or drink anything*. And he hadn't. That was the one thing, the only thing, he knew for sure. So that meant everything else had to be some kind of trick. What the doctor did with that woman, that piece of paper, it was all a trick. Simon dared a quick glance at Dr. Reina and saw he looked tired. As if playing that trick on Margaret had exhausted him. He still sat upright, but his hands held the steering wheel tightly and his cheerful expression looked fixed in place. Simon thought how it didn't tire *him* when he "read" people's minds (as Dad called it). It made him feel better.

So, if Dr. Reina cheated, or even just played tricks, was it okay for Simon to cheat, too? He leaned back, closed his eyes and slowly, carefully, like someone opening a dangerous box, he felt his way inside Dr. Frederick Reina . . .

. . . and found himself surrounded by stone walls, in a room with no door and no windows, nothing but a rectangular slab of iron the height and shape of the butcher's block in Jerry Lowe's mom's kitchen. Simon turned around and around, ran from wall to wall, searching, feeling for a way out, a door, anything . . .

. . . and was back in the car seat, staring at Dr. Reina, who turned to him and smiled. "A beautiful day!" the doctor said, gesturing with his hand at the sunshine that shone on the endless trees along the side of the road. "Soon we will come to the Institute. And then the real healing will begin."

Chapter Thirty

MATYAS

Matyas knew very little about the College of Trees, only that it occupied the eastern slope of a small mountain in a country across the Northern Sea. The Unwilled Stride could hardly take Matyas over water, and so he realized he would have to negotiate passage on a ship. And that of course would require money, more than his precious ten florins. He made his way to the port, a place he'd never seen, however many times he and Royja had talked about it, and took lodging in a large inn near the docks.

The inn was called the Green Lion, a title that intrigued Matyas, for in the Transmutation of Metals a green lion was said to appear and devour the outer form of base metal to release what was called True Gold. For two days Matyas sat on an outdoor terrace, sipping tea and thinking how if he'd only studied the Transmutation he would not have to sit here like some sort of performer waiting for a patron.

He sipped marigold tea and tried to ignore the inn owner's nervous looks at the empty tables—who would sit next to someone who could freeze your tongue in your mouth if you talked too loudly, or turn you into a frog if you blocked his view of the Sun?—or the people who turned their faces away as they hurried past him, or the boys who dared each other to go and speak to him but always ran away. Matyas did not care about such things (or so he told himself). He only cared that he was still in the wrong place. He tried to pass the time by imagining what a True Ladder might be but nothing came to him.

Finally, a man in black and gold livery approached Matyas' small table. Tall, and very thin, with slicked-back gray hair, he made the usual sign of protection, but more as a mark of respect than fear. His employer, he said, was in need of a Man of Knowledge, and might it be possible to beg the Master's help? Matyas had no idea if he was supposed to feign a lack of interest, or maybe even offense, so he simply stood up and allowed the servant to walk him to a black and gold carriage drawn by six black horses with gold bridles.

Matyas never learned the name of the woman who'd sent her servant to hire him. A shield on the gate to the tall, narrow building on top of a hill bore the name "Storkhaven," and indeed, at least four of the stone building's seven chimneys appeared given over to stork nests. The woman herself, however, gave no name or title, nor did she ask exactly who it was she had hired. Matyas had no idea if people here in the port city had heard of "Matyas the Young." Tall and thin, like her servant and her house, the woman wore a plain, pale yellow dress with a simple gold chain. Her long white hair was held behind her by an ivory clip in the shape of a swan. Matyas wondered if she didn't tell him her name, or ask his, for fear that such an exchange would give him power over her. As if he would need to know who she was to place any of twenty spells on her!

What she wanted turned out to be almost childish. She hoped to expand her business, she said, and an opportunity had caught her by surprise. Her analysis, or rather the analysis of her experts, told her to trust the enterprise and the man who had presented it. But she was a cautious woman, used to acting slowly, and analysis was not enough to change a lifetime's habit. She wanted knowledge, not just opinion.

Matyas tried not to laugh. He was searching for the secret of flight, and this—this merchant . . . He told her to bring him a clear glass bowl, a pitcher of fresh water and two swan eggs. She was about to send her servant when Matyas told her she had to do it herself. Her face stiffened into a blank mask and Matyas wondered if she guessed he'd just made that up, but she didn't challenge him.

The "investigation," to use the proper term, took no more than five minutes to uncover the information that she needed certain commitments and then everything would go smoothly. The only real challenge for Matyas was when she asked his fee. Nervously he said two hundred florins, and immediately regretted it, for her eyes widened and she immediately said yes, of course, and sent her servant for the money. All the way down the hill, and then the next day as he paid his bill at the inn and found a ship to give him passage, he experienced over and over the humiliation of that moment, her contempt at how cheaply he valued his services. Even as he was settling into his cabin on the boat, he was wondering if he should have said he'd made a mistake, he'd meant to say *five* hundred. And as the boat slipped from its moorings and he saw a pair of storks overhead, he had to fight the urge to take control of them and send them to attack her house. He knew it was unimportant—two hundred was certainly enough, given that the passage was only fifteen, and it was clearly very easy to earn more—so why did it bother him so much?

Matyas expected the sailors to try to avoid him, the way the patrons of the Green Lion had done, maybe even refuse to sail with a wizard on board. Instead, they looked pleased, even saluted him as they went past where he was standing at the rail. It took him some time to realize that sailing was a dangerous life and a Master meant a layer of protection. It surprised (and disturbed) him how good that made him feel.

When Matyas first arrived at the College of Trees, he thought he must have made a mistake—that, or the wood spirits he'd conjured to guide him had misunderstood, for while the mountainside they led him to was dense with trees, there were no buildings he could see. The trees were old and bent, twisted like a net, making it hard to see more than twenty yards or so in any direction. It reminded Matyas of the dark grove, but without the sense of malevolence. Nor could he detect a hidden light or song that might have signaled the presence of an imprisoned Kallistocha. (If he found one, he wondered, would he feel some need to return home and tell the High Prince he was not alone?)

There *was* something there, something complicated that he could not quite understand. Despite the bright sunlight of a summer morning, a chill moved through him. He'd charged his robe with a spell to keep him warm or cool, as the season required, but now he still hugged the fabric against himself.

It took him a while to notice the people. It wasn't just the way they moved softly in and out of the trees, or the way their robes appeared to be made out of twigs and leaves, or even that there were so few of them.

They simply took no notice of him, did not appear to care that a stranger had invaded their world.

Matyas stood and watched. Because of their rigid robes and their long hair worn down and uncombed, Matyas found it hard to tell if they were male or female, young or old. They moved at varied speeds but never in a straight line, and when they stopped their bodies settled into odd angles, never convoluted, but never just upright. Like trees. They'd lived in the forest so long they'd started to imitate the trees—no, not an imitation. The more he watched them, the more he could sense some energy or intelligence flowing between the people and the forest.

He stood, and waited in what he hoped was a respectful manner, but no one moved to greet him, so finally he just strode up to someone who had stirred from the odd postures they all took on when they were standing still. He thought this one might be younger than the others, and probably female by the softness of her face under the tangle of hair. Moving quickly, to catch her in the open, he said, "Greetings. I come in search of the College of Trees." She said nothing, only nodded slightly. Behind her, two trees rustled their branches. He said, "My name is Ma—"

"Matyas. Of the tribe of Florian."

Matyas' eyes widened. He'd never thought of himself that way, but he liked it. "Yes. Will you help me?"

"Help you how?"

He took a breath to control himself. Did all female wizards twist everything into riddles? If he shook her, he wondered, would leaves and berries fall out of her hair? He said, as patiently as he could, "Help me find the College."

She said, "I cannot help you do something you have already accomplished." When he just stared at her, a quick smile softened her face. "This is the College of Trees. You are standing in it."

"But there is nothing here. Where do you all live?" She shrugged, and he imagined them all sleeping among the branches, plucking leaves and small red berries for their meals. "Then where is the library?" he asked. "Where do you study? Where are your texts, your secrets?" He could not bear that he had come all this way just to meet a group of deranged people who imitated trees. Another wrong place.

"Look," the woman said. She turned away from him and moved her head from side to side, slowly, as if asking Matyas to follow her gaze. He stared, trying hard to see what she did, angry at himself for his dullness and at her for exposing him, until suddenly he saw it. The trees! The trees themselves were the College. Words appeared, coded into the branches, stored in the trunks, sung in the leaves. Matyas laughed and clapped his hands. The humans here appeared insignificant because they were. Here were trees whose knowledge stretched back before the Academy, before Florian, before even Joachim. The right place! He turned to thank the woman but she'd already blended back into the trunks and branches.

Matyas spent most of the summer on the mountain. It took him only a few days (but a very uncomfortable few days) to learn how to recognize food, or sleep among the leaves. It took quite a bit longer to grasp what really mattered, how to follow the ancient mind of roots and branches. That too came, the first glimpses building on each other, until he began to see patterns and structures. The great library at the Academy, the piles of books in Veil's tower, these were all written by people, compiled by people, used by people. Here was something very different—wonders and secrets, and a whole way of seeing the world that was ancient when the Kallistochoi first migrated to the Earth.

Only—

Nothing in these vast wonders taught him what he'd come to find out.

After months of frustration, he finally sought out the woman who'd first revealed the College to him. "Please," he said, then thought to fall on his knees and grasp her legs, something he'd seen the people do with the trees. "My time has been blessed by wisdom. Thankfulness fills my heart." She said nothing, did not appear to react at all to his body against her legs. Matyas said, "And yet, there is one small thing that eludes me. It is the thing I came to discover but cannot seem to find. Please—where can I find the secret of flying? Where can I find a True Ladder?"

She looked down at him now, and Matyas thought he saw a flicker in her eyes. *Finally*, he thought. Then suddenly she lifted her head and laughed. Matyas jumped to his feet as the branches shook wildly. All around him people he couldn't even see were laughing! The woman said, "You came *here* to study flying? *Here?*"

Matyas stared at the trees, the solid trunks, the low branches that always twisted back toward the ground, and above all the roots— clutching the Earth, embedded deeply in the dirt and the rock. He tried to say something, only to feel all the words empty out of his head.

He left that day.

Thus began what later scholars and wizards would call the Great Journey, or even NUAB, the New Union of Above and Below—though, as the more cynical would point out, if Master Matyas had found the means to extend his journey *above* he would have ended his travels and all the mysteries he revealed would have stayed hidden, all the doorways remained closed. "Failure is the doorway to success," the more pious Matyasans would answer. And yet they never could exactly delineate just what the Master himself experienced, for the fact was, Matyas never wrote anything down, never passed anything on directly to students. It was only later, when wizards, adventurers and historians attempted to retrace the Journey, that the Secret Wonders found their way into books and oral teachings.

He traveled to great centers of learning, huge libraries of stone or glass, some with Masters so old and deep in study they were barely visible. In one place, each wizard perched alone, naked, on top of a stone pillar engraved with ancient texts; in another, the teachers themselves had long ago vanished, leaving only anthills to protect their scrolls and parchments. He dived into a lake whose surface was so still it served as a mirror of the sky for scholars to study the Sun without blinding themselves. At the bottom of the lake, he came to a library that only wizards might enter, simply because no one else could maintain a single breath long enough to reach the entryway and step into a dry courtyard filled with flowers.

On a mountain halfway around the world from the College of Trees, he found a library that changed its shape whenever he turned his back on it. After a time, he realized it was made out of people's thoughts, those of the ancient wizards who'd created it, but also the attentions, expectations and random distractions of anyone who wished to enter it. Any laxness of attention could cause it to change shape or disappear altogether. Matyas stayed there three weeks.

Again and again he followed rumors, stories, promises of a new, greater, more secret center of learning. In a desert where water had to be magically summoned from the dry rocks, he found a community of scholars without any books at all. Convinced that writing caused true learning to evaporate, they took in orphans (according to some, they "encouraged" the orphaning of bright children) and taught them to memorize texts that on paper would have run to thousands of pages.

In all these places, Matyas found himself drawn into wonder and beauty and the joy of knowledge. And yet, in each place there would come a moment, whether in the middle of the night, or while reading a text, or lifting a spoonful of soup to his mouth, when he would remember— abruptly, as if someone had slapped him—just why he had come to this place. Then he knew it was time to ask the great question. *How can a man fly?*

No one could answer him. It was always the wrong place. The wrong people.

He gave up on centers of learning and sought out hermits, wise beggars, teachers who had abandoned teaching and lived in caves, or slept in doorways of buildings they scorned to enter. He located a sorceress who had found the Secret of Endings when she was five years old and made sure never to get any older. He met an old man who limped every day through the dirty streets of a grand city, collecting scraps of cloth and paper which he endlessly arranged and rearranged, for each configuration, he said, described a different way the world might die, and each time he created such images and then destroyed them, he was closing the door on another calamity.

But as with the scholars in the libraries, no one could help him.

If all these places were wrong, he decided, then maybe the right place was somewhere older than the Wise and all their traditions. He began to trace his way through forests and rivers, deserts and mountains, searching for the oldest tribe, the truest teachings. He followed stories and rumors, moving from one tribe to another. He watched ceremonies where people danced with drums, dressed in long carved masks and layers of cloth, all to invite the First Ancestors to enter their bodies. When he stood up in the dance, however, and demanded that these leaping, howling spirits teach him to fly, they were as useless as the wizards and scholars.

Chapter Thirty-One

SIMON

They arrived at the Institute on a cloudy afternoon. The sky pressed the long stone building into the earth. It reminded Simon a little of his school. Like the school, the Institute had pearly gray walls and a clock tower rising above the second story, with a lawn and scattered trees in front, and what looked like a wood behind it. Maybe it was supposed to look reassuring. Like going to a new school. It didn't work. Simon just stared at it and sank down into his seat. Dr. Reina came and opened the door for him. "You may leave your backpack and suitcase in the car," Dr. Reina said. "Someone will bring them to your room."

As they walked toward the entrance, wide wooden doors with brass handles, Simon wondered where everybody was. Where were the other children, the doctors and nurses? The wide lawn, the flowers along the front of the building, the oak and silver birches along the sides—they all looked cared for yet somehow ragged, as if the woods behind the building would rise up and reclaim the land and the Institute at any moment. And everything was silent.

Inside looked nothing like school. It was more open and fancier, with wide windows, black and white tiled floors and ivory-painted walls, with occasional carved chairs or small marble statues of children standing or running. The whole place appeared to be very nice, yet at the same time cold and kind of *slippery*. The statues—they all looked happy at first, but if you looked closer they seemed scared, or maybe desperate. "Where are all the other kids?" Simon asked.

Dr. Reina nodded. "A good question. Now I will tell you a secret." He smiled, with what Simon guessed was supposed to be reassurance "You, Simon, are the only one here. Do you see now that you are very special?"

"I don't understand."

"I wish to give you my full attention. And so I have sent home all my other cases." He bent toward Simon, who had to fight not to run, because really, where could he go? The doctor's teeth were so white they glowed, but there were dark spots, as if he'd brushed and brushed but couldn't remove old stains. Simon couldn't stop staring at them. The ones at the back looked chipped.

The doctor said, "I have even sent home the other doctors and the nurses. It will be just you and me, working together to make all the bad dreams and bad feelings disappear." He spread wide his fingers like a magician releasing a bird. "Gone forever. Do you see?"

Simon didn't answer.

Simon's room was large, slightly bigger than his dad's bedroom at home, but simple where the hotel rooms had been fancy. There was a wooden bed covered with a green bedspread, an oak desk with nothing on it and a high-backed plain wooden chair. There was a small bathroom off to the side. There was so little in the room, just those few pieces of furniture, no telephone, computer or television. Simon wondered what he was supposed to do here. Stare out of the window at the lawn and trees off in the distance? The room's only decoration was a painting in a gold frame. About two feet high, it showed a pair of trees, one with long white flowers that looked about to burst, the other with blackened leaves on droopy branches. Simon couldn't help staring at it. He did his best not to look at the dead leaves and see only the bright flowers. Except, as he held his eyes on them, the flowers looked over-ripe, almost diseased. He made himself turn away.

"Can I call my dad?" he asked.

"Later," Dr. Reina said. "First you must settle in. Rest. Have dinner. This is very important."

"I want to speak to him. He's going to worry."

Dr. Reina held up a finger. "Simon," he said, "your father has given you to me. You must follow and do what I say so that healing will come."

"When can I call him?"

"We will see tomorrow. And that is all we will say about it for now." When he smiled, this time the white teeth reminded Simon of the flowers, the ones on the edge of rotting. "Now, you must be hungry," the doctor said. "Rest, please, and in a little while we will eat." He left the room and closed the door behind him.

As soon as he was alone, Simon took out his cell phone to try to call his father. "No signal" read a box, and below it a picture of an old-fashioned table phone had a red X over it.

He tried to open the window but it wouldn't move. Could he break it with the chair? It was the ground floor, he could just climb out, run for it. But where would he go? He started to cry. *No*, he told himself, and wiped his eyes. Crying like a baby wasn't going to help. He needed to pay attention. That's what his mother had said. Pay attention and not eat anything.

He lay on the bed, trying not to cry, until Dr. Reina returned, now dressed in a white suit. "Come, Simon," the doctor said, "it is time to eat." At that moment, Simon discovered he was terribly hungry. He jumped up, filled with desire for fried chicken or hamburgers or ice cream. Or chocolate cake! Wouldn't it be wonderful to eat a big, thick slice of cake? He'd gone *days* without eating—wasn't that enough?

Simon followed Dr. Reina down a long corridor lined with statues. Children again, in odd poses, about to jump, crouched down, reaching for something. Simon ignored them, drawn by the smells of hot food. The dining room was large, with big windows overlooking the lawn, and several long tables with red-lacquered wooden chairs. Simon looked only at the table in the center, for it was filled with everything he wanted— chicken and cheeseburgers and hot dogs and ice cream and the biggest, gooiest slice of cake he'd ever seen. He felt a surge of happiness and would have hugged Dr. Reina if he hadn't wanted to start eating right away. Dr. Reina said, "It's all for you, Simon. Special, just for you."

Simon was about to pile food on his plate when suddenly he heard a soft whisper inside his head. It said:

Simon, Simon,
Rhymin' Simon,
Take the time an'
Stop the crime an'
Set the children free.

But I'm so hungry. I'll be sick if I don't eat something.

"Pay attention," the voice said. "Do not eat or drink. Not anything."

Simon put his hands under the table and clenched his fists. His body shook a little as he said, "I'm sorry. I don't think I'm very hungry right now."

Dr. Reina stared at him with a look that made Simon turn away. "Not hungry? After so long a journey? And eating so little on the way? This is foolishness, Simon. I have tolerated your refusals while we were on our travels. But now we are arrived. We must be serious. We cannot begin your cure if you refuse to eat. Your father will be very disappointed in you."

Though delicious smells filled Simon's whole body, he said, "No, thank you. I'm not hungry." As soon as he said the words he discovered it was true. The hunger had vanished, and now the smells disgusted him.

Dr. Reina pointed a finger at him. "You must eat."

Right then, Simon heard a scratching noise at the window. He looked and almost shouted with joy. The squirrels were there. They stood on the windowsill and clawed the glass as if they were trying to break in. *She sent them*, he thought. His mother.

Dr. Reina was furious. "Get away!" he shouted, and swept his arm across his body. The squirrels continued to *tap-tap* at the window. Dr. Reina opened the window to grab them, but they only ran to the next sill. He rushed to the doorway. "Stay here," he ordered Simon. "I will chase away these pests. It is your father's wish. And it is his wish also that you eat, so you can make yourself strong." He ran down the hall.

Simon dashed to the window and was about to climb out when a soft voice said inside him, "No, you cannot escape that way." When he looked at the squirrels, the red one nodded. The voice said, "Use your napkin to put some food on your plate, then drop it out of the window. Make sure you don't touch it."

With the white cloth napkin, Simon grabbed a chicken wing, a cheeseburger and a hot dog. Even through the cloth the touch made Simon feel a little sick. He thought of the pieces of children from his dreams, the fingers and tongues. "No," the voice said, "this is not them. But nothing here is what it appears to be. Hurry." When Simon had dropped the food out of the window, the voice said, "Now pour some of the drink into your glass, then out of the window. Don't let a drop touch you." There was a large pitcher on the table filled with red fruit juice. Very carefully Simon poured some into his glass then walked it to the window and spilled it out.

He was just back in his seat when he saw Dr. Reina come around the side of the building, shouting something Simon couldn't understand. The squirrels ran away while Dr. Reina shook his fist.

When the doctor returned a minute later, Simon was at his place, his hands folded neatly on the table. Dr. Reina still looked angry, but when he saw that some of the food and juice were gone, he smiled. "Good, good," he said. "You have eaten. Soon we can begin your treatment." Then he narrowed his eyes and looked at Simon, who did not dare to look back. He picked up the plate, stared closely at it, even sniffed it. He did the same with the glass. When the doctor went and looked out through the window, Simon had to fight the desire to run. To his surprise, Dr. Reina smiled happily, then patted Simon's shoulder. "Good boy," he said, and Simon shivered. Dr. Reina said there was nothing more to do that day and sent Simon back to his room.

Chapter Thirty-Two

MATYAS

Matyas kept searching. In a distant, forgotten library, he heard of a place known as the Birth of the World. He set out immediately, across oceans, on a grand ship, and then along rivers and streams in a small, hand-paddled boat made from a dead tree. After that came a desert where he had to dig insects out of the cracked dirt to have anything to eat. Finally he found it, a giant rock so big it would take hours to walk around it. It sat all alone on a flat desert of red sand that blew all over the rock so that it shone like blood in the evening sunlight.

There were paintings on the rock, circles and lines and spirals and dots, so old even Matyas couldn't decipher them. When he tried to trace one of the designs with his finger, his skin became so hot he thought it had burst into flames, but as soon as he pulled his finger away it was fine. That was his right hand. When he tried with the left, his fingertip froze. He smiled, and after that was careful just to look. After he'd seen all the signs at ground level, he found cracks and handholds where he could climb up to the top. The wind flapped his robe around him, and he had to weave a quick shield to avoid being coated in dust that would fix him in place so that future wizards who might come here would think him a statue, or just an extension of the rock.

He closed his eyes to try to speak to the elementals in the rock. All he could hear was a rumble that might have been thunder. Or the growl of some huge animal, as if the rock itself was a sleeping beast. Then he heard a loud buzzing sound, and when he looked again he discovered himself surrounded by men and women sitting in a circle, chanting in a tuneless drone.

Matyas stared at the group, trying to understand how they could have come up here and settled into whatever it was they were doing in the short time he'd had his eyes closed. They were naked, but covered in paintings and scars. Daubs of color, jagged lines, angular boxes and concentric circles all formed some kind of code Matyas could not begin to decipher. So old—and then it struck him. *Maybe they knew the secret!* Maybe he'd finally found the right place. For an instant, excitement made him forget his shield and the wind nearly carried him off the rock, but then he steadied himself.

The people didn't look at him or speak to him, only sat on the rock and continued that nasal drone. Matyas wanted to wait for a chance to speak to them but his head began to hurt, his skin tingled and soon his bones were vibrating so intensely it felt like he was going to break apart.

Savages, he thought. How dare they threaten him? It was some kind of trick to keep him from finding out how to fly. He stared at the paint on their bodies. It was all for show, he decided, ignorant squiggles that didn't mean anything. How could they? There were no sacred names, no sigils, just blotches and lines. Fantasies of ignorant children.

Damn them. His head hurt so much he nearly screamed. He tried to call up fire demons to force them to their feet. Nothing happened. He shouted for lightning. Nothing.

He stared again at the paint on their bodies, trying not to see it as writing or individual symbols but instead as something whole and complete. Then he understood. The lines and blotches were not about flying, they were the history of the Earth. Their chant was the song the world sang to itself when it first awoke. But didn't that mean they would know all the secrets? As so many times before, Matyas felt the pull of knowledge. If he just surrendered his purpose there was so much to learn. He could stay and study with them until he surpassed everyone, even Veil.

No! No more distractions. He focused his eyes on what he hoped was the leader, an ancient woman, short, lumpy, with drooping breasts and layered hips, her face a mass of black stone painted with red and yellow ochre. "You!" he said, and sent a sharp jab of energy directly at her forehead.

If it hurt her, she gave no sign, but she did open her eyes and get to her feet. None of the others took any notice. The woman herself just stared calmly at him.

Matyas opened his mouth before he realized he had no idea of her language. He could gesture, or try to draw a picture, but maybe she understood the Old Tongue, the common language of wizards that Joachim was said to have learned from the plants and stones. He said, "My name is Matyas."

"Yes," she said, her accent surprisingly soft. "I have been waiting for you."

Ridiculous. He knew nothing of her or her strange tribe, so how could she possibly—? She was just trying to impress him, of course. She was no different from Veil, and indeed, when she smiled, it was so slight, and quick, she really did remind him of the old woman hidden away in her tower.

"I want to fly," he said. "Tell me the secret of the True Ladder." The wind blew so hard he could barely hear his own voice.

"I cannot do that," she said.

"You can!" he shouted. "Don't lie to me! Do you want to become part of this rock that you love so much? Do you want to stay here forever? A living statue? Tell me how to fly."

She looked at him for a long time, calm and unafraid, while the chants continued, and all around them blew the red desert wind. Finally she said, "I cannot satisfy your desire. Forgive me. But I can tell you something almost as precious."

Matyas started to say there was nothing else he cared about, but curiosity stopped him. "Tell me," he said. "What is so rare and wonderful that you can compare it to the one thing everyone hides from me?"

"The name of the Child Eater."

His mouth opened so wide bits of sand flew into it and he had to spit them out on the rock. Finally he laughed. "No one can possibly know that. He removed it from the world."

Her head moved from side to side on her wattled neck. "No. Buried, not removed. If he removed his name, he would have destroyed his power. His knowledge. And then he could no longer perform the Spell of Extension."

Matyas thought back to when Veil told him about the spell, and Joachim's *other* disciple. What were her actual words? *He buried his name inside a great red rock.*

No, Matyas thought, *it's not possible,* then foolishly stared down at his feet. When he looked up, he worried he'd see the woman laughing at him but her face had hardened, as smooth as if he really had turned her into stone. He said, "Why would I want that? What good is it to me?" She didn't answer, didn't move, until finally his own mind answered him. Knowledge. Truth. Things he'd come to love just for themselves. "Tell me, then," he said. "What is it? Tell me the name of the Child Eater."

"His name is Federaynak."

For a moment Matyas held his breath, as if the sky would open, or the rock pour forth demons. When nothing appeared to have changed, he began to laugh, only stopping when the rock shifted under him and he nearly fell off. No, it wasn't the rock, of course not, it was just a wave of dizziness. He was fine now. He squinted at the old woman. Was she laughing at his clumsiness? No, she just stood there, dumb and stolid, her dense hair and black face lit up by the afternoon sun. What was going on?

Images flooded him, words, histories. He could hardly see as everything whirled around him. The Spell of Forgetting! Veil had said there was a spell all around the history of the Child Eater to keep people from remembering whatever they might learn about him, but she was wrong. It wasn't a spell at all, it was just an effect. From when he hid his name from the world. When he buried his name, he buried his history. And now Matyas could see it, all of it. All the murdered children, their screams, their terror, the stone knife rising and falling, over and over and over.

"Stop it!" he cried, and fell to his knees before the unmoving woman, who just stared at him. Matyas heard again the voices, the long-ago prophecy. Not the part he'd obsessed over all this time, where it said he could fly, but the second part.

Or will you try as
Ancients cry, as
Children die, as
No one dares to talk?

Was *that* why he'd come here? Not to fly but to stop the Child Eater? He had no idea what he could do, but he had the name and that must mean something or why would *Federaynak* hide it?

But what did it have to do with him? Why did *he* have to be the one? The woman knew it, didn't she? Why didn't *she* stop him? Why should Master Matyas give up his life, his destiny? He stood up now, stared back into her mountain range of a face. For it was clear to him that it had to be one or the other, fly or fight Federaynak. Wasn't that what the prophecy said? "*Or* will you try." He could choose.

And after all, what did the Child Eater have to do with him? For hundreds of years the great Masters in all the Colleges and Academies and hermitages had allowed themselves to forget as they pursued their own knowledge, their power. He took a step toward the woman, but if he'd hoped she might step back, frightened, he was disappointed. "Why me?" he said. "Why should I have to give up everything?"

She spoke so softly the wind nearly carried her words away before they could reach him. "You found the hiding place. You found us."

Yes, Matyas thought. He'd done what no one else could do. Didn't that mean he was better than all of them? "What if I do both?" he said. "Fly, and then fight the Child Eater."

She said, "There are times we may take our desires and times we must choose."

"Exactly! *My* choice. *I* get to choose." And why couldn't flying be the right choice?

They all said no one could fly. All the teachers, all the scrolls, all the books. Even Veil said it, over and over. If he could show them they were wrong, didn't that give the world something just as valuable? And suppose he sacrificed his own deepest purpose and *tried* to stop the Child Eater—and couldn't? What good would he have done? If the Creator Herself had to accept that She could not create a world without the Spell of Extension, how could one wizard, even the greatest of them, imagine he could put a stop to it? All he knew was a name. Maybe once he left the rock he would forget again, just like everyone else. And if this stone woman did tell him the secret of flying, would he forget that as well? Tricks. Too many tricks.

Suddenly he almost laughed. Why should he think about the Child Eater at all? He wasn't a child anymore, *it had nothing to do with him*. The whole thing was just another excuse to keep him from finding out how to fly.

When he was sure he could control his desire to burst out laughing, he told the woman, "You said I could choose. So this is my choice. I don't care about the Child Eater. Do you hear me? He has nothing to do with me. I only care about flying. *That's* my choice."

The woman closed her eyes a moment, and when she opened them again Matyas was astonished to see she was crying. In a gentler voice than Matyas would have believed possible for her, she said, "Then there is nothing I can give you."

"I don't believe you. Teach me the True Ladder." She said nothing, and her silence seemed to make the drone louder all about them. Matyas wanted to walk around the circle and slap their blank faces, one after another. Or maybe just cast a silence spell to freeze their vocal cords. Instead, he turned back to the woman and said, "If this is the wrong place, send me to the right place. Send me where I can get what I want. Now!"

Still no answer. Furious at ancient women who refused to tell him what he needed to know, Matyas stepped toward her, his hand raised. As he got closer, the colors on her body began to shift, move together, flow into forms. Matyas felt dizzy, sick. Another step and he no longer saw a human form at all, but a picture of a garden, with bright flowers and a waterfall. One more step and he was staring at grass, surrounded by poppies and calla lilies. Sweet perfume ran through his body, mist from the waterfall moistened his face and arms which had become dry and cracked in the desert winds.

Matyas lost his balance and fell against a tree. Confused, he stared all around him. There were actually two trees among the flowers, very old and bent. Where was he? How had he got here? He squeezed his eyes shut, tried to think. He'd been traveling. A long way, a long time. There was something he was supposed to remember. Something he was supposed to do.

When he stood up again, a naked boy and girl were looking at him. The boy had golden hair, the girl silver. "Who are you?" the boy said. "What are you doing here?"

Matyas ignored him. He looked around, sniffed the air so light and sweet, stared up at a sky that was layers of color and light. "I know what this is," he said. Florian, his great Master, had written about this. She'd come here. Florian, and Joachim himself, and . . . and the other one. They'd come in a group, as if it needed all three of them, but now Matyas had come by himself.

He smiled at the two trees that looked like grand old dames at a manor house. "Those two," he said, "they're called the Tree of Constancy and the Tree of Variance, yes? Am I right?" The children said nothing. "And this place," Matyas said, "it's where Joachim and the first wizards came, when they changed the world. This is the Garden of Origins."

The children backed away a step, and Matyas thrilled at the fear in their faces. "Yes. You didn't think anyone would ever find you again, did you? You thought you could hide here and be safe. But I found you. You're the Guardians. The ones who didn't leave. The Day and the Night. The Sun and the Moon."

The boy said, "We don't know who you are but you don't belong here. You have to go."

Matyas stood up straight, nearly twice as tall as the children. "I am Master Matyas!" he cried out. "I have traveled the world, I have searched out its mysteries. And now I have come to learn how to fly. *I will not be refused.*"

"No," the girl said. "That isn't possible."

"Don't lie to me. I am sick of lies." He began to pace back and forth, like an impatient wolf. "You don't have any choice. I've penetrated your secrets, just like Joachim did. You can't refuse me."

The boy said, "We cannot give you what we don't have."

"I told you! No more lies." Matyas pointed a quivering finger at him. "No more great powers telling me what they can't do for me. Do you have any idea what *I* can do? I am Master Matyas!"

"Please," the girl said, "if you know what this place is, and who we are, then you must know that what we do is important. Please don't disrupt that."

He looked up and down her flat, hairless body, smiled as she winced and turned her head. "Don't think you're so valuable. Or pure. Do you think no one knows what you two really do with each other? Do you think the world still needs you? The wizards broke you. We took away your power. I could kill you and the Sun would still get up and fall down, the Moon would still grow and die and grow again. No one needs you anymore. Don't you know that?

"Joachim knew he couldn't trust you, so he created laws. The world runs on geometry and numbers now, remember? Not games and stories. You're only good for one thing now. To teach me to fly."

"I'm sorry," the girl whispered. "We can't do that."

"Then you don't deserve to live."

The boy fell to his knees, held up his hands, palms forward. "Take me," he said. "Let my sister go."

Matyas laughed. "Aren't you afraid you'll unbalance the world? Take the sun away? Or make the Moon too ashamed to show her face? *Teach me to fly.*"

The girl said, "We cannot give you what we cannot give you."

"Don't tell me that! That's what Veil told you to say, isn't it? You think I don't know? You were there that night. In the courtyard. You and . . . and the trees." He could see it again, himself at the window, Veil far below, and all the buildings gone, replaced by the trees, the children—the Guardians. He didn't understand then. He let himself forget. Not this time. "She told you to lie to me, didn't she?"

"No," the boy whispered. "It wasn't about that."

"Liar! *Teach me to fly.*"

"We cannot."

"Stop lying. I'm so sick of lies."

Matyas looked around wildly. He saw the two trees, bent, as if they hoped he wouldn't notice them. He jabbed his right arm straight out, first at one, then the other. Power surged through him, fire and ice.

"Please," the boy said, "you don't know what you're doing."

"I know exactly what I'm doing." Now he raised his left arm, and pointed the first and last fingers at the sky, with the other fingers and the thumb turned into the palm. Colored fire ran between the extended fingers.

The boy and girl hugged each other. They looked at each other and cried, and then their faces moved closer and they began to kiss. Light and dark shimmered up and down their bodies.

"Well, well, your true selves," Matyas said. It was time to punish them, at long last, time to punish everyone who'd refused him. And yet as he watched them, he knew he couldn't kill them, though he had no idea why. They deserved to die. Even after what Joachim had done, they still thought themselves superior to a lowly human. He should kill them and free the world from the Guardians once and for all. But he couldn't do it.

His body shook with the energy built up in his hand. What should he do? A thought came to him. Of course! They weren't worth death. He should just do to them what village witches do to bratty children who steal a taste from the cauldron.

He lowered his hand. The fire leaped from his fingers to flood the boy and girl, who cried out—and in their place a pair of green and black toads gulped the air! Matyas laughed, gestured again, and the frogs changed into swans frantically waving their wings. Again and again he changed them, goats, hedgehogs, foxes, until finally it all began to bore him. Something trivial, he thought, something . . . He had it! Laughing wildly, he moved his hand elaborately through the air, and then, with a final gesture he turned them into . . . squirrels. "Stay that way," he said. "Stay forever." Then he walked away.

He found himself at the foot of a mountain. Confused, he looked up at dark, tangled trees, then down at dead grass all around his feet. Wasn't he just in a garden? A queasiness ran through him. He could hardly stand. He needed food, he told himself. That's all it was, this strange state, he just needed something to eat. That and a place to rest. In the valley below the mountain, he could see a town. He started to walk toward it, though he could not gauge how far away it was.

His legs hurt and he limped slightly. Wasn't there some way to move more quickly? He couldn't remember. If only he could fly. He smiled at the thought. What a wonderful idea. What would it be like to just open your arms and lift up into the air? A lot less painful than walking!

The Sun set and it grew cold. He looked down at the thin, useless robe he was wearing. Why didn't he have something warmer? He made a face at the designs that filled the fabric. There were pictures—a tree, snakes—and a bunch of lines and curls that made no sense to him. Maybe they were some kind of writing. He made a noise. What use would that be to *him*? How would *he* ever learn to read?

Below the mountain, the town lit up with hearth fires and torches. He longed to be there, where he hoped some kind person would take him in. But it was too far away for him to reach it that night, so he piled up leaves against an old tree and hoped the animals would leave him alone.

Chapter Thirty-Three

SIMON

Simon sat in the chair or walked back and forth or lay on the bed. Every few minutes, he looked out of the window to see if he could spot the squirrels, but there were never any there. "I want to go home," he whispered. "Please, please, can't I just go home?" He tried again to call his father, and when the cell told him once more "No service," he threw it at the wall. It bounced off and landed on the bed where Simon ran to pick it up and make sure his dumb act hadn't damaged it. When he saw that it was okay (though still without service), he squeezed it in his right hand like some kind of magic talisman. A talisman that might work if he just trusted it.

When night came, Simon put on his pajamas and got into bed. He didn't dare to wash his face or brush his teeth for fear he would swallow something.

He began to feel sleepy, and even though he was scared of what he might dream, he thought how sleep would at least take him away for a while. Then he remembered his mother telling him to pay attention. He shook his head, and just as the hunger had vanished earlier, so now did his tiredness. He lay in bed and waited. At home he sometimes lay awake for hours, scared of his dreams. He listened to the wind in the leaves outside his window, or occasional cars, or the furnace or water heater in the basement going on and off. Here there was nothing.

No. There was a sound, very faint: crying. Crying children. At first Simon wasn't sure he heard it, and then, when it became unmistakable, his first impulse was to cover his ears, make a noise. Sing, something, anything to block it out. But then he made himself take his hands away, made himself listen. Pay attention. What should he do? He went to the door, reached out to open it, then pulled back his hand. What if something terrible was waiting on the other side? He imagined seeing the hallway littered with fingers, bones, the pieces of children he saw in his dreams. But this wasn't a dream, was it? If you wondered if it was a dream, then you weren't dreaming.

He was just reaching for the handle again when the noises stopped. Shaking, Simon listened for a long time before he let himself go back and sit on the bed.

It was difficult to keep track of time here, but after what felt like hours, he became sleepy once more, unable to keep his eyes open. Just as the sky was getting brighter, Simon slept.

He woke to daylight but no sense of how much time had passed. Panicked, he jumped up to see if anything had happened, if he'd missed something by letting himself sleep. Pay attention, his mother had told him, that was all he had to do, and he'd blown it! But when he glanced around the bedroom, and out of the window, everything looked the same. *It's okay*, he told himself. *I didn't do anything wrong.*

He had just got dressed when Dr. Reina opened the door. "At last you're awake," the doctor said. "You were very tired, I think, to sleep so long, almost the whole day." Simon glanced out of the window again. Was it really that late? Dr. Reina said, "You must be very hungry."

Just as the day before, Simon thought he would fall down if he didn't eat something. How could he be so foolish as to go days without food? What if he was too weak to pay attention? Wouldn't his mom want him to keep his strength up? When they came to the dining room and he saw watermelon and cookies and macaroni and cheese and barbecued steak, he wanted to grab all of it at once. It looked so wonderful! And the smell!

But just as the day before, he made himself sit and say, "No, thank you. I'm not hungry," and the hunger immediately vanished, replaced by disgust at the piles of food, the odor which now smelled more like decay, as if everything had suddenly turned rotten.

"You must eat," Dr. Reina said, and leaned forward so that his face appeared to float inches away from Simon's eyes. "You eat and become well." Then, just as the day before, the squirrels appeared, and Dr. Reina, enraged, ran to chase them away. Simon put food on his plate, filled his glass, then dropped it all out of the window. When he looked down to see if the food had disappeared or the ground had covered it, it just lay there. Yet when Dr. Reina looked, he once again nodded his satisfaction.

That night the crying was louder. Simon tried to ignore it, or cover his ears, but it beat at him. What did that poem say? *Take the time and stop the crime. Set the children free.* But how? Simon was just a kid. What could he do? Just as the night before, he put his hands over his ears, but this time it didn't work; the noise only grew louder. Finally he got off the bed and put on the moccasins his father had bought him for the trip and stepped into the hallway.

No horrible pieces of children littered the clean carpet. It all looked the same as during the day. Trying to move toward the sound, and at the same time check that Dr. Reina wouldn't catch him, Simon made his way through the building.

The house confused him. There were so many turns and corridors, all hazily lit, although he couldn't see any lamps. He kept rehearsing in his mind what he would do if Dr. Reina jumped out at him. Run? Better to have some excuse ready. He thought of sleepwalking, or just curiosity, or even saying he'd heard someone and wanted to check who it was. But none of them were necessary. Wherever the doctor was, he apparently paid no attention to the sad cries that filled his empty hospital.

At the top of a flight of stairs, Simon came to a room with a dark red door. When he touched the handle it was very hot and he jerked his hand away twice before he could open it. Inside, instead of a hurt child, he saw only rows of what looked like very old wooden stands, each with a stack of small papers on top—no, not papers. Cards. Despite the urgent cries that still surrounded him, Simon could not resist going closer. Yes, they were Tarot cards. A whole roomful of them. He reached out for the nearest pack.

And stopped. Something about it felt wrong, even more scary than the poisonous food. He stood there for what felt like a very long time. Finally he dropped his arm and looked closer without touching. The top card on each pack was the Fool, his favorite, the one he always thought of as the Beautiful Boy about to Fly even after he found out its true name.

On each one the head had been cut out, slashed away with a jagged pair of scissors or a knife.

Simon ran from the room so fast he nearly tumbled down the stairs. If someone had asked him why it scared him so much he couldn't have answered, but he knew he had to get out of there. On the ground floor, he discovered he could find his way back to his room as easily as if he'd left a trail of breadcrumbs. When he lay down, he discovered that the crying had stopped, and gratitude surged through him. It was okay, there'd been nothing he could do anyway. It was okay to go back to his room. But as soon as he closed his eyes, he immediately saw those cards with the heads cut out so savagely a wild beast might have attacked them. *I want to go home*, he thought to himself, *I just want to go home*.

The third day was a repeat of the others. Simon wondered how Dr. Reina let himself get tricked like that—the thrown-out food was right there, right under the window. But really, Simon didn't care. He was just hoping he could do whatever it was he needed to do and go home.

That night the crying was worse than ever. Simon got straight out of bed and tried to follow the sound. He came to the room with the Tarot cards and kept going. At what felt like the very top of the house, he saw a door as dark blue as the other was red. The crying was so loud here that Simon's whole body shook, and he was scared he might break apart just from the sound. He stared at the door a long time before he reached for the handle. It was cold, colder than the red had been hot, but he managed to get it open.

At first he thought the room was empty. It was dark, lit only by the light from the stairs, but Simon couldn't see any furniture inside, let alone crying children. When his eyes adjusted to the dimness, he saw in the center of the room a single metal stand, dark and plain. It stood about as high as a grown-up, and on top of it was something like a ball. Simon stared and stared at it, while his mind yelled at him, *Run, get away*.

Then he cried out, for he realized—or just admitted to himself—that the thing on top of the column wasn't a ball. It was a head. A child's head.

Simon cried out again, just a noise. Right then the weeping stopped. Simon almost fell, for he'd been bracing himself against the sound as if against a powerful wind. But who had been crying like that? It couldn't have been the head—it was dead, and murdered children don't make any noises. Suddenly he thought of Eli, the kid who'd disappeared, and how he'd called out to Simon for days, until suddenly the voice in his head just stopped and Simon had known it was over. He looked around. "Hello?" he called.

"It's you," a voice said. "You're next, aren't you?" The voice was young and old at the same time, and sadder even than when it was crying.

Simon looked around again but he knew now he wouldn't see anyone. Any *body*. He walked up to the head. Like the voice it was old and young, the features those of a girl about Simon's age, yet with wrinkled, cracked skin. There were marks on the cheeks and a dark smudge like a burn on the forehead. Somehow she looked familiar and Simon wondered if he'd dreamed about her, or was it just that he dreamed about so many? He said, "Who are you?" It felt safer than anything else he might ask.

"I thought I might be the last," the head told him. "I'm almost done, and I hoped, I hoped so much—I don't know why, I guess I just wanted to hope that somehow I would be the last one. That maybe he wouldn't find another one. That it would be over, finally, finally."

"What would be over?"

"This. What he does to us."

"I don't understand," Simon said, though he was terribly scared that he did. "Do you have a name?"

"I think I was named Caroline. It was a long time ago, I think. You see? I'm almost finished."

"I'm Simon."

The head—Caroline—made a noise, then squinted at him. "There's an old poem." Softly she recited, "Simon, Simon . . ." The voice trailed off.

"I know that one," Simon said. "My mother said it. I think it was my mother. It was kind of in a dream." He didn't recite the rest of it.

"Come closer," Caroline said. "I want to look at you." Simon hesitated, then walked up. "Is it possible?" Caroline said. "Do you have protection?"

Protection. Maybe, even with whatever terrible thing was going to happen, he was safe. Then, suddenly, Caroline began to wail and Simon realized there would be no safety.

"Oh no, no," Caroline said, "there's a hole in the shield. Someone—a woman—tried to protect you. When you were a baby. She knew, she knew. But she wasn't able to finish. Some stupid person stopped her! Your foot—she didn't manage to protect your foot. He can get you that way. As long as there's an opening. Now nothing can stop it."

Simon didn't want to ask but he couldn't keep it in. "Stop what? What's going to happen to me?" *Will he cut off my head? Will he make me like you?*

"I'm getting old," Caroline said. "I'm wearing out. Tell me, does Reina seem at all weak to you?"

"Doctor Reina?"

"Doctor. Yes, that's a title he would use. Have you seen any weakness?"

"No. Well, maybe. Not really weak, you know, but he sort of misses things." Simon told Caroline about throwing the food out of the window and Dr. Reina not seeing it.

"You didn't eat anything? Or drink?"

"No. Nothing. I was really hungry but then it went away."

"Oh, thank God," Caroline said. "Then you still have a chance. Listen to me, Simon. Whatever that food looked like, it wasn't real. Reina feeds you pieces of himself. His body. And if you take any of it you belong to him."

"I didn't!" Simon said. "I didn't even touch it."

Caroline didn't seem to hear. Her eyes flickered and she spoke softly, with a shake in her voice, "Then he comes to you. With that stone knife. Oh God. He cuts and cuts, a piece at a time, until there's nothing left but your head! And then he writes things on your face, and oh God, the last thing is the picture. He cuts it and burns it into your forehead."

The Fool, Simon thought. That was why all the Tarot decks had the faces cut out of the Fool! Sickness came over him and he almost fell. "I want to go home," he said. He started to cry. He was trying to be strong, but it was all so scary and worse even than any of his dreams.

"You can't," Caroline said. "None of us can. You're on the other side now."

"Why? Why does he do this? Who is he?"

"He used to be a man. Many centuries ago. Then he discovered the great secret. He could live forever if he created the heads."

"Then why does he need me? If he's already got you." Maybe Dr. Reina would let Simon go if he realized he still had Caroline.

"I'm weakening, and so *he's* weakening. That's why you were able to trick him. My time is almost up and he needs a replacement."

"I'm sorry," Simon whispered.

"No, no, no. I want to end. Finally. But you! You must save yourself, Simon. If you can keep him from taking you, *he* will finally end. So many years, so many children. And we're the special ones. He takes others, devours them, just because . . . because he can. But we're the special ones, the ones who keep him alive."

"What do I do?"

"I don't know. No one has ever escaped him. Ever."

"I'll run away. I'll climb out through the window or something. I just have to get to where my phone works and then I can call my dad."

"You don't understand. This is not really a place. It's hard to describe. It's his world."

"No!" Simon said. "You're lying. You just don't want me to get away because you never could. I'm going and you can't stop me." He ran for the door. He just had to reach his dad. His dad would send the police or something.

Behind him he heard Caroline's sad whisper: "Go, Simon. Maybe you can do it."

Simon turned around. "I know you," he said. "I mean, I've met you. Before I came here. But you were old." He could see her so clearly now. The old woman sitting all alone in the attic that wasn't really there. Just a dream, his dad had said, but it wasn't, it was Caroline!

Caroline's eyes opened wide. "I don't know," she said. "Maybe . . . maybe that was who I was, who I would have been. If Reina hadn't caught me. If I'd been allowed to live and grow old." She began to cry now. "Go!" she said suddenly. "Run!"

Simon ran down the stairs so fast he hit the walls of the stairwell four times on his way to the ground floor. *Out. Get out. Get to the woods. Find a place where the phone works. Call Daddy.*

He hit the front door and fell back, then got up and fumbled it open. *Go, go*, he told himself. Then he was outside the house and he just had to keep going, run for the woods. It was daylight, how did it get to be daylight? He couldn't think about that. There were the trees, they looked a couple of football fields away. His sneakers slapped the dirt, faster and faster.

"Simon!" Dr. Reina's voice filled the sky, shook the ground. "*It is time for you to begin your treatment.*"

Simon couldn't help it. He had to see. He turned and there was Dr. Reina, in his white suit, his face bright and his hair sparkly. In his left hand, loose at his side, he carried a gray stone knife. It looked very, very old. The sun flickered off red spots along the blade. Dried blood. Caroline's blood. The blood of all the children over so many years.

"Come, Simon," Dr. Reina boomed out. "Soon we will make you a healthy boy."

Simon ran for the woods.

Chapter Thirty-Four

MATYAS

He dreamed he was walking in a withered garden, past a pair of bent and broken trees. Something had happened to them, he knew, but he could not seem to remember what that was. They looked abandoned, lonely. In the dream, he was called Matyas, and that felt important somehow, something to hold on to when he woke up. "Remember," he told himself, and immediately thought, *Remember what?* The name, yes.

At the far end of the garden, he saw a stone house, long and gray, with wide windows and a red door. He walked toward it, something that for some reason felt both very difficult and important. As he got closer, he saw a tall man in front of the doorway. The man wore a white tunic and pants, and red boots. His gray-brown hair was brushed back and his face was bright and strong, the eyes shiny, the teeth sharp and gleaming. His right hand held a stone knife pointed at the dirt. It was dripping blood onto some shapeless object at the man's feet.

Matyas stared at him, terrified. He had never seen this man before but he knew who he was. How could he not? He'd known him all his life, seen him in dreams. He'd tried to forget him but could never quite do it.

"Ah, it's you," the Child Eater said.

Matyas made a noise and tried to back away, but the hand with the knife waved him closer. "There's no need to run," the Child Eater said. "You can't do anything to me, and I won't hurt you."

Against his will, Matyas stepped closer. Now he saw what the object on the ground was—a boy, ten or eleven years old. He looked emptied out, with no life, no trace of life in the crumpled mass. And yet, Matyas thought he knew him, recognized what was left of him. *Rorin?* he thought.

And then, as Matyas remembered the boy's name, he realized suddenly there was something else he remembered. The name! *He knew the name of the Child Eater!* He could destroy this ancient evil and then he could fly. He'd done it at last. He'd found the right place.

In the dream, Matyas raised his hands, fingers spread wide to gather power. Nothing happened. *It doesn't matter*, he told himself. He had the name. "Federaynak!" he shouted, "I am Master Matyas. I've come to destroy you."

Federaynak laughed. "Why? You're just like me."

He woke up with a cry of pain, though he couldn't remember what caused it. He couldn't seem to remember anything, really, not how he got here or where he was going. In fact, when he thought about it, he discovered he couldn't even remember his own name! He felt like this should bother him much more than it actually did. He didn't know why, but he felt almost a relief about losing his name. There'd been something . . . something he was supposed to do, and now he didn't have to.

The Sun shone without heat, as if the Sun itself couldn't get warm. He stood up all stiff and hungry, with no idea how to find food. Looking down at this strange, green robe he wore, he saw again the lines and squiggles and wondered what they were. Then it struck him and he almost burst out laughing. Writing! He was wearing a robe with writing on it. How did *he* ever come to wear something like this? Suddenly he looked around nervously. Had he stolen it? Were people searching for him? He might have thrown it off and hidden it, except there was nothing else to put on, and he didn't think it was a good idea to walk around naked. He felt around the robe and discovered there were pockets, subtly made so that they were hardly there. Hoping to find some money, he reached inside, but all he came up with were scraps of paper with marks on them—more writing—and some leaves, and an envelope. He opened it, still hoping to discover money, or maybe gold, but all he found was a foul-smelling yellow powder. If it hadn't reeked so badly, he might have tried to sell it, but he couldn't imagine anyone would want it so he threw the envelope away. A little of the powder got onto the heel of his hand and it itched for most of the morning.

He shook his head and sighed. He wasn't going to solve anything just standing here so he began to walk.

He walked for many hours, until he finally came to a city.

It was very large, with grand buildings of all sizes and colors, some with gold roofs, others made of stone or glass or iron. There were simpler houses as well, made of dried mud bricks or wood.

In the center stood a castle and he almost set out in that direction, but then he noticed another structure off to the side, at the top of a steep hill. There was a stone wall with a large gate that he could just make out from so far away, and the elaborate tops of what must have been elegant multi-story buildings. Off to one side, but higher than everything else, stood a simple stone tower whose top was lost in the bright Sun. He discovered he wanted very much to go there. He took a few steps in that direction only to stop. How could he even think of just walking up to something so rich and important? He was only . . . he was nobody. Someone who couldn't even remember his own name.

And besides, he was hungry. He hadn't eaten in . . . a long time. Instead of going to powerful places and presenting himself as if he was some kind of great prince, he should just try to feed himself.

He wandered aimlessly, confused, wondering what to do. When he saw people with food, he asked if he could have a little. Some laughed, as if he'd made a joke, others hurried away, still others looked angry, as if they wanted to say something nasty but didn't dare. He couldn't understand why people would act that way—what had he done to them? He didn't even know them.

As he tried to figure it out, he realized that whatever the reaction, they all appeared to look first at his clothes. Maybe he was someone rich or important! Maybe people were afraid of him. More likely he really had stolen the robe and people knew it. He didn't feel like a thief, but how could he be sure when he couldn't remember anything?

Nevertheless, if his robe really was the problem he should get rid of it. It would be a shame, it was so well made, but it clearly wasn't doing him any good.

When he came to a street with vendors selling old clothes and broken tools from blankets on the ground, he looked around until he spotted an old woman wearing a robe a little like his own. It was much thicker, lumpier, with crude designs, but there was a resemblance, as if . . . as if she had in fact copied the one he was wearing. He became suddenly very frightened. Had people reacted so strangely not just because the robe looked wealthy, but because they actually recognized it? He must have stolen it, because how could someone as worthless as he be wearing a robe that was not only rich but famous? But how had he got it? The horrible thought struck him that he might have killed the original owner. Snuck up on him when he was sleeping, crushed his head with a stone or something. No wonder people were afraid of him! If only he could remember. Could he really have done something so terrible? All he knew was that he had to get rid of it.

"Please," he said to the woman, "would you like to buy this?" He fingered the front of his robe, praying silently she would say yes. "It's like yours," he said, "but nicer." Her eyes narrowed and he was scared he'd insulted her, but she said nothing, just stared at him so long he wondered if she might not speak his language. Finally she held up a few tarnished coins. "Here," she said. She thought a little, then reached over to her neighbor's blanket for a brown tunic and pants. "And this to change into," she said.

He heard laughter as he walked away in his brown clothes but at least he had money. He was very careful with it, buying only the simplest food and eating as little as possible. At night, he slept in alleys or under stars. Vivid dreams troubled him, but he could never remember them when he woke up. At least people had stopped staring at him.

His money ran out just as winter brought the first frost to the city. Now he needed warmth as well as food. All he had for his feet were the sandals he'd been wearing when he came there. He should have told the old woman she had to give him boots along with the money. Maybe if he found her again . . . No, she'd only laugh at him. Sometimes he looked up at the sky and thought how wonderful it would be if he could just fly away, disappear and then come down again somewhere warm and safe.

He tried begging but never seemed to make enough in a day for even the most meager meal, let alone extra for new shoes. There was something about him that made people turn away, even now that he'd got rid of the robe. Oh, he knew he was dirty and smelly, but so were the other beggars. Something in him bothered people, maybe they didn't realize it themselves, but they rushed away as soon as he approached them.

He would have to steal. He didn't want to. The thought of whatever he must have done to whoever had owned the robe made him queasy, and now he was going to steal again. But what choice did he have?

He watched people walk by and wondered how he could knock them out and take their money. When he realized he could never do that, he began to stare at shops closed for the evening or darkened houses. This too he didn't dare. Finally, one evening, almost delirious with hunger, he attempted to pick someone's wallet from his pouch. The man was out with two friends and he stopped to buy a bottle of wine from a street vendor. When the would-be pickpocket saw the tan leather wallet full of coins bounce back into the open bag, he could not help but follow them.

They caught him immediately. The intended victim did nothing, only smiled while the others beat and kicked him and threw him back and forth like a toy. When they left, all he could do was stagger a few feet away, spitting blood, until he fell into a snow bank against the wall of a small inn.

Chapter Thirty-Five

JACK

Jack Wisdom knew something was wrong almost immediately, but it took him three days to admit it. As soon as the car had gone around the corner, he'd wanted to run after it, open the door and pull out his son, before ... before it could swallow him. That was the image that filled his mind, Dr. Reina's Mercedes was like a monster that would gulp down his helpless little boy.

Ridiculous, he told himself. If he seriously thought that Simon was in danger, he wouldn't have let him go, right? If he really thought he'd made a mistake he would get in his car and chase him down, or call the cops, not fantasize a sprint down the block like some character out of a comic book. Separation anxiety, that's all it was. Possessiveness. Maybe he didn't want Simon to get better. Maybe he was scared he'd lose his tight hold on his son. Maybe he was jealous. *Selfish bastard*, he told himself. *Care more about yourself than your own child*. But that wasn't how he felt. How he felt was terrified.

For two days, Jack used anger at himself to ignore the alarm bells that rang up and down his body. The surges of panic that almost doubled him over. The tears that finally caused his boss to tell him to take some time off. The prayers that ran through his mind when he was watching TV or washing dishes. He found himself thinking of that horrible night when Rebecca had tried to kill their baby. Strangely, it wasn't the horror of the fire or his wife's insanity that caught him up, it was the peculiar poem or lullaby she'd been chanting.

Simon, Simon,
Rhymin' Simon,
Take the time an'
Stop the crime an'
Set the children free.

What the hell was that about? And why was he thinking of it now, when he'd forgotten all about it for twelve years?

Strangest of all was the sense that Simon was actually very close. Right in the next room. Just outside the door. On the other side of the wall. As if Reina had not really taken his son, but only hidden Simon in some secret passage, like in an old movie. Jack would wake up in the middle of the night, think, *Simon*, and reach out to touch his son, then gasp with sorrow and fear when there was no one there. *I'm losing my mind*, Jack thought, and told himself he had to pull himself together, for Simon's sake.

On the third day, Jack woke with a certainty that Simon was not only close but in danger. He could almost hear him crying to come home. *Just a dream*, he told himself. Simon was safe. It was hard, but it was for the best . . . They'd all discussed it, Jack and Howard Porter and Dr. Reina. He just needed to trust.

No, he thought. Simon was *not* safe. He was sure of it. What Jack Wisdom needed to trust was himself. He sat up and grabbed the phone.

For two days, Jack had made no attempt to call the Institute. Whenever he thought about it, he told himself that Dr. Reina had asked for no contact in the initial stage of treatment. Now he had to admit that the real reason was fear he might hear exactly what he was hearing now. "The number you have dialed is disconnected or not in service." Jack's hands shook and he had to steady himself to dial again. He tried two more times, then Information in case the number on Dr. Reina's card was out of date or misprinted. No listing. He had the operator check every variation he could think of, as well as other towns in the area. Nothing. "Oh God," Jack said as he hung up the phone. "Oh God. Help me."

He ran to the computer, slammed the keys for the website. No such address. This too he tried over and over, and then used search engines for the Institute or Dr. Reina himself. Nothing. *This is crazy*, he told himself. He'd spent hours reading and rereading everything on that site. The testimonials. The fucking videos! Where were they? Where was Reina's goddamn Institute? *Where was his son?*

He called Howard Porter, asked him for everything he knew about Reina and the Institute. Howard started to speak then stopped himself. "Jesus, Jack," he said. "I don't . . . I don't think I really know anything about him. Jesus Christ."

Jack began to cry. "How could we do this?" he said. "How the hell could we do this?"

"I don't know. It's like I was hypnotized or something."

If Jack hadn't needed Howard so much, he might have wanted to travel through the phone lines and strangle him. Instead he said, "What am I going to do, Howard? That son of a bitch has got Simon. I don't even know what he is, but he's got my little boy."

"I'll be right there," Howard said. "You better call the police."

Jack and Howard Porter spent all day with the police: local, state, FBI and on the phone with the cops in Wisconsin, who knew nothing about Reina or his Institute. In the middle of his panic, Jack worried they would blame him, maybe even charge him with something. He kept expecting them to say, "You gave your son away to some pervert with a fake website and a fancy brochure? What the hell kind of father are you?"

In fact, they were kind, patient and thorough. They were also helpless. There were no files on a Frederick Reina, no information about his supposed Institute. When Jack and Howard worked with the sketch program to come up with a picture, it brought no connections from the state or FBI's lists of pedophiles. There were men who stole children, not for themselves but to sell them, and they checked that, too, including searches of the pedophile websites where predators advertised such things. These sites were heavily guarded, they explained, but their undercover people had infiltrated them. Nothing.

The police managed to track down the organizer of the conference where Howard had met Reina. They too knew nothing, were not even sure how they'd come to invite him to speak. One of the organizers laughed nervously as she talked to the detectives. She said, "I don't know how we could do that—accept a speaker no one really knew anything about. It was like we were hypnotized or something."

After nearly twelve hours, Jack finally allowed the police to fill him with hopeful reassurances and send him home. They told him he should eat, get some rest. *Try not to worry*, they said. They would call him as soon as they had any news.

At home, Jack stared at the telephone. *Any moment*, he told himself. Any moment the phone would ring, and it would be the police, or the FBI, to tell him it was all a mistake. They'd found Simon and he was fine. It would all be okay. *Try not to worry*, the police had said.

Worry! Fuck, worry was what you did when your son's grades went down. This was so far beyond worry—what could he do? He had to do something. He thought of what his mother would tell him to do. Pray. He'd been sitting in the kitchen, and now he walked stiffly to the living room, as if God might appreciate the more formal setting. He got down on his knees alongside the couch, in imitation of how his mother had taught him to kneel by his bed at night. Hands clasped, he said, "Please, God, spare my son. I know I don't deserve your help. I haven't gone to church or anything for years. But please. Not for me, for him. He's just a little boy. Whoever this Doctor Reina really is, don't let him hurt Simon. *Please.*"

He stayed there for a little while, then got up. Who was he fooling? He didn't know how to pray. He'd never really done it, not seriously. Was it even fair to ask God for help after ignoring Him for so long? Should he offer something? Jesus, he thought, he'd already given up his firstborn. What the fuck else could he offer?

In a wild gesture of despair he spun around. His eyes fell upon the photo of Rebecca on the piano. Even in his time of deepest anger he'd never taken it down. He picked it up in both hands, sighed at the memory of her eyes. She was sitting almost formally on the bench he'd put in the back yard in honor of their first meeting, that time in the park. Both feet were on the ground, her hands were in her lap and she was staring right through the camera.

"Bec, Bec," he said. "What have I done? Oh God, Rebecca, I've screwed everything up. I've killed him. I know it, I know it, *I've killed our little boy*. That's what I thought you were going to do, and now *I've* done it. I got it all wrong. I got it all so fucking wrong." Tears gushed from his body. "Help me, Rebecca! Please!"

Exhausted suddenly, he sat down on the sofa with the photo still in his hands. Lights flickered around the picture but he only half noticed them. He didn't think he could sleep, but he closed his eyes and in seconds was gone.

He dreamed he was outside, behind the house, but it also was the lawn of Dr. Frederick Reina's Institute. He could see the huge building, just past the trees, just like in the picture. And then he saw Simon. His son was running toward him, mouth open in terror. Behind Simon stood Dr. Reina, calm and sleek in a white suit. He held something gray and sparkly but Jack couldn't make out what it was.

Jack wanted to call out to Simon, tell him Daddy was coming, but Dr. Reina said, "No, no, Mr. Wisdom, you must not interfere. Simon's treatment has begun." Jack wanted to shout him down but couldn't, for Reina's words had taken on solid form, a syrup that covered Jack's body and filled his mouth. He fell down and couldn't get up, could hardly breathe or see. He would die here. He would suffocate and die, unable to help his son.

It was then that the squirrels appeared. With quick efficiency they gnawed away at the thick coating, first around his eyes and mouth, then his arms and legs—

Jack woke to see Rebecca standing in the living room.

Chapter Thirty-Six

MATYAS

He might have died there, against that wall, with snow all around him, and inside, the sounds of people laughing, warm, safe. Vaguely he thought of entering and asking for help, but what good would that do him? He was a beggar. His whole life he'd been beaten, kicked, thrown out, and now he would die where he belonged. He was ready, he told himself. He'd tried to fight back and he couldn't do it. He'd never had a chance, he was just a child, a helpless boy. It made sense he couldn't remember his name, or anything else about his life. He was nothing. He'd always been nothing. He sat down against the wall, arms wrapped tight around his cold, hurt body.

And yes, he might have died there, alone and broken, except . . . he heard a noise. Weeping. Somewhere nearby someone was crying, a sound so piteous the boy could not seem to shut it out. So he pushed himself to his feet and as best as he could he followed the sound, moving along the wall, around the corner. There he saw a man on the ground, his head in his hands. The man looked old or sick. He might have been burly once, but now his skin sagged, and the muscles along his arms shook like strings as he rocked back and forth. He'd had red hair, apparently, and a thick beard, but now most of his hair had fallen out and his beard had grown irregularly and both looked the color of rust on old metal.

Despite the man's withered shape, he wore a heavy robe and some kind of moth-eaten animal skin thrown over his shoulders. And boots. Warm, fur-lined boots. The boy stared at them, the boots, the cloak. He could just take them and run. The weeping man looked too weak to put up a fight.

Instead, he knelt down and said, "What's wrong? What happened to you?"

The man shook his head. "I can't do it anymore," he said. "I'm finished. I can't do it."

"Do what?" No answer. The boy said, "Maybe you need some rest. Maybe if you go inside they can give you a room." The old man cried out as if in pain, but the boy had no idea why. Awkwardly he put his arm around the man and tried to lift him to his feet.

"No!" the man said, and twisted away.

"It's all right," the boy said.

"You don't understand," the man said. "I slept there last night."

"And what, you made them angry?" The boy thought how he was starting to get pretty angry himself, but he just said, "It doesn't matter. When they see how much you need to be inside they'll have to take you." And what about himself? When did anyone ever take *him* in?

"No, no," the man said. "It's the curse. The spell."

Spell, the boy thought. Was this man some kind of wizard? He scrambled backward, frightened at what the man might do to him. Could wizards read people's minds? Would he know that the boy had wanted to rob him? He looked around, nervous that the man whose wallet he'd tried to steal might come up and denounce him. There was no one there, but he noticed something odd in the snow near the old man. A broken stick lay there, or the remains of one, for it was just a splintered shaft around two feet long. It looked like there had been some kind of red stone attached to the top, but it too was broken now, just a jagged, dull red shard at the end of the wood.

The boy stared at it, then again at the boots, the fur. Maybe he could sell the stone. Keep the boots and the fur. He might even get the robe off and sell that, too. But he looked at the man, slumped over and helpless, and the thought of hurting him, even just leaving him there, made the boy feel sick. He didn't know why. What had this man, this *wizard*, ever done for him? All the great wizards in the world, and none of them had ever protected him.

And yet, he bent down and reached out carefully to touch the man's shoulder. When no lightning bolt of magic knocked him backward he laid his arm more firmly over the ragged fur. "It's all right. I'll take you inside and you'll be safe."

"No! You ignorant, stupid . . . Get out of here. Let me die."

Rage shook the boy. They were all the same, wizards, innkeepers, old women . . . He looked around for a weapon, something to give the old man what he deserved. He saw the broken stick with the jagged stone and grabbed it. A stabbing pain went through him, but only for an instant. The stone seemed to brighten, casting a glow over his hand. Or did the effect come from the swarm of small lights that suddenly had appeared in the air, darting every which way all around him? What a strange sight. If it hadn't been winter, he might have thought they were fireflies.

The man stared, open-mouthed, at the boy, the lights, the boy. In a rough whisper, he said, "How . . . what are you . . . how can you—?" He stopped, only to say a moment later, more loudly, "My God. *It's you.*"

The boy ignored him. He wanted to ask what the man meant—could he possibly know who the boy was?—but he knew he had to go ahead and do whatever he was supposed to be doing. Even though he had no idea what was going on, he felt sure this was his only chance to help the old man. He raised the stick in his left hand with the jewel pointed at the night sky, then reached out to place his right palm on the old man. He tried the forehead first but that felt wrong, and he moved his hand to lay it over the man's heart.

"No," the man said, "you don't know what you're doing. No one can help me. You'll just hurt yourself."

The boy thought he should jerk his hand away, but he didn't move. Instead, he looked at the swarm of lights and whispered, "Please. Help us."

Heat ran through his body, hotter and hotter, and he kept telling himself to drop the stick and run. He didn't move. Suddenly the stone broke, shattered into dust, and in that same instant something heavy and dark lifted from the old man's chest. It hung in the air for less than a second then blew away.

The boy dropped the stick and pitched forward onto his hands and knees. When he'd caught his breath and could look at the old man again, he saw him slumped against the wall and for a moment he was terrified that instead of helping the man he'd killed him. But no, his chest was rising and falling—he was just asleep.

Exhausted, the boy almost lay down next to him, but then all his effort would have been wasted. So he shook the old man awake and said, "Get up. It's time to go inside." The man looked about to object again but all he did was nod and allow the boy to raise him to his feet then lead him to the door.

Inside, the inn was bright with oil lamps, and crowded with travelers and drinkers. They were laughing, arguing, whispering. Over in a corner, a group of men were playing cards, with small stacks of money in front of them, and something about that made the boy—the young man—uneasy, but he ignored the feeling. More important was how people might look at him. Some did glance at the old man held up by the ragged young beggar, but they soon returned to their sausages and beer. The only one to pay any real attention to them was the landlord, a bald, skinny man in a stained apron. "Well," he said to the man, "so you've changed your mind and will stay another night with us after all. Good, good. And you've brought a friend?" He smirked at the young man, taking in his wretched condition but not looking particularly worried. The old man must have money.

The boy—the young man—looked longingly at the plates of food, the fireplace with its eager flames. He turned to the old man, hoping to be invited to stay, but instead the man took his hands and said, "Bless you. May the Creator and all the Guardians bless you forever."

Guilt, like a shock of pain, made the young man pull his hands away. *Guardians*. He'd done something—something terrible . . . The memory slid away from him but it made no difference. The truth remained. He did not deserve a warm fire or food or even the hope to sit quietly among people. He ran outside, back to the snow. Behind him, the old man called, "Wait!" and the innkeeper laughed. He paid no attention.

Now he knew it would be a race for what would kill him first: hunger or cold, or maybe even blood loss, for he was still injured from the beating he'd taken when he tried to steal the wallet. He collapsed into a deep snow bank, hoping he would fall asleep and miss the actual slide into death.

If he'd been hoping for a soft bed, he didn't find it. There was something hard in the snow, just where his head lay. Something small and rectangular, with sharp corners. Groaning, he pushed himself up and stared at it. It looked like a package wrapped in blue cloth, about the width of his hand and not quite as long.

And then he began to shake, and it was not from blood or hunger or cold. He shook as if the world itself was breaking apart. Memory was returning to him, wave upon wave. He knew who he was. Knew what he'd done. He knew why he did not deserve to live. But most of all, he knew what *this* was. He knew it even before he fumbled off the blue wrapping. Before he saw the stack of painted cards. Before he looked at the first picture, a joyous man hanging upside down by one foot over an abyss of light.

He knew who he was. Matyas, the most undeserving of men. And he knew what these cards were. A miracle.

For this was the Tarot of Eternity: the original, painted by Joachim the Blessed thousands of years before Matyas' birth, and hidden from the world for nearly as long.

Matyas clutched the cards against his chest and wept. He wept with all his might and all his heart and all his soul. His blood became tears, the snow became tears, the fires of the city became a river of tears.

There was a saying about these cards, from Joachim himself. Medun had told it to him, long ago, but he'd forgotten it, just as he had forgotten everything important. But now it had come back. *Whosoever touches the Tarot of Eternity, he shall be healed of all his crimes.*

Strength was returning to him now. He knew that no one would harm him and he should rest. It was what the cards wanted, he could feel it. He clutched them tightly against his chest and fell asleep.

He woke to sighs of sorrow. He looked around, only to discover he was sitting at the end of a quiet cul-de-sac of dirt houses. He understood then that it was the Earth's pain he was hearing. This was what Veil heard, he realized. All those times she sat in her chair, hands in her lap, eyes on nothing, she was listening to the world's sadness. He shook his head. How could he not have known that?

He reached into Eternity and pulled out a card. It showed a woman sitting up in bed weeping with her hands over her face. The night sky was behind her, black with pinpoints of stars, and suspended in the air were nine swords, all horizontal and one above the other, like the steps of a ladder. The bottom sword was dark and heavy, a weapon of stone, and then each one became successively lighter, until the last was not a sword at all but a blaze of brightness stroked across the night.

Who is she? he wondered, as if somehow he should know her. It was just a drawing, wasn't it? How could it—? He cried aloud. Of course! It was Florian! All those years he'd studied her works, thought of himself as her greatest disciple, he hadn't understood anything. Her doctrines, her discoveries, all her achievements, they weren't driven by glory, or even just a yearning for wisdom. They came from her deep understanding of the world's pain. What was it she'd put over the Gate of Light leading into the Academy? "Beg the aid of the Masters, for they alone shall help you."

Matyas stared and stared until the bed vanished, and the woman, and only the swords remained, huge before him, a ladder to the sky. A True Ladder, for what was truer than sorrow for the world's suffering? He wrapped up the cards and put them in his waistband, then slowly began to climb, clumsy at first, then with determination, even grace, until he reached the final rung, the beam of light, and stepped off.

He was soaring over the city, wind in his face, trouser legs flapping like flags in a storm before he even realized he was doing it. Flying! He was doing it. At last, after all these years. Down below, the lights and stones of the city ran together, and in the midst of the wind, he could hear human voices, and the chatter of birds. He laughed and his body vaulted upward, he inclined his head and tilted back toward the ground. When he closed his eyes, the air swirled all around him and he could almost believe that he himself did nothing and the world was simply turning beneath him. *So this is it*, he thought. It was never a trick, or a spell, or anything a teacher or a power could give you. It was simply a way of being.

Hovering in the air, he laughed suddenly. Florian had told him he was looking in the wrong place and he'd run across the world searching for the right one. But what she'd meant was any place but inside himself. And the other thing? The one he didn't hear? The wrong time. It could only happen when he was ready.

He laughed again and spun joyously in the air.

Chapter Thirty-Seven

JACK/SIMON

Jack stared, afraid to move or speak. Rebecca was right there, in the room. She wore the purple dress she'd had on when he'd first met her. Her hair shone brightly as it flowed over her shoulders. And it wasn't just her hair—there were lights all around her, her clothes, her face. No, he realized suddenly, she *was* light. A thousand tiny lights, like butterflies, had taken the shape of his beloved Rebecca. "It's just another dream," he whispered, sad now, for that meant he was about to wake up. He'd read that somewhere, when you're dreaming and you realize it you wake up.

"No," Rebecca said, as if she'd heard his thoughts (but that was what she did, wasn't it? She and Simon?). "This is not my body but I am here. The Splendor have given me this gift so that I can talk to you."

"The Splendor?"

"The name for the lights you see. Jack, you must listen to me."

He sat up now. He wanted so much to lie to her, to tell her everything was all right. Instead, he said, "Bec, I've killed him. I killed Simon."

"No! Simon is alive but he needs your help. He is trying to escape Reina right now, but he can't do it without you."

Jack jumped up. "What do I do?"

"He needs the cards and you're the only one who can take them to him."

"You mean the Tarot cards? Oh my God, Bec, I got rid of them."

She shook her head. "No, no, no. The Tarot of Eternity can never be destroyed. Didn't I tell you that?"

"I tore them up. I burned them."

"Please, Jack, you have to listen to me. Whatever you or I did doesn't matter. Only right now matters. Do you understand?"

"Yes."

"Then go around the back of the house. You will see the cards there, wrapped in blue cloth. As soon as you pick them up, you will see Simon. You won't be able to hand him the cards, but you can throw them to him. That is all you have to do. Do you understand?"

"Yes. Yes I do."

"Good. I love you, Jack Wisdom. I love you forever."

"I love you, too," Jack shouted. He was already running for the door.

Outside, it was evening but the sky was bright and red. Had the Sun just set? He couldn't remember what time it was. Jack pushed any such thoughts away as he searched the backyard. There it was, a small blue package lying in the grass. To his amazement, the squirrels were there, standing on either side, like guards.

For a moment, Jack's old fears stopped him. Something in him tried to say, "This is insane," or even, "It's a trick, she's trying to hurt you." *No*, he told himself, the trick was Reina's. He made Jack doubt himself. Doubt Rebecca. Doubt *Simon*. It was as if Reina was whispering in his ear, telling him lies. He'd done it all Jack's life, ever since that day on the baseball field. It was Reina, Frederick Reina, who'd felt all over his head only to say, "You're not ready," and sent him home. Jack had thought he was safe but Reina had never left him. He'd been there all Jack's life, whispering to him, making him doubt.

Instead of freeing Jack, this knowledge just weighed him down. All the terrible mistakes he'd made—turning against Rebecca, giving Simon to the monster—they'd all come about because of Reina. How could Jack hope to beat him?

And then something rose up in Jack. This wasn't about him anymore, it was about Simon. That's what Reina had meant when he'd said Jack wasn't ready. He was waiting for Simon.

"You son of a bitch!" he shouted. "You can't have him!"

Jack Wisdom picked up the cards and the sky caught fire.

He screamed and jumped back. A wall of flame had appeared in front of him but he was okay, he wasn't hurt.

He squinted into the blaze. He could see shapes on the other side . . . Simon was there! His precious boy was running right toward him. Only . . . Simon was running with all his might but he couldn't seem to get any closer. Behind Simon, Dr. Frederick Reina walked slowly forward, gaining on the boy with every step. Reina was smiling, and in his right hand he held a stone knife.

Through the fire, Jack called, "Simon!"

"Daddy," Simon cried, "help me!"

Jack didn't know what to do. He tried again to get through the fire but the heat pushed him back. If he tried to throw Simon the cards, would flames burn them up? *Trust Rebecca*, he told himself. *The Tarot of Eternity can never be destroyed*. He hurled the package toward his son.

Chapter Thirty-Eight

MATYAS

He rolled through the air, he sped forward, he darted back, he turned over like a swimmer so he could watch the sky instead of the Earth. Below him the forests and villages, the rivers and mountains, rolled out like a ribbon off a spool. He remembered all the times he'd imagined flying, all the times he'd demanded the secret, and realized it was always to become better than everyone else. To escape his past, escape himself. He'd never thought about the absolute joy.

Even though he knew it was cold, the way you know the Sun rises in the east, he didn't feel it. He no longer felt hungry, and the wind appeared to have cleansed his wounds and washed away the blood from the beating the men had given him when he'd tried to steal their lord's wallet. He laughed and gave thanks that he'd been so bad a pickpocket.

Where should he go? No, that wasn't the question, he knew very well where he needed to go, what he had to do. But how? How could he even figure out the direction? It was only when he looked down and saw the twisted forest of the College of Trees, and not long after that the Library of Ants, that he realized he didn't need to control where he went. The flying carried its own knowledge.

Streams of red dust clung briefly to his face and arms, only to let go and be carried off behind him. He looked down and saw the Great

Rock, the Child Eater's hiding place. When he saw the circle of chanters and the mountainous woman and then the man in the thin green robe, arm raised as if to draw down lightning, he realized that flying could free you from time as well as the Earth.

If he thought that he might go back before his great crime, he soon gave up the hope when he came to a place of very cold air and discovered himself drifting down to a small valley. As the ground became clearer, he could see withered trees and dull flowers. *I did this*, he thought, and an immense sadness weighed him down. Maybe they escaped. Maybe he'd ruined the garden but the Guardians had shaken off his foolish, hateful spell as soon as he'd stepped away. Then he saw them and all hope vanished.

Two squirrels, one red, one gray, stood facing him, side by side, each with a glittering walnut in its front paws, one of silver, the other gold. Matyas spread himself face down in the dirt. "Forgive me," he said, "though I do not deserve it."

From somewhere inside him, he heard the girl's voice. "It is not for us to forgive."

Matyas raised himself to his knees, bowed his head. "I understand. What I have done cannot be undone and therefore never forgiven."

The boy said, "No, no, Matyas. You understand nothing. You did what was necessary."

He lifted his head to squint at them. He remembered Veil, years ago, telling him that everyone has a purpose and sometimes that purpose belongs to something bigger than themselves. He clung to this idea only for a second before he realized he had to let it go. The crime was still real. He said, "What is given cannot be taken back. I cannot break my own spell."

"Of course not," the girl said.

"But I can give you something new. A Spell of Alleviance." He tried to think, but no magic came other than a statement that somehow felt right. "Freedom will come with the one thousandth child."

The voice of the boy sighed. "Thank you, Master Matyas."

The girl added, "You have given and we have accepted. We release you and bless you."

"I don't understand," Matyas said. "All I do is cause pain."

The red one shook its head, and the gold walnut flashed with light. Within Matyas, the boy's voice said, "Your understanding is not necessary. Only your actions. But if you wish, you may go to the One Who Knows." With that, both squirrels ran off behind the trees.

"What do I do?" Matyas said. He looked all around but they were gone. Maybe, he thought, the Tarot of Eternity would help him. He took the wrapped cards from his waistband. But when he tried to remove the blue cloth, the cards gave off such intense light that he could hardly bear to hold them, and he wrapped them up again.

The One Who Knows. Veil? Panic seized him at the thought of facing her, but then he realized they meant someone else. Someone older.

Matyas closed his eyes, moved his arms away from his sides and let himself become lighter than dust. He flew for a long time now, empty of distractions, with nothing more than glimpses of the blurred Earth below him. Only when he saw a low stubble of hills and a stand of dark trees did he let himself descend.

The trees were so entwined there was no way into them, but he knew what to do. Hadn't he seen it years earlier? "Come around me," he said, and the Splendor appeared, a thousand dazzling lights. "Open the way." As soon as he'd said it, the lights touched the trees and a path opened. He walked inside without hesitation, though he dreaded what he might hear.

The Kallistocha burned so brightly Matyas could not look at it but only stared at the ground, where pebbles of a hundred colors lay all around the black stick. "My lord," Matyas said, "help me. Once you called me Master and told me I would fly. I gave my life to that dream and all I have done is destroy what is good and necessary. You spoke of darkness and I thought you meant the color of the sky. Now my soul is black as ink. Help me."

The Prince looked directly at him, all mockery gone from the golden eyes. "You did what was necessary, Matyas. And now you are free. Accept it."

"No! How can you say that? I cursed the Guardians. I met the Child Eater and I did nothing. I knew his name and I still did nothing."

"Matyas. Listen to me. There was nothing you could have done. Knowing his name allows you to create a spear but you are not the one to hurl it. The Child Eater is beyond you. He was beyond the Guardians as well—there was no way for them to touch him, either. But now your foolish spell has put them in a form where one day they will help the thousandth child. That is all that matters. All things do what they must. Be at peace, Matyas. Your anger has served the future."

"Thank you," Matyas said. He bowed his head in preparation for leaving. About to back away, he stopped. "Master of Wisdom," he said. "Great holy Prince. May I ask a question?"

"Yes," the Kallistocha said.

"Federaynak. He came here, didn't he? This is what the Victors did to you?"

Light flashed in the Prince's face so brightly Matyas had to force himself not to look away. They had been speaking in the Phase of the Fifth Chamber, but now the Prince moved to the Shattered Face, the tongue reserved only for the deepest pain. He said, "When they put me here, this place was the most blessed on all the shining Earth. I could sing and the woods would carry the song to my sisters and brothers across the world. Like a child, I thought the Angels had tempered their punishment with mercy. Do you see, Matyas? You are not the only foolish one."

Matyas whispered, "In the world of men, beauty attracts ugliness."

"Yes. He came, just after he found the Spell of Extension. He had taken the first child and was looking for a place to . . . consume her."

"And he thought of you because Joachim had come here, yes?"

"Joachim and I revealed the Tarot of Eternity here."

"Revealed?"

"Of course. Did you think Joachim created it? Did you think I invented it? The Tarot of Eternity has always existed. The Creator used it to shape the world. It was Eternity that told Her She could not create a world without the Spell of Extension."

Matyas rocked back and forth, holding his arms. He discovered he could understand the Child Eater, for if it was him he would have come here as well. For Federaynak, what better way to show he had gone beyond his teacher, his Master Joachim?

"Matyas," the Prince said softly, "you are not him."

A great shudder ran through Matyas, so powerful he thought at first it was the Earth. "Thank you," he said again.

"Now go. Veil would like to see you."

Veil. Matyas left the grove, feeling the trees close behind him. As soon as he stood under the clear sky, he opened his arms and left the ground. For a moment he was aware of a filthy boy who had hidden behind a rock and now was trying to sound important as he did his best to summon the Splendor. He laughed as he moved through the night sky. *We will meet three times, though two shall be one.*

Matyas came down in the courtyard, with no idea what time it was, what *year* it was, only that it was night and no one was there. He ran up the narrow stairs, aware for the first time that every step was a story, whether of pain or joy, for the Tower of Heaven was built with human passions.

He found her in her wooden chair, back straight, hands on her knees as she stared out of the window. Her hair flew around, tangled up in itself, while a yellow and blue dress hung loosely on her skeletal shoulders. She was nearly transparent now, as thin as air, and he knew that time had caught up with her. A sweet smell filled the room.

Matyas knelt down and took her hand, so feathery he had to look to make sure he was holding it. "Mistress—" he began, but her free hand waved him to silence as gracefully as a silk stream.

"Please, child," she said. "No apologies. You did what I needed you to do. You always did what was needed."

He smiled. "You haven't called me 'child' in a long time."

Her laughter was dry and faint. "I didn't want to insult you."

"I brought you a gift."

"Ah. How nice. Old ladies like presents, you know."

He removed the blue package and held it out to her. "Oh good," she said. As she began to unravel the cloth, Matyas averted his eyes but no flash came out, and when he looked they were just painted cards spread out in her narrow lap. Softly, she said, "Hello, Joachim. It's been a long time." She held up the card that showed a young man on the edge of a cliff with spirals of light behind him. A little louder, she said, "Do you know, Matyas, that light travels? I suppose that's why it can be dark in one place and light in another. And here's the curious thing. Light always travels at the same speed. Time can slow down or accelerate, people can get bigger or smaller, but light always remains the same. Isn't that wonderful? What do you suppose it tells us?" She put the card with the others and set the pack in her lap.

Matyas began to cry, for he knew very well what she was telling him. For each of us, time must end. To deny this can only banish us from the light. He said, "What will happen now? Here, with the Academy?"

She shrugged, the gentlest movement. "No doubt Lukhanan will become undisputed Master. It's all he desires."

"Lukhanan is a fool."

"Of course. Remember, Matyas—the scholar hears of the Gate and tries every day to undo the lock."

Matyas responded, "The student hears of the Gate and tries to squeeze between the bars."

"The Fool hears of the Gate and laughs."

"Without laughter the Gate would never open."

Veil clapped her hands. "Well done," she said. "I've missed you." She leaned back now and closed her eyes. "Brush my hair?" she said.

"I will be very happy to brush your hair." The old brush felt heavy and cold at first, but it warmed up as he ran it through the fine strands, careful to separate the tangles rather than pull at them. At first it was difficult, for no one had brushed her hair in a long time, but after a few minutes he could slide the brush in smooth, easy strokes, moving her hair down her back like a waterfall.

Eyes closed, Matyas began to sway in time with the strokes of the brush. Light streamed over him, light and images, as if the cards had lifted from her lap to be caught up in her hair. Sweet aromas filled him, bouquets of flowers mixed with a distant smell of the sea. Sounds drifted to him from very far away, voices, wind in mountains, a bell as pure and clear as the sky, a cry of delight.

He dropped the brush and opened his eyes. Veil was gone. Only the chair remained, and the table, and the books, and the bed in the alcove where he'd slept for what now felt like a few precious nights. And Eternity, quiet now, wrapped in its cloth the color of the sky.

With both hands, he picked up the blue package and held it against his chest. He bowed his head a moment, then went to the window. Below the tower, the tops of the buildings shone faintly in the dawn. Matyas stood there a long time, watching the stones change color with the sunrise. From below, in the courtyard, he heard voices, sounds of amusement, anger, pride. Finally, he stepped out onto the narrow window ledge, took a deep breath and lifted into the sky.

He came down at the edge of a small group of houses near a lake. The houses looked odd, large and neat and clean, and all very alike, as if one person had been put under a spell, compelled to build the same house over and over. There were trees by the lake, and impossibly even grass.

Matyas paid little attention to these things. Instead, he set down the blue package by the water and stared at it. Finally, he held his breath and undid the cloth. The pictures glowed, but not so brightly he couldn't look at them, and for that he said a prayer of deep gratitude.

He made his right hand into a fist, stared at it for a while, then extended his index finger. One by one, on each card, his finger traced a word. The same word, over and over, seventy-eight times. Federaynak. Federaynak. *Federaynak*.

When he had finished, he wrapped them up again and set them in the hollow of an ancient tree. "For the thousandth child!" he said. Then he closed his eyes and tilted back his head and rose once more into the air.

Chapter Thirty-Nine

SIMON/JACK

Simon didn't know why his dad wasn't coming to him. He could see Daddy try, but something pushed him back. And he didn't understand why he couldn't get away from Dr. Reina. He was running as hard as he could and Dr. Reina was walking so slowly, yet Simon remained as far away from his father as ever, and Dr. Reina kept getting closer.

Then Simon saw his dad throw something. He couldn't see what it was, but he knew it was important, Daddy wouldn't have done it otherwise. It looked as if it was about to fly right over his head, but he jumped up, just like when they played catch and Daddy threw wild, and he grabbed it.

Even before he looked at it, he knew what it was. He could feel the blue cloth. The cards. Somehow Daddy had brought him the Tarot cards. On his knees now, he fumbled at the wrapper.

Only some twenty yards away, Dr. Reina laughed. "Simon, please," he said. "Tarot cards? What will you do? Tell my future?" Suddenly his voice shook the ground. "I *am* the future! I am Frederick of the Other Side. You have eaten me, body and blood. Three times, and now *my* mouth is open. I am the teeth of death, Simon Wisdom. You are my food. I will eat you and live forever."

Simon fell down in terror. At the same time, he thought, *He doesn't know. He thinks I ate the food.* He had a chance, but what should he do? What?

Run, he thought, then, *No, the cards*. He fumbled through them, dropped half, fell over as he tried to pick them up.

From just ten yards away, Dr. Reina laughed. "Simon, Simon," he chided. "Are you going to read your cards? What do you think they will tell you?"

Open-mouthed, Simon stared at him. *Simon, Simon*. He remembered now! What his mother had said that night in the living room.

Simon, Simon,
Rhymin' Simon,
Take the time an'
Stop the crime an'
Set the children free.

He had to take the time, not try to run. But what would that do? How would taking time stop the crime? Simon, Simon. What else did his mother say? "You're my perfect poem." A poem! He'd thought she was being nice but she was telling him he had to make up a poem. Rhymin' Simon. A magic poem could stop the crime.

Dr. Reina was only a few yards away now, his smile as sharp as his knife. Simon could hear his dad yelling at him to get away but he couldn't listen. He closed his eyes and wished he could close his ears as well. "Tarot, Tarot," he whispered, then a little louder, "long and narrow."

Dr. Reina laughed—so close now. He said, "Verse? For your last breath? Do you hear your father? He wants you to say goodbye to him." Simon opened his eyes. Dr. Reina had stopped just a few feet away. Simon could see the bloodstains up and down the stone blade, he could hear the crying children, all the ones Dr. Reina had killed. Caroline was there, and nearly a thousand more. "Set the children free," his mother had said.

As strong as he could make it, Simon called out:

Tarot, Tarot,
Long and narrow,
Be like knives—

Dr. Reina's laughter choked off Simon's voice so that he couldn't finish his poem. "A spell?" the doctor said. "How clever. But you're missing something. Do you know what it is?"

What? What was he missing? Simon stared again at the cards. There was something written on them, faintly, but there it was, on every card, the same strange letters. A name. Simon was sure of it. That's what was missing, the thing to make the spell work—Dr. Reina's real name!

But how was he supposed to read it? The letters were in some funny language. How could he—? And then he laughed. He was Simon Wisdom. He didn't need to read letters. *He could read minds.* He held up the cards, half of them in each hand, fanned open to act like shields.

The doctor stared at them. "No," he said. "No, it can't be. He sent them out of the world! I was there. I saw it."

In that moment of fear, Simon found his way inside, past the dark cloud, the terrified screams, feeling his way, searching. And there it was, small and hidden, covered with centuries of blood. Simon didn't have to read it, or hear it, he just knew.

"Federaynak!" he cried. Stunned, the monster stared at him. He opened his mouth to speak, but nothing came out.

Simon called out:

Federaynak, Federaynak.
The time has come to take our souls back.

And then:

Tarot, Tarot,
Long and narrow,
Be like knives
To save our lives!

With all his terrified might, Simon Wisdom threw the cards at the Child Eater.

The cards separated as they sliced through the air. Simon could see each one before it hit, and so could Federaynak, for he stared at them, unable to move, head shaking slightly, as if he was trying to say, "No, no, this is wrong." The first card to hit was the Fool, the Beautiful Boy about to Fly. It cut right through his throat, sending forth a jet of blood so thick and dark it looked like oil. The Child Eater held his hands up in front of his face, only to have the next group of cards cut off his fingers. More cards attacked his legs, his arms, his chest. Parts of him fell on the ground where they turned into black crystal, clothes and all, then broke into small, sharp pieces that sank into the grass.

The very last card to hit him was the man hanging upside down by one foot with light all around his face. It hit the eyes and light exploded from it. For a moment, Simon could see the faces of children, layer upon layer, neither happy nor sad but quiet, eyes closed, lips slightly open in a long collective sigh. At the very last, he saw Caroline. The eyes looked at Simon, then closed in gratitude. Finally they were gone.

Simon could never remember exactly when it all disappeared. One moment he was looking at the pieces on the scorched grass and the cards scattered on the ground. Something must have hurt his eyes, for he squeezed them shut, and when he opened them again everything had vanished—the black crystals, the cards, even the Institute itself and the wide lawn. Instead, he saw his own backyard. There was Mr. Carlys' house with the covered-up swimming pool, and there were the two pine trees that Grandma called "the gateway to happiness." Amazed, Simon turned around. There was his father. Simon wasn't making it up. Daddy really was there.

On either side of his father stood the boy and girl, their gold and silver hair sparkly in the sun. Simon was happy to see them, and at the same time he thought, *They're not supposed to be here.*

As if they could hear him—could read his mind—they smiled and nodded. They took a step back. At that moment, as if someone had hit the play button on a DVD, Simon's dad called out, "Simon? Are you really there? Oh God, Simon!"

They ran at each other so hard they bounced off and fell down. Daddy grabbed him, held him so long he couldn't breathe. "Oh, Simon," Daddy said, "my beautiful boy. My precious boy." Finally they stood up and Daddy took his hand as they walked to the house.

They were almost at the door when they heard singing: glorious liquid joy, sounds beyond anything they could imagine. All across the world, voices hidden for centuries were calling out, rediscovering each other. In dark woods and busy streets, on glaciers, in rainforests, in the mud and gore of battlefields, in the secret corners of schools and hospitals and cemeteries, in lonely houses and noisy sweat shops, the

Great Abandoned Ones, the Kallistochoi, had found their brothers and sisters.

Simon and his father had no idea how long it lasted. Even when it seemed to stop, when they could no longer hear it, they knew it hadn't really ended. And never would.

Jack Wisdom kept hold of his son's hand as he led him into the living room. There he picked up the picture of his wife. Faint lights sparkled around it. "It was your mother," he said to his son. "She told me what I had to do."

"Me too," Simon said. "She told me I had to make up a poem, so that's what I did."

Jack smiled. "Your mother is a very smart woman, Simon. She loves us both very, very much. And I love her. I love you more than anything in the world, but I love your mother, too."

Simon said, "I know, Daddy."

Jack looked startled for a moment, then laughed. "Of course you do," he said. "Of course you do." He laughed again and hugged his son. Later, he knew, they would sit down and talk about it, maybe try to understand what had happened. But right now they were together, and safe, and that was all that mattered.

ACKNOWLEDGMENTS

I owe a great debt of gratitude to Karen Mahoney and Alex Ukolov of Magic Realist Press for publishing the original collection, *The Tarot of Perfection*, and to Chris Priest, for always being there. And to Alisa, Darrah and Carol, the best writers' group there is, and to Paula Scardamalia, superb editor and writing coach. Without them, this book might never have come to life.

The original draft of this book was written by hand, using antique fountain pens, in particular a 90-year-old Wahl pen, gold, and inscribed on the side with the name of its owner: **M. Matyas.**

Rachel Pollack
Hudson Valley, 2012

ABOUT THE TYPE

Typeset in Garamond Premier Pro at 11.5/14 pt.

Garamond Premier Pro is a product of type designer Robert Slimbach's study of Claude Garamond's type designs. This interpretation of the Garmond extensive typeface is refined, versatile, and yet contemporary with current typography.

Typeset by Scribe Inc., Philadelphia, PA